p6

"Sorry," she apologized. "I can get a little defensive."

"Yeah, well." He pulled a rag from his back pocket and wiped his hands on it. "Me too. I suppose."

She peered at him through lowered lashes.

"Truce." He stuck out his hand.

"Truce." She accepted it.

The contact was electric. Tuck's head reeled, his body stiffened and his gut clenched in a wholly enjoyable way. Damn, damn, damn. She smelled like freshly laundered linen, crisp and clean and cozy. He thought immediately of a turned-down bed.

Her eyes widened. She dropped his hand.

Tuck was just as shocked. He couldn't believe he was reacting this way.

"Did you find somewhere else to stay?" Tuck ventured, praying she would say yes.

"I did."

From the way she was looking at him, he wasn't getting good vibes about this. "What's the address?"

Her gaze was steely. "Fourteen-fourteen Enchantment Lane."

Hell, he knew that's what she was going to say. "No, no."

"Yes, yes."

"You can't stay with me."

"From a legal standpoint, I can. Like it or not, I'm your new roommate."

PRAISE FOR

Rocky Mountain Heat

(PREVIOUSLY PUBLISHED AS

All of Me)

"Delicious details, a small town full of memorable characters, great dialogue, and humor all combine to make this a highly enjoyable tale about two people who find healing—and each other—in a story honest about grief without being maudlin."

—*Booklist*, starred review

"Wilde's clever combination of humor, sorrow, and love brings a deeply appealing sense of realism."

—*Publishers Weekly*

"Light and charming, this is a pure romance... a satisfying read with excellent characterizations and real-life issues."

—*RT Book Reviews*

Rocky Mountain HEAT

Also by Lori Wilde

License to Thrill

Charmed and Dangerous

Mission: Irresistible

You Only Love Twice

Kiss the Bride

Happily Ever After

Mad About You

Double Trouble

Valentine, Texas (previously published as *Addicted to Love*)

Long, Tall Texan (previously published as *There Goes the Bride*)

Second Chance Hero (previously published as *Once Smitten, Twice Shy*)

Rocky Mountain HEAT

Lori Wilde

NEW YORK BOSTON

Forever
Hachette Book Group
1290 Avenue of the Americas, New York, NY 10104
read-forever.com
twitter.com/readforeverpub

Originally published as *All of Me* by Forever in April 2009
Reissued: December 2019

Forever is an imprint of Grand Central Publishing. The Forever name and logo are trademarks of Hachette Book Group, Inc.

The publisher is not responsible for websites (or their content) that are not owned by the publisher.

ISBNs: 978-1-5387-0019-8 (mass market reissue),
978-0-446-55199-1 (ebook)

Printed in the United States of America

OPM

10 9 8 7 6 5 4 3 2 1

Michele Bidelspach—the most insightful,
understanding editor I have ever worked with.
Thank you for the *Gilmore Girls.*
May you find that grand love of your very own.

Acknowledgments

Thanks to Lou Ann King for showing me around her quaint little Colorado lake town. I love you like a sister. Thanks to legal eagles and fellow writers Dorien Kelley and Jamie Denton for all their help with the legal mumbo jumbo. Any mistakes are solely my own. You guys rock!

Jillian's Story

Chapter One

Houston deputy district attorney Jillian Samuels did not believe in magic.

She didn't throw pennies into wishing wells, didn't pluck four-leaf clovers from springtime meadows, didn't blow out birthday-cake candles, and didn't wish on falling stars.

For Jillian, the Tooth Fairy and the Easter Bunny had always been myths. And as for Santa Claus, even thinking about the jolly fat guy in the red suit knotted her stomach. She'd tried believing in him once, and all she'd gotten in the pink stocking she'd hung on the mantel were two chunks of Kingsford's charcoal—the kind without lighter fluid.

Later, she'd realized her stepmother put the coal in her stocking, but on that Christmas morning, while the other kids rode bicycles, tossed footballs, and combed Barbie's hair, Jillian received her message loud and clear.

You're a very bad girl.

No, Jillian didn't believe in magic or fairy tales or happily-ever-afters, even though her three best friends, Delaney, Tish, and Rachael, had supposedly found their true loves after wishing on what they claimed was a magic wedding veil. Her friends had even dared to pass the damnable veil along to her, telling Jillian it would grant her heart's greatest desire. But she wasn't falling for such nonsense. She snorted whenever she thought of the three-hundred-year-old lace wedding veil shoved away in a cedar chest along with her winter cashmere sweaters.

When it came to romance, Jillian was of the same mind as Hemingway: *When two people love each other, there can be no happy ending.* Clearly, Hemingway knew what he was talking about.

Not that Jillian could claim she'd ever been in love. She'd decided a long time ago love was best avoided. She liked her life tidy, and from what she'd seen of it, love was sprawling and messy and complicated. Besides, love required trust, and trust wasn't her strong suit.

Jillian did not believe in magic, but she did believe in hard work, success, productivity, and justice. The closest she ever came to magic were those glorious courtroom moments when a judge in a black robe read the jury's guilty verdict.

This morning in late September, dressed in a no-nonsense navy-blue pin-striped Ralph Lauren suit, a cream-colored silk blouse, and Jimmy Choo stilettos to show off the shapely curve of her calves and add three inches to her already imposing five-foot-ten-inch height, Jillian stood at attention waiting for the verdict to be read.

On the outside, she looked like a dream prosecutor—statuesque, gorgeous, young, and smart. But underneath the clothes and the makeup and her cool, unshakeable countenance, Jillian Samuels was still that same little girl who hadn't rated a Christmas present from Santa.

"Ladies and gentlemen of the jury, have you reached a verdict in this case?" Judge Atwood asked.

"We have, Your Honor," answered the foreman, a big slab of a guy with carrot-colored hair and freckled skin.

"Please hand your decision to the bailiff," the judge directed.

Jillian drew a breath, curling her fingernails into her palms. Before the reading of every verdict, she felt slightly sick to her stomach.

The bailiff, a gangly, bulldog-faced middle-aged man with a Magnum P.I. mustache, walked the piece of paper across the courtroom to the judge's bench. Judge Atwood opened it, read it, and then glared at the defendant over the top of his reading glasses.

Twenty-three-year-old Randal Petry had shot Gladys Webelow, an eighty-two-year-old great-grandmother, in the upper thigh while robbing a Dash and Go last Christmas Eve. Gladys had been buying a bottle of Correctol and a quart of 2 percent milk. He'd made off with forty-seven dollars from the cash register, a fistful of Slim Jims, and a twenty-four pack of Old Milwaukee.

"Will the defendant please rise?" Atwood handed the verdict back to the bailiff, who gave it to the jury foreman to read aloud.

Head held high, Petry got to his feet. The man was a scumbag, but Jillian had to admire his defiance.

"Randal LeRoy Petry, on the count of armed robbery, you are found guilty as charged," the foreman announced. As the foreman kept reading the verdicts on the other charges leveled against Petry, Jillian waited for the victorious wash of relief she always experienced when the word *guilty* was spoken. Waited for the happy sag to her shoulders, the warm satisfaction in her belly, the skip of victory in her pulse.

But the triumph did not come.

Instead, she felt numb, lifeless, and very detached as if she were standing at the far end of some distant tunnel.

Waiting . . . waiting . . .

For what, she didn't know.

People in the gallery were getting up, heading for the door. The court-appointed defense attorney collected his papers and stuffed them into his scuffed briefcase. The guards were hauling Petry off to jail. Judge Atwood left the bench.

And Jillian just kept standing.

Waiting.

It scared her. This nonfeeling. This emptiness. Her fingernails bit into the flesh of her palms, but she couldn't feel that either.

"You gonna stand there all day, Samuels, or what? You won. Go knock back a shot of Jose Cuervo."

Jillian jerked her head around. Saw Keith Whippet, the prosecutor on the next case, waiting to take his place at her table. Whippet was as lean as his name, with mean eyes and a cheap suit.

"Chop, chop." He slammed his briefcase down on the desk. "I got people to fry."

"Yes," Jillian said, but she could barely hear herself. She was a bright kite who'd broken loose from its tether, flying high into a cloudless blue sky. Up, up, and away, higher and higher, smaller and smaller. Soon she would disappear, a speck in the air.

What was happening to her?

She looked at Whippet, a weasly guy who'd asked her

out on numerous occasions, and she'd shattered his hopes every single time until he'd finally given up. Now he was just rude. Whippet made shooing motions.

Jillian blinked, grabbed her briefcase, and darted from the courtroom.

Blake.

She had to talk to her mentor, District Attorney Blake Townsend. He would know what to do. He'd tell her this feeling was completely normal. That it was okay if the joy was gone. She would survive.

Except it wasn't okay, because her job was the only thing that gave her joy. If she'd lost the ability to derive pleasure from putting the bad guys behind bars, what did that leave her?

The thing was, she couldn't feel happy about jailing Petry, because she knew there were thousands more like him. She knew the prisons were overcrowded, and they would let Petry out of jail on good behavior after he'd served only a fraction of his sentence to make room for a new batch of Petrys.

The realization wasn't new. What was startlingly fresh was the idea that her work didn't matter. She was insignificant. The justice system was a turnstile, and her arms were growing weary of holding open the revolving door.

She was so unsettled by the thought that she found it difficult to catch her breath.

Blake. She needed to speak to Blake.

Anxiety rushed her from the courthouse to the district attorney's office across the street, her heels clicking a rapid rhythm against the sidewalk that matched the elevated tempo of her pulse.

By the time she stepped into the DA's office, she was

breathing hard and sweating. She caught a glimpse of her reflection in a window and saw that her sleek dark hair, usually pulled back in a loose chignon, had slumped from the clasp and was tumbling about her shoulders.

What was happening to her?

The whole room went suddenly silent, and everyone stared in her direction.

"Is Blake in his office?" she asked the DA's executive assistant, Francine Weathers.

Francine blinked, and it was only then that Jillian noticed her reddened eyes. The woman had been crying. She stepped closer, the anxiety she'd been feeling morphed into real fear.

She stood there for a moment, panting, terrified, heart rapidly pounding, staring at Francine's round, middle-aged face. She knew something bad had happened before she ever asked the question.

"What's wrong?"

The secretary dabbed at her eyes with a Kleenex. "You haven't heard?"

A hot rush of apprehension raised the hairs on the nape of her neck. "Heard what? I've been in court. The Petry case."

"I . . ." Francine sniffed. "He . . ."

Jillian stepped closer and awkwardly put a hand on the older woman's shoulder. "Are you okay?"

Francine shook her head and burst into a fresh round of tears. Jillian dropped her hand. She'd never been very good at comforting people. She was the pit bull who went after the accused. Gentleness was foreign.

"This morning, Blake . . . he . . ."

Jillian's blood pumped faster. "Yes?"

"It's terrible, unthinkable."

"What?"

"Such a shame. He was only fifty-six."

Jillian grit her teeth to keep from taking the woman by the shoulders and shaking her. "Just tell me. What's happened?"

Francine hiccoughed, sniffled into a tissue, and then finally whispered,

"Blake dropped dead this morning in the middle of Starbucks while ordering a grande soy latte."

THE NEXT FEW DAYS passed in a fog. Jillian went about her work and attended her cases, but it felt as if someone else was in her body performing the tasks while her mind shut down, disconnected from her emotions. She'd never experienced such hollow emptiness. But she could not cry. The tears stuffed up her head, made her temples throb, but no matter how much she wanted to sob, she simply could not.

Francine had learned from Blake's doctor that he'd had an inoperable brain tumor he'd told no one about. That new knowledge cut Jillian to the quick. He hadn't trusted her enough to tell her he was dying.

The morning of Blake's memorial service dawned unseasonably cold for the end of September in Texas. Thick gray clouds matted the sky, threatening rain. The wind gusted out of the north at twenty-five miles an hour, blowing shivers up Jillian's black wool skirt.

She still couldn't believe Blake was gone. Speculation about who would be appointed to take his place swirled through the office, but, grief-stricken, Jillian didn't give the issue much consideration. Blake was gone, and no one could ever replace him in her heart.

Learning of her mentor's death compounded the feelings of edge-of-the-world desolation that had overcome her during Petry's trial. She'd met Blake when he'd been a guest lecturer in her summer-school class on criminal law at the University of Houston. He'd found her questions insightful, and she'd thought he was one of the smartest men she'd ever met.

Their attraction was strictly mental. They admired each other's brains. Plus, Jillian had lost a father, and Blake had let a daughter slip away. When Blake had been elected district attorney about the same time Jillian graduated from law school, his offer of a job in the DA's office was automatic.

Jillian didn't question if it was the right step for her. Blake was there. She went. Other than Delaney, Tish, and Rachael, Blake was the closest thing to family she could claim.

The memorial service was held in an empty courtroom at the Harris County Courthouse. Law was Blake's religion. Saying farewell in a church didn't seem fitting. Francine had made all the arrangements. The room was jam-packed with colleagues, opponents, allies, and adversaries. But there was no family present. Blake had been as alone in the world as Jillian.

A poster-sized photograph of Blake sat perched on the judge's bench. Beside it was the urn that held his ashes. The smell of stargazer lilies and chrysanthemums permeated the courtroom. Jillian took a seat in the back row of the gallery. Her head hurt from all the tears she'd been unable to shed. Her throat was tight. Her heart scraped the ground.

Suddenly a memory flashed into her head. One night, four months earlier, she'd gone over to Blake's house for dinner to celebrate putting a cop killer on death row. She'd expected Blake to be in a good mood. He was supposed to be cooking her favorite meal, spaghetti and meatballs. She'd brought a bottle of Chianti for the occasion. Instead, after he'd invited her in, he told her he'd ordered takeout Chinese and then he'd gone to sit in the bay window alcove overlooking the lake behind his property, a wistful expression on his face.

She sat beside him, waiting for him to tell her what had happened, but he did not. Finally, after several minutes of watching him watch the birds landing on the lake for the evening, she'd asked, "Blake? Is something wrong?"

He tilted his gray head at her. He looked so tired, and he gave her a slight smile. "You should get married," he'd murmured.

"Huh?" She'd blinked.

"You shouldn't be here hanging out with an old man. You should be dating, forming relationships, finding a good guy, getting married."

She hadn't expected the hit to her gut that his words inflicted. "You know I'm not a big believer in marriage."

Blake had looked away from her then, his eyes back on the birds and the lake. "You deserve love, Jillian."

She had no answer for that. "Marriage didn't work out so well for you."

"Because I screwed it up. God, if only I could go back in time . . ." He let his words trail off.

"Did something happen?"

He glanced at her again, and for just a second she saw the starkest regret in his eyes. Regret tinged with fear. The look vanished as quickly as it had appeared, and she convinced herself she must have imagined it.

"Nah." He waved a hand. "Just an old man getting maudlin."

The doorbell had rang then. The delivery driver with their kung pao chicken and steamed pork dumplings. The rest of the evening Blake had been his usual self, but now, looking back on the moment, Jillian couldn't help wondering if that was the day he'd been diagnosed with the brain tumor.

She blinked back the memory. Her nose burned. *Oh, Blake, why didn't you tell me you were dying?* He'd worked up until the last minute of his life and then died so tritely in Starbucks.

Jillian's heart lurched. She felt inadequate, useless. And guilty that she hadn't seen the signs. She remembered how his vision seemed to be getting worse. How lately he'd been making beginner mistakes when they played chess. She thought they were close friends, and yet he hadn't told her about his illness. Hell, she might as well admit it. She felt a little excluded. He hadn't trusted her with his darkest secret.

Just before the service began, the doors opened one last time and Mayor Newsom swept inside with Judge Alex Fredericks, followed by Alex's beautiful young wife with a towheaded toddler on her hip. The minute Jillian spied Alex and his family, she felt the color drain from her face.

Nausea gripped her.

The last time she'd seen Mrs. Fredericks had been on

Christmas Eve of the previous year. At the same time Randal Petry had been shooting Gladys Webelow at the Dash and Go, Jillian had been ringing Alex Frederick's doorbell in the Woodlands, dressed only in a denim duster and knee-high cowboy boots. Learning for the first time that her new lover was married with a family.

Jillian sank down in her seat and prayed neither Alex nor his wife spied her. Newsom ushered them to the front of the room, where they sat side by side in three empty folding chairs. The service lasted over an hour as one person after another took the microphone to remember and honor Blake. Jillian had prepared a speech, but when the officiating minister asked for any final farewell words, she stayed seated. She couldn't bear standing up there in front of Alex.

He had been the biggest mistake of her life.

Her friends urged Jillian to open herself up to a relationship. They'd made her start to hope that she could find love, that there *was* a man out there for her.

And hope was such a dangerous thing.

Alex was handsome and charming and at just thirty-six already a criminal court judge. They looked good together, both tall and athletic. Her friends were all falling giggly in love, and Jillian dared to think, *Why not take a chance*? For the first time in her twenty-nine years on the planet, she'd put her fears aside, opened herself up, and let a man into her heart.

And then she'd found out about Mrs. Fredericks.

Idiot.

She should have known better. No matter what anyone said, there was no such thing as magic. No happily-ever-after. Not for her anyway.

"If there's anyone else who'd like to say something about Blake, please come forward now," the minister said. "If not, Mayor Newsom has an announcement he would like to make, and then we'll conclude the service with a closing prayer."

The minister stepped away from the microphone and the mayor took his place. Newsom shuffled his notes, cleared his throat, and then launched in.

"We've lost a great man in Blake Townsend. He's irreplaceable. But life goes on, and Blake wouldn't want us standing in the way of justice," Newsom said as if he had a clue what Blake wanted. "Since all his friends and colleagues are gathered here in one place, it seems the best time to announce the appointment of our new DA before my formal press conference this afternoon."

A murmur rippled through the crowd.

It was crass and inconsiderate, announcing Blake's successor at his memorial service, but classic Mayor Newsom. The guy had the class of a garden trowel. Jillian caught her breath and bit her bottom lip. She sensed what was coming and dreaded hearing it.

"Judge Alex Fredericks will be the new Harris County district attorney." Newsom turned to Fredericks. "Alex, would you like to say a few words?"

Anger grabbed her throat and shook hard. No, no! It could not be true.

Jillian would not sit still and listen to this. Bile rising in her throat, she charged for the door. Reality settled on her shoulders, even as she tried to outrun the inevitable. She hurried across the polished black marble floor of the courthouse, rushing out into the blowing drizzle, gulping in cold, damp air.

She didn't see the Tom Thumb delivery truck. She just stepped off the curb and into its path.

A horn blared. Tires squealed.

Jillian froze.

The truck's bumper stopped just inches short of her kneecaps.

She stared through the windshield at the driver, and he promptly flipped her the bird. She smiled at him. Smiled and laughed and then couldn't stop.

The driver rolled down the window. "Get out of the road you crazy bitch."

Great, terrific, you almost get run over and you're laughing about it. The guy's right. You are crazy.

She wandered the streets, not paying any attention to where she was going and ending up walking the path through the city park she and Blake had walked many times together, engaged in friendly legal debates. She wondered what he'd think of Alex as his replacement. Blake hadn't known about her relationship with Alex. She'd been too ashamed to tell him.

Her mind kept going back to the memory of the night Blake had told her she should get married, and the more she thought about it, the more convinced she became that had to have been the day he'd gotten his diagnosis. The death sentence he'd shared with no one.

The rain pelted her, and Jillian realized she'd been walking in a big circle for the last thirty minutes. Ducking her head against the quickening rain, she hurried to her office. The place was empty. Everyone else had probably gone to lunch after the services were over. She shrugged out of her coat, dropped down at her desk, and closed her eyes.

"Blake," Jillian whispered out loud. "What am I going to do without you?"

All her girlfriends were married now, getting pregnant, having babies, living lives so very different from her own. She'd used Blake to fill the void. Every Thursday night, they'd played chess together. He'd make dinner, because Jillian didn't cook, or they'd go out to eat, her treat. He was the one she called when she had trouble with a case, and she was the escort he took to political functions. Many assumed they were having an affair. But she'd never felt any of those kinds of feelings for Blake, nor he for her. He'd always been like the dad she'd never really had.

Except now he was gone.

"Ms. Samuels?"

She opened her eyes to see Alex Fredericks standing in the doorway.

His gaze was enigmatic, his stance intimidating.

Jillian thrust out her chin, refusing to let her distress show. "Yes?"

"I want to see you in my office."

She stared. Was the bastard about to fire her? Ever since she'd ended their affair, whenever she appeared in Alex's courtroom, their relationship had been adversarial. She'd lost more than one case she might have won if there'd been another judge on the bench.

"Don't you mean Blake's office?"

"I'm the new DA," he said. "It's my office now, and I want to see you in there immediately."

Jillian wanted to tell him to go to hell, but she held her tongue and got up.

Other employees were filtering into the building. She followed Alex into Blake's office. A fresh surge of anger pushed through her as he commandeered her mentor's chair.

Alex was a very handsome man, with just enough flecks of gray in his black hair to make him looked distinguished. He possessed glacier-blue eyes and a dimpled chin. His shoulders were presidential, his waist lean. He nodded at a chair across from the desk. "Sit down."

"I'd rather stand."

"Suit yourself."

She crossed her arms. His smirk irked the hell out of her. "What do you want?"

"Aren't you going to congratulate me on my new position?"

"No."

He leaned forward, rested his elbows on the desk, and pressed the tips of his fingers together. "You know, things don't have to be this way between us."

She glared.

This was the scumbag who'd bruised her ego and usurped her mentor's place. It wasn't so much that he'd lied to her about his wife. If she was honest with herself, she'd admit she wasn't even that upset over losing him. What really hurt was his betrayal. Just when she'd decided to finally trust a man and put her heart on the line. She'd taken a chance and it had blown up in her face. Plus, he'd made her an unwitting partner in his adultery. She couldn't forgive him for that.

The bastard.

Shame. That's what she felt when she looked at Alex Fredericks. Shame and remorse and self-loathing.

"I'd like to give you the benefit of the doubt, Jillian.

We can start over fresh, you and I." Alex raked his gaze over her, his eyes lingering on her breasts.

Her fingers twitched to reach across that desk and smack his smug face. "Give *me* the benefit of the doubt?"

"I'm merely saying there are ways we can repair our tattered relationship." Alex got up and came around the corner of the desk toward her. Surely he was not suggesting what she feared he was suggesting. Was he hinting about resuming their affair?

Jillian held her ground. She was not about to let him make her back up, but she hated being this close to him. Hated the familiar smell of his cologne in her nostrils. Hated that she'd ever thought he was worthy of her caring.

He stood right in front of her, his eyes predatory.

"I've missed you, Jillian," he said.

She snorted.

"It's true."

"Does your wife know how much you've missed me?"

Alex shifted his weight. "My wife and I . . . we have an understanding."

"What? You screw around and she doesn't understand?"

"I've especially missed that sarcastic wit." He reached out and stroked the back of his hand across her cheek.

"Don't." Jillian grabbed his wrist and flung his hand away from her. "Don't you ever touch me again."

"I *am* your boss."

"And this is sexual harassment. I can file charges."

Alex's expression was hooded, inscrutable. He was too good of a politician to acknowledge her accusation. He didn't move.

Jillian sank her hands on her hips and stepped forward

until their noses almost touched. She'd seen this man naked, done intimate things with him that she now sorely regretted. She couldn't believe she'd slept with him and even stupidly imagined having a future with him. She felt like a complete idiot. She'd been right all along—love was for suckers and fools.

He blinked and she saw a flicker of contrition in his eyes, but the whisper of humanity was gone as quickly as it appeared. "Ms. Samuels," he said coldly.

"Yes?"

"I wouldn't recommend that course of action. It would be my word against yours, and I could make your life here quite miserable, indeed."

He was right and she knew it. Blake was gone, and even before that she'd been feeling a strong sense of unease. Now with Fredericks in charge, it was too much to bear.

She experienced that end-of-the-tunnel sensation again she'd been feeling ever since that day in court with Randal Petry. The same day Blake died.

"I don't have to put up with this," Jillian said, injecting her voice with steel as cold as his.

"What do you intend on doing about it?" He drew up his shoulders, puffed out his chest.

"You're a real ass, and I can't believe I slept with you."

"As I recall, we didn't do much sleeping. I miss you, Jillian. Your fire and your guts and your passion. Seriously, I'd really hate to demote you."

That did it. She wasn't going to put up with his threats. She'd had enough. "You know what, Alex? Shove this job up your ass. I quit."

Chapter Two

Back in her own office, Jillian opened her desk drawers and chucked her belongings into a cardboard box. She thought about calling Delaney or Tish or maybe even Rachael, who was living in the isolated terrain of southwest Texas.

But Jillian did not pick up the phone. Her friends all had their own lives, loves, husbands, and children.

They would listen to her, of course. And sympathize. But they couldn't really understand. They could never know what it was like to grow up the way she'd grown up. They'd try to get her to laugh and tell her everything was going to be all right. But she knew that wasn't true. Nothing was ever going to be the same again.

Blake was really gone.

It hit her then. That she really didn't have anyone. She was alone and it was her own fault. She'd wanted to stay unattached. Her job had been her excuse, but in truth, intimacy of any form scared the hell out of her.

Maybe in the back of her mind, she'd always known Alex was unobtainable. He was too good-looking and accomplished to be single, plus she'd never come right out and asked him if he was married. Why not?

You've got to stop this line of thinking. You can't let yourself get dragged down.

She feared that if the dark cloud chasing her ever caught up with her, the depression would swallow her whole. She had to do something. She had to get away from her life, think this thing through, formulate an action plan.

Two security guards appeared in her doorway. "DA Fredericks sent us. We're here to escort you off the premises, Ms. Samuels," the tallest one said sheepishly.

"Fine." Jillian snapped her briefcase closed and straightened.

"I'll carry that box for you," said the second security guard.

"Thank you."

They escorted her down the corridor, past the curious eyes of her colleagues. Jillian held her head high. A few minutes later, hands shaking, she slid behind the wheel of her red Sebring convertible, the cardboard box stowed in the back behind her, her briefcase stashed on the passenger seat. With trembling fingers, she tried to stab the key into the ignition. After several fumbling attempts, she finally got the engine started.

Were all men cheating bastards? Lying pigs? Even Blake had cheated on his wife. He'd told her his infidelity was what had destroyed his marriage. He regretted it. He was ashamed of what he'd done, but he'd done it. If a good guy like Blake couldn't keep his pants zipped . . .

I'd like to give you the benefit of the doubt, Jillian. We can start over fresh, you and I. Alex's words rang in her head.

Jillian gritted her teeth. Had he honestly thought she'd jump at the chance to resume their affair? God, how she regretted sleeping with the man, but even more, she regretted feeling as if they'd had something special.

Fool. In your heart you knew better.

It was her own fault for daring to think she deserved the same kind of happiness her friends had found. They'd all wished on the wedding veil. All met the loves of their lives. They'd told her it was worth the risk. That she could find love too. So she'd dared to take a chance.

And it had exploded in her face. Dammit, she'd known better.

Blake dropped dead in Starbucks of the brain tumor he'd hidden from me.

He had abandoned her as well. The only man she'd ever really trusted. Jillian stared unseeingly through the windshield as she drove from the parking lot, her mind numb. Losing Blake hurt so damned much.

Tears, hot and unexpected, burned the back of her eyelids, but she refused to let them fall. She sucked in air, sucked up the pain, closed off her heart. Never again. She'd been hurt too many times by men to ever truly trust one.

It didn't matter that her three best friends had found true love and happily-ever-after. They were different from her. They believed in magic.

No matter how hard she tried, Jillian couldn't believe.

Without even knowing how she got there, numb from everything that had happened in the past week, Jillian drove to the condo she rented in a trendy area of Houston not far from downtown. Her lease was up at the end of the month; she'd planned on renewing it, but now she realized there was nothing holding her here. She'd lost everything. Her mentor, her job, her self-respect.

She wanted to curl into a tight ball and howl from the pain. She hated herself like this. Vulnerable, taken advantage of, used, disregarded. She'd spent her life trying to rise above the victim mentality, to prove she deserved better than the way she'd been treated by her stepmother.

But now she felt stupid, deceived, cheated. And worst of all, the defensive mechanism that had kept her safe all these years, the guard she kept around her heart, had failed her miserably.

She walked into her quiet, lonely house, aching to her very core. She didn't know what drove her, but she tossed her purse and her briefcase on the table and stalked to the bedroom. She went to the cedar chest at the end of her bed, started yanking out sweaters and tossing them heedlessly about the room. At the bottom of the chest she found what she hadn't consciously known she was looking for.

The magical wedding veil.

Rachael had passed it on to her months earlier. It was a floor-length mantilla style made of Rosepoint lace. She remembered the day Delaney had found the veil in a consignment shop just before her wedding to the wrong man, and she remembered the fanciful story the store owner had told.

According to the lore, in long-ago Ireland, there had lived a beautiful young witch named Morag, who possessed a great talent for tatting incredible lace. People came from far and wide to buy the lovely wedding veils she created, but there were other women in the community who were envious of Morag's beauty and talent.

These women lied and told the magistrate that Morag was casting spells on the men of the village. The magistrate arrested Morag but found himself falling madly in love with her. Convinced that she must have cast a spell upon him as well, he moved to have her tried for practicing witchcraft. If found guilty, she would be burned at the stake. But in the end, the magistrate could not resist the power of true love.

On the eve before Morag was to stand trial, he kidnapped her from the jail in the dead of night and spirited her away to America, giving up everything he knew for her. To prove that she had not cast a spell over him, Morag promised never to use magic again.

As her final act of witchcraft, she made one last wedding veil, investing it with the power to grant the deepest wish of the wearer's soul. She wore the veil on her own wedding day, wishing for true and lasting love. Morag and the magistrate were blessed with many children and much happiness. They lived to a ripe old age and died in each other's arms.

Delaney had wished on the veil to get out of marrying the wrong man, and in the end, she'd found her heart's desire in her soul mate, Nick Vinetti.

Then Delaney had passed the veil on to Tish.

Tish had wished to get out of debt, and the granting of her wish had brought her back together with the husband she'd lost but never stopped loving.

And then Tish had passed the veil on to Rachael.

Rachael had wished to stop being so romantic, and she'd ended up marrying the hero of her dreams.

Jillian didn't believe in magic, but the wedding veil was all the hope she had left. She'd lost everything else.

"What a load of crap," she muttered, but even as she muttered it, she took the antique veil from its protective wrapping and settled it on her head. Compelled by a mysterious force beyond her control, she stared at herself in the mirror.

"I wish," she muttered, "I wish I'd been born into a loving, trusting, giving family. I wish . . . I wish . . . I wish . . ." Her words trailed off as she realized what it was she really wanted.

Finally, she whispered, "I wish I had a brand-new life."

The second the wish was out of her mouth, her scalp began to tingle and she felt her body grow suddenly heavy. With the wish on her lips, the veil on her head, and utter despair in her heart, Jillian curled up on the floor and fell into a deep, exhausted sleep.

UNTIL TWO YEARS AGO, Tucker Manning had led a magical life.

People said he was charmed, and it was true. Born the youngest child and only son to James and Meredith Manning, he'd been spoiled by his parents and his three older sisters straight from the get-go. He'd possessed an easygoing personality and a bad-boy smile women simply couldn't resist.

And when he discovered he'd not only inherited the famed Manning carpentry skills, but that he had a natural flare for architecture as well, the world beat a path to his door. He had put himself through architectural school with his carpentry skills. For his senior class project, twenty-two-year-old Tuck had designed and constructed an innovative learning center for elementary schoolchildren. Then something amazing and bizarre happened.

The grade point average of every single child enrolled in Tuck's new learning center shot up.

Tuck brushed if off to coincidence. But educators seemed convinced it was the building. They claimed something about the lighting and the open-air blueprint stimulated learning. Other schools heard what had happened, and they commissioned Manning Learning Centers.

Tuck designed them. Each and every time, test scores rose and grade point averages shot up. Tuck figured it was a self-fulfilling prophecy. People thought their children would get smarter in his buildings, so they did.

Architectural Digest ran a feature story on him, dubbing him "Magic Man." He traveled the world building schools and getting rich.

Then he met Aimee Townsend in Albany, New York. A kindergarten teacher by trade. Beautiful girl. Petite. Honey-blond hair, big blue eyes, creamy porcelain complexion. Wearing a *Wizard of Oz* green sweater and a short brown wool skirt. Nice legs. No pantyhose. Wholesome and heartwarming.

Tuck had designed and built *that* classroom as if it was just for her.

Two months later, they were married and bought a loft in Manhattan. He loved city life, but Aimee was a small-town girl at heart, and she made him promise that when they were ready to start a family, they would move to the place where she'd spent her summer vacations as a kid before her parents got divorced. The place she loved most in the world.

Salvation, Colorado.

Tuck had said glibly, easily, "Sure. Why not?" Kids were a long way off.

Then Aimee got very sick with a deadly form of ovarian cancer. He took her from doctor to doctor. Private clinic to exclusive hospital. They consulted experts in Europe and Japan. They went through most of his money, but Tuck didn't care. All he wanted was to save his wife.

In the end, Aimee had whispered, "Take me to Colorado, Tuck. That's where I want to die. At the lake house. In Salvation."

And that was where the magic had run out.

Now Tuck hunkered alone in a small rowboat in the middle of Salvation Lake in Salvation, Colorado. In spite of his down coat, the wind sliced through him, as cold as a ceramic blade. To warm himself, he took another swig from the bottle of Johnny Walker Red at his feet. The whiskey neatly seared the back of his throat.

"Look at the stars, Aimee," Tuck whispered into the midnight sky carpeted with a thousand points of starlight. "Brilliant as the night I asked you to marry me. Remember?"

The water stretched out around him, inky black and vast. He was a good fifty yards from shore, where the first snowfall of the season clung to the pine trees, looming up like ghostly giants.

"I know I didn't get started on renovating the lake house this year like I promised. A lot of things got in the way. Chick Halsey hired me to add a bedroom onto his house, because he and Addie are expecting another baby. Their fourth. And before that, Jessie Dolittle had me build a pole barn for some new mules. Then there were the special-order cabinets for an older couple that just moved up here from Denver. Now the lake house will have to wait because of winter. I'm sorry to disappoint you again, babe. I'll get started on it come spring, I promise."

Another slug of the Johnny Walker and he was a regular furnace inside.

He could picture Aimee sitting across from him in the rowboat. Her long blond hair trailing down her back, her blue eyes aglow, looking the way she'd looked the night he proposed. Right here on this lake. It had been summer then, Fourth of July, actually. Fireworks going off all around the lake, a picnic basket of fried chicken sitting in the bottom of the boat between them. The taste of watermelon on their tongues as they'd kissed.

He'd slipped a four-carat diamond sparkler on her hand, and she'd said, "Yes, yes, yes. You just have to promise me one thing."

"Anything," he'd breathed.

"You can never, ever cheat on me the way my dad cheated on my mother. I won't stand for it. Promise you'll never break my heart."

"I promise," Tuck had sworn. It was an easy promise. He loved her so much, he'd never jeopardize what they had over another woman. His mistake, he realized now, was that he hadn't made her swear not to break his heart.

Tuck's breath frosted in the chilly air. "I miss you, babe. I miss you so damn much. I'm not worth shit without you."

If Aimee were here, she would have chided him for cursing. She was so sweet, so innocent. Too innocent for this sorry world.

Grief knotted his throat.

It was bad today.

Some days it was better. Some days he was almost his

old self again, flirting innocently with the waitresses at the Bluebird Café, whistling while he sanded down cabinets or planed doors, smiling at people on the streets. Forgetting for hours at a stretch. Some days the sorrow didn't hit him until he was underneath the covers with the lights turned off, and the empty spot in the bed beside him stretched out as wide as the lake.

Then the grief would sledgehammer him. His beloved Aimee was gone, and he was alone.

Some days, like today, were so bad that the only thing that could dull the pain was good old Johnny W. He put the whiskey bottle to his lips. Took another sip and wondered if it was against the law to drink and row.

When the hell did it ever stop hurting? When would he wake up and not listen for the sound of her moving about the kitchen, cooking him egg-white omelets, which he despised but had eaten anyway to make her happy? She'd told him he had to watch his cholesterol, because she wanted him with her until they were stooped and gray. Tuck had eaten the loathsome egg-white omelets, but she'd been the one to break the pact. Aimee would never grow stooped and gray. She was forever twenty-five.

He threw back his head and howled at the starry sky. "Fuuuuck!"

The sound of his mournful curse carried on the crisp night air, echoing up and down the lake. The outburst made him feel a little better so he did it again.

"Fuuuuck!"

Wind rushed into his lungs, freezing the pipes the whiskey had previously warmed. He got to his feet, threw his arms wide, and embraced the icicle breeze. Bring it on, Mother Nature.

"Fuuuuck!"

The boat wobbled. Tuck stumbled. Johnny Walker played fast and loose with his balance. He tried to sit back down, but gravity already had him in a choke hold.

Next thing he knew, Tucker Manning, the former Magic Man of Manhattan, was tumbling headlong into Salvation Lake.

EVIE MANNING RED DEER was locking up the Bluebird Café when her husband, Ridley, came up the sidewalk and slipped his arms around her waist. He pressed his face into her hair and pulled her up flush against his body so she could feel his arousal pressing into her backside.

"Mmm," he murmured. "You smell like fry bread."

She turned in his arms. His shoulders were as broad as beams, his ebony hair longer than hers, and she slipped her arms around his neck, tilting her lips up for a kiss.

Ridley crushed his mouth against hers. Evie breathed him in. God, how she loved this man.

When she'd come to Salvation to be with her younger brother in his time of grief over losing his young wife, she could never have imagined that she would fall in love with a native, marry him, and end up running the Bluebird Café. She was a pastry chef who'd trained at Lenotre in Paris. She'd trotted the globe. Seen the world. Met royalty and movie stars. She'd had far more than her share of lovers. But Salvation, Colorado, was where she'd lost her heart, and she'd freely surrendered her old life to be with this man. Ridley Red Deer was everything Evie had never known she wanted.

Ridley was kind and generous, strong and understanding. While he was truly masculine, he had a tender heart as big as the sky. He grounded her, calmed her in a way no one else ever had.

He broke the kiss, nuzzled her neck, and slipped his hands up underneath her coat.

"Ridley." She giggled.

"Uh-huh?" He lowered his eyelids suggestively.

"We're out on the street for everyone to see. Save it for when we get home."

"Everyone knows how crazy I am about you." He ran his tongue along her neck, sending shivers of delight darting down her spine. "How I can't keep my hands off you."

Panting, she pulled away. "Down, boy."

He chuckled and let her go but reached out to take her hand. She looked at his profile in the lamplight. Proud Native American nose, ruddy skin, high cheekbones, intelligent dark eyes. Her heart did an instinctive little hopscotch the way it always did when she caught sight of him.

Ridley linked his fingers through hers, and they started down the street, swinging their arms in unison, heading for their house on the next block over. Every night, he came to walk her home from the café.

"So how was your day?"

"We cleared four hundred dollars."

"Not bad for a Thursday in down season."

"We had a caravan of recreational vehicles stop in, snowbirds on their way south for the winter. They'd seen the feature story on us in *RV Today*."

"That's great."

She could hear his pride for her in his voice. Evie

leaned into him, inhaled his familiar scent. "So how was Tucker when you left him?"

"Um, I wasn't with Tuck tonight."

"What do you mean?" She punched her husband playfully on the upper arm. "Are you teasing me?"

"Dutch dropped by and we watched college basketball. UNLV trounced the hell out of USC."

Evie stopped walking and sank her hands on her hips. "Ridley, please don't tell me you forgot."

"Forgot what?"

Worry grabbed hold of her. "Rid, it's the second anniversary of Aimee's death. I told you this morning to go hang with Tuck when you got off work."

"You didn't tell me."

"I did." She heard her voice rise an octave.

"When did you tell me?"

"You were in the shower, and I was putting on my makeup, and I clearly told you—"

"If you told me when I was in the shower, then I didn't hear you. Running water and all that."

"Never mind." Evie spun on her heels and started walking in the opposite direction. She wrung her hands. "I can't believe you forgot the day Aimee died."

"You're overreacting," Ridley said, chasing after her. "Tuck's been a lot better lately."

She stopped and spun around. "Am I? What about last year?"

A sobering look passed over her husband's face. "That was last year. Tuck's come a long way since then."

"But it's the anniversary of her death."

Ridley pressed a hand to the nape of his neck. "Look, I'm sorry. I should have remembered."

"We've got to get over to the lake house. No telling what kind of shape he's in." She started running down the street, then cut across the town square, an odd sense of urgency pressing down on her. Tuck was in trouble; she just knew it.

"Evie, hang on," Ridley called out. "I'll go get the car."

Ten minutes later, they pulled up into the driveway of the lake house where Tuck had been living. All the lights were out, and the place was silent.

"It's dark," Evie said, anticipating the worst.

"It's nine-thirty. Is it possible he just went to bed early?"

Evie hopped out of the car, dashed up the front steps, and twisted the knob. The door sprang inward. No one locked their doors in Salvation except during tourist season. Evie flicked on the light in the foyer. "Tuck?"

Ridley came up behind her. "Tuck!"

"Tucker, are you here? It's me and Ridley."

No answer.

"Check the upstairs bedrooms; I'll check his workshop," Evie instructed her husband.

They split up and searched the house. Minutes later, they met up again in the kitchen. Ridley was shaking his head.

"He's gone and done something stupid again," Evie said. "I just know it."

"You don't know that." Ridley slid his big arm around her shoulder. "Don't jump to conclusions."

"We've got to check the dock."

"Why would he be on the dock? It's freezing cold out on the water."

Evie strode out onto the redwood dock, feeling the boards vibrate as Ridley came up behind her. She tried to imagine what she would feel like if something happened to her husband, but the thought was too horrible to bear.

"I see your brother's rowboat," Ridley said.

"Where?"

Her husband pointed out across the lake stretching as dark as midnight.

Evie squinted. She could barely make it out, but the boat looked empty. Her hand strayed to her throat.

Oh, little brother, what have you done?

The next thing she knew, Ridley was stripping off his coat, kicking off his shoes.

"What is it?"

"I see something. I see him. He's out there."

"Tuck's in the water?"

In answer to her question, Ridley dove in. Evie's blood thundered in her ears as she watched her husband disappear underneath the icy black water.

Chapter Three

Tuck coughed up a lungful of Salvation Lake.

He opened his eyes and looked up at his sister and brother-in-law. He was lying on his back on the dock, soaking wet, shivering so hard he could barely breathe.

"Thank God, he's alive." Evie burst into tears.

"Go start the car, crank the heater," Ridley instructed.

Evie ran ahead of them.

It was only then that Tuck realized his brother-in-law was as wet as he. Ridley slipped an arm underneath Tuck's shoulder and helped him to his feet. "Lean on me."

"Wh-wh-wh—" His teeth chattered so hard he could barely speak, so he just gave up trying and let Ridley half drag him to his Toyota 4Runner.

Evie had the engine running and the heater blasting by the time Ridley deposited Tuck in the backseat. She draped a blanket over her husband's shoulders and then folded another one around him.

She wrinkled her nose. "You smell like a brewery."

Tuck didn't defend himself. His sister was right. He smelled—and felt—like a skid-row bum.

Glowering, she hopped behind the wheel and drove to her house. They arrived and got out of the car.

"I can't believe you tried to drown yourself," she

scolded, following along beside them as Ridley helped Tuck in the back door. His damned legs didn't want to bend.

"I . . . didn't." It was all Tuck could manage.

"No?" Evie worried her bottom lip with her teeth and sank her hands on her hips.

Tuck shook his head and slumped into the kitchen chair.

"Then what were you doing out on that lake?"

He didn't have the energy to answer.

Evie turned. "Rid, get out of those wet things and take Tuck with you. I'll have hot soup waiting when you get finished."

"I'm taking him to the sweat lodge," Ridley said.

She made a face. "He needs to get dry first."

"He needs more than that, and the sweat lodge will warm him up," his brother-in-law said firmly. "If ever a man has needed a vision quest to set him on the right path, it's your brother."

"He doesn't believe in that stuff. You know we were raised Roman Catholic."

"You're the one who doesn't believe," Ridley said.

Tuck knew Ridley used the sweat lodge as part of his religious practices, but he'd never been invited to take part. He'd been mildly interested and had asked a few questions, but Ridley and Tuck had the kind of relationship where you didn't pry.

"Your brother has an open mind," he continued. "You get Tuck some soup. I'm going to go start a fire in the sweat lodge."

"Not in those wet things you're not."

"Woman," Ridley growled. "I know you get bossy

when you're upset, so I'm not going to fight with you. Heat your brother some soup. I'll be back in a minute."

Ridley disappeared out the back door, leaving Tuck alone with his second oldest sister. Evie turned her back on him, went to the refrigerator, pulled out a plastic container of homemade chicken noodle soup, and stuck it in the microwave to heat.

Tuck sat dripping water all over her kitchen floor and shivering into the blanket. "I'm sorry, Evie. It wasn't my intention to upset you. It was just . . . I couldn't stop . . . Aimee."

She shuddered and tears gleamed in her hazel eyes. "Tuck, I know you're still grieving, especially today, but I can't bear to think of what would have happened if we hadn't come along when we did. I don't mean to lecture, but it's been two years. At some point, you've got to let go of Aimee. You know she wouldn't want you to keep hanging on, jeopardizing your own life."

Tuck drew in a shaky breath as the gravity of the situation hit him. He *had* almost died tonight, and he didn't even know how he felt about it.

"You've been doing so well lately, and I'd thought you were finally healing and—" The microwave timer dinged, and Evie broke off what she was saying. She took out the soup, plucked a spoon from the silverware drawer, and slid the Tupperware bowl across the table toward him.

Grateful for the soup, Tuck reached out for it as Ridley came in the back door. "The sweat lodge is ready," he said. "You can bring the soup with you."

He got up, holding the bowl, and followed his brother-in-law into the backyard toward a white domed structure with a small hole in the roof. A thin plume of gray smoke swirled through the opening, sending the smell of mesquite into the air.

"Go in and take off all your clothes," Ridley instructed. "Sit down on the bearskin rug, and breathe in the smoke. Make your mind empty. Pick a word that resonates with you. A mantra like love, peace, serenity. Repeat it over and over as you breathe slow and deep. Stay in here until you have a vision."

"You're not coming in with me?" Tuck met his brother-in-law's eyes.

"This is your vision quest. You're the one who's searching for meaning, my friend."

"Umm . . . from what I can tell, there is no meaning."

"Exactly. Now go find it." Ridley gave him a shove. "I'm tired of your sister fretting about you. It's time you took responsibility for your own healing."

Anger crouched inside Tuck, a tiger ready to spring, but he knew Ridley was right. He'd worried Evie long enough. Who knew, maybe a vision quest was precisely what he needed. "I . . . How will I know if I'm doing it right?"

"Let whatever happens be okay," Ridley said cryptically. Then he turned and went back into the house.

Tuck ducked into the sweat lodge. There was a small fire in the middle of the room and radiant sauna stones circling the fire pit. Other than bearskin rugs, quilted blankets, and oversized throw pillows, the place was empty. But there were stereo speakers bolted to the walls, and they spilled low, steady sounds of Native American Indian drumming.

He stripped off the wet clothes. The temperature in the

sweat lodge climbed. His primary objective was warmth and dryness. He didn't give a damn about a vision quest.

The bearskin rug tickled his naked butt. He sat cross-legged in front of the fire. Smoke swirled upward, funneling through the flue and out the hole in the roof.

Johnny Walker Red was still doing a number on his head. He closed his eyes. Took a deep breath.

Let whatever happens be okay.

He sipped the soup, feeling the liquid warm him up inside. He sat and sipped, inhaling smoke and listening to drum music and waiting for something to happen.

But nothing did.

Tuck thought of Aimee and how'd he'd promised to buy the lake house from her dad and renovate it. She believed the house held special spiritual powers. It had given her peace in her final days. She believed it could restore his inspiration, reignite the creative magic her illness had stolen from him if he'd give it the chance. But he'd lost his faith in magic.

"Fix it up, Tuck. Fix up the house and you'll see. It will come to full life again, just as you will in the process of rebuilding," she whispered to him on the day she'd died. "Promise me, please."

He'd promised, but he hadn't had the heart to follow through with it yet.

Tuck thought of his rowboat still out on Salvation Lake. He thought about Evie and Ridley and how they spent too much time worrying about him. Hell, Evie had moved to Salvation because she'd been so worried about him, and then she'd met Ridley and married him. He thought of how easy life used to be for him—the Magic Man.

But the magic was long gone. He'd used up his share.

He took a deep breath and felt a slow, languid heat snake through his body. His muscles relaxed. His head spun.

Dizzy. He felt dizzy.

Dreamily, Tuck set aside the cup of soup. It was hot in here, steamy, and getting hotter all the time. Sweat beaded his brow. Smoke grew thicker in the room. He coughed, blinked, and then he could have sworn he saw someone step out of the smoke.

It was a woman. High breasts, narrow waist, curvy hips, walking straight toward him, cloaked in shadows and smoke.

"Aimee?" he croaked.

She came closer and he could see it wasn't Aimee. His Aimee had been petite, small-boned, blond.

This woman was an Amazon. At least five-ten, maybe taller, black Cleopatra hair, chocolate brown eyes.

"Who are you?" he whispered, but she didn't answer.

Instead, she started to perform a slow, deliberate striptease, and it was only then that he realized she was clothed in veils. White veils. Wedding veils. She twirled in time to the drumming, peeling off a veil with each turn. The music got faster and so did she, whisking off veil after veil until she was a whirling dervish, spinning around the sweat lodge.

The music stopped.

And she spun to a halt in front of him.

All the veils were gone, strewn about the sweat lodge. She was totally naked.

Instantly, he got an erection.

God, she was a beauty. The cut of her shiny ebony hair accentuated her high cheekbones. Ivory skin smooth as glass. Full, crimson lips. The high thrust of her pert pink nipples. The flat of her belly. The springy dark triangle of hair above her thighs.

Her gaze was bold, but her eyes . . . her eyes . . . they were *lonely*. As lonely as Tuck's.

The music started again. A slow, thumping beat. Like the heart of an athlete.

Thud. Thud. Thud.

She sauntered toward him; she was as leggy as a runway model.

Was she real? Was he dreaming? It didn't feel like a dream. Was he on a vision quest? Was this supposed to be happening?

Let whatever happens be okay, Ridley had said.

What did that mean? Was he just supposed to go with it no matter what transpired? Have sex with a stranger?

She dropped to her knees in front of him, reached out, and walked her fingers up his forearm.

Tuck gulped.

If this was some kind of hallucination, it was a damned good one. She felt so real.

"Who are you?" he asked again.

A sly grin lifted her lips. "Don't you know?"

"No."

She laughed, a low sexy sound, and then she said the strangest thing. "Why, I'm the other side of you."

"Other side of me?'

"Uh-huh. Mirror image."

Her answer made no sense. He was just about to tell her that, when she leaned in close and ran her tongue along his lips. She tasted like dark chocolate—rich and sinful.

He hadn't been with a woman since Aimee, and he

didn't want to be with this one, but his body had other ideas. His cock grew even harder.

She noticed. Purred. Touched him.

He was granite in her hands.

Shame shoved Tuck's heart into his stomach. He felt as if he was cheating on Aimee.

It's just a dream.

Was it?

And besides, Aimee's dead. You're not cheating on her. You're a young, healthy man. You're allowed to have sexual desires.

Where were these thoughts coming from? What was happening to him? This was a bad idea. He had to get out of the sweat lodge. He tried to get up, but the naked woman with the exotic brown eyes was throwing her legs around him, straddling his lap.

"No, no. I don't want you." He settled his hands around her waist to pull her off him, but her skin felt so warm and soft beneath his palms that he just held on.

"Shh," she murmured, like a mother soothing her baby. "Shh." She put her lips against his throat and kissed him so lightly that it felt as if she was tickling him with a feather. "It's okay. It's all right."

He closed his eyes, battling against his desire. "I'm not in a good place. I'm—"

"Shh." Her arms went around him, and she cradled his head to her breasts.

Tuck shifted, his resistance melting. He laid back against the bearskin rug and took a deep breath. Smoke swirled in his lungs. His head spun. The room was so hot. His body was drenched in sweat.

Lower and lower she kissed, heading for dangerous territory.

He threaded his fingers through her hair. "No, no," he protested weakly.

"Yes . . ." She kissed him. "Yes."

Another kiss.

Then her hand was on him. Stroking his throbbing head. She laughed a smooth laugh that loosened something in his belly.

"It's just a dream anyway; it's not real," he muttered, all the fight gone out of him.

She closed her mouth over him, and overwhelmed, Tuck simply surrendered.

JILLIAN WOKE UP from her naughty sex dream with a flushed face and a pounding heart. She shivered, remembering him. Tall and muscled, but not overtly so. Straight nose, strong chin, a trustworthy jaw ringed with a stubble of beard. His eyes had been the color of expensive whiskey. His hair like winter wheat.

He'd seemed so sad. As if he'd been carrying the weight of the world on his shoulders for a very long time and didn't possess the strength to take one more step.

And then she'd seduced him.

Gulping, Jillian shook her head to dispel the image and threw back the covers. And that's when the realization hit her. She had nowhere to go and nothing to do. In all her twenty-nine years on earth, it was a first.

She fell back against the pillows, staring at the ceiling, thinking of the sex dream. It had seemed so real that she wouldn't have been surprised to find the man beside her. Yet, while her body felt strangely electrified, the other side of the bed stretched empty.

What did surprise her, however, was the fact she still wore the mourning clothes she'd worn to Blake's funeral. And she still had that stupid wedding veil on her head.

Chagrined at having put the veil on in the first place and being desperate enough to make a wish, she yanked it off and sprang to her feet. She could have lingered in bed, tried to get back the wisp of the smoking hot dream, but Jillian was not a woman who lingered, even when she had nowhere to go or nothing to do.

She folded the veil and stuffed it in the cedar chest, wanting it out of sight, out of mind. She stripped, leaving her clothes lying in the floor, and took a hot shower, washing away the last remnants of the haunting dream, the man with the whiskey eyes.

There. It's over. Forgotten.

But as she poured herself a cup of coffee from the automatic-drip coffeemaker on her kitchen cabinet—it was the only kitchen appliance she owned beyond the major ones that came with the place—she thought of him again.

He'd seemed so damned sad.

The guy wasn't real. Move on. It was just a dream.

God, but he'd had some kind of body.

Haven't you had enough of men after what Alex—

Enough.

Determined to stop thinking about the dream man, she took peanut butter—the smooth kind—from her pantry. She slathered it on a slice of wheat bread, folded it over, and called it breakfast. Balancing the peanut butter sandwich on her coffee cup, she opened the back door and walked out onto the stoop of her condo, where she liked to sit and watch the sunrise and eat her morning meal on the few days in Houston when the weather allowed such indulgences.

Jillian had just settled onto the first step and stuck the sandwich in her mouth when she saw him.

Hunkered in the corner behind the yaupon holly. Watching her like a fugitive. Correction. He wasn't watching her; he was watching the sandwich.

She took the peanut butter sandwich out of her mouth. "You hungry? You want this?"

He leapt from the shrubbery and trotted over.

Up close, she could see his mixed heritage—Lab, Doberman, collie, German shepherd, and with those ears, maybe even a bit of basset hound. He possessed big brown melancholy eyes, a sharp nose, and a tail that was too long for his body. He looked like a five-hundred-piece jigsaw puzzle put together by a three-year-old.

Nothing fit.

The mutt stopped at the bottom of the steps, nose twitching, oversized tail wagging. Jillian extended the sandwich, and he took it from her hand with surprising gentleness.

It was gone in two quick bites.

He looked hopeful.

"You still hungry?"

Of course he was still hungry. His flanks were so lean that she could count his ribs. His hair was matted, and she feared he had fleas and ticks, so she was leery of letting him into the condo.

"Hang on," she said. "I think I've got a can of chunked white albacore in the pantry."

He hung on.

She got the tuna. He scarfed it down as quickly as he'd disposed of the peanut butter sandwich. When he was done, he sat on his haunches and looked at her. She was not a pet person. Had never owned one. Not even a goldfish. Her stepmother wouldn't allow it, and she had no idea what to do with him.

You need to find his owner.

She knocked on her neighbors' doors. The dog followed. No one claimed him. After an hour of canvassing the neighborhood, she ended up back at her condo.

"Right back where we started."

The expression on his doggy face seemed to say, *Story of my life.*

She took him to the vet. She had nothing else to do, and it helped keep her mind off Blake and Alex and quitting her job and her crazy, wedding-veil-induced sex dream with a whiskey-eyed man in a sweat lodge.

"The dog's been neglected," the veterinarian told her. "He needs medicine."

"That's why I'm here."

"We'll give him shots, clean him up, check his blood work, and he needs to be neutered."

"I'm not going to keep him. I just want him healthy while I look for his owners."

"I seriously doubt he has an owner. If you keep him, look into the neutering thing."

"I'm not keeping him. I'm not a pet person. I don't do pets."

The vet prescribed medication. "Give him these pills once a month to prevent heartworms."

"Hello, not keeping him."

He pressed the prescription into her hand. "In case you change your mind."

She wasn't going to change her mind. She couldn't change it if she wanted to. Her condo didn't allow dogs.

When she got home, she called the *Houston Chronicle* and took out an ad. Then she went on the computer and posted on craigslist. *Lost dog.* She detailed his vital statistics and added her cell phone number.

"Now we wait," she told the mutt.

He gazed at Jillian as if she was the most impressive person on the face of the earth.

"Remember, Mutt, I'm not a pet person, so don't get attached. I'll just break your heart."

He looked as if he didn't believe her.

"I will. I'm mean that way. Ask anyone."

Her cell phone rang.

"Hey," she told Mutt. "This could be it. Your long-lost family." She flipped open her phone. "Hello?"

"Jillian Samuels?"

"Yes?" She hadn't put her name on the craigslist ad. The call couldn't be about the dog.

"This is Hamilton Green. I'm Blake Townsend's attorney," the man said.

At the mention of Blake's name, she curled her fingers tighter around the phone. "Yes?"

"I need to speak with you in person."

"What's this about?"

"Mr. Townsend has left you an inheritance and a sacred responsibility. May I have my secretary pencil you in for a three-thirty appointment on Tuesday?"

"HOW WAS THE SWEAT LODGE?" Ridley asked Tuck as they drove to the construction site on the other side of the mountain the following morning. They were both working as contract labor—Ridley hired as an electrician, Tuck as a carpenter for a new spec house going up.

Ridley was behind the wheel of his SUV. Tuck was ensconced in the passenger seat wishing he'd driven alone. But he'd woken up in the sweat lodge that morning, and Ridley had just assumed they'd carpool to the job site.

Tuck shrugged.

"Did you have a vision?"

"I don't want to talk about it."

"You sure? Because sometimes vision quests can be pretty intense."

"Mule deer in the bar ditch." Tuck pointed not so much to warn his brother-in-law just in case the animal decided to dart into the road as deer often did in that part of the country, but to distract him from the conversation. That damn vision was imprinted on his brain. It made him feel horny and guilty as hell. He was afraid of his own subconscious, and the last thing he wanted was to have Ridley Red Deer analyze it.

His brother-in-law slowed.

The doe raised her head as they motored past, and she stared Tuck squarely in the eyes. The deer looked accusatory, as if she knew all about those shameful sweat lodge happenings.

You're losing your marbles. Snap out of it.

"You sure you don't want to talk about it?" Ridley asked. "It might help to powwow."

"I'm good, thanks."

"That bad?"

"We're not talking about this."

"So you *did* have a vision?"

"That constitutes talking."

"Gotcha. No talking about the vision quest."

"Thank you."

A long moment of silence stretched out. Tuck let out a relieved breath. Ridley was gonna drop it. He stared out the window, studying the fall scenery. This time of year, most of the leaves were gone. The snow on the ground was light, but there would soon be more.

"So how'd you end up in the lake last night?" Ridley ventured. Apparently, he just wasn't going to let it go.

"My sister put you up to this conversation, didn't she?" Tuck asked.

"How'd you know?"

"You're not usually so intrusive."

"Come on, dude. Throw me a bone. You know Evie. She'll gnaw my ear off with questions if I don't bring her something."

"Sort of like what you're doing to me?"

"So you can see how annoying it is."

"She's my sister. I know how annoying it can be."

"About the lake . . ."

Tuck sighed. "I was feeling sorry for myself. Took a boat ride on the second anniversary of my wife's death. That's not so crazy."

"In the middle of the night? In Colorado? In October?"

"Hey, at least it wasn't February."

"Valid point. Although if it had been February, you could have just skated out on the lake."

Ridley shut up again, but this time Tuck was afraid to count on the silence. *Note to self: Find another carpool buddy.*

"Your sister loves you. She worries."

"I know."

"We both care about you."

"I know that too."

"There is life after Aimee."

That one he wasn't so sure about it. He might be breathing, but it sure as hell wasn't much of a life. Walking around with only a small shred of heart left inside him.

"You should start dating again."

Tuck folded his arms over his chest and stared determinedly out the window. "I'm not ready."

"Evie and I could double-date with you. If that'd make it easier." Ridley stopped at an intersection behind a green garbage truck.

Tuck focused on an banana peel dangling from a crack in the truck's tailgate. "Not interested."

"How about Sissie Stratford?"

"Aimee didn't like her, and she's got that phony laugh."

"Too bad Lily Massey got engaged to Bill Chambers. Aimee liked her and she's really pretty."

"I'm sure Bill isn't thinking it's too bad Lily said yes to his proposal."

Ridley snapped his fingers. "I know. What about Lexi Kilgore? She's nice."

"She's older than I am."

"Please, by what? Three years? Evie's two years older than me, and it makes no difference at all."

"Lexi's nice enough, but there's just no spark there; besides, she talks too much."

"What about that new bartender at the Rusty Nail? Have you see her?"

"I haven't been at the Nail in weeks."

"She's cute. Blond. I know you have a thing for blondes. I think her name's Tiffany or Amber or . . ." Ridley snapped his fingers. "Brandi. It's Brandi. Her name is Brandi."

"How very bartendery of her."

"So, you want me to introduce you?"

"Rid," Tuck growled. "I appreciate the effort, I really do. But I'm just not interested."

"You do know what my cultural beliefs are in regard to the vision quest, right?"

Tuck shrugged. "You might want to make that a little clearer for me."

"When you're a young man entering adulthood, or you're at a crossroads in your life, my tribe believes the vision quest guides you on to the next phase in life. You, my friend, are at a serious crossroad."

He couldn't argue with that. "Okay."

"The dream you had in the sweat lodge is a harbinger of what's ahead," Ridley continued. "Not what's behind you."

Tuck pondered that one. A harbinger of what lay ahead. Hmm. So he was going to be sexually molested by a wedding veil–draped dervish? The thought made him both uncomfortable and excited.

The excitement disturbed him.

"So about this vision. Maybe you're confused by the symbolism and you need me to interpret—"

"I'm turning on the radio now. What program is it that you really hate?" Tuck reached for the radio dial and snapped it on. He didn't want to discuss this. "Yeah, here it is—*Rush Limbaugh*."

Chapter Four

All weekend long, no one called about the dog.

By Tuesday, Jillian was convinced no one was going to claim him. Poor baby. She knew what it was like to be unwanted. "I guess I'm stuck with you, Mutt."

The dog didn't seem to mind.

Jillian was starting not to mind so much either. Sure, he shed hair all over the place, so she had to vacuum every day, and he had the bad habit of chewing on her shoes, but she was surprised by how much the dog lifted her spirits.

It was a pity. She'd found someone worse off than she was and that cheered her up.

"I'm only keeping you around because you make me feel good about myself," she told him.

Mutt seemed cool with that too.

"Can you behave yourself while I'm off to see Blake's lawyer? No shoe chewing? Especially stay away from the Jimmy Choos. If I'm unemployed much longer, I might have to sell those suckers on eBay for some quick cash."

Mutt wagged his tail.

"Okay, I'm taking you at your word. But to be on the safe side, I'm shutting you out of the bedroom. And fair warning—if I'm keeping you, we *are* looking into that whole neutering thing."

The dog lowered his head. Amazing how he seemed to understand her. Who knew that dogs could be so cool?

At three-thirty on the nose, Jillian walked into Hamilton Green's office. She'd tried not to think too much about what Blake could have left her in his will. Thinking about it made it too real. She still wasn't ready to fully accept that he was gone.

Maybe he'd left her his marble chess set. She'd like to have that to remember him by. As she settled into the chair across from the lawyer in his plush scholarly looking office, the tears she'd yet to shed thickened behind her eyelids.

"Thank you for coming, Ms. Samuels, and please accept my condolences on the loss of your mentor." Hamilton Green had a broad flat face, a Jay Leno chin, and salt-and-pepper hair that gave way to male pattern baldness. You could tell he'd never been handsome, not even in youth.

"You knew Blake was my mentor?"

"We golfed together. He spoke of you often and with great fondness."

The pressure behind her eyes tightened. She realized she'd known Blake longer and more thoroughly than she'd known her own father.

The lawyer steepled his fingers. "I'm certain his fondness for you is the reason he appointed you as executor."

Her throat constricted. "He did?"

"Blake also left instructions in his will that you be the one to scatter his ashes over Salvation Lake."

The announcement took her by surprise. "Me?"

He nodded. "The will still has to be probated, of course, and as executor, you'll be checking up on everything. But as it stands in Blake's current will, he left the bulk of his estate to legal aid charities. You were the only individual mentioned in his will. He had a new will drawn up the week after his daughter's death."

Jillian's nose burned. She bit down on her bottom lip. Honestly, while Blake had been her mentor and they'd been close, she hadn't truly realized she'd meant so much to him.

"He left you his property on Salvation Lake."

"Where is that?" Blake had never mentioned anything to her about owning lake property.

"Salvation, Colorado. It's a small tourist town north of Denver. The house was built in the sixties, and it has never been renovated. It's been vacant for years. I have no idea what condition it's in or even the approximate value of the property."

"Blake left me a lake house?" she repeated, still unable to believe it.

"He did at that."

"And he wants me to scatter his ashes on the lake?"

"Yes."

It was a lot to absorb. Emotion clotted her throat at the notion of scattering Blake's ashes. Alone. Suddenly, her world seemed very small, indeed. She had no experience with this sort of thing. She didn't even have anyone she could ask. Blake would have been the person she would have turned to for such advice.

"Here's a copy of his will and the keys to the house." Hamilton Green pushed a manila envelope across his desk toward her.

"The house is paid off?"

"Free and clear."

She took a deep breath, determined to do her duty firmly and without negligence. This is what Blake wanted. She would not disappoint him.

"And here are Blake's remains." The lawyer picked up an urn that had been sitting on the floor beside his desk and handed it to her.

At the weight of the urn, a tumult of emotions flipped through her. Sorrow and surprise, uncertainty and confusion, despair and yet at the same time, a small unexpected flicker of hope.

Blake had left her a lake house in Colorado.

It was almost as if he'd thrown her a life preserver in her moment of greatest need.

Salvation.

A fresh start. From the grave, Blake was offering her a fresh start. He'd given Jillian her first job; now he was giving Jillian her first home.

She stared at the urn and the manila envelope and the keys, and in that moment, she just knew what to do.

Accept Salvation.

RIDLEY RED DEER was worried about his wife's little brother.

He shouldn't have put Tuck in the sweat lodge. Clearly, from the way he had been acting, he hadn't been ready for whatever had happened in there. It had been like sticking a six-year-old on a Harley without a helmet and telling him to take off. A vision quest was heavy-duty mojo.

On the second anniversary of Aimee's death, Ridley had felt guided. He thought the spirit had spoken to him, telling him to shove a soaking wet, drunken Tuck into the sweat lodge to renew his ragged soul. But he could see that Tuck had been unsettled by whatever he'd experienced.

Doubt gnawed at Ridley. Evie had been right.

His wife was always right. It was damned aggravating.

Thing of it was, Ridley couldn't undo it. Tuck had already been initiated. He'd seen something. The only way Ridley could help him was to get him to discuss what he'd seen.

But Tuck was not inclined to talk.

Ridley picked up a six-pack of Michelob on his way home from work and dropped by the lake house. He found Tuck huddled on the dock in a deck chair, staring at the sunset with a University of Colorado blanket thrown over his lap.

"Are you remembering how cold the water is this time of year?" Ridley asked.

"Hey, buddy," Tuck greeted. "Have a seat."

Ridley dusted snow from the deck chair beside Tuck and plunked down. He twisted the top off a longneck bottle of Michelob and passed it to his brother-in-law before opening a second one for himself.

They said nothing for a long time. Just sipped and watched the sun slide down the sky. Finally, Ridley broke the silence. "You still planning on staying at the lake house?"

"Yes," Tuck said fiercely. "Starting next spring, I'm renovating the house the way I promised Aimee. I should have started it when Blake deeded the place to me four months ago, but I just couldn't summon the energy."

"It was pretty weird how Blake just deeded you the land out of the blue," Ridley said.

"I guess he felt guilty." Tuck's voice caught. "Blake

never came back to Salvation after the divorce. I suppose he held on to the cottage simply because he planned on giving it to Aimee one day. She had her own key, and he'd given her permission to use it anytime, but their relationship was so strained that she didn't want him to know we were here. She wouldn't let me tell him that she was dying."

"That's hard-core."

"Aimee just couldn't forgive her father for cheating on her mother and busting up the family. I tried to talk to her about forgiving him, but as sweet as she was, forgiveness was not one of Aimee's virtues. If you ever got on her shit list, you were banned for life."

"That must have been really hard on her dad," Ridley mused. Thinking about becoming a parent was causing him to consider things in a different light. He wondered what he would do if he ever found himself in a situation like Blake Townsend's relationship with his daughter, and he couldn't fathom it.

"She never gave him a chance to make amends. She didn't want him to know about her cancer."

"Why?"

"She didn't want his pity. Nor did she want him to suddenly start trying to be a father when he hadn't been around all those years."

Ridley was still puzzling it out. "Aimee cheated her father out of precious time with her. Looking at it from her father's perspective, she was pretty cruel to the guy."

"I know." Tuck looked glum. "But she had her mind set, and I couldn't change it. Sometimes you've just gotta stay out of it."

Ridley nodded. "You have no desire to ever go back to architecture? No more Magic Man of Manhattan?"

Tuck snorted a harsh laugh. "I was so full of shit back then. It took something like losing Aimee to make me see what matters most in life. The people you love. Like you and Evie. Aimee's ashes are scattered on this lake. I'm not going anywhere. Salvation's home."

"Aw, dude, tell me you're not getting mushy. Here, have another beer."

"I'm thinking I should hold off."

"Probably wise." Ridley nodded and noticed that fresh snowflakes had started drifting from the sky.

After another long moment, Tuck spoke. "I saw a woman."

"Huh? Are you dating someone?"

"No, no. I saw a woman. In the sweat lodge. In my vision. At least I hope it was a vision."

Ridley tensed. His stomach knotted. A woman could be a good omen or a bad one. It depended on the circumstances. He prayed it wasn't a bad omen. Evie would skin him alive if Tuck had had a vision with a bad omen. He didn't want to push. He was afraid his brother-in-law would pull back in like a truculent turtle.

"It probably wasn't even a vision," Tuck continued. "Probably just some weird Johnny Walker dream."

"Yeah, you gotta stay away from that stuff."

"I know. Usually I do . . . it's just that . . . anniversaries hit me hard." Tuck exhaled audibly.

Ridley's butt was getting cold, but he knew Tuck was on the verge of opening up, and he didn't want to break the tenuous thread. "So this woman you saw. She wasn't Aimee?"

Tuck shook his head.

"That bothered you? Seeing a woman and it not being Aimee?" He rubbed his palms together to warm them. It was cold on the dock, yes, but that wasn't the only place the chill was coming from.

"Yeah."

"This woman, what'd she look like?"

"Dark hair, pale skin, tall. I mean, really tall. Close to six foot. Beautiful in a smart, high-class kind of way. Like Cleopatra."

Ridley grunted. Uh-oh, that didn't sound good. Not good at all. He took a swig of his beer, afraid to ask what needed to be asked next.

"And," Tuck added, "she was naked."

Ridley choked on his beer. He sputtered, coughed. His braid fell forward across his shoulder.

"You okay?"

Ridley couldn't stop coughing, and tears of strain misted his eyes.

Tuck pounded him on the back. "Rid? You need the Heimlich?"

He shook his head. Oh shit. Evie was gonna kill him dead. "I'm okay."

"You sure?"

"This woman you saw," Ridley croaked. "Was she an . . . um . . . a temptress?"

Tuck's head jerked up. "How did you know?"

"The temptress is quite common in folklore and mythology," he said, not wanting to tell Tuck what seeing a temptress in a vision quest really meant. His brother-in-law simply wasn't ready to hear about that. "Did she . . . um . . . did she tempt you?"

"It was a sex dream, if that's what you're asking."

"Were feathers involved?" Ridley asked hopefully. Feathers were a good omen. Maybe feathers could temper the ominous naked-temptress-sex-dream thing.

Tuck frowned. "No, not feathers."

"But something?" Ridley fisted his hands. This was getting worse by the minute. He should stop asking questions, but he couldn't. He had to know exactly how bad it was.

"Veils."

Uneasiness took hold of him. Ridley's blood thickened in his veins, and his breath went thin. Hurriedly, he took another swallow of beer. "What kind of veils?"

"Wedding veils. Lots and lots of white lace wedding veils." Tuck slapped a hand on Ridley's thigh. "So, Red Deer, you're the Native American here. What does the vision mean?"

"Mean?" Ridley asked, hearing the nervousness in his voice. "Who says it means anything?"

"It doesn't mean anything?" Tuck sounded oddly disappointed. "I thought by the way you were choking on your beer that it probably meant something."

"Naw, not really," he lied. "I just swallowed wrong."

"You're a lousy liar, Rid."

"Who says I'm lying?"

"Me. When you lie, your nose twitches. Word to the wise—stay away from poker."

"It does not." Ridley put a hand to his nose.

"Then why are you touching your nose?"

"Bastard."

"So what's the big woo-woo sweat lodge secret?"

"No secret."

"Then why'd you come sit out here with me in the cold if you weren't trying to get me to tell you about the vision?"

"Because I'm worried about you."

"Ease my troubled mind. Tell me what the damned vision means."

"I'm no expert," Ridley hedged. He was in over his head.

"What does being visited by this wedding-veil-wielding temptress portend for the Magic Man of Manhattan?"

"It probably doesn't mean a thing."

"But if it did mean something . . ."

Ridley rolled off a shaky laugh. No point in alarming Tuck when he didn't have any strong evidence that something untoward was going to happen. "Hang loose, dude. You're blowing this all out of proportion. Sometimes a cigar is just a cigar."

"WE STILL CAN'T BELIEVE you're moving to Colorado lock, stock, and barrel," Delaney Cartwright Vinetti told Jillian as they shut the door closed on the rented U-Haul trailer and tucked a lock of hair behind her ear. "And in October. Autumn doesn't seem like the prime time for a move to a mountainous state."

"It's the perfect time," Jillian assured her. "I've got nothing else to lose."

Delaney was a pretty brunette with a people-pleasing personality. She'd been the one to find the three-hundred-year-old wedding veil in a consignment shop, and she'd immediately fallen under its spell. She'd believed in the fantastical story that went with the veil. She'd wished on it just before she was about to marry the wrong man and ended up finding her true love. Nick Vinetti was a detective for the Houston PD. They had a daughter, Audra, three and a half, and one-year-old twin sons, Adam and Aidan.

"But Blake's will hasn't even been probated yet."

"I'm the executor; I have to go check out the property."

"But you're moving. Visiting I could understand, but you're moving to the place sight unseen."

Jillian shrugged. "The lease was up on my condo. I couldn't justify signing up for a second year."

"It seems so sudden," Tish Gallagher Tremont added. "You don't even know what you're getting into."

"Now, come on, Tish, you're supposed to be the adventurous one of the group. Don't tell me motherhood has changed you that much," Jillian said.

Tish was an auburn-haired beauty who was almost as tall as Jillian. Delaney had passed the wedding veil on to her, and Tish had reconnected with the love of her life, former secret service agent Shane Tremont. They had a son, Max, who just turned two, and a three-month-old daughter, Samantha.

"And you're not eligible to practice law in Colorado," Tish said.

Her friends might not realize it, but she'd thought this thing through. "Not yet. But I have some money saved, and I'll sit for the Colorado bar as soon as I can. In the meantime, I'll take a job as a law clerk. It won't hurt to brush up on the basics."

"Jilly, are you really sure this is what you want?"

Rachael Henderson Carlton asked. "We're all going to miss you something terrible."

When Tish had remarried Shane, she gave the wedding veil to blond-haired, blue-eyed Rachael, who—after she'd started Romanceaholics Anonymous—ended up falling madly in love with Brody Carlton, the sheriff of her hometown of Valentine, Texas. Rachael was roundly and radiantly seven months pregnant with their first child due sometime around Christmas.

"I'm going to miss you guys, too, but come on, let's be honest. You've all got your own lives now. It's time I found my place in the world."

They'd been friends since they were suitemates at Rice University, and Jillian loved them all dearly, but they'd moved on with their lives, and she'd been the one left standing still. But the minute she'd told them she was going to Colorado, they'd organized a moving party and shown up, even pregnant Rachael, who lived four hundred miles away. They truly were special friends.

"You're going to be so far away from us," Tish bemoaned.

"We'll call each other every week. Plus, you can come visit me during the summer or during ski season. There's a ski resort on the other side of the mountain from Salvation."

Rachael's eyes misted with tears. She was the most emotional of the four and Jillian's polar opposite. "Oh, Jilly."

Jillian pointed at her. "Now, now, no waterworks, missy."

"B-but . . . you're going to be up there all alone. No friends, no family."

"Except for you guys, I haven't had a real family since I was five," Jillian said. "And besides, I've got Mutt now."

At the sound of his name, the dog trotted up, wagging his tail. He'd just come back from the vet after having his little snip-snip operation, and he wasn't his normal peppy self.

"And isn't he adorable," Tish cooed, and scratched Mutt under the chin. The dog ate up the attention.

"Where'd you get him?" Rachael asked.

"He just showed up the day after Blake's funeral," Jillian said.

"No kidding?" Tish looked uneasy.

"Oh my." Rachael sucked in her breath.

"Oh my, what?"

"The dog, it's Blake's way of sending you a message that he's okay," Rachael said as if she completely believed what she was saying and it made perfect sense.

"What?" Jillian frowned.

"You've never heard that?" Tish asked. "I've heard it."

"Heard what?"

"That if a dog shows up right after a loved one dies, it's the loved one communicating to you from beyond the grave. It's a sign telling you everything is okay," Delaney added.

"You too?"

"It's a common folklore," Rachael said. "Google it when you get a chance."

"You said the operative word. Folklore. As in fable, old wives' tale, blarney."

"She has such little faith." Rachael sighed to Tish. "What's it going to take to make a believer of her?"

Jillian looked at Delaney. "Speaking of folklore, I've got something for you."

"Oh?"

She stepped to her car, picked up the sealed garment bag, and handed it to Delaney.

"What's this?"

"The wedding veil. Please take it."

"No, no, Jilly. It's yours."

"I don't want it."

"How do you know? You're starting a new life. It might be exactly what you need."

"The bride thing?" Jillian splayed a hand over her chest. "So not me."

"Jillian . . ." Delaney made a you're-being-difficult sound in the back of her throat.

"Delaney . . ." She mimicked her friend's tone.

Delaney gave her the sweetly tolerant look a mother gives a willful child. "It's going to hit you one day; you *do* know that."

"What? A bus? A train? A milk truck? Should I up my life insurance?"

Delaney ignored her sarcasm. "Love. You can't outrun it."

"Not even in Nikes?"

Delaney smiled and shook her head. "Salvation's not going to know what hit them."

"Seriously, take the veil." Jillian thrust the bag toward her. "You bought it; it's yours."

"I don't need it anymore."

"I don't need it either."

"On the contrary. You've never needed anything more. You're at a crossroads in your life. Make the wish, Jilly."

"Too late, I already did and nothing happened."

Delaney exhaled and her eyes widened. "You? You wished on the veil?"

"Yep, and like I said, nada, zip, zero."

"I can't believe you wished on the veil. You swore you'd never wish on it."

"Like you said—crossroads, desperation. I had a moment of weakness. Lost my head."

"And . . ."

"And nothing."

Delaney's smile grew sly. "I get it. Something *did* happen, and it scared the underpants off you."

"Hey, hey." Jillian spread her arms. "Check it out. I'm completely clothed here, people."

But her underpants sure as hell hadn't been on in that dream. She wanted to fan herself just thinking about it, and she hoped the expression on her face didn't give her away.

Delaney giggled and clapped her hands. "It happened. You saw him."

"Did not." She heard the defensiveness in her voice.

"You saw your soul mate."

"Pfttt."

Rachael came around the side of the moving van to where Jillian and Delaney were standing. "What happened to you?"

"Jilly made a wish on the veil," Delaney said gleefully. "And she saw her guy."

Oh great, tell the romanceaholic.

"There was no guy. I saw no guy," Jillian lied.

Rachael rubbed her palms together. "So what did he look like? Handsome? Hot?"

"There's no guy."

"You put on the veil," Tish joined in. "Made the wish and absolutely *nothing* happened?"

Dammit. She knew she should have just thrown the stupid veil in the trash. "That's right. I just fell asleep."

"With the veil on?" Tish quizzed.

"Um . . . yeah. So what?"

Tish and Delaney and Rachael all exchanged meaningful glances as if they were party to something significant that Jillian could never understand.

"What?" Jillian demanded.

"Did you have some kind of dream?" Delaney raised her eyebrows.

"I don't remember," Jillian lied.

"She dreamed about him." Tish nodded her head knowingly. "She dreamed about him, and it scared the underpants off her."

"Why does everyone keep accusing me of losing my underpants?" Jillian sighed in exasperation. "I'm not Britney Spears."

"I bet it was a sex dream. Was it a sex dream, Jilly?" Rachael leaned in closer. "Tell us all about your sex dream."

"Geez, you people . . ."

"It was a sex dream," Tish said.

Jillian rolled her eyes. "And you wonder why I'm moving a thousand miles away from you lunatics."

"Fourteen hundred away from me." Rachael made a sad face.

"We're just teasing you, Jilly." Delaney touched her forearm. "If you really don't want the veil, I'll take it."

"Good. Thank you." Jillian sighed again, this time

with relief as Delaney accepted the bag. "It's all I ever wanted."

"That and the hot guy from your sexy dream." Rachael giggled, her eyes crinkling merrily.

Despite their good-natured ribbing about the veil, Jillian knew her friends truly cared about her. She was closing a chapter in her life. She could see the significance of it reflected in their faces, and she knew they could see it on hers. These three women were the closest thing she had to a family.

"I'm gonna miss you guys," she said earnestly.

"Group hug." Rachael held her arms open wide.

Normally, Rachael's insistence on group hugs got on Jillian's nerves, but this time, she let it happen and didn't even blink away the mist of tears.

Chapter Five

Two days later, at five forty-five in the morning, Jillian drove into Salvation.

She'd made poor time, what with the drag of the U-Haul on her Sebring's bumper hitch and having to make frequent pit stops for Mutt. But since no one was expecting her, the time of her arrival wasn't much of an issue. The weariness of two days on the road clouded her brain. Yellow asphalt stripes disappearing beneath strumming tires. Eighteen-wheelers jockeying for position. The dry flat taste of too-strong coffee. The sitting-too-long ache in her knees and tailbone.

Jillian rounded the last curve in the road, and there it lay dead ahead. Through the damp windshield, she watched the streetlamps wink off as the orange wash of morning scrubbed the horizon a hazy blue.

Salvation.

Small, sleepy, and so adorably cute she almost turned the car around and headed straight back to Houston. Jillian didn't do adorable or cute, but Rachael would have loved the place.

The first thing that came into view was the picturesque town square. Decorated quaintly with festive pumpkins and hay bales and scarecrows. There was a faint dusting of snow on the ground mingling with the fallen autumn leaves—orange, yellow, red.

The architecture was a mix of Swiss Chalet, French farmhouse, and Queen Victoria. There were carved window boxes and wrought-iron streetlamps and quirkily painted wooden park benches positioned outside the shops—bookstore, green grocer, novelties and souvenirs, yarn and fabrics, drugstore and sundries.

On the corner was a diner dubbed the Bluebird Café. A clot of SUVs and pickup trucks were parked outside. Ninety percent of them American made. Smoke swirled from the chimney, filling the air with the scent of mesquite. She'd had breakfast on the interstate an hour earlier or she might have stopped, eaten some eggs, met a few of the residents.

Her new town.

Jillian drew in a deep breath. This was where she was going to be living. Salvation, Colorado. Population 876, according to the sign she'd just passed.

She'd never lived in a small town.

A warm gush of sudden panic swept aside her stubborn resolve. Anxiety hunkered on her shoulder. What in the hell was she doing? Yanking up her life to relocate to a place she'd never been. She was jumping the gun. Blake's will wasn't even probated yet, and she'd moved all her earthly possessions up here. She'd quit her job, given up her condo, and taken on a dog.

What if the townsfolk didn't like her? What if she didn't like them? Was she crazy? Was she having a midlife crisis twenty years early? Was this all just a knee-jerk reaction to losing Blake?

What's done is done. Make the best of it.

Resolutely, she shrugged off her doubts and reached for the hand-drawn map on the seat between she and Mutt. The map that she'd found in the envelope Hamilton Green had given her. According to the directions, Salvation Lake was a half mile outside of town. She would be there soon.

Butterflies fluttered in her stomach.

"This is it," she told Mutt. "Our new home. What do you think?"

The dog put his paws on the side of the door and licked his lips as they passed by the Bluebird Café. Apparently, whatever they were serving for breakfast smelled tastier than the kibble he'd just eaten.

The houses on the road to the lake were just as adorable as the buildings circling the town square. The place was a fairy-tale town. Like something from the books she'd read when she was a kid and dreamed about but was too afraid to hope such places really existed. Honestly, it was too perfect for words.

"I don't trust perfect," she muttered under her breath. "There's no such thing as perfect."

Mutt looked at her.

"I know what you're thinking. Okay, so I'm not the most trusting person in the world. Especially when it comes to men. Consider yourself very lucky I adopted you."

Mutt barked.

"You're welcome."

A garbage truck rumbled past. The driver waved.

Jillian didn't wave back.

Mutt's ears dipped.

"What? Don't look at me like that. I know what you're thinking. Get to know the garbageman, maybe he'll throw you a bone. But you don't know this guy. He could be a serial dog killer. He could throw you poisoned meat. Best motto—trust no one."

Okay, it was official. Too many days on the road with only a dog to talk to had made her nuts. Once she got settled in, she simply had to introduce herself around town.

And maybe see if she could hire someone to help her unload the U-Haul.

Off to the right, she spied the lake in between gaps in the pine trees, the deep blue of the water melding with the orange cream sky. The lush evergreens were dusted with powdered-sugar snow. The paralyzing beauty took her breath away, and she fell instantly in love.

"It's incredible," she murmured, and her earlier misgivings were swept away by the azure majesty of the early morning sun shimmering off the lake.

"Maybe we can go fishing in the spring," she told Mutt. "You'd like that. Lots of sitting in the sun."

One of the few memories she had of her father was when he'd taken her fishing. She'd been quite small, three or four at most, and all she could remember of the trip was the tiny pink plastic tackle box with yellow daisies on it and the way her little hand had felt in his big palm as they'd walked to the water.

"Oh, oh, here it is. Enchantment Lane." She made a right. "Is that a corny name or what?"

Mutt yawned.

"Are you bored already? But we're only three weeks into this relationship, buster." She carefully navigated the twisty one-lane road. "Hey, be on the lookout for number 1414."

Most of the summerhouses appeared shuttered and

locked for the winter season. She expected number 1414 to be boarded up as well.

It wasn't.

However, the hedges were long past the point of needing a trim, and the cottage begged for a fresh coat of paint. Several pickets in the wooden fence had rotted out, and the rainbow-hued wind sock on top of the house was tattered. Dead tree branches littered the yard, and the mailbox was dented and rusting.

Home sweet home.

Jillian let out her breath. When had Blake last visited here? She'd known him for eight years and had never heard him once talk about his summer house or even taking a vacation. And why hadn't he hired someone to see after the place?

"Looks like we've got our work cut out for us, Mutt. You up for it?"

Disappointment anchored her to the seat, car keys in her hand. She didn't know what she'd been hoping for. Hamilton Green had warned her the property wasn't in the best of shape.

"But, hey, let's look at the bright side. We've got a killer view."

Mutt whined.

"I know, I know, you gotta pee." Jillian sighed and shrugged off her disenchantment with the house on Enchantment Lane. "Let's go."

She got out and walked Mutt around the side of the house so he could take care of business. From this angle, Jillian could see the redwood dock leading down to the water. The sight of the lake cheered her up a bit. This was her place. She owned it. Or at least she would as soon as Blake's will was probated.

Home.

"Home," she said out loud. She'd never had a real home.

Yeah, okay, the place needed work, but she wasn't afraid of manual labor. On that score, her stepmother had trained her well. Who knew a childhood spent as an indentured servant had an upside? A coat of paint, trimmed hedges, new boards in the fence and the place would be good as new.

"In nice weather, we can have breakfast on the dock and watch the sun come up," she told Mutt. "Would you like that?"

The dog paid her no mind; he was too busy sniffing the ground, exploring his new surroundings.

"Gird your loins. It's time to see the inside." She tugged on Mutt's leash and led him up the cobblestone walkway to the front porch. There she found a porch swing with a busted chain, the back corner resting on the ground. "Add that to the list."

She took the key from her pocket and slipped it into the lock, but before she ever turned the key, the door eased opened.

"It wasn't locked," she murmured. "Why wasn't it locked?"

She hesitated, not sure if she should go in or not. Everything was unnervingly quiet, but Mutt didn't seem alarmed. Jillian wasn't a coward, but neither was she a fool. Should she call the sheriff? She didn't want to look like an idiot on her first day in town. Maybe some teens had broken into the place and were using it as a make-out spot.

That thought sunk her spirits. She had to investigate. If someone was inside, she had Mutt to raise the alarm. Tentatively, she pushed the door all the way open and stepped over the threshold.

Hamilton Green had told her the summerhouse was furnished, but she hadn't expected it to look as if someone was living here. A pair of men's muddy work boots sat on a newspaper in the tiled foyer. Mutt sniffed them. A brown all-weather men's coat hung on a hook above the boots. The small foyer table held a blue glass bowl filled with pocket change, car keys, and breath mints. Not to mention an inch of dust.

A sudden thought occurred to her. What if she had the wrong place?

Nervously, Jillian stepped back out on the porch to double-check the numbers on the house. Yep. 1414. This was it.

"Why do I feel like I'm suddenly in a Stephen King novel?" Jillian asked.

Tongue lolling, Mutt looked up at her.

"Right, I got it, you have no idea who Stephen King is. But let me assure you this is seriously spooky."

Jillian hauled Mutt back inside, shut the door, and unclipped the leash from his collar. Then she edged into the living room.

Water stains dotted the ceiling, letting her know the roof leaked, and she noticed the walls needed painting even worse than the outside of the house. The back of an oversized brown leather couch faced the foyer. A red and white crocheted afghan was draped over it. Across the room sat a stone fireplace. There were a couple of flat-bottomed chairs, both heaped high with newspapers and magazines. An empty pizza box lay open on the coffee table.

Someone *was* living here.

Had Blake been renting the place out and neglected to inform Hamilton Green? Or had some vagrant wandered in and made himself at home?

She skirted the edge of the couch, looked down, and saw the most gorgeous naked male back she'd ever seen. Startled, Jillian slapped a hand over her mouth and jumped backward.

Her gaze focused on every minute detail. The tanned spine disappeared into the waistband of a pair of black briefs barely covering a firm gorgeous ass. The delineation of his taut musculature, the slope of the small of his back, the masculine thickness of his thighs all served to shove her libido into hyperdrive.

Mutt growled low in his throat, pricked up his ears, and cocked his head.

The guy snored, oblivious to the fact he had company.

Jillian's gaze tracked from the exquisite butt, up the curve of the small of his back, to his broad shoulders that barely fit on the couch, to the shaggy thatch of wheat-colored hair sticking out all over his head and back down again. His muscular calves were tangled in a blue quilt, and a pillow without a case lay on the floor beside the couch.

That was some kind of body.

A skitter of excitement ran through her. Once upon a time, she wouldn't have minded waking up to find a backside like that in her bed. But since Alex, she'd sworn off men. The creatures did nothing but cause misery and heartache.

She didn't know what to do. If he was a vagrant, she should call the police and have him evicted. If he'd rented the place, then she needed to wake him and tell him about Blake dying and leaving her the house.

Either way, he had to go.

But how to rouse him? If she tapped him on the shoulder, he was sure to turn over, and she really didn't want to see what was on the flip side.

Or did she?

Mutt was still growling at the guy in a low menacing tone she'd never heard the dog use.

Jillian cleared her throat. Loudly.

Nothing.

Apparently, the interloper could sleep through an avalanche.

Okay, she was going to try the tapping-on-the-shoulder thing. But first she had to cover him up so she would stop staring at him. She caught her bottom lip between her teeth, dropped her purse on the floor, and tiptoed toward the couch.

She leaned over, going for the red and white afghan, intent on tossing it over him, when a strong hand reached up and grabbed her wrist.

Jillian shrieked.

He had a vise grip like the Incredible Hulk.

In one fluid motion, he rolled off the couch onto the floor, taking Jillian with him. He made a guttural noise as his butt smacked against the rug.

The red afghan had fallen over Jillian's head, and she couldn't see a thing. All she could do was feel. Everything about him was hard. His grip, his chest, his thigh, his . . . his . . . oh God.

Jillian fought, shoving the afghan from her face, batting back the hair that had fallen into her eyes, and sputtering and struggling against him.

"Let go of me," she howled.

"Who in the hell are you? What do you want? Why are you in my house?" He peppered her with questions in a voice as deep as a scattergun blast.

Jillian was in his lap, and he wasn't letting go. She finally got her vision cleared and found herself peering straight into whiskey-colored eyes, fringed with long dark lashes. His silky, wheat-brown hair was rumpled, his jaw shadowed with beard stubble. His entire face bespoke bone-deep sadness.

His gaze met hers.

All the breath left her body. Her heart leapfrogged into her throat. Her stomach dropped to her knees, and her jaw unhinged. Panic bulleted through her veins.

Impossible. Unbelievable. This simply could not be happening.

It was him.

In the flesh.

The rugged, hunk of a man from her wedding veil–induced sex dream!

TUCK STARED into the eyes of the woman from his vision quest and felt the earth shift beneath him.

This was impossible, illogical, but here she was.

Dream. Gotta be a dream.

But it sure as hell didn't feel like a dream with her warm, firm ass parked in his lap.

Was there such a thing as vision-quest flashbacks? He'd have to ask Ridley.

Her eyes were bright, her lips so temptingly close. He couldn't help but think about kissing her. He slid his arms around her waist and she—

Slapped him.

"Ouch!" He raised a hand to rub his stinging cheek.

Okay, neither a dream nor a flashback. If it was a flashback, she'd be kissing him, not smacking his face.

So if it wasn't a dream or a flashback, that meant . . . Holy shit, holy shit, holy shit, this was real.

There was a strange woman in his house—and not just any strange woman but one whom he'd had sex with in a sweat lodge vision. And she was far more beautiful in real life than she'd been in the dream. Her hair was blacker, glossier. Her eyes more intelligent. Her skin creamier. Her scent spicier.

"Let go of me." She splayed a palm against his bare chest and shoved him.

Hard.

Tuck tipped backward and his head hit the floor.

Her stare fixed on his lower anatomy, and she let out a squeak of surprise at the sight of his cock burgeoning against the seams of his undershorts.

Quickly he grabbed the afghan and flung it over his lap. Just as quickly, she jumped to her feet and ran to the opposite side of the room. He secured the afghan around his waist with his fingers and scrambled onto the couch, placing a pillow strategically over his lap.

They were both breathing like marathon runners at the twenty-fifth-mile marker.

"Who the hell are you?" they asked in unison.

"I'm Jillian Samuels," she said.

At the very same time, he said, "Tucker Manning."

And then they both said, "What are you doing here?"

It was a very strange moment. It wasn't every day that a man met his fantasy woman.

She's not your fantasy woman. You just had a dream about her.

Except that apparently hadn't been just a run-of-the-mill dream but a portentous vision, just as Ridley had claimed. Flippin' freaky.

"This simultaneous talking isn't getting us anywhere. You go first, Jillian," he said, being polite. "You're the visitor here."

"Actually, Tucker . . ."

"Call me Tuck. Everyone calls me Tuck."

"Actually, Tuck . . ." She drew herself up to her full height, which had to be close to six foot. She was almost as tall as he was. "I'm not."

"Excuse me?"

Her expression grew somber and her voice softened. "I'm sorry to be the one to tell you this . . ." She hesitated, drawing in a deep breath.

He couldn't help noticing her chest rise with the inhalation. If the vision he'd had of her was in any way accurate, she had a great pair of breasts underneath that fluffy red sweater. "Yeah?"

"Why are you staring at me like that?" she snapped.

"Like what?" Tucker forced his eyes off her breasts and onto her face. She was the kind of woman who made a man think about midnight skies and four-poster beds. And for a guy who hadn't thought about any woman like that since his wife, it was damned disconcerting.

"Like you know what I look like without any clothes on."

"Sorry, nasty male habit." He wasn't about to let her know about his sweat lodge vision. If he did, he had no doubt she'd slap him again. Probably even harder this time and he would deserve it for the lascivious thoughts circling his brain.

"Well, knock it off and pay attention. I'm delivering bad news here," Jillian said.

"Oh." He straightened on the couch, stabbing his fingers through his mussed hair. "I'm listening. Whatcha got?"

"There's no other way to break the news than to just say it. Blake Townsend's dead."

"Huh?" Her words didn't register.

"Blake's dead." Tears glimmered in her eyes.

"Blake's dead?" he repeated, hearing his own words come out hollow and strange. Her words still weren't registering. "How . . ." Tucker's chest tightened and his brain fogged. "When?"

"Two weeks ago."

"What happened?"

Jillian sank down on the fireplace hearth. He saw her bottom lip was trembling, and he realized she'd cared deeply about Blake. "It was all so trite. One minute Blake was mundanely ordering a grande soy latte at Starbucks just like it was any other morning, and the next minute he was on the floor dead from a brain tumor. Turns out he'd had it for months. Inoperable. He never told anyone."

The pain written on her face told him that Blake keeping his illness a secret hurt her deeply. "That's awful. How come . . ." Tuck broke off, unsure of what he was feeling. He swallowed past the lump in his throat and tried again. "Why didn't someone tell me?"

"No one knew you were living here. Blake's lawyer thought the place was vacant. He told me the place hadn't been occupied in years. Who are you, by the way?"

"I'm his son-in-law."

Jillian sucked in her breath. "Aimee's husband."

"Yeah."

"I . . . I'm sorry for your loss," she said. Their eyes met and damn if Tuck didn't see empathy in her gaze. That pissed him off. She had no right to look as if she understood his pain. "I know what it's like. Blake was . . . We were close."

"Ah . . ." So *that* was the lay of the land.

"Not *ah*." She glowered. "There's no 'ah.'"

"You and Blake were lovers."

"God no!" she exclaimed as if the thought horrified her. "We were friends. He was my mentor. A father figure."

"Lucky you." His turn for sarcasm. This woman had usurped Aimee's father.

"Don't get angry," she said. "It's not my fault that Blake and Aimee had a tumultuous relationship."

Tuck scowled. He didn't like hearing her speak Aimee's name. He sat there in his underwear feeling pretty damned exposed when he spied the dog for the first time. Or what passed for a dog. Apparently it had been snooping around the house, making itself at home, before coming over to plop down at Jillian's feet.

"What's that?" he asked.

"That's Mutt."

"Aptly named."

"Thank you. I thought of it all on my own."

He grinned. "Hey, folks, who knew? She's beautiful and imaginative too."

"Yep, the total package, that's me. Like DIRECTV."

Their banter must have struck her as inappropriate at the same time it occurred to him how out of place it was, and they simultaneously glanced away.

She gazed down at her hands. "So, anyway, Blake left me the lake house in his will."

"What?"

"The lake house. It's mine."

He jumped to his feet, barely hanging on to the afghan, fighting the rage pushing at him. He thought about dropping the blanket simply to intimidate her, but something told him this woman did not intimidate easily, and he'd end up being the one feeling embarrassed if he exposed himself.

She stood up as well, looking calm and cool and completely emotionless. In that moment, Tuck hated her.

"Listen," she said. "I don't know the understanding you had with Blake—why he was letting you live here—and it's really none of my business. But the house is mine now, and this is your official eviction notice. I'd appreciate it if you could be out of the house by the end of the week."

And with that, she turned, whistled to her dog, and walked out.

Chapter Six

Jillian made it to her car before Tuck caught up with her. He was hopping around on one booted foot while trying to jam his other foot in the remaining boot. He'd pulled on a pair of faded jeans, the fly unzipped, and he'd thrust his arms though a blue flannel jacket, but he didn't have a shirt on underneath.

"Whoa, wait just a damn minute there, sister!" he shouted.

She turned to face him.

He got his boot on and zipped up his jeans. His cheeks were flushed, his scruffy hair mussed, his eyes flashing fire. He slammed a palm against her car door just as she reached for the handle to jerk it open.

"Take your hand off my car," she demanded as calmly as she could in the face of her rising ire. She'd had a rough few weeks, and her nerve endings dangled on a precarious thread.

"Not until you hear what I have to say," he growled.

Tuck stepped closer, crowding her space, but Jillian knew all about those kinds of intimidation tactics and she didn't budge.

Sinking her hands on her hips, she glared. "Fine. Speak your piece."

"You don't own this lake house."

"Maybe not technically. Not until Blake's will is probated, but he left it to me."

"No, he didn't."

"Are you deaf?" She reached in her purse and pulled out the will. "I have it right here."

"When was that will drawn up?"

She told him.

The anger in his eyes deepened. "The week after Aimee died," he muttered, seemingly more to himself than to her.

"Yes."

"You can't inherit the lake house."

Jillian drew in a deep breath. She realized he was still hurting from the loss of his wife. It was written all over him. She didn't know what his relationship with his father-in-law had been like, but she supposed it wasn't good. Blake had only mentioned him a time or two, and he'd only referred to him as "Aimee's husband," never by name. "Look, I'm not heartless. I understand you're still recovering from your wife's death and—"

"Don't"—he shook a finger at her—"don't you dare pretend you know anything about me or what I'm going through."

Something in his tone had Jillian raising her hands in surrender. "Okay, all right. I did just spring this on you. You need time to process. I'll give you two weeks to find someplace else to live."

"You're not listening to me," he said. "You can't inherit the lake house, because Blake deeded the place to me four months ago."

His words yanked the air right out of her lungs. "What?"

"You heard me."

Four months ago. About the same time Jillian suspected Blake had been diagnosed with the brain tumor. But if he'd deeded the lake house to Tuck, why hadn't he changed his will?

Maybe he forgot. He did have a brain tumor.

Or maybe Tucker Manning was lying his ass off.

"Impossible."

"Au contraire. Not only is it possible, but it's also true."

Jillian narrowed her eyes. "I'd like to see the deed. I am the executor of Blake's estate."

"I . . . um . . . don't have it."

"Imagine that." Jillian snorted. "Did you really think you could pull one over on me, Manning? I am a criminal prosecutor."

Tuck looked mad enough to spit nails. "I'm not a liar. Blake deeded me the house."

"Easy enough to prove. Simply produce the deed."

"It's with my attorney."

Was he seriously trying to con her? She tilted her head, studying him. He seemed sincere. And pissed off.

Just then Jillian's cell phone rang.

Tuck turned and headed back for the house.

"Where are you going?" she called after him.

"To see my attorney."

"It's Sunday." Her phone rang again.

"Take care of your own business." He tossed the comment over his shoulder as he disappeared into the house.

Glowering, Jillian flipped open her phone, saw from the caller ID that it was Delaney, and put a pleasant tone in her voice. "Hey."

"Hi, Jilly, did you get there yet?"

"Yes, I arrived in Salvation safe and sound."

"Oh . . . wonderful . . . glad . . . there."

The cell phone reception was spotty in the mountains, plus Delaney's kids were hollering in the background. With her index finger, Jillian plugged up the ear that wasn't pressed to the phone. "Huh? What did you say?"

"Let me close the door to the playroom," Delaney shouted.

Static crackled. A few seconds passed.

"There, is that any better?"

"Some, yeah. Sounds like the natives are restless."

"That's life with three little kids under the age of four," Delaney said cheerfully.

"How do you make it through the day?"

"Turn them over to their father the minute he comes home from work." She chuckled. "So how was the trip?"

"Good. Although it took longer to get here than I expected," Jillian said, wondering what Tuck was doing.

"How's the house?"

Jillian wasn't ready to tell Delaney about the snafu she'd just encountered. She didn't know for sure that Tuck's claim to the lake house was true. "Do you remember that movie with Tom Hanks and Shelley Long?"

"*The Money Pit*?"

"That's the one. That's my house."

"I'm sorry."

"Yeah, well, life's a grand adventure or it's nothing, right?"

"Like having three toddlers."

"I'll take the money pit. Listen . . ."

"Yes?"

"About that veil."

"You want it back. I knew you'd change your mind."

Jillian leaned back against the passenger seat and propped her booted feet on the dashboard. "I don't want it back."

"Jilly, you still there?"

"I'm here."

Jillian watched Tucker come back out of the house, raise the door to the garage, get into a red four-wheel-drive extended-cab pickup truck, and burn rubber out of the driveway. He didn't even glance over at her as he shot past.

"Bat out of hell," she muttered.

"What?"

"Not you, Laney."

"What's wrong?" Delaney snapped her fingers. "Hey, hey, Audra, quit whacking your brothers with SpongeBob."

"I thought you shut the door."

Delaney sighed. "They opened it. Bunch of little Houdinis the Vinetti offspring."

"Doesn't Nick have extra handcuffs lying around?"

"They're locked on my bedposts." Delaney giggled.

"Okay, that classifies as way too much information. Anyway, about this veil . . ."

"Uh-huh?"

"As you know, I had a sex dream when I fell asleep with it on," Jillian said.

"You wished on the veil, right?"

"I did."

"What did you wish for?"

"A new life."

"And it's coming true." Delaney sounded positively giddy. "The veil is never wrong."

"That's not the half of it."

"What's the whole of it?"

"You're not going to believe this, but when I got here, there was this nearly naked guy asleep on the couch in my house."

"Excuse me?"

"He was in his underwear."

"Seriously?"

"We're talking heart attack material. He's that good-looking."

"That cute, huh?"

"There's more."

"More?"

"Laney, he's the guy from my sex dream."

"Jilly, I just got chill bumps."

Jillian plucked at a loose thread on her sweater. "I'm wigged out."

"And you didn't believe in the veil."

"I still don't."

"So how do you explain the guy?"

Jillian sighed. She'd been asking herself the same question. "There's got to be some kind of logical, rational—"

"There is. The veil's magic."

Jillian faked a cough. "Ahem, let's not go down that road."

"Face it. You're fated. He's your soul mate."

"That's so bogus."

"What about me and Nick?"

"Right place, right time."

"I saw Nick's face when I wished on the veil. Saw him before I ever met him."

"Self-fulfilling prophecy."

"And what about Tish and Shane and Rachael and Brody?" Delaney asked.

"Mass hypnosis. Maybe mass psychosis."

Delaney laughed. "Deny it all you want. This man is your destiny, and there's nothing you can do about it, so you might as well accept it."

Jillian blew out her breath to keep from saying something to Delaney that could damage their friendship. "Tucker Manning is *not* my destiny."

"Tucker? That's his name?"

In the background, Jillian heard one of Delaney's kids wail. "Oops, sounds like they're reenacting the story of Cain and Abel. You better get a jump on it."

"You're just trying to get out of this discussion . . . Aidan, you take that toilet paper out of your mouth right this minute."

"Bye, Laney."

"Tucker's your destiny."

"He is *not*."

"Oh ye of little faith."

"Crazy woman."

"Skeptic."

"I'm hanging up now."

"Don't run away from love, Jilly. The wedding veil is waiting right here for you when you need it."

"This reception is really bad. You're cutting out. Gotta go." Jillian turned off her cell phone and blew out her breath. She looked over at Mutt. "Coming here was a very big mistake."

TUCKER STALKED into the Bluebird Café looking for his brother-in-law. On Sunday morning, the place was packed with the before-church breakfast crowd. He paused a moment to scrape his boots on the welcome mat.

"Hey, honey," Evie called out from behind the counter when she spied him. "What'll you have? Chocolate-chip waffles are on the special."

"Where's Rid?"

"He's playing fry cook."

Tuck went around the counter and headed for the kitchen.

"Put on a hairnet if you're going in there." His sister was such a stickler for hygiene.

"I'm just gonna stand in the door and talk to your husband. I won't be hanging over the food."

"Don't distract him. He'll burn himself."

Tuck stuck his head in the kitchen and saw Ridley flipping bacon on the griddle. The smell was enticing. His stomach grumbled, but his mind was too preoccupied to think about food right now. "I gotta talk to you and it won't wait."

"Sure, what about?"

"Can we go outside?"

Ridley raised his head. "You sound serious."

"I am serious."

"Dutch," Ridley said to the sad-faced, fortysomething prep cook with a prison tattoo on his forearm. "Flip the bacon for me, will ya? I'm taking a quick break."

Dutch grunted.

Ridley slid an anxious gaze toward the front counter. "Let's make it snappy. Your sister's on the warpath."

"What'd you do?"

"I didn't do anything. Honest. Those fertility drugs she's taking make her like she's got a triple dose of PMS."

"Yeesh."

"You better believe yeesh." Ridley led Tuck out the back door into the alley, yanking off his hairnet as he went.

"I grew up with three sisters. I have a clear picture. You have my sympathy."

"So what's up?" Ridley fished a single cigarette from his shirt pocket and lit it up.

"I thought you quit."

"I'm trying. It's not working. Don't tell Evie." Ridley took a deep puff.

Tuck paced the alley. "Listen, about this vision I had in the sweat lodge. The temptress."

"Yeah?"

"She's here."

Ridley frowned. "Whaddya mean she's here?"

"I mean she's in Salvation."

"Your temptress is here? In Salvation? In the flesh?"

"That's what I'm telling you."

"Can't be. A vision isn't real, Tuck. It's a prophecy. A metaphor for the future."

"Well, this metaphor is real, and she's got legs that won't quit. She walked into my house this morning and found me sleeping in my BVDs on the couch."

"You mean you dreamed about her walking into your house."

"No, I mean she literally walked into my house." He told Ridley about Jillian and then he told him about Blake.

"Blake died?"

"Yeah. Explains why he deeded me the lake house out of the blue. Guess he knew he was dying. What I can't figure out is why he left the house to the temptress in his will."

"The temptress has claims on your house?"

"Looks like it. But my deed postdates her will."

Ridley splayed a palm to the back of his neck and looked worried. "For real?"

"For real."

"No shit." Ridley whistled.

"No shit."

"How come you were sleeping on the couch?" Ridley took another hit off his cigarette. "You've got a king-sized bed."

Tuck threaded his hand through his hair. "I can't sleep in there. It's too big. Too empty."

"Without Aimee."

"Yeah," he admitted. "So I had a vision about this temptress woman, and now she shows up at my house claiming it's her house. I'm thinking it means something important. What does it mean, Rid?"

"Um . . ." His brother-in-law avoided his eyes. "I better get back in there. Evie's gonna come looking for me." He crushed the cigarette butt under his boot and turned to leave.

Tuck put out a hand to stop him. "Tell me."

"Tell you what?"

"The prophecy."

Ridley laughed, but it was a hollow sound. "You don't believe in any of that stuff, remember?"

"Having her show up has made a serious believer out of me. What does it mean?"

Ridley looked uneasy.

"Is it bad?"

His brother-in-law shrugged, but he looked alarmed. "I'm no expert."

"You can tell me. I can handle it. How much worse can it be than losing your wife to ovarian cancer when she's only twenty-five?"

"I guess there's going to be a legal battle over the lake house."

"Looks that way."

"But you've got the deed, right?"

Tuck swallowed. "Sutter Godfrey's got it. He was supposed to file the damned thing, but then he broke his hip. . . ."

"Sutter never filed the deed?"

"I don't think so. I wasn't paying that much attention."

"That sucks. You could lose your house."

"Tell me. In the meantime, I think she's planning on moving in. She's pulling a U-Haul."

Ridley hissed in a breath. "Where you gonna go? This time of year there's not a lot of places for lease in Salvation."

"I don't know. This whole thing caught me off guard."

"You could come stay with me and Evie."

Tuck shook his head. "You guys are trying for a baby. I'd cramp your style."

"Family's family. We'd make do."

"Why should I be the one to leave? She's the interloper." Tuck stuck his fingers through his belt loops. "So are you going to tell me what it means to have a vision about a temptress?"

Ridley swallowed audibly. "Having a vision about a temptress is bad luck."

"I'd already sort of figured that out."

"The temptress signifies broken plans, broken hearts,

broken dreams. But seeing a temptress in real life that you've already had a vision about . . ." He shook his head. "Out of my sphere of expertise, but I'm betting it ain't good. The woman is bad luck. A jinx."

Tuck looked him squarely in the eyes. "You're telling me."

AFTER JILLIAN got off the phone with Delaney, she decided to take inventory of the house. She was the executor of Blake's will, after all. It was her job. She had the right.

By lunchtime, Jillian had a list as long as her arm of things that needed repairing in the house, and she'd only made it through the downstairs kitchen, living area, and bathroom. She hadn't even ventured into the bedrooms upstairs.

Feeling overwhelmed, she plunked down onto the couch and stared glumly at her surroundings. What had she gotten herself into?

This behavior wasn't like her. She wasn't impulsive or spontaneous. So why had she thrown everything away and just moved up here on a whim? In retrospect, it was quite stupid. Especially since she might not even have a legal claim to the house. What in God's name had she been thinking?

What? Why? Because her life in Houston had stopped working. She'd needed a change and needed it badly. But she hadn't bargained on feeling so . . . so . . . What did she feel?

Jillian sighed. Well, there was nothing to do but make the best of the situation. She'd clean the house, that was a first step. And she'd start by throwing away the piles and piles of magazines and newspapers stacked all around the living room. Apparently Tucker Manning was something of a pack rat.

She rummaged through the kitchen, found black plastic garbage bags, and returned to the living room. She picked up a stack of magazines. *Architectural Digest* mostly. She tossed them into the garbage bag and then reached for another handful.

Her gaze fell on the cover. There was a picture of Tuck looking quite debonair in a tuxedo. He was winking, arms folded across his chest, biceps bulging at the seams of his suit, a sly grin on his face.

The caption read MANNING MAGIC.

This was the scruffy naked bum she'd found sleeping on the couch in her house?

Unbelievable.

Correction. It's not officially your house yet.

Fascinated to uncover this new information, she sat cross-legged on the floor and flipped to the page with the article about the brilliant young architect the media had dubbed the "Magic Man." He designed classrooms so conducive to learning that test scores and grades shot up in students who attended classes in a Manning school.

The article heaped praise on his talent, citing him as one of the most influential young architects of his generation. There were detailed photographs of the learning centers he designed and pictures of his exclusive Manhattan loft. According to the piece, he dated starlets and heiresses and traveled the world.

Why had he given it all up to live like a vagrant in Blake's summerhouse? Yes, he'd lost a wife, but that was two years ago. Why hadn't he gone back to his former life?

Jillian flipped back to the cover and saw the magazine had come out four years earlier.

"Wow, you're a lot more complicated than appearances led me to believe, Tucker Manning," she muttered.

"And you're a lot snoopier than you look," growled Tuck from the living room archway.

Startled, Jillian let out an "Eeep" and tossed the magazine in the air.

Glowering, Tuck "Magic Man" Manning marched across the living room and scooped up the magazine from the fireplace hearth where it had landed. "Mind your own damn business. And keep your hands off my magazines."

"Why are you so testy?"

"Um . . . let's see. I have some strange woman claiming to have inherited my house. You think that has anything to do with my sour mood?"

"So get another place and leave this one to me. According to that magazine, you're rolling in dough."

"Not anymore," he snapped.

"Went bankrupt, did you?"

"What part of 'mind your own business' do you not understand?"

"So you're the Magic Man."

"Don't go there."

"Imagine," she teased. "I've seen the Magic Man in his BVDs."

He snorted. "Only because you were breaking and entering."

"Door was open, no breaking involved. I was merely

entering. And in case you've forgotten, I was operating on the assumption that it was my house."

"As if you'd let me forget that."

"What happened to the tux?"

"Huh?"

"The tux you were wearing on the magazine cover. What happened to it?" she asked.

"I sent it out to have it cleaned along with my Rolls-Royce."

"What would *Architectural Digest* say if they knew how truly crabby the Magic Man could be. Not so magical after all."

He chuffed out his breath. "I'm not that guy anymore, so can we just drop the whole thing?"

"Aw, but we were just getting to know each other."

"You're a smart-ass, aren't you?"

She batted her eyelashes. "Thanks for noticing."

"Hmm," he said.

"Hmm what?" She canted her head.

"I can see why you're not married."

Ouch, that was a low blow. Clearly he was getting even with her for the Magic Man teasing. "How do you know I'm not married."

"Are you?"

"No." She looked away so she wouldn't have to meet his eyes, and she saw how badly the corners needed dusting. There were so many cobwebs that John Carpenter could set a horror flick in here.

"Okay, then, let's go."

"Excuse me?"

"Let's go."

"Go where?"

"To the Bluebird."

"Bluebird?"

"What are you? An echo? It's a café."

"What for?"

"For one thing, it's lunchtime," he said. "And I know you haven't eaten, because there's no food in the house."

"But plenty of beer in the fridge," she noted.

"You've been going through my things."

Jillian hazarded another glance at him. That blue flannel against his olive complexion . . . *well* . . . totally breathtaking. "Hey, you were the one who took off."

"The second reason we're going to the Bluebird is to see Sutter Godfrey. He has lunch there every Sunday."

"Sutter Godfrey?"

"My lawyer."

"We're not bothering the man on his day off, especially when he's eating a meal. It'll keep until tomorrow."

"No." Tuck's eyes flashed darkly. "No, it won't. I want this thing settled right now. I have a feeling you don't believe me about the deed."

He was right, she didn't.

"Let's go," he repeated.

Jillian shrugged into her jacket. "Just to be clear, I'm not going with you because you ordered me to go. I'm hungry."

"Don't worry, I didn't mistake you for someone who took directions well," he said.

"As long as that's settled." She flipped her hair out from under the collar of her jacket where it had gotten caught. "What kind of food do they serve at the Bluebird?"

"It's a café. They serve café food."

"Now who's the smart-ass?"

Silence fell and she instantly had a flashback and saw the firm shape of his bare back as it disappeared into the waistband of his undies. Briefly, she closed her eyes and willed the image away.

"You with me?"

She opened her eyes and shot him a surreptitious glance. He had long, extravagant eyelashes that were in sharp contrast to the rest of his thoroughly masculine face. Those lashes kept his rugged looks from being too harsh. His lips were full but angular. Her gaze just hung there. Spellbound, she wondered if his lips tasted as good in person as they had in her dream.

"Are we taking separate cars?" she asked.

He pulled his keys from his pocket. "I'm driving. You've got a U-Haul attached to your Sebring."

"Oh yeah." She'd forgotten about that.

"What should I do with Mutt?"

"Bring him along. The Bluebird keeps a leash clip chained to a pole outside for four-legged visitors, along with a water bowl and complimentary dog biscuits."

"Wow, imagine. Pet pampering in the wilds of Colorado."

"It's not Antarctica."

"The cell phone reception *is* pretty bad."

"Mountains. They're tall."

"Ooh, there's that smart mouth again."

They reached his pickup truck, and he walked around to the passenger side to hold the door open for her. It felt weird, and she realized she couldn't remember a guy ever opening the car door for her. Surely someone had, but the memory escaped her. A funny, unexpected feeling she couldn't define swooped through her.

Hell, he impressed you.

No, no, she wasn't impressed; she was just . . . just what?

He opened the back of the extended cab and whistled for Mutt, and the dog hopped inside.

"So," she said when they were in the car together and headed up Enchantment Lane. "What happened with the big, splashy architectural career?"

"The topic isn't open for discussion."

"Oookay. How do you make a living these days?"

He paused for so long that she thought he wasn't going to answer the question, and then finally he said, "Carpenter."

"Seriously?"

"Is that so hard to believe?"

"From the shape the lake house is in? Yeah. How come you didn't fix it up, if as you claim, Blake deeded the place to you?"

"I was getting around to it."

"Ah," she said.

"Ah, what?"

"The Round-to-It. Bane of homeowners everywhere."

Tuck grunted and ignored that comment, but his eyes were on her. She tried not to notice, but she couldn't help seeing the interest there. His tousled hair fell sexily over his forehead. Just like in her dream. Nervously, she fingered the bracelet on her wrist.

Stop looking at him. Stop thinking about him. Find something else to occupy your mind.

Jillian thought about all that work that needed doing on the house. Thought of his carpentry skills. He couldn't be all bad. He'd opened the car door for her and brought her dog along on their outing.

And he'd given her one hell of an orgasm in her dreams. Two orgasms if she was being technical.

That was reason enough to stay as far away from him as she could manage. But how was she going to do that while he was living in the house she'd inherited?

Except for the fact that maybe she hadn't inherited it after all.

As Tuck pulled into the parking lot of the Bluebird, Jillian had the sudden realization that moving to Colorado might have been one of the dumbest mistakes of her life—even dumber than her ill-fated affair with Alex Fredericks.

Chapter Seven

Evie watched Tuck return to the café with Jillian in tow. One look at the woman and she thought, *Uh-oh.*

She didn't understand the uneasiness in her stomach or her sudden mother-bear need to protect her little brother at all costs. All she knew was the interloper looked like Warrior Woman—with her tall imposing height, her sharp dark eyes, and the I-dare-you-to-cross-me set to her shoulders. She was a scrapper, and the last thing Tuck needed was a fight.

Who was she, and what was she doing with Evie's baby brother?

Wiping her hands on her apron, Evie came around the front counter, her gaze sizing up the Amazon.

The Amazon's return stare was cool and emotionless.

Evie narrowed her eyes. "Hey, Tuck. If you're looking for Ridley again, he went down to Fielder's Market. We ran out of eggs. Dutch had a mishap with the eggs Benedict."

"Nope, we're here to see Sutter."

We're here? As if they were a couple. Looking for the town's only lawyer. Something smelled fishy.

"He's in the back at his usual table with the usual suspects." The curiosity was killing her. Apparently Tuck wasn't going to introduce her. Evie pasted on her best hostess smile, even though she wasn't feeling the love, and thrust out her hand. "Hi," she said to the Amazon. "I'm Evie, Tuck's big sister."

The Amazon barely cracked a smile. "Jillian Samuels." She shook hands like a logger. Firm and strong and serious.

"Nice to meet you."

"Same here."

"You passing through town?"

"Evie, could you cut us some slack? We just want to see Sutter," Tuck said. "Then later we'll grab some lunch."

Evie's fingers tingled and she jammed her hand into her back pocket. "Is there a problem?"

"Nothing Sutter can't handle," he said, and turned for the back room, Jillian at his heels like a shadow.

Evie felt a stab of something closely akin to jealousy. For the last two years, she'd essentially been the only woman in her grief-stricken brother's life. She deserved more info than that. Blast it, she'd changed his diapers and pulled his first baby tooth and taught him how to whistle and snap his fingers. She trailed them to the door of the other room.

Tuck walked up to Sutter, who was surrounded by his cronies—the town elders—who kept counsel in the Bluebird most days of the week and introduced the old barrister to Jillian.

Evie cocked her head, trying to eavesdrop on the conversation, but the lunch crowd was booming. The diner hummed with the noise of buzzing voices and clanking silverware and the Hank Williams CD Dutch had stuck on, now playing. "Hey, Good Lookin'."

She started to slip farther into the room, but a pair of masculine hands coming to rest on her shoulders stopped her in her tracks.

"Mind your own business, big sister," Ridley whispered into her ear.

Evie stiffened. "Tuck is my business."

"He's a grown man."

"A heartbroken grown man."

"Still . . ." Ridley turned her around and pointed her in the direction of the kitchen.

"Who's that woman he's with? Did you know he was seeing someone? How come you didn't tell me?"

"I don't know who she is for sure, but I imagine it's the temptress."

"The who?" Evie jerked her head to stare up at him as he guided her away from the group in the back room.

Ridley sighed. "Promise me you won't get upset."

"Upset? What's there to get upset about?" She twisted from Ridley's masculine grip.

"Remember the night I put him in the sweat lodge?"

Evie didn't like the sound of this. "Uh-huh. . . ."

"Well, your brother had a vision."

"A vision, huh?"

"In the vision he was visited by a temptress."

"Meaning?"

Her big husband nodded his head toward the back room. "Meaning she's his destiny, and there's not a damn thing you can do to change it."

SUTTER GODFREY was holding court.

The elderly lawyer sat in a wheelchair at the head of

the table, dressed in a blue seersucker suit straight out of the 1940s, complete with a blue and white polka-dot bow tie.

He was a thin man, with a thick flush of white hair and a dapper Charlie Chaplin mustache. He had to be pushing eighty downhill. He was surrounded by five other men, four of whom were in his age group and dressed in the usual hunter regalia—camouflage clothes, down vests, and orange baseball caps. A couple of them looked to be of Native American ancestry. The fifth appeared to be a decade younger than the rest of the bunch. He had on jeans, a starched button-down white shirt, and a gray tweed jacket.

The minute Sutter spied Jillian, his pale blue eyes lit up. "Scoot over, Bonner, Carl, and let the young people have a seat."

She and Tuck took the quickly vacated positions to Sutter's right; "Sutter," Tuck said, "This is Jillian Samuels. Jillian, Sutter Godfrey."

"It's rare for Salvation to be graced with the charm and beauty of one so refined as you," Sutter drawled in a deep South Carolina accent.

Her bullshit meter clicked rapidly. "You have a gift for flattery, Mr. Godfrey. A handy talent for a lawyer."

"Let me introduce my associates." Sutter went around the table naming off the men. The guy in the tweed jacket was Salvation's only practicing physician, Dr. Bonner Couts. The two Native Americans, Tom Red Deer and Sam Soap, were the elders of their tribes. One was a retired mechanic, the other a still-practicing accountant. The remaining two men were Carl Fielder and Dub Bennet, town counsel members and local merchants. Carl owned

Fielder's Market, and Dub ran a hunting and fishing guide service.

They might be fading into old age, but it was clear that this group still held a lot of power in the community.

"So what might I do for you and this lovely lady, Tucker?" Sutter took a sip of coffee, eying them over the rim of his cup as he waited.

"Could you please confirm for Ms. Samuels that Blake Townsend deeded me his lake house?"

Jillian clenched her hands in her lap. She didn't want to know why her throat suddenly squeezed so tight she could barely breathe.

Sutter pursed his lips and set down his cup. "I do recall having that conversation with Blake, yes, indeed."

Tuck exhaled audibly. "So you filed the deed?"

"Hmm." Sutter paused. "I do believe so, yes. But as you recall, that was about the time I took a nasty fall down the steps of the Peabody Mansion and broke my right hip."

"I recall."

Sutter nodded as if that explained everything.

"So you have a copy of the deed on file in your office?" Jillian asked.

"Most likely," Sutter drawled. The guy spoke as if a simple yes or no would kill him.

"I'm the executor of Blake's will. Is it possible to get a copy for the probate?"

"Surely, my dear." He smiled. "Anything for a beautiful lady."

"That would be helpful, thank you."

"Of course," he went on, "you'll have to go find it for yourself. I can no longer climb the stairs to my office."

"You don't have an assistant?"

"Sadly, my previous assistant took up with the wrong kind of fellow, found herself in a family way, and left town in shame."

"What about a computer? Don't you have electronic files?"

Sutter shook his head. "I never learned to use those infernal machines. My assistant had one, but I have no idea what she did on it."

Good grief, had she been jettisoned back to 1950? If she turned around, would she see Sheriff Andy Taylor and Deputy Barney Fife walk through the door? Would Aunt Bee come rushing in with a homemade apple pie? Would Opie tag along, fishing pole cocked over his shoulder?

Tuck leaned over to whisper, "Most people go to Boulder for their legal needs."

She shot him a why-the-hell-didn't-you? look, at the same time Sutter cleared his throat. Jillian glanced back to see the elderly lawyer was dangling a set of keys from his index finger. "If you plan on riffling through my office, you'll be needing these."

"Thank you, Sutter," Tuck said as he pushed to his feet. "We'll be back in a bit."

"I'll be here." He gave a wave of his hand.

Carl and Bonner resumed their seats while Sam broke out the dominoes. Yep, Andy, Barney, Bee, and Opie had to be around here somewhere.

The Peabody Mansion turned out to be the large turn-of-the-twentieth-century Victorian in the town square. Before they left the diner, Tuck got Evie to make them a sack lunch while Jillian retrieved Mutt from where he'd been attracting the attention of passersby on the sidewalk.

He was eating up the strokes and scratches behind the ears with his usual extroverted glee.

They didn't bother taking Tuck's truck. It was a short walk from the Bluebird to the Peabody. The wind was brisk, and Jillian found herself wishing for a thicker sweater. She suppressed a shiver, but the next thing she knew, Tuck's flannel jacket was around her shoulders.

It smelled of him. Manly, comfortable.

"What—"

"You looked cold."

Disconcerted by Tuck's gentlemanly manners and the way his masculine scent disturbed her senses, she wanted to shrug off the jacket and give it back to him, but she was cold, so she drew it closer around her and managed a grudging, "Thank you."

"You're welcome."

An awkwardness settled between them as they mounted the steps of the Peabody. The once-stately manor had been converted into office space. Besides Sutter's office, the sign out front told her the place also housed the offices of two certified public accountants, a used bookstore, and a business specializing in flooring and window treatments.

She also noticed there were no parking meters. A town where you didn't have to pay to park? Too damned charming.

Tuck unlocked the front door and they stepped inside.

The house smelled nostalgically of old boards, old books, old wallpaper, and lavender potpourri. It was a get-comfy-snuggle-up kind of smell. Like rain on a winter's day. Like cedar chests and autumn leaves and thick cable sweaters. Between that and the lack of parking meters and the feel of Tuck's jacket on her shoulders, Jillian was about to overdose on quaint.

"Wanna have lunch down here before we tackle Sutter's office?" Tuck asked, pointing to seating in the bay window between the flooring store and the CPA's offices that overlooked the town square.

She wanted to get this over with, but her stomach rumbled. She was hungry. "Sure," she said, slipping off his jacket and handing it back to him.

Tuck pulled sandwiches from the white paper sack. "Tuna on rye or turkey on whole wheat?"

"Whichever one you don't want."

"Evie cut them in half; why don't we mix and match?"

It sounded too damn cozy, but he didn't wait for an answer, just started taking out the sandwiches. Mutt sat on the floor at their feet, thumping his tail and licking his lips.

"Okay," Tuck said. "I can see the sandwiches have got to be divided three ways. He broke off a chunk of his tuna on rye and passed it to Mutt.

Jillian didn't know why she found the gesture touching, but she did. *This town is making you feel sappy. Snap out of it.*

"Sit." Tuck patted the cushion beside him, then held out a wax-paper-wrapped section of turkey on wheat.

She sat beside him on the seat. "Just to be clear, I'm not sitting because you told me to."

"Gotcha. Independent, strong-minded, you don't need no stinkin' man telling you what to do."

When he said it like that, it made her sound like a stone-cold bitch. Did she really come off that way?

"As long as that's settled," she said, trying to act like

she'd been teasing. "Are there any chips in that bag to go with the sandwich? I like the crunch."

"Yep, we've got the barbecued variety or salt and vinegar."

"Ooh, salt and vinegar, my favorite."

"Tart, I should have figured." He tossed her the bag of chips.

"Is there something you want to say to me?"

"Nope. Evie stuck some colas in the sack as well. You want one?"

She nodded and he popped open a Coke for her. Avoiding his gaze, Jillian unwrapped the sandwich, took a bite, swallowed. The turkey was succulent, roasted, hand carved. "Honestly, Tuck, I know we got off on the wrong foot, but thanks for lunch."

"You're welcome."

Silence fell and it wasn't the good kind.

Hurriedly, she ate the sandwich, giving Mutt the last few bites; then she dusted her fingers with a napkin and sipped her soda while she waited for Tuck to finish his meal. He seemed to be taking an extraordinary amount of time eating. Did he normally eat so slow, or was he trying to aggravate her?

"Look," she said, "I'm sorry about all this."

"Nothing to be sorry about," he said, dabbing mayonnaise from his bottom lip with a napkin. For some unfathomable reason, her gaze hung on his mouth, and she couldn't tear her eyes away. "It's my house, and we're going to find the document that proves it. You're the one who's going to be inconvenienced."

"If Sutter didn't file the deed, it's murky legal territory. The vague testimony of a doddering old man will not hold up in court. You need a proper legal document to lay claim to the lake house."

"I've got them."

"Do you?"

"I'll fight you on this," he said, his voice taking on a steely edge she'd never heard before.

She met his gaze. "I fully expect you to. But I have to tell you, back in Houston, I'm known as the Bulldog, because when I sink my teeth in, I never let go. I never give up. I never surrender."

"Is that a threat?"

"No," she said, alarmed by the sudden rapid pounding of her pulse. "It's a fact."

He held her gaze, turned it into a stare, didn't even blink. "You want a battle, I'll give you a battle. Just know before you get into this, Bulldog, that I've got the home-field advantage."

TUCK COULDN'T SAY WHY he'd challenged Jillian. The confrontation hadn't been a conscious decision. It had just come pouring out of him on an emotional current so strong it took his breath away. As if all the pent-up anger that had been lying dormant underneath his grief couldn't be stomped down any longer. He needed a target for his resentment and Jillian was it.

"Let's get this over with," he said, picking up the remains of their lunch and tossing it in the trashcan positioned inside the front door. "The sooner we find that deed, the sooner I'll get rid of you."

Jillian inhaled audibly.

Tuck turned to glance at her, and for the briefest of

moments, he spied utter hurt in her eyes. Instantly, she wiped the emotion away, but he saw it and felt like a complete shit for having said what he did. Jillian Samuels was more vulnerable than she wanted anyone to know.

He should have realized that. Should have been more attuned to her feelings and what was going on with her. Aimee would have been ashamed of his behavior. Not only had Jillian's mentor just died, but she'd also packed up her belongings and moved to a place she'd never even visited. A lawyer, picking up lock, stock, and barrel when Blake's will hadn't been probated?

Something wasn't right. She did not seem the kind of woman who acted on whims. Something was driving her. She was running away, and the lake house had been her refuge.

"I'm sorry," Tuck apologized. "I shouldn't have spoken so rudely to you."

"Never apologize for being honest," she said lightly, but he heard the brittle edge in her voice. She *was* in emotional pain.

Damn it all.

He couldn't deal with his own feelings, much less hers. Tuck pivoted on his heel and started up the carpet-lined staircase to Sutter's second-floor offices. Jillian and her dog followed.

The key fumbled in the lock, giving her time to catch up with him. Mutt was running the halls, entirely too cheerful. He tried not to be pissed off at the dog. It wasn't his fault Tuck's life was so screwed up.

He shoved the door inward. The hinges shrieked. The minute they stepped over the threshold, they both stopped in their tracks, mouths agape.

The phrase "looks like it's been hit by a tornado" was a serious cliché, but in all truthfulness, it was the only phrase that fit. Papers were strewn about the room; piles of manila folders lay in haphazard stacks. Musty old law tomes were spilling off the bookcase and shelved in the oddest places—cluttering the floor, the sofa, the top of the radiator. The drawers of the file cabinets were open, briefs and deeds and accident reports hanging from them willy-nilly.

But that wasn't the worst of it. In the middle of the floor was a murky puddle of foul-smelling water. Directly above the puddle was a serious water stain on the ceiling that also ran down one wall, and there were telltale signs of mold. No telling how long Sutter's roof had been leaking.

A sigh seeped out of Jillian.

"I hope you weren't in a hurry," Tuck said.

She laughed. A short, humorless sound full of weariness, disappointment, and defeat. "Sutter has no idea the place looks like this, does he?"

"I'm guessing not."

Jillian chuffed out her breath and crossed the room to sink into the leather desk chair. Dust rose up around her. She sneezed.

"Bless you," Tuck said automatically, before he remembered she was the enemy intent on kicking him out of his home.

"Thanks. I need all the blessings I can get."

"You're not the only one."

Her eyes met his. "We are in something of a pickle, aren't we?"

"It's not a good day," he agreed.

"This was supposed to be my fresh start," she said, her shoulders sagging in a dejected slump. She looked like a prizefighter going down for the last count.

Why did he have a sudden compulsion to make her feel better? It was a good thing she was feeling overwhelmed. She'd be all the more likely to get into her Sebring and head that U-Haul back to Houston. The thought made him feel a bit sad. He wanted her to stay and fight.

But why? Why would he feel that way?

"Look," he said. "You've had a long day. Let's just call it quits until tomorrow."

Another one of those rueful nonlaughs escaped her. "I don't even have anywhere to stay, and from the look of it, at this time of year, Salvation isn't exactly flush with lodging options."

She was right. In the summer, Salvation did a big tourist trade. But come the end of September, the motels and B and Bs closed for the winter and didn't reopen until May. There was ski season, yes, but people preferred to stay on the slopes rather than an hour's drive down the mountain to Salvation.

He didn't know why he said it. He didn't mean to say it. But the next thing he knew, Tuck opened his mouth, and the words simply tumbled out. "You can stay at the lake house until we get this thing sorted out."

THEY WENT BACK TO THE LAKE HOUSE, Tuck built a fire, then quickly left her alone after mumbling something under his breath about meeting some friends of his. He didn't offer to let her tag along, but why would he? Just because she was alone in town and didn't know anyone. She'd usurped his home. He was bound to be upset.

Jillian sat on the couch staring into the fire, Mutt sleeping at her feet. She felt out of place and offtrack. What the hell was she doing here? She didn't belong in Colorado. She belonged . . .

Where did she belong?

That was the thing. She didn't belong anywhere, but Salvation was supposed to have been her new beginning. Her chance to find her place. To fit in. To finally achieve the love and belonging that had been so elusive for most of her life. She'd found it temporarily, in college, with her three friends. Then again, in Blake. But while she'd had their love, she'd never had that sense of community or permanence. Never lived in a place where everyone knew you and accepted you anyway.

Until this very moment, Jillian hadn't realized how much she wanted that. She shivered, even though she wasn't cold. Mutt raised his head from his place on the floor and looked up as if sensing her vulnerable mood. He sighed and rested his chin on her foot.

"Okay." She laughed, reaching down to scratch him behind the ears. "I'm not completely alone. I have you. We're in this together, Muttster. It's you and me, kid. Homeless wanderers."

He made a whining noise in the back of his throat.

"What's the matter, boy?" She kept scratching his ears. "I just took you outside, and it's too early for your supper."

He looked sad.

"You want me to stay and fight?"

His eyebrows went up. Who knew dogs had such expressive faces?

"You like it here, don't you? Much nicer than the city. Woods to run through. A lake to play in. Rabbits to chase."

He thumped his tail. His fur was soft beneath her fingers.

"I like it here too."

So fight for it.

"Do we have mental telepathy going on here, Muttster? Or am I cracking up?"

Another thump of his tail.

This was a damnable situation. She'd found out Blake had left her paradise, then in the same breath taken it away. Why would he do something like that? If he deeded the land to Tuck, why not change his will as well?

He wasn't thinking straight. He had a brain tumor.

Or . . .

An elusive thought chased through the back of her mind. It made her sit up straight, but before she could fully wrap her head around the notion nudging around, it was gone.

Oh well, perhaps it would occur to her later. In the meantime, she knew what she had to do next.

First thing tomorrow morning, she was calling Hamilton Green and getting to the bottom of the property dispute.

AFTER BUILDING A FIRE in the fireplace to warm the house for Jillian, Tuck had taken off. He felt agitated, confused, guilty, sad, and aggravated with himself. He didn't know where to go, and he wasn't in the mood to talk to anyone about what he was feeling. The only person whose opinion mattered to him at the moment had been dead for two years, her ashes scattered over Salvation Lake.

He hadn't been on the water since the anniversary of Aimee's death, the night he'd fallen in, and he shouldn't be out on it now, but here he was, bobbing in the little red rowboat, wrapped in a parka, a wool blanket across his lap, his cheeks numb from the cold damp wind, staring listlessly at pine trees lining the dock and wondering where in the hell his life had gone.

It was just beginning to sink in that Blake was dead. Even though he'd never really known his father-in-law, he couldn't help feeling a deep, underlying sense of loss and regret. For what could have been. For what would never be. Fences would never been mended. Past hurts would never be forgiven. Misunderstandings would never be resolved.

It made his gut ache. More death, more sorrow.

And then there was Jillian.

Being around Jillian unsettled him, and it wasn't due to any of Ridley's bad-luck-temptress stuff. Well, all right, maybe it was a little, but there was more to his unexpected emotions than that.

He was attracted to Jillian, and that disturbed him because he hadn't been attracted to a woman since his wife. And then he'd gone and told her she could stay with him at the lake house.

How stupid was that?

Why?

He didn't really know why. Maybe it was because Jillian didn't look at him as if he was one of the walking wounded. Everyone else in town treated him as if he was an amputee. No one in Salvation—except for Evie—had known him before Aimee. It was nice, at least for a little while, not to be defined by his status as a widower. It felt good to flirt. To feel like his old self again. And that made him guiltier than ever.

Maybe it was because Jillian seemed to understand, being close to Blake and losing him. She had an underlying sadness in her eyes that tugged at something inside him.

Maybe it was because on some level he felt sorry for her. Apparently, she didn't have anyone else in her life. If she did, why would she have moved up here with all her worldly possessions without first coming to check the place out? Why didn't she have anyone with her, helping her move?

But maybe—and this is the one he really didn't want to admit—just maybe, a part of him wanted to explore the attraction.

Tuck studied the lake house. It was starting to look its age. It needed renovating, updating. On her deathbed, he promised his wife that he would rebuild it. He'd also promised her he would marry again and have the kids the two of them would never have together, but he'd lied about that too. For the life of him, Tuck couldn't imagine getting married again. No one could ever take Aimee's place in his heart.

"I can't believe your father left the lake house to *that woman,*" he spoke out loud to Aimee. "And then he turned around and deeded it to me. Why would he do it? Why would he mess with our heads that way?"

If Aimee were here, she'd probably say, "That proves he's an asshole."

But if Aimee were here, this whole mess wouldn't be an issue. If she hadn't gotten sick . . .

If Aimee hadn't gotten sick, he wouldn't be in Salvation. He'd still be the Magic Man living their Manhattan lifestyle. It was only Aimee's illness that had brought him here. And it was his devotion to her and the small peace he'd found in this odd little town that rooted him.

Now everything was changing. Blake Townsend was dead, and Jillian Samuels had arrived laying claim to Aimee's beloved lake house.

What did it all mean for his future?

Blake deeded the place to you. Even if Sutter forgot to put through the paper work. He wanted you to have it.

But Jillian was a lawyer. She knew how to fight. She was a prosecuting attorney from Houston; she was accustomed to bare-knuckled brawling. She'd slice him to ribbons in a court of law. Unless he could find proof Blake had deeded him the property, he was going to lose the place that had meant so very much to his beloved Aimee.

One thing was clear—he had to get Jillian out of his house.

Chapter Eight

Jillian and Mutt ended up bedding down in one of the upstairs bedrooms after the ten o'clock news. She'd heard Tuck come in around midnight, and she'd tried unsuccessfully not to picture him stripping off his clothes and tumbling onto the couch.

She'd seen him in the nude in her dream and then almost naked in real life, and the man certainly lived up to the fantasy. She'd heard him. Thought of him. And then she'd touched herself in the darkness and pretended it was his hand.

Jillian awoke at seven feeling unsettled and out of place, with the smell of fresh-brewed coffee luring her downstairs. She found Tuck in the kitchen fully dressed, making eggs. She felt oddly disappointed to see him in blue jeans and flannel instead of the way she'd pictured him in her mind.

It's official. You're a pervert.

"Coffee," she demanded.

"My, you're bright-eyed in the morning."

She just glared. "Coffee?"

Tuck chuckled, filled a cup, and pushed it gingerly toward her. "Cream? Sugar?"

"Do I look like a lightweight to you?"

"Black it is."

"Thank you."

"You're welcome."

"I need to take Mutt out," she mumbled after she'd had a few sips. "And give him some kibble."

"Already taken care of."

"That was nice of you."

He shrugged. "Mutt wouldn't leave me in peace until I did. How do you like your eggs?"

"You're cooking? For me?"

"Why not?" His grin dazzled.

All at once, she felt a little woozy, like she'd been running too hard and too long. She couldn't ever remember any man cooking for her, other than Blake.

Jillian plunked down on the barstool across from the stove and sipped her coffee. She couldn't help but notice Tuck's long, masculine fingers.

"Eggs?" he asked.

"Over easy."

Their eyes met; then Tuck looked away, but not before she caught the lingering glance he slid down her body. The look ignited the sparks shooting between them.

Suddenly she realized she was still in her pajamas, and her hair was mussed, and she just felt . . . *exposed.* Her hand trailed to her collar, and she fastened the top button.

"Are you cold? 'Cause I can crank up the heater."

"No, no. I'm fine." Sitting here, looking at him, she was the antithesis of cold. She was a bonfire.

He dished up the eggs on a blue Fiesta ware plate and slid them across the bar toward her.

"Gracias."

"You speak Spanish?"

"I'm a lawyer from South Texas. Even when you don't speak Spanish, you speak a little Spanish."

He put his eggs on a green plate, leaned his back against the counter, and ate standing up. Was he that reluctant to take the barstool next to her?

"So how come you're really here?"

She shrugged. "I thought I'd inherited this house."

"If that's the only reason you came here, why not just sell it through Blake's lawyer?"

"I'm the executor of his will. I came here to settle things."

"In a U-Haul?"

"Hey, you wouldn't tell me about the Magic Man thing. Why should I tell you my sob story?"

"Point taken."

"These are good eggs."

"Thanks. I added shredded cheddar."

They ate in a silence punctuated only by the clinking of forks against Fiesta ware.

"Now that you know the place isn't legally yours, what are you going to do?" he asked.

"I don't know that. I haven't seen this mysterious deed."

"You calling me a liar?"

"I'm just saying that in the eyes of the law, at this moment in time, you have no proof Blake deeded you the property, and I have a copy of his will that gives it to me."

"Okay," he said, tossing his plate in the sink and crossing his arms over his chest. "Let's play what if. What if we can't find the deed? What if you take me to court and win and the place is yours? Then what? You're seriously planning on living in Salvation?"

"Yes," she said mildly, although her muscles tensed, and she didn't know why.

"What are you going to do for work?" Tuck asked. "It's pretty hard to make a living up here, especially during the winter."

"You seem to manage."

"My needs are modest."

"Mine are too."

He raked his gaze over her and snorted. "Not if your hundred-dollar haircut is any indication."

Irritated, Jillian ran a hand through her hair and glared. "In answer to your earlier question, I'm setting up a law practice. I have to take the Colorado bar first, but until then, I have some money socked away."

Tuck's eyebrow raised in surprise. "You're going to open a law practice in Salvation?"

"Why not? Is that so far-fetched? If Sutter's the only lawyer, the town is in desperate need of competent legal counsel."

"Sutter's competent."

"The man's over eighty and healing from a broken hip."

"Most people go to Boulder for their legal needs."

"With me here, they won't have to."

"Listen," he said abruptly. "I've gotta get going. New job starting today."

"Um, okay. Thanks for breakfast."

"No big deal." He headed for the door, turned, paused.

"What?"

"Maybe you could find another place to stay. There's

plenty of motels in Boulder, or you can try contacting Jefferson Baines. He's a local realtor. He'd know if there was anything for rent in Salvation at this time of year."

"Excuse me? Wasn't it just yesterday that you asked me to stay?" She tried to sound teasing, but damn if it didn't come out accusatory.

"I'm unaccustomed to roommates," he said gruffly. "Of course, you can stay until you find a place of your own. I'd just appreciate if it was sooner rather than later."

"I understand," she said, even though she was a bit confused by his about-face.

After Tuck left, Jillian took Mutt for a walk, then came back inside to wash the breakfast dishes before jumping into the shower. Showering was a bit tricky, since the faucet handle was broken off and she had to use a pair of pliers she found on the bathroom counter to adjust the water temperature.

"Totally brilliant, Jillian. If you really do end up inheriting this place, it's going to cost a small fortune to get it renovated." Maybe she should just let Tuck have the lake house and forget all about it.

And do what? Go where?

A sudden rush of grief washed over her, and she bowed her head against the flow of hot water, sucking in great sobs of air. Her entire body shook. She fisted her hands against the pain. She missed Blake so damned much.

She wished he were here. Wished she could ask him what he'd been trying to do by willing her the lake house in Colorado. Making her think it was the answer to her prayers, then getting here and discovering he'd given the place away to someone else.

It hurt.

Another betrayal in a lifetime of betrayals.

If he'd just bothered to change his will, she would never have gotten her hopes up, never had any expectations, never dared to start wanting something she'd always been afraid to want.

A place to call home.

Her throat constricted. Despair wasn't like her. She was tough, she was resilient, she didn't wallow in self-pity. And she wasn't going to give up without a fight. All her life she had to scrap for everything she'd ever gotten. Why should this be any different?

Determination pushed out the grief. Tenacity dried her eyes. A sense of purpose stilled the echoes of past hurts and betrayals.

She got out of the shower, dressed, and found her cell phone. Steeling her jaw, she called the courthouse in Boulder and identified herself as the executor of Blake's will and asked if the lake house deed had been filed to Tucker Manning. Once she determined that it had not, she dialed Hamilton Green's number.

His secretary answered and put her on hold. Jillian paced the living room while she waited, palm splayed against her forehead.

Finally, Hamilton came on the line. "Miss Samuels?"

She didn't bother with pleasantries; she just launched right in and told him about Tuck and his claims on the house Blake had willed to her.

"But you said Mr. Manning doesn't have the document and his lawyer didn't file it."

"That's correct. He can't find the deed."

"If he doesn't have a deed, he doesn't have a case," Hamilton said. "The house is yours. Of course, you know he can choose to contest the will. My guess is that it's a shakedown."

"His lawyer backs him up."

"The lawyer could be in on it. Be careful, Jillian. People in small towns stick together, and they're distrustful of outsiders."

"I'm not getting that kind of vibe from him. Are you certain Blake never said a word to you about deeding the property to his son-in-law?"

"Never. I didn't even know Blake had a son-in-law. That's what makes me so suspicious. Why would Blake go through some small-town attorney to deed the property instead of coming directly to me? Why not then change his will?"

"That's what I keep asking myself."

"Are you certain this guy was Blake's son-in-law?" Hamilton asked. "Maybe he's an imposter. Stranger things have been known to happen where money and property are involved."

Was he? Jillian frowned. She remembered Blake telling her Aimee was married, but for the life of her, she couldn't remember him mentioning Tuck's name. Could Tuck just be some guy living in the lake house, pretending to be Aimee's husband?

She dismissed the idea as soon as it occurred. Something bizarro like that might happen in Houston, but not in Salvation. It was too small, too insular. Unless the whole town was in on the subterfuge, and that thought was too ridiculous to entertain for even a second.

"I'm sure he's Aimee's husband, and I imagine that he's telling the truth about the deed. It's probably buried somewhere in his lawyer's hellhole of an office," she said.

"Excuse me?"

Quickly, she explained about the ransacked condition of Sutter's place of business.

"Egads," Hamilton said. "Incompetence at its finest."

"The guy's old and recovering from a fractured hip," Jillian said, feeling an unexpected urge to stick up for Sutter. "And his secretary apparently plundered the place. There are extenuating circumstances."

"So he let you into his office carte blanche?"

"Yes."

"That doesn't sound very prudent."

"I was with Tucker at the time."

"Hmm."

"Hmm, what?"

"Nothing . . . just . . ."

"Just what?"

"If you had access to his office and he never actually filed the deed, you have the power to make sure it's never found."

"Are you suggesting I destroy the deed if I find it?" Jillian put steel in her voice, unable to believe what he was hinting at.

"No, no, of course not," Hamilton backtracked. "That would be unethical."

"Not to mention criminal."

"Right, right. Just pray you don't find the deed."

"And if I do?"

Hamilton paused. "When did this Manning say Blake deeded him the property?"

"About four months ago."

"That's about the same time Blake learned he had a brain tumor."

Jillian could see where Hamilton was headed with this. "You're going to claim Blake wasn't in his right mind when he deeded the lakehouse to Tuck."

"If he was in his right mind, why not go through me?"

"I can't answer that, but we both know Blake wasn't mentally impaired."

"Do we?"

She considered what Hamilton was saying. Blake had been forgetful before his death. Distracted. But who wouldn't be with a diagnosis of an inoperable brain tumor hanging over them?

"Honestly, Jillian, you're in the driver's seat. This man doesn't have a deed, and unless it's found, he has no legal claim on the house. And even if the deed is found, we can take him to court on the grounds Blake didn't know what he was doing when he deeded him the property. We stand a good chance of winning based on Blake's brain tumor and the fact that he, a lawyer, didn't draw up a new will to reflect the deed change. Question is, do you want to fight?"

Did she?

Jillian stopped her pacing and glanced out the window at the supreme beauty of the lake stretching out in front of her. Just looking at the calm water, the pine trees, the purple-blue of the snowcapped mountains instantly quieted her mind. Serene, peaceful, the place called to her soul in the way no place ever had.

Home.

"I want to fight."

"Then get in that house and set up camp there. You've got the power of the will on your side, and right now he's got nothing. Remember, possession is nine-tenths of the law."

AFTER SPENDING the remainder of the morning unloading her possessions from the U-Haul into the garage, Jillian drove to Boulder and dropped off the trailer as prearranged with the moving company.

Then she returned to the lake house, stopping to pick up a fast-food salad for her and a junior-sized hamburger for Mutt on the way. After finishing her lunch, she dressed in a gray wool suit, white silk blouse, red Hermès scarf, red and gray Jimmy Choos, and conservative gold jewelry. Perfect attire for winning over a jury. Hopefully it would have the same effect on Sutter Godfrey.

As Jillian motored up Enchanted Lane, heading toward town, it occurred to her that no one here knew her. She could become anyone she wanted. This was truly a fresh start. A clean slate. No one had to know about her past. A liberating thought.

Jillian parked in front of the Bluebird and went inside. It was almost two, but the place was still half full with customers, most of them over sixty. The minute she stepped through the door, every eye in the place was glued to her.

"Afternoon," several people called out. She noticed a bunch of old coots were giving her legs the once-over.

Note to self: In the future, wear pants.

She raised a hand. “Hi.”

“You looking for Tucker?” asked Evie from behind the counter.

“Actually, I’m looking for Sutter. Is he here?”

“Always.” Evie nodded toward the back room and the sound of dominoes being shuffled.

“Thanks.”

She found Sutter Godfrey in exactly the same position he’d been in the previous day, surrounded by his cronies. The doctor was gone, but in his place sat another buddy. She wondered if Sutter ever moved from the spot.

Sutter glanced up at her, but the welcoming light that had been in his eyes when she was with Tucker had vanished.

“Hello, Mr. Godfrey.”

“Miss Samuels.” He played a domino, earned ten points.

Jillian shifted on her heels, suddenly feeling very awkward. “Might I have a few minutes of your time in private?”

He paused, and for the longest moment, she thought he was going to refuse. An unexplained panic grabbed hold of her, but she forced herself to remain calm on the outside. She’d had lots of practice cloaking her feelings.

“Fellas,” he said to his companions, “can you give us some space?”

They all looked at her a bit suspiciously but got up from the table and headed into the main part of the café. She was beginning to feel like the business suit had been a huge miscalculation, clearly marking her as a foreigner in their community. Jillian took the vacant seat to Sutter’s right.

Sutter steepled his fingers. "How might I help you, Miss Samuels?"

She forced a smile. "The question is, Mr. Godfrey, how can I help you?"

He shook his head.

"Did I say something wrong?"

"You don't need to pull any of those big-city sales tactics with me, young lady. Just tell me what you want."

Okay, so he wasn't going to be the pushover she'd imagined. That was fine. She lived for challenges. "I want to work for you."

"I'm not hiring."

"You're not even going to hear me out?"

He pressed his lips into a straight line and leaned back in his wheelchair. "Let's have it."

"You need an assistant."

"Maybe," he said grudgingly.

"No maybe to it. I saw the inside of your office yesterday with Tuck. It's in shambles."

"So Tucker told me."

"A man of your stature—"

He held up a hand. "Normally, I am a fan of flattery, but cut the bullshit. What do you want, and why?"

"I need a job, and I'm trained as a lawyer."

"Exactly. Why would you want a position as my assistant?"

"For one thing, I haven't taken the bar in Colorado. For another, I want to start a legal practice here in Salvation, and when I do, I think it would work out to both our advantages if you agreed to take me on as a partner and mentor me in family law, as opposed to me setting up a competing practice."

He laughed. "Sweetie, all it would take from me is one word, and no one would darken your door."

"Are you that sure of yourself?" she asked. "You're over eighty, in a wheelchair, and you never filed Tuck's deed. Some people—especially the young people—in this town just might think you're losing your touch."

"Spoken like a true lawyer." There was admiration in his voice.

"So you'll consider taking me on?"

He paused again. "Your scenario sounds all well and good in theory."

"What are your reservations?"

"Why do you want to set up a practice here?"

"I inherited a lake house."

"A lake house that's already been deeded to someone else."

Jillian blew out her breath. "Still haven't seen a deed yet."

"It's there."

"Then why not let me straighten out your office and find it?"

"What? Put a fox in the hen house?"

Jillian drew herself up straight. "I resent the implication. If the deed exists, I'll honor it."

"The deed exists."

"Your word isn't legal proof."

He cocked his head. "You want to work for me and yet you don't trust me."

"Trust isn't my strong suit," she said, figuring her answer was going to end the interview, but to her surprise, he nodded.

"I get that. You been kicked around a lot."

She didn't know how to respond to that, so she said instead, "I graduated top of my law school class. I've worked in the Harris County DA office ever since. I've—"

He held up a palm. "I don't doubt your credentials."

"No?"

"It's your motives I have issues with."

"Let me clear it up for you. I want a new start, in a new place, and even if the lake house isn't mine, I intend on staying—"

"Why?" Sutter interrupted.

"Salvation is quiet and serene and—"

"Exactly what are you running from?"

Jillian hardened her chin against his question. Was he insinuating she was a coward? "I'm not running from anything."

"Right."

"I'm not."

"High-powered assistant DA chucks it all to move to the mountains. You're running from something. What's his name?"

Damn! The old man was too good. "Who says it's a him?"

"Okay, then, what's her name?"

"It's a him," she admitted, not really knowing why she did. "His name is Alex Fredericks."

Sutter nodded. "I suspected as much."

Confused, Jillian blinked at him. "You know Alex?"

"I know he took over Blake's job. I also know Blake was worried about you after your affair with Fredericks went sour."

"Blake talked to you about me? Blake knew I had an affair with Alex?" The news completely ambushed her.

"He did."

Jillian recovered quickly. "So you should know he wanted me to have the lake house."

Sutter shrugged. "Maybe he wanted Tuck to have it more."

"Then why didn't he change his will?"

"I don't know. That's one for you to puzzle out on your own."

"So, you'll give me the job as your assistant, and when I pass the bar, you'll consider making me your partner?"

"You don't have to push so hard."

"Then you're considering it?"

"You're persistent," he mused. "Determined. Not one to give up even when it's clear you've made a huge mistake. I'm considering taking December tenth in the pool."

Jillian frowned. Just when she thought the old man was sharper than she thought, he said something completely off the wall. "Excuse me?"

"The town has a pool," he said.

"For swimming?"

He laughed. "For betting."

"I'm not following you."

"We're taking bets on how long it will take you to hightail it back to Houston."

"Seriously? They're already taking bets on when I'll leave town?"

"Oops, that stubborn look in your eye means you'll last at least a couple of weeks longer. I'm putting twenty dollars on December twenty-fourth. Holidays get to the best of 'em."

"Think again—Christmas means nothing to me."

"Smart, fiery. I like that."

She slammed a hand on the table, making the dominoes jump. "Then hire me."

Sutter just sat there grinning at her like she was the best entertainment he'd had in weeks. It irritated the hell out of her. "I'm not getting tired of this town."

"You ever spend the winter in the Rockies?"

"No."

"I thought as much."

His smile took on a knowing quality that made her want to do something to rattle his smug certainty. "No, but I spent thirteen years being raised by a stepmother who treated me like her personal servant. I had a biological mother who abandoned me and a father who died when I was five. I put myself through college and law school, sometimes working three jobs to make ends meet. I'm not a spoiled, pampered rich kid, nor am I a weak-willed whiner. I'm tough and I'm strong, and when I make up my mind to do something, it gets done."

"Hmm," he said mildly. "I guess I better take February first."

"Dammit, I'm staying. From now on, Salvation is my home, and I have a lake house to prove it."

"You don't have the lake house yet."

"Then you prove that I don't. Oh wait, you can't because you can't get upstairs to your office." She was mad now and was past the point of caring if he gave her a job or not.

His laughter infuriated her. She jumped from the chair, grabbed her purse, and headed for the door.

"Wait," Sutter called.

With her pulse throbbing furiously in the hollow of her throat, Jillian turned. "Yes?"

"I'll tell you what, Miss Samuels. I can see you're quite earnest, and I admire industriousness. I'll pay you fifteen dollars an hour to get my office in order, and when you find Tuck's deed, we'll talk again about hiring you for real."

Chapter Nine

With that one comment, Sutter had ensnared her in a catch-22. He would take her on as his protégé only if she found the deed that would spell her own downfall. With the deed, she'd have no lake house and no real reason to stay in Salvation. But without the deed, she'd have no entry into the town's business community.

She had a choice to make. Was she going to stay in Salvation no matter what happened with the lake house?

Sutter sat, arms crossed, awaiting her decision.

Either way, it wasn't going to hurt to take the temporary job. It would give her something to do and bring in a little money. Besides, she had nowhere else to go. "I accept," she said.

"All right." He motioned for his friends who were hanging around the door. "Carl, put me down for February first in the pool. This one's a scrapper. She'll outlast most."

Jillian couldn't help smiling as she left the Bluebird and headed across the street to Sutter's office in the Peabody Mansion. "You're going to lose that bet, you old goat. I'm not going anywhere."

The flooring store and the CPA offices were open when she walked through the front door. Before Jillian got to the staircase, a diminutive, bespectacled woman about Jillian's age, with light auburn hair and a nose dusted with freckles, popped up from behind the counter at the entrance to the flooring store.

She waved a plump hand at Jillian. "Come here, come here."

The woman sounded so excited that Jillian trotted over.

"Come around, come around, and kick your shoes off."

This was starting to feel a little weird, but she walked around the counter to see three different kinds of floor padding behind the counter. She noticed the woman was dressed in a bulky purple knit sweater with Holstein cows appliquéd on the front and a long denim skirt. She was also barefooted.

"The shoes, the shoes." The woman waved again.

Obediently, Jillian kicked off her shoes.

"Now, walk on all three samples and tell me which one feels the cushiest. I've been testing them out for so long that I've lost all objectivity."

"Um, okay." *That's not all you've lost.*

"Really get after it. March. Get the feel for how it's going to hold up under traffic."

Jillian stomped the floor padding. "Like this?"

"There you go." The woman whistled and picked up one of Jillian's stilettos. "Hey, are these Jimmy Choos?"

"Uh-huh."

"Classy." The woman eyed Jillian and handed her the shoe. "From head to toe, I might add."

"Thank you."

"You're new in town."

"How'd you know?"

"I know everyone in Salvation, and it's the wrong time of year for tourists." The woman shoved her bangs back off her forehead and extended a hand. "Lexi Kilgore, and you are . . ."

"Jillian Samuels."

"Nice ta meet ya, Jillian. So, what do you think?"

"About what?"

Lexi gazed at Jillian's feet.

Jillian glanced down. "Oh, the padding."

Lexi sank her hands on her hips. "Give it to me straight. Which is the softest? Number one, number two, or number three?"

Jillian considered the question for a moment. "Number three."

"Ah." Lexi raised a finger. "But is it too soft? Will it hold up to the demands of heavy foot traffic?"

"I don't know."

"Of course not. How would you? You're not in the flooring business." Lexi looked at her. "Are you?"

"No, no."

"Whew." Lexi splayed a hand across her chest and blew out her breath. "That's good, 'cause it's hard enough making a living in town without more competition."

"You're safe where I'm concerned. No interest in the field of flooring whatsoever."

"That's why I had to branch out into window treatments," Lexi went on. "Can't be too specialized in a town this small."

"I can appreciate that."

Behind the frames of her glasses, Lexi's eyes perked up. "So, Jillian, if you're new in town, do you think you might be needing new flooring? Or window treatments, maybe? I just changed suppliers, and he's got killer connections for Roman shades. Straight from Florence."

"I might be interested at that."

Lexi clapped. "Really? That's great. Where are you living?"

"I inherited a house on Enchantment Lane."

"Fantastic location. Which house?"

"Number 1414. It was owned by—"

"But that's Tuck and Aimee's place." Lexi looked confused.

"Tuck and Aimee," she repeated, fully realizing for the first time that in everyone's mind, Tuck was still linked with his late wife.

"Oh yeah. You didn't know?" Lexi touched her arm. "It's so sad. Tuck's wife died of cancer. She was only twenty-five, poor girl. Aimee was so sweet," Lexi went on. "Everyone loved her. She and her mother and father came here every summer from the time Aimee was small. Then after her parents got divorced when Aimee was thirteen, they just stopped coming."

"Sad," Jillian echoed, not knowing what else to say.

"But that lake house has been in the Townsend family for three generations. It sat empty for years, until Aimee got sick and Tuck brought her here. She'd made him promise that one day, when they were ready to have kids, they'd leave New York City and come home to Salvation and renovate the lake house. But Aimee died before Tuck could do that."

Jillian's chest tightened. "So tragic."

Tears misted Lexi's eyes. "But tragic in a romantic way. Like *Love Story* or *The Notebook*. Tuck is such a great guy." Lexi sighed. "He's having trouble letting go, moving on."

"I imagine it is difficult."

"So how'd you get the house?"

"Aimee's dad, Blake, was my mentor. He recently passed away and left it to me."

"Blake's dead?" Lexi wrung her hands. "I hadn't heard. Oh, that's such a shame. I imagine the fact he never reconciled with Aimee before she died took a toll on his health."

"I imagine."

"So what's going to happen to Tuck? Where's he gonna go?"

"Doesn't his sister live here?"

"Yes, but she and Ridley are trying for a baby. Tuck would never impose on them."

"Tuck doesn't have the money to buy his own place?"

Lexi shook her head. "Aimee's medical bills blew through his fortune. He took her to all kinds of specialists and alternative medicine doctors, looking for that last-ditch cure."

She considered telling Lexi about the missing deed and the erupting property dispute, but she decided against it. Word would get out soon enough.

"So what do you do for a living, Jillian?" Lexi changed the subject.

"I'm a lawyer. At least in Texas I am. I have to sit for the Colorado bar. Until then, I'm Sutter Godfrey's new assistant. And speaking of which"—Jillian waved at the upstairs—"I better get to work. His office is a disaster zone."

Lexi nodded. "His last secretary was a real piece of

work. Took advantage of the poor old guy. Embezzled from him. Nasty business."

"He said she got pregnant and left town."

"That too. I'm happy to see Sutter's got a real professional helping him now."

"It's been nice chatting with you, Lexi, but I better get to work." Jillian made a motion for the door.

"Wait, wait, let's exchange cards." Lexi plucked a business card from a gold-plated holder on the counter. "For when you're ready to put new flooring in Aimee's place."

Jillian exchanged cards with her and wandered out into the hallway, Lexi still following her and talking ninety miles an hour. The CPAs were standing in their doorway, eying Jillian with curiosity. They were twins. Two men in their late thirties, dressed alike in matching long-sleeve burgundy polo shirts and black Dockers.

"Jillian, Bill and Will Chambers. Guys, this is Jillian Samuels. She's a lawyer, and she inherited Tuck and Aimee's place," Lexi chattered.

Seriously? Bill and Will?

Suddenly, Lexi burst out laughing.

"What?" Jillian asked.

Lexi splayed a hand over her mouth. "Oops, sorry. I just had a thought. Now we've got Bill, Will, and Jill all working under the same roof."

"I never go by Jill," she said.

"But it gets better." Lexi waved a hand. "Bill's getting married this Christmas at Thunder Mountain Lodge, and his fiancée is . . . drum roll please . . . named Lil."

"Come on, Lexi, you know Lily doesn't like to be called Lil," Bill said.

Lexi grinned impishly. "Maybe not, but it's fun to say.

Bill and Lil, Will and Jill. Hey, Jill, are you single? Will's single."

"It's Jillian," she corrected.

"Aimee was such a sweet girl," Will said, quickly changing the subject. "Bright as sunshine." The one she thought was Will shook his head, clearly ignoring Lexi's sidebar into rhyming names. "So sad what happened. And poor Tuck, two years later and he's still having trouble moving on."

"Everyone adored her." Bill sighed. "Such a tragic loss."

Yes, yes, Aimee the saint. Immediately Jillian felt bad about her uncharitable thoughts. What in the hell was wrong with her?

"So where are you from, Jillian?" Will asked.

"Houston."

Bill's gaze met Will's. "I've got dibs on Halloween."

Will eyed Jillian. "She'll last at least until Thanksgiving."

Jillian couldn't believe this. "You guys are betting on me too?"

"What bet?" Lexi asked.

"It seems the whole town is betting on when I'll leave, and I just got here yesterday."

"Ooh," Lexi said. "I want in. Who's running the pool?"

"Not you too!"

Lexi shrugged but didn't look the slightest chagrined. "Hey, not much happens in Salvation. We have to take our excitement where we can find it."

Jillian had to laugh. What else was there to do? "I've got to get to work, guys."

"See ya later." Lexi wriggled her fingers.

"If you need a good accountant," Will said, "please, keep us in mind."

"I will do that, thanks."

"And don't forget your flooring needs," Lexi sang out.

"Never fear, when I'm ready to retile, you're on my speed dial." Finally Jillian escaped and climbed the stairs to the second floor.

The old wooden staircase creaked underneath her feet. Once she reached the second floor, it was easy to locate the frosted glass door with SUTTER GODFREY ESQUIRE stenciled on it in dramatic black script. She pulled his keys from her purse, but the door wasn't locked. She turned the handle and stepped inside to find a plastic drop cloth covering the floor and a blue-jean-clad man on a ladder. All she could see was from the waist down. The rest of him was sticking up through a pretty big hole in the ceiling.

His butt was at Jillian's eye level.

She'd seen that butt before. Jillian looked up at the same time Tuck looked down.

"This is your new job?" she asked, at the same time Tuck said, "Sutter hired me to repair his roof and the water damage to his office."

"I'm working for him too. As his assistant."

Tuck stared at Jillian, unable to believe his crappy luck. He was going to be stuck with Jillian at home and at work? "Found a job on your first day in town. That's a coup. Congratulations."

"How am I supposed to get anything done if you're hammering and running saws?" She sank her hands on her hips.

"How am I supposed to get anything done if you're underfoot?" he groused.

"This isn't going to work."

"You're telling me."

"Sheetrock dust."

"Clacking, clacking on the keyboard," he countered.

"What have you got against me?"

"Other than the fact that you've invaded my house?"

"It's not my fault. Besides, it's *my* house."

"Just until the deed turns up."

"I'm beginning to think there is no deed. I called the Boulder courthouse and learned a deed hasn't been filed in your name. I called Blake's attorney, and he says Blake never mentioned a word to him about deeding you the lake house. In fact, Blake never mentioned you at all." She sank her hands on her hips. "How do I know you and Sutter aren't in cahoots, trying to bilk me out of my inheritance? Believe me, if that deed does turn up, I'm going over it with a fine-tooth comb."

"*Your* inheritance?" Tuck gave an angry snort. "That house belonged to Blake's daughter, not some skank who wormed her way into Blake's bed." He folded his arms over his chest. He shouldn't have said that. The second the words left his mouth, he knew they were low and mean and untrue. He'd lashed out in pain and anger at the only target around.

Jillian clenched her jaw. She looked as hurt and angry as he felt. He felt like even a bigger butthead. "Excuse me, I did not sleep with Blake Townsend!"

He wanted to apologize, but he was entrenched in his position. "So you say."

"I'm so mad at you right now that I could grab this

ladder and shake it until you fall off and break your stupid neck, but I won't because . . ." Her voice trailed off.

Tuck put a hand on the ladder just in case she decided to carry out her threat. In his other hand, he held the flashlight. "Because of what?"

She pursed her lips.

Tuck climbed down the ladder. "Because of what?"

Her dark eyes softened. "Because I don't want to go to jail for manslaughter. The momentary sense of pleasure wouldn't be worth the consequences."

"That's not what you were going to say."

"It doesn't matter what I was going to say."

"I want to hear it. Spit it out."

She arched an eyebrow. "You sure you can take it?"

He jerked his chin upward. "I can handle whatever you can dish out."

"I'm overlooking your attitude because I know how much you're hurting over the loss of your wife."

That got him square in the gut. "I don't want or need your sympathy. I'm acting like a jerk because I'm a jerk, not because my wife died."

"You're not a jerk."

"You don't know me."

"I know you've been through a lot of pain."

He hated the way she was looking at him. Just like everyone else did. As if he was an emotional cripple. "No more than the next Joe."

"Losing a spouse is not trivial."

Anger rose in his chest. "Oh yeah, and you're so well versed on what it feels like to lose a spouse? Don't even try pulling that empathy crap on me. You don't have a clue what I've been going through."

Jillian recoiled as if he'd slapped her, and immediately Tuck wanted to kick his own ass. "You're absolutely right," she murmured. "I don't, but I do know what it's like to lose the only person who truly gets you."

"Blake."

She nodded and without another word, turned on her heels and stalked over to the desk he'd swathed in a plastic drop cloth to protect the papers from falling ceiling debris. She batted back the plastic.

"Here, let me help." He went toward her.

She picked up a letter opener off the desk and wielded it. "Back off. Don't do me any favors. I can take care of myself."

He raised both arms in a gesture of surrender and cocked her a grin. "Don't stab, I'm backing away slowly."

She giggled then, and it was such an odd sound coming from her that he laughed too. What an emotional roller coaster they were both on. Tuck didn't quite know what to make of her. She had this tough, no-nonsense way about her, but then unexpectedly, like now, he'd glimpse another side of her. A softer side he imagined she didn't often show.

Jillian put the letter opener down. "Sorry," she apologized. "I can get a little defensive."

"Yeah, well." He pulled a rag from his back pocket and wiped his hands on it. "Me too. I suppose."

She peered at him through lowered lashes.

"Truce." He stuck out his hand.

"Truce." She accepted it.

They shook hands.

The contact was electric. Tuck's head reeled, his body stiffened and his gut clenched in a wholly enjoyable way.

Damn, damn, damn. She smelled like freshly laundered linen, crisp and clean and cozy. He thought immediately of a turned-down bed.

Her eyes widened. She dropped his hand like she'd just learned he had leprosy.

Tuck was just as shocked. He couldn't believe he was reacting this way, and he felt ashamed. *I'm sorry, Aimee.*

"Did you find somewhere else to stay?" Tuck ventured, praying she would say yes, especially after she'd just electrocuted his hand.

"I did."

Hallelujah, he could have his life back. "Boulder?"

"Right here in Salvation."

"Convenient for your new job. Jefferson Baines hook you up?"

"Nope."

From the way she was looking at him, he wasn't getting good vibes about this. "What's the address?"

Her gaze was steely. "Fourteen-fourteen Enchantment Lane."

Hell, he knew that's what she was going to say. "No, no."

"Yes, yes."

"You can't stay with me."

"From a legal standpoint, I can. Since I'm executor of Blake's will and he left the house to me—unless you produce documentation that says otherwise—I *can* stay in the house. I've unpacked my U-Haul. Like it or not, until you have that deed, I'm your new roommate."

* * *

JILLIAN HELD HER BREATH as Tuck snorted, fisted his hands at his side, pivoted on his heel, and then stalked out of Sutter's office, slamming the door behind him.

In the wake of his obvious anger, she felt as if she were standing alone in the desert with a hot blast of sand pelting her as she stared at miles and miles of empty landscape.

What? You thought taking over a man's home was going to be easy?

No, but she hadn't expected to feel so . . . What was she feeling?

Jillian swallowed against the vacant, lost sensation surging inside her, and she flashed back to that day in court where the same emotions consumed her. Coming to Salvation was supposed to fix this hollow feeling. It was supposed to make her whole. Fill her up.

Instead, she was adrift, unsure of herself, isolated. But that was no different than she'd been for most of her life. Maybe she should reconsider staying at the lake house.

And go where? Back to Houston? There was nothing left for her there.

She sucked her bottom lip between her top teeth and stared dismally at the shambles around her.

This is where you start. This is square one. This is your new beginning.

The sound of footsteps tromping on the roof drew her gaze upward. *Stomp, stomp, stomp.* Had to be Tuck and from the sound of it, he was still steamed.

Too bad.

It was time to take a stand. Sure, she could just pack up and drive away, but no matter where she went, she now realized things wouldn't be any different. She'd feel the same sense of loneliness. There was only one way to overcome it. Step from her aloofness. Entrench herself in a community. Make friends. She loved the town, loved the house, and by gosh, if she made an effort, she could love these people and they could come to love her.

Really? whispered the ugly little voice in the back of her head. *You really think that anyone is going to love you? Your own mother didn't love you. Why would these people?*

Jillian closed her eyes against the sudden rush of tears. She would not cry. She would not. Gulping, she sniffed, blinked.

No, she would not cry, but neither would she run. For better or worse, she'd made her decision. She'd come to Salvation to find a home, and that's what she was going to do. Come what may, she wasn't going to let Tuck Manning stop her.

LATER THAT DAY, Tuck stalked into the lake house, planning on laying down the law and telling Jillian why she simply could not stay there. He had the arguments all prepped in his head when he heard her singing at the top of her lungs from the direction of the bathroom. The cheerful sound stopped him in his tracks.

He canted his head, listening to identify the tune over the sound of the shower running—"I Can See Clearly Now."

The tune reached out and smacked him. He sucked in his breath.

Aimee used to hum it when things were going badly. She'd told him once it was the song her father hummed just before he went into court for his final summation.

She recalled sitting on the bed in her parents' bedroom, watching Blake knot up his tie in front of the mirror while belting out the old Johnny Nash tune.

Tuck had asked, "If it's a song favored by your dad, why do you sing it?"

"It gives me courage and hope."

"But you and your dad don't get along."

She shook her head and looked at him as if he were a naïve child. "I love my father with all my heart, Tuck. I just can't forgive him for destroying our family."

And that was Aimee's greatest flaw. Her inability to forgive if you'd wronged her. He'd never wronged her, so he'd never been on the receiving end of her unforgiving nature, but suddenly he had an unexpected empathy for Blake. And a deep sadness for Aimee, who'd been unable to let her father make amends.

Had Jillian picked up the song from her mentor? Did she, too, hum the tune when things were going badly? Was it the equivalent to whistling in the dark, pretending you weren't scared of the boogeyman?

The thought dissipated his anger.

And before he could move, the bathroom door opened and Jillian stepped into the hallway, wrapped in nothing but a beach towel while she busily dried her hair with a bath towel.

"Oh," they exclaimed simultaneously as their eyes met.

And for one long moment, time just hung.

Tuck stared at her, his throat muscles paralyzed. He couldn't speak or swallow.

She stared back, her dark eyes glimmering in the light from the hallway bulb, rich as cocoa beans dipped in Swiss chocolate.

Something inside Tuck slipped. An awareness that he'd never felt before. For the first time, he noticed the little imperfections on Jillian's face. The tiny half-moon-shaped scar in the center of her forehead. The way her eyelashes were so long they looked fake. How the hair-line on her left side grew farther back than on the right side. Oddly, those imperfections served to make her more appealing.

Her cheeks were flushed pink from the hot water of her shower, contrasting sharply with her otherwise creamy white complexion. With that dramatic dark hair and her pale skin, she would have made a hell of a Goth girl if she'd wanted.

He expected her to duck into her bedroom for cover—Aimee would have under similar circumstances—but Jillian just stood there, appraising him with her best prosecuting attorney gaze. He forgot every word that had been in his head just minutes earlier.

"Your mouth is hanging open," she said coolly, rubbing her hair between the terry cloth fold of her towel.

"Um . . ." He grunted, unable to push anything resembling civilized conversation over his tongue.

"Is there something you wanted?"

You, I want you.

The thought raced through his mind and took him completely aback. "Um . . ."

"Yes?" She fluttered those dynamite lashes.

He cleared his throat. *Remember, you were going to lay down the law, tell her she had to hit the road.*

She waited.

Dammit, he couldn't help himself; his gaze dropped

to where her towel was knotted just above her breasts. "Um . . ."

Droplets of water spattered the hardwood floor at her feet. His eyes tracked downward to her bare toes painted fire-engine red. He'd never seen anything more erotic.

"Tuck?"

His gaze shot back to her face. "Huh?"

"You were trying to say something to me?"

"Yeah, yeah." He nodded, trying to shake off the mental fog that had befallen him. "There's only one way this arrangement is going to work."

"If you move out?" Jillian asked with a hopeful tone in her voice.

"You wish," he said. "I'm not going anywhere."

"Well, neither am I. So if you want me gone, you better find that deed."

"Believe me, I'm on it. But in the meantime, since you're so determined to hang around where you're not wanted—"

Jillian tossed her head. Wet strands of hair slapped lightly at her cheeks. "I'm determined to take possession of what's mine."

The hot look in Tuck's eyes sent a shiver of ice straight down her spine. "That's still in question."

"So until it's settled, we need to find a way to live together." Her heart was pounding. She was trying so hard to look cool, calm, and collected. She didn't want him guessing just how much courage she'd had to summon to stay here rooted to the spot in nothing but a beach towel when she wanted nothing more than to dart upstairs to the guest bedroom where she'd spent the previous night.

"Agreed."

Was it her imagination or did he sound as off center as she felt? "I could live upstairs; you take the downstairs."

It was official. She'd lost her marbles. She should either leave or throw him out, but here she was proposing a live-in relationship.

He eyed her. "You sure?"

"We're both adults. We can make this roommate thing work."

"Roommates, huh?"

He smiled and she saw he had a cosmically cute dimple in his right cheek. She could see why he'd been christened the Magic Man. There was something very compelling about that grin.

Mutt trotted over and sniffed at Tuck's shoes. The traitor.

Tuck leaned down to scratch the dog behind the ears, and Mutt sighed like he was in heaven. He'd won over her dog.

She didn't like that. "Let's get the ground rules straight."

"Yes, ma'am."

"Smart-ass."

"You started it."

"I hate getting up early in the morning," she said, ignoring his quip.

"That's good, because I'm an early bird. We can avoid each other."

"No bringing women back here. You want to make out, go to her place."

"You don't have to worry about that."

"Okay, then no bringing guys back here. You want to make out, go to his place."

"I'm not gay."

She could tell that, but she hadn't wanted to assume anything. "So you're what? Celibate?"

"Something like that. But the same goes for you. No bringing guys over."

"Agreed."

A dark look crossed his face. Abruptly, he turned. "I gotta go. I just remembered I have another job."

"After working on Sutter's place all day?"

"Carpentry never sleeps." He was shrugging into his coat, avoiding looking at her.

"What does that mean?"

"A man's work is never done?"

"Okay, so I'll see you when I see you."

"Yeah." He moved toward the door with purposeful strides, leaving her wondering exactly what she'd said to send him scurrying for freedom.

BY FRIDAY, the tension between Tuck and Jillian was so thick it would have given a chainsaw a run for its money.

She spent as much time as possible in the office, going through Sutter's files and pending cases, trying to make order out of chaos. It wasn't easy in the midst of Tuck's construction. She'd gotten the bulk of it tamed to manageable tasks, but she hadn't stumbled across the deed to the house on Enchantment Lane. Which was both a blessing and a curse.

Added to this, whenever she got home, Tuck would leave and come back long after she went to bed. He got up before she did, and he was out the door before her feet hit the floor.

It was more difficult avoiding him during office hours, although as long as he was patching the roof, she only saw him when he came down for lunch or to go to his truck for supplies. However, yesterday, he'd finished the roof and today he would move on to repairing the office ceiling.

Jillian realized she simply couldn't take it anymore. Not when she kept having fevered dreams about him. Not when she kept entertaining inappropriate sexual thoughts about a man who was emotionally unavailable. Today, she'd tell him that he had to go.

She walked into the office to find him on the ladder again, impressive butt on display as it was the first day. She tried to ignore him, but it was like ignoring a persistent toothache.

Apparently he was trying to ignore her as well, because he didn't say a word. Not even "good morning." Neither did she.

The room was deadly quiet.

The clock on the wall ticked loudly. Jillian cleared her throat.

"I'm going up into the attic," Tuck said. "Looks like Sutter's got termite infestation, and they're eating up the support beams."

"Thanks for the update but don't feel obligated to keep me apprised of your comings and goings."

"Just trying to be courteous," he said tightly.

"No need." She kept her gaze focused on her laptop even though she wasn't seeing a word of the codicil she was drawing up for Tom Red Deer's will.

He left the room, his boots clomping loudly, letting her

know she irritated the hell out of him. Well, it cut both ways. He got on her nerves as much as she got on his.

TUCK CLIMBED INTO THE ATTIC, his thoughts in turmoil over Jillian. Living with the woman for the past several days had been tough. He'd never lived with anyone other than Aimee, and it felt strange, unnatural.

He shone the flashlight through the attic and shook his head. It would take him forever to replace all the damaged timber. After he assessed the damage and started to work on the water-damaged Sheetrock, he poked his head through the hole in the ceiling and stared down at Jillian below.

Sitting there in her chair, attention honed on the computer screen, she looked the epitome of an accomplished businesswoman. But he'd seen another side to her. Knew she wasn't near as tough as she wanted everyone to think. Jillian Samuel's had a soft underbelly she struggled hard to hide. But Tuck wasn't fooled.

"How 'bout some tunes?" he said after a long minute of watching her.

"Huh?" Jillian raised her head and met his eyes, but immediately her gaze skittered off his like striking marbles. He fully understood her reluctance to make eye contact. He wasn't exactly thrilled with the jolt of awareness that passed through him every time their gazes met.

"Music," he said.

"Music?" she echoed.

He nodded toward the radio perched on the top of the bookshelf behind her.

"Oh, okay." She got up and turned on the radio. She

played with the dial. Classical music poured from the speakers. She sat back down.

"You gotta be kidding me."

Jillian heaved an exaggerated sigh. "Something wrong?"

"You're seriously going to listen to that?"

"Mozart. It'll boost your IQ."

"Maybe I don't want my IQ boosted. Maybe I like being dumb."

"Clearly. What would you like to hear?"

"Country and western."

Jillian made gagging noises.

"What? You're from Texas. Aren't you required by law to like country and western?"

"Precisely why I don't like country-and-western music. Force-fed Merle Haggard and George Jones and Dolly Parton as a kid. Scarred me for life."

"All right, then. I'll settle for rock or pop or hip-hop. Anything but that mind-numbing Mozart."

"I can't listen to music with lyrics while I work. It messes with my concentration."

"Okay, so forget the tunes."

She snapped the radio off. "Go ahead, be culturally bereft. See if I care."

Tuck watched her go back to her laptop, his gaze trailing over the gentle slope of her ass.

Tell her the real reason you don't want to listen to Mozart. Tell her about all the times you took Aimee to the symphony. How she loved classical music and the sound of it reminds you too much of her.

"Jillian, I . . ."

"Yes?" She looked at him expectantly.

"Nothing," he mumbled. He didn't even know her. He couldn't tell her this private stuff.

She went back to her laptop.

Tuck tried to return to his work, but time and again, he found his eyes drawn to her. In spite of himself, he kept thinking about the vision he'd had of her in the sweat lodge. The temptress. It was damned eerie and unsettling.

She got up and made her way over to Sutter's filing cabinets. He couldn't help admiring the way her hips swayed when she moved.

After riffling through the top drawer a moment, she bent lower, going for the bottom drawer. Tuck canted his head, appreciating how the conservative gray wool skirt tightened over the curve of her ass.

Very nice.

He shifted for a better look.

His knee slipped off the support beam. He tried to right himself, but it was too late; his balance was compromised, and the Sheetrock was weakened from water damage. Tuck heard the ceiling crack ominously beneath his weight at the same time he felt it give away.

Next thing he knew, gravity had hold of him and it was all over.

Chapter Ten

Tuck fell through the hole in the attic, slamming onto Sutter's office floor with a resounding *bang*.

Jillian let out a startled scream, sucked in a deep breath, and tasted Sheetrock dust. She spun around to find Tuck lying on his back at her feet.

"Tuck, Tuck, are you okay?" She squatted beside him.

His eyes were closed and his breathing shallow. He moaned softly when she touched him.

"Tuck, look at me."

He opened his eyes, peered up at her, and blinked.

Jillian raised her palm. "Tell me, how many fingers am I holding up?"

Groggily, he shook his head, grunted.

Oh dear, this wasn't good. "Speak to me."

He grinned up at her. "Hi."

"Hi? That's all you have to say? Hi?"

"You look worried. Why are you worried? You get the cutest little wrinkle line between your eyebrows when you frown."

Jillian pressed the pad of her thumb between her eyes and stopped frowning. "Of course I look worried—you just came crashing through the ceiling."

"I did?"

"You don't remember?"

He reached up to finger her hair.

"What are you doing?"

"You have such pretty hair," he murmured. "Black like a raven's wing."

Alarm spread through her; his eyes looked glassy. Should she move him? Should she call an ambulance? Did they even have an ambulance in Salvation? She was unprepared.

Jillian wrung her hands. She might be a killer in the courtroom, but when it came to medical stuff, she was useless. She fainted at the sight of blood. Thank God he wasn't bleeding.

She plucked his hand from her hair. "Tuck, try to concentrate. Do you know what day it is?"

"You're a pretty temptress."

"Temptress?"

"Ridley says you're a jinx, but I don't believe it."

"Ridley? Who's Ridley?"

"Evie's husband and my best friend."

"Ridley's your brother-in-law?"

Tuck nodded. "That's it."

"Why does Ridley think I'm a jinx? He doesn't even know me."

"Shh." Tuck placed an index finger to his lips. "It's a secret."

"What's a secret?"

"You're the vision."

"Huh?"

"I know." Tuck winked and his voice took on a suggestive tone.

Startled, Jillian pulled back. "Know what?"

He grinned. "What you look like naked."

All at once, Jillian *felt* naked. Clearly the man was addled, and he had no idea what he was saying. Actually, neither did she. "You must have a concussion. We need to get you to a doctor. Can you stand?"

"And lips. The color of raspberries. Beautiful, beautiful lips."

"Tuck," she said sharply. "Listen to me. You've got to concentrate. You fell through the ceiling and hit your head. We have to get you to the doctor. Can you get to your feet?"

"Okay. Can do." He smiled at her like someone who'd had one drink too many.

"Here." She pulled his arm around her neck. "We're just going to stand you up."

"Hey," he said.

"What now?"

"You smell pretty too."

"Okay, I have pretty hair and lips, and I smell good too; we've established that," she said. "Can we please move on?"

"Absolutely." His jovialness scared her. He seemed far too happy under the circumstances.

"On the count of three. One, two, three . . ." She leveled him off the floor.

He muttered a string of curse words.

Ah, that was more like it. "What is it, what's wrong?"

"My foot."

"What about it?"

"Hurts."

"Can you bear weight on it?"

"Yeow!"

"Obviously not." Jillian sighed. "Can you hobble?"

The color drained from his face. "Hobbling's a good option."

"Lean on me."

He leaned into her, and Jillian became aware of exactly how big he was. She was plenty tall, but he was still a head taller, and his chest grazed against her breast. Through the material of both his flannel shirt and her silk blouse she could feel his hard, honed masculine muscles flexing, and she could feel her own nipples tightening at the contact. She slid an arm around his back.

She was so aware of him. His weight, his scent, his sinew and bones. She gulped, felt the movement slide all the way down her throat, leaving her feeling dry and breathless. She'd never been so acutely aware of a man's body before.

Or her own.

Her heart hammered. She moistened her lips, but the dryness hung on. Arid Colorado air.

And hot Colorado he-man.

Her thoughts were totally inappropriate.

Stop this. Stop thinking about his body. You're a perv. The man needs a doctor. Get your head out of the gutter and on your goal.

"Here we go," Jillian said. "You ready? Out the door and down the stairs."

"Stairs." He grunted.

"You can do this. I'll help you do this." Jillian looked at Tuck's face to make sure he was all right. He was staring at her as if she was the most fascinating thing he'd ever seen. He must have really whacked his head if the attraction was stronger than pain. His gaze drilled into her, as penetrating as a buzz-saw blade, slicing right through her, causing her nipples to strain even tighter against the lace of her bra.

Totally, completely inappropriate. Lusting after an injured man. *Concentrate on getting him down the stairs without too much jarring.* Without too much lusting.

They clumped down the stairs together, Tuck hanging on to the banister with one arm, his other arm slung over her shoulder, his leg bent to lessen the likelihood of him whacking his injured foot against the steps.

She was so close, his warm breath feathered the fine hairs on her neck, causing shivers to run down her spine.

"I damn well hate this," he grumbled.

"Hurting yourself?"

"Well that, but mostly I hate looking like a big pansy in front of you."

"You don't look like a pansy."

"Right. This is exactly what every woman wants, a big strong guy who has to lean on *her*."

"Hey, you're not superman. Everyone needs someone to lean on now and again. I'm here. I'm tough and tall. It's okay to lean."

He grunted his disagreement, although he did say, "The tallness is a plus."

Jillian realized that with having a wife who'd had a long illness, Tuck had played the role of caretaker for so long he felt uncomfortable when he was in the position of needing someone to take care of him. Well, too bad, he could just get over his macho need to be the rescuer.

Before Jillian and Tuck reached the bottom of the stairs, Will and Bill, who must have heard the commotion, came running to help load Tuck into his pickup. She was relieved to step back and let the twins help out. Lexi came out of her store as well, fluttering anxiously about and asking a hundred questions.

"Is there a hospital in town?" Jillian asked.

"You'll have to take him to Boulder," Bill said.

"Just take me back to the house and call Dr. Couts," Tuck said. "I'll be okay."

"Forget it," Jillian barked. "You're going to the emergency room. End of discussion."

"You sure are bossy," Tuck said.

"Damn straight. You bust yourself up in front of me, you're stuck with me until you're officially patched up."

"I'll keep that in mind."

"See that you do."

Once Tuck was sitting in the passenger seat, relief washed over her. She'd gotten him past the first hurdle. She thanked the accountants and Lexi for their help and climbed in behind the wheel.

"Give me your keys," Jillian said to Tuck. "And the directions to the hospital."

"Can you drive a stick?"

"I can," she said. "I'm multitalented."

Tucker winced and lay his head back against the headrest.

"Does it hurt badly?"

"Not gonna be doing the Cotton-Eyed Joe anytime soon."

"How's your head?" She started the engine. "Still dizzy?"

"Better."

"That's good." She angled for the highway and promptly smacked a pothole.

Tuck sucked in his breath through clenched teeth.

"Sorry, sorry. I don't know where all the potholes in town are yet."

"S'okay, but talk. Distract me from the ankle."

"All right, all right. What should we talk about?"

"I dunno, what do you do for fun when you're not being a lawyer?"

"I go running. I've run a couple of marathons, do three or four ten-kilometer races a year."

"That's exercise, not fun. How do you relax?"

It was a legitimate question and one she didn't really have an answer for. "I do yoga occasionally."

"Again, exercise."

"Maybe I haven't yet conquered the concept of relaxing," she admitted.

"You're going to have a hard time acclimating to Salvation until you learn how to slow down."

"I'm getting that."

"You may never be able to reduce your speed. The slow lane might not be in your nature."

She shot a glance at him. "It's not going to work. You're not running me out of town."

"I have been thinking," Tuck said. "If that deed never turns up, how 'bout you sell me the lake house?"

"What? No."

"Why not?"

"For one thing, I'm not a quitter. For another thing, I need this change of pace. As you pointed out, I don't know how to relax."

"You can learn to relax anywhere. I've lived here two and a half years. It's where I . . ."

Lost my wife.

He didn't say the words, but she heard them just as clearly as if he had. She felt sorry for him, but she wasn't going to let him guilt her into leaving the lake house. The only way she was leaving was if he produced the deed. Blake had left the lake house to her. It was as if he'd known the place was exactly what she needed. She was rebuilding her life here in Salvation. She wanted a fresh start, and this was her chance.

"I'll pay you more than it's worth," Tuck enticed.

"Why would you offer that if you knew the place had been deeded to you?"

"I want it."

"Sorry." Jillian shook her head. "It's not for sale."

"The place needs major work. It's gonna cost you a mint to fix it up."

"Then why would you pay more than it was worth?"

"Because the place means that much to me. Sentimental value."

Guilt, that nagging emotion, knocked around her head. He certainly knew how to twist the knife. "It's got sentimental value to me as well. My mentor left it to me."

"He left it to me too."

"Which you can't prove. I feel for your situation, truly I do—"

"But you don't care."

"Look, I don't even really know you."

"And yet you're driving me to the hospital. What's that all about?"

"Common courtesy. You'd do the same for me."

"How can you be so sure?"

"You wouldn't?"

"Of course I would, but if the roles were reversed, I'd

take your word for it about the deed and get out of the lake house."

"Easy for you to say—the roles aren't reversed."

"Why is it so important to you? It's gotta be more than the fact that Blake left you the house. If you were keeping it strictly for sentimental value, you would just have it as a summer place. You wouldn't have pulled up stakes, left your job in Houston as assistant district attorney."

"I don't owe you an explanation."

"Come on, we're living together. And besides, don't you want to help me take the focus off my pain?"

This was the longest conversation they'd had in a week of living under the same roof. "I was feeling burned out," she surprised herself by admitting.

"And?"

"There's no *and*."

"There's an *and*. I can hear it in your voice. What are you really running away from?"

"That's none of your business."

"Okay, fine, keep it bottled up inside." He shifted in the seat beside her and let out a small groan.

"It hurts a lot, doesn't it?"

"Of course it hurts a lot, and you won't even help distract me."

"Okay, all right, I'll distract you."

"You're a peach."

Jillian snorted. "I don't know why I'm telling you this. I could do something else to distract you."

"Oh yeah? Like what?"

She didn't miss the wicked tone of innuendo. "Sing 'Ninety-nine Bottles of Beer on the Wall.' "

"A favorite of yours?"

Jillian narrowed her eyes. "I should just let you suffer in silence."

"Please don't. We've got twenty miles of highway stretching in front of us," he said.

"I'm not even sure I like you. Why should I tell you my secrets?"

"It's a man," he guessed. "Broke your heart."

"More like bruised my ego," she admitted.

"What happened?"

She hesitated.

"Come on," he wheedled. "You can tell me. I won't judge."

She shrugged. "Really, it's nothing you want to hear about."

"How do you know unless you tell me?"

Drawing in a deep breath, Jillian realized she did want to tell him, even though she was afraid of what he might think of her. She felt awkward, self-conscious. She didn't know why she was telling him this except that he was a stranger, and she hadn't told anyone about Alex, and the dirty secret was burning her up. Finally, she just blurted it out.

"I had an affair with a married man." Furtively, Jillian angled a glance over at Tuck to see how he took the news.

His expression didn't change.

That encouraged her to go on. "I didn't know he was married," she continued, realizing that she sounded defensive. She felt defensive. No, that wasn't true. She felt guilty, ashamed. "But he was married just the same."

"That must have been a blow when you found out the truth."

"It was horrible." She shuddered. "Last year. Christmas Eve. I thought I'd surprise him. We'd been dating about a month, but we'd never gone to his place. That should have been a tip-off. I was dense. Or I didn't want to see the warning signs. I got his address from his employee file and went to his house. I dressed up. Victoria's Secret underneath a denim duster. I wore cowboy boots. I even had toy six-shooters strapped to my hips."

"Sounds sexy in a cowgirl kind of way."

"Thank you, it was."

"I would have liked to have seen you in it."

"You can't. I burned the outfit."

"Darn my luck."

He was sounding pretty damned chipper for a man with a busted ankle. "So anyway . . . I rang his doorbell . . ." She trailed off. Did she really want to go there?

"And?"

"A woman comes to the door. Younger than me. Hell, she barely even looked twenty-two. Beautiful, beautiful girl. Dressed in a sweet Christmas outfit. A vest with Santa faces on it. She had an infant on her hip, and she was smiling and smiling and smiling like I was bringing her a big fat Christmas present. In the background, I hear *his* voice. 'Who is it honey?' he asks her."

"Kick in the teeth."

"To say the least. 'Who are you?' his baby wife asks me. She's trying so hard to keep the smile on her face. Then *he* comes up behind her in the foyer. I'm tall. The baby wife isn't. Our eyes meet over wifey's head. His face goes pale, he knows he's busted. It hits me all at once. I am so stupid, so clueless."

"So what didja do?"

"What could I do? I'm feeling like I went fifteen rounds with Mike Tyson, but I figure there's no reason for two of us to feel that way. I didn't do it to protect him. Buzzards could peck his eyes out and I wouldn't shoo them away, but I couldn't bear to crush little Miss-Santa-Claus-Vest's heart, so I simply said, 'Sorry, wrong house.' I turned and ran back to my car."

"That was kind of you, sparing the wife's feelings."

"It was very uncharacteristic of me. My impulse was to cold-cock him right in front of her. I don't know why I didn't rat him out. Or maybe I do. I remember looking into her face and thinking, 'She believes she's got the world on a string. She thinks she's landed this great guy who's given her a great life, and she's in for a world of hurt when she finds out the truth.' But I couldn't be the one to knock the house of cards down on her. Yes, I'm tough. In the courtroom, I take no prisoners. But there, on that porch, I knew opening my mouth would be like kicking a puppy."

"The guy sounds like a complete prick. You're better off without him."

"Yeah."

"Why were you with him in the first place?"

"He was handsome and could be very charming and witty. I have a thing for witty men."

"I'll try to remember that. Were you in love with him?"

"I was trying to be in love with him."

"You can't try to be in love with someone," Tuck said. "You either are or you aren't."

"Okay, then, I wasn't. But I wanted to be."

"Why?"

"Because I've never been in love, and I just wanted to know what it felt like."

"You've never been in love?" He sounded incredulous. "Honest?"

"No. Not romantic love. I mean, I loved Blake, but in a daughterly kind of way."

"Why haven't you ever been in love?" he asked.

She shrugged. "I guess I never let myself. I had dreams—big dreams—and I wasn't going to get sidetracked."

"Not even a high school crush?"

She bit her lip. "Not that I can recall. I've always felt like an outcast because of it. Like there's something wrong with me because I didn't feel . . . this . . . this *thing* everyone else carries on about. But all my friends were falling in love, and they seemed so happy and I . . . I wanted that too. I wanted to be normal."

"That's understandable."

"It's pathetic. Trying to force myself to love someone."

"Jillian?"

"Yes?" She looked over at him again.

Tuck's smile was genuine, even though his eyes were tinged with the pain he was trying to hide. "It's okay. You didn't know he was married. You're not a terrible person."

"Yeah, well, it doesn't feel that way."

"You're not," he reiterated.

"Then Blake dies and the mayor appoints this same guy—the guy I had the affair with—as the new district attorney."

"Shit."

"You can say that again. How could I stay there and work for him?"

"You couldn't."

"I didn't. I quit. Then I find out about Blake's will, about this place, and I take it as a sign I'm supposed to be here."

There was an awkward pause in the conversation. Jillian sneaked a peek at Tuck from her peripheral vision. He had a faraway expression on his face. What was he thinking about? Probably how much his foot hurt.

"I had an affair with a married woman once," he admitted. "Except I knew she was married. She was separated, getting a divorce, but she was still married."

The scenery whizzed by the window. Mountains blue and majestic. Pine trees tall and green. Air so thin it made your heart hurt.

"What happened to the relationship?" she asked him. "With the married woman who was separated and getting divorced."

"She went back to her husband."

"Ah."

He shrugged. "It happens."

"How'd that make you feel?"

"Used."

"Exactly."

"It's not easy being the dirty little secret."

"I've never told anyone about Alex. Not even my best girlfriends," she confessed.

"I've never told anyone about Kay."

"I'm glad I told you." She smiled at him. "I do feel better."

He smiled back. "Me too."

Jillian felt something warm and melty inside of her. "Does this mean we're starting to become friends?"

"Do you want to be friends?"

"We *are* living together."

"But in a strictly platonic way," he hastened to add.

Message received loud and clear. Friendship was all he could offer her.

But that was good. That was fine. Splendid even. After Alex, she was taking a break from sexual relationships. "Friends would be nice. I need friends. I'm friendless in Salvation," she said.

"Not totally friendless," he said. "You have me."

"And Lexi who runs the flooring/window treatment store. She wants to be friends."

"Lexi's nice. And you'll make other friends. Salvation is a friendly place."

"I dunno. Everyone I've met seems really attached to Aimee and possessive of you." The minute she said his wife's name, Jillian could have bitten off her tongue.

Tuck said nothing.

She sneaked a look over at him. Noticed the strength of his profile. The firm jaw line, chiseled cheekbones, masculine nose. He was staring out the passenger side window, and his breathing was quick and shallow.

"I'm sorry," she apologized. "I shouldn't have said that."

"Nothing to be sorry for," he said lightly. "Turn here. The hospital is just up ahead."

Jillian slowed, but her heart was pounding. Why was her heart beating so fast? "How's the ankle?"

"Numb."

"Your boot's probably cutting off the circulation."

"Probably."

"Good thing we're here."

"Good thing," he echoed.

An odd feeling hit her then. One she couldn't name but didn't like. It made her feel all jumbled up inside, and she was afraid that if he saw her face, he would know exactly how much he'd unsettled her.

Art of the bluff.

She could hear Blake inside her head. He'd taught her a lot about hiding her feelings. She was a lawyer and a damned good one. Jillian put on her game face. She parked his pickup in the emergency room parking lot and looked over at him. "I'll be right back with a wheelchair."

"RELATIONSHIP?" the emergency room clerk asked Jillian as she wheeled Tuck into an examination room. "Sister, girlfriend, wife?"

"Friend," Tuck said at the same time Jillian said, "Lawyer."

"So which is it?" asked the clerk, nervously giving Jillian the once-over.

"She's a lawyer and a friend," Tuck said. "But don't worry, we're not suing anyone. The accident was my own fault."

"Although the Peabody Mansion *is* falling apart." Jillian followed them into the examination room. "You could sue Sutter."

"That's not the way we do things in Salvation. Besides, he's your boss. Wouldn't suing him be a conflict of interest?"

"I'm just outlining your options. It's an unsafe work environment."

"I accepted the risks when I took the job." *And when I stared at your ass.* "I'm not suing."

He had to admire the way Jillian held it together. Getting him out of the mansion, calmly driving him to Boulder, throwing her weight around to get him seen as soon as possible.

Tuck tried to imagine Aimee handling a minor emergency like this, and he couldn't do it. One time he'd accidentally cut open his palm with a utility knife, and when Aimee had seen the blood, she'd passed out. He'd ended up getting her in bed and then calling a neighbor to come stay with her while he'd driven himself to the emergency room. It was kind of nice, he realized, having a woman who could hold her own in the face of an emergency.

That's not fair. Aimee was a trooper when it came to facing cancer. She was tough as hell, just in a different way.

True. Aimee had been a saint. Tuck bit the inside of his cheek and focused on the pain in his ankle. It wasn't hard to do. A doctor had come into the room and was working off his boot.

Jillian sat in the corner on a rolling stool, watching while the young doctor, not long out of medical school, diagnosed a broken ankle. He sent Tuck for X-rays to confirm it; then he put him in a fiberglass walking cast and handed him crutches and a prescription for Vicodin.

The entire time, Jillian watched the doctor like a hawk—serious, watching for mistakes. The doctor told them he'd once been a ski bum but decided to go to medical school and specialize in emergency medicine after his best friend was killed on the slopes right in front of him. As he talked, the guy slid flirtatious glances at Jillian.

Tuck couldn't blame him, although he felt a sudden urge to tell the guy to keep his scintillating glances to himself. The woman was stunning. But maybe Tuck was being unfair, misreading the signals. Maybe the doctor was just worried because the clerk had told him Jillian was a lawyer, and he was terrified of being sued.

"He hit his head too," Jillian said, her eyes on Tuck's face, but her fingers were worrying the bracelet at her wrist. "Check him out for that. He didn't know where he was for a minute or two. He could have a concussion."

"Thank you for calling that to my attention." The doctor did a quick neurological exam, then turned to Jillian. "I think you're worried for nothing. Your friend checks out fine. No sign of a concussion."

"You're certain?" She narrowed her eyes at the doctor, and Tuck got a small whiff of what it would be like to face her in the courtroom. The effect was unsettling. She'd never get a chance to use those kind of interrogation skills in a place like Salvation.

"I . . . ca . . . could get a CAT scan if you like," the doctor stammered, and blinked.

"Do that."

For the first time, Tuck noticed how pale she looked, how her forehead knitted in worry. She was really concerned about him. That was unexpected.

"I'm fine, Jillian," he said. "There's no need for an expensive CAT scan."

"You're sure?"

"I'm okay." Tuck didn't know what compelled him, but he snugged the crutches up under his arms and reached

Chapter Eleven

"You were right," Tuck told Ridley as he sank down next to him in a back booth at the Rusty Nail the day after his accident. He propped his crutches against the wall beside him. He'd had to get out of the house; he was going stir crazy with nothing to do but watch television and think about Jillian.

"Right about what?"

"The temptress is a jinx."

Ridley's eyes widened as someone put a Carrie Underwood tune on the jukebox. "What in the hell happened to you?"

"Jillian Samuels happened to me."

"Huh?"

"The temptress."

"Yeah, I get that, but how'd she jinx you?"

"I was so busy staring at her butt that I fell through the ceiling."

"Back up, back up, I'm not getting this."

Quickly, Tuck filled his brother-in-law in on what happened the previous morning at Sutter Godfrey's office and how he ended up at Boulder General Hospital with Jillian.

"You know," Ridley said, "If she hadn't been there, you'd have been in a real fix."

"You're not listening. I was in the fix because she was there. You were absolutely right. She's cursed."

"That seems a bit strong. I never said she was cursed. Plus, I might have been hasty in my interpretation of your vision," Ridley said.

"What do you mean?"

"I was talking to my uncle Tom about what you saw, and he said the temptress isn't necessarily a bad omen," Ridley explained.

"No?" Tuck swept a hand at his casted foot. "What do you call this?"

"Bad luck?"

"Isn't that the same thing as a jinx?"

"Not really."

Ridley waved at the passing waitress, and she stopped by their table.

"Hey, Rid." The petite blonde smiled.

"Hey, Brandi."

"What'll you have?"

"My *single* brother-in-law here would like . . . what?"

"Draft beer," Tuck said. "Whatever's on tap."

Brandi laid a napkin on the table in front of Tuck. "We've got Coors and—"

"It'll do."

Brandi's eyes widened.

"Don't mind his gruffness," Ridley apologized for him. "Tuck's wife died. He's a widower."

"Oh, you poor thing." Brandi sighed. "I'm so sorry. I'll be right back with your beer." She scurried off.

Tuck glared at his brother-in-law. "Why did you tell her that?"

"Sympathy date."

"I don't want to date her. She's a child."

"She works in a bar; she's at least twenty-one."

"Yes, and I'm almost thirty-one. If she'd be interested in me at all, it's because she's got eyes for my Social Security check."

"Aimee was younger."

"By only five years."

"So the temptress, is she younger?" Ridley took a sip of his beer.

"We're close to the same age. But you're right. She's a jinx. I've got to find that damned deed. Sutter claims it's in his office. Jillian's straightening the place up, but she hasn't run across it. Is the offer to bunk with you and Evie still open? I'm asking you because I know my sister will automatically say yes."

Ridley shifted in his seat. "Um . . . the doc has her on a different dose of fertility hormones, and it's made her voracious, if you catch my drift. Why do you think I'm hiding out here? I'm exhausted."

Tuck plugged up his ears. "That's my sister you're talking about. I don't need to hear any of this."

"Just letting you know what you're stepping into if you come stay with us."

"Okay, never mind, forget I asked. I'll sort out my living arrangements some other way."

Ridley's eyes lit up, and Tuck turned to see what he was looking at. Evie had come through the door. She spotted them and walked over to cozy up on the bench beside her husband.

"What happened to you?" she asked Tuck.

"Fell through Godfrey's attic and broke my ankle."

"The Peabody Mansion is a hazard. It should be torn down." Evie reached for the bowl of peanuts on the table.

"Bite your tongue, woman." Ridley slipped his arm around her shoulders. "That house is the very foundation of Salvation."

"Then the town is on very shaky ground."

"She's right," Tuck added. "It's eaten up with termites."

"But it's the first house ever built in Salvation," Ridley protested.

Evie leaned across the table and whispered to Tuck, "He's such a sentimentalist."

"Not that I'm not happy to see you," Ridley said, "but who's manning the Bluebird?"

"Dutch." Evie crunched a peanut and leaned against her husband. "And before you get alarmed, beef stew is on the dinner special, so all he has to do is dish it up and make cornbread. Gives us plenty of time to go home for a quickie before the trivia tournament starts."

"I really do not want to know about this," Tuck said.

"Uh-oh." Ridley's eyes were fixed on the door.

"What? Am I wearing you out?" Evie chuckled and patted Ridley's chest. "Where's that famous Native American stamina you love to brag about?"

"Your jinx is here," Ridley told Tuck.

"What?" Evie asked.

"Tuck's new roommate."

"Oh, Jillian," Evie said. "I like her. She's sharp."

As a razor blade.

Tuck searched the crowded bar for Jillian and finally saw her standing next to the door. He couldn't help himself—his eyes clung to her. Her straight, symmetrical haircut swung about her shoulders like a swaying curtain as she moved, giving her a patrician appearance. Her cheeks were windblown, and she had on a pair of black slacks, black boots, and a snug-fitting, white V-neck sweater that made him drool.

He felt like one of those cartoon characters whose eyes bug out of their heads when seeing a gorgeous woman. It was all he could do not to let loose with a wolf whistle. Oo-ga, oo-ga.

Queenie, he thought. *Mistress of all she surveys.*

He realized this was the first lustful interest he'd seriously entertained about a woman since Aimee. His libido had come kicking back to life—and in big way.

Great, this was exactly what he did not need.

Then stupidly, Tuck raised his hand and waved at her. *Dimwit.*

She smiled then, and it felt like the sun coming out after a long winter storm.

Tuck slid across the bench, making room for her at the booth. Evie raised an eyebrow and exchanged a look with Ridley. He shrugged.

Jillian sauntered over.

"Have a seat," Tuck patted the cushion beside him.

"Just for a second," Jillian said, sliding in beside him. "I'm waiting for someone."

A male someone? he wondered, then hated himself for wondering. What did he care if she had a date? It was nothing to him. He barely knew her.

"What'll you have?" Brandi asked Jillian and Evie as she brought Tuck his beer.

"Cherry Coke for me," Evie said.

"I'll have a glass of the house Chardonnay." Jillian folded her hands on the table and leaned forward, unwittingly exposing her cleavage.

Tuck ogled.

Jillian turned and caught him. She frowned and drew her shoulders back.

He grinned and lounged insouciantly against the booth. It felt good, feeling lusty again.

"Slow learner, huh?" she said.

"What?"

"Falling through the ceiling because you were paying more attention to my ass than what you were supposed to be doing didn't teach you anything?"

Evie hooted. "I like her." She reached across the table and shook Jillian's hand. "I like you."

Tuck scowled. "The women are ganging up on me, Rid. We guys gotta stick together. Help me out here."

Ridley held up his palms. "Hey, you're on your own, dude. I gotta go home with Evie."

"Smart man." Jillian grinned.

"I've got him trained." Evie plucked the cherry from the glass of Coke the waitress deposited in front of her and popped it into her mouth.

"No, no," Ridley disagreed. "I just let you think you have me trained."

"What difference does it make?" Evie asked. "As long as things work out the way I want them to?"

Ridley rolled his eyes. "Do you hear your sister?"

"Hey," Tuck said. "Don't look at me. I was stuck with her from birth. You married her."

"And it was the happiest day of my life." Ridley smiled.

Evie patted her husband's hand. "Did I mention he's a very smart man?"

On the jukebox, Carrie Underwood gave way to Merle Haggard and Jillian covered her ears.

"You want me to go fix it?" Tuck offered. "I can find something to replace Merle, but I doubt I can scrounge up *A Little Night Music.*"

"You've been holding out on me," Jillian teased accusingly. "You are familiar with Mozart."

Tuck measured off an inch with his thumb and forefinger. "Never underestimate the Magic Man."

Evie groaned, but in a good-natured way. "Watch out, my little brother is feeling cocky."

"I for one am happy to see it," Ridley commented. "His eyes haven't had this much spark since . . ."

Ridley broke off as Tuck mentally filled in the blank. *Since Aimee got sick.*

Silence fell over the group.

"So this is the local watering hole." Jillian rushed to fill the emptiness and swung her gaze about the place.

Tuck appreciated the rescue at the same time he felt resentful. It wasn't her place to ease his emotional tension. Her hair flowed over her shoulders like water over rocks when she swiveled her hair. The cut was so stylish and artistic he had no doubt she'd forked over big bucks for it. For some reason, he resented that too. He shouldn't have. Back in the days when he was the Magic Man, he'd splurged on haircuts as well.

"Looks like half the town is here," she went on.

It was after five now, and people were stopping in for happy hour on their way home from work. It was the only saloon in town. Although the Rusty Nail also served sandwiches, hamburgers, and appetitzes, it was first and foremost a drinking establishment. Pool hall in the back. Video games, trivia tournaments, and eternal ESPN on the plasma-screen televisions throughout the front.

Tuck saw it through Jillian's eyes. Peered into the past to remember how the Rusty Nail had looked the first time he'd come here with Aimee one summer before they were married. In happier times. Before the ovarian cancer diagnosis.

Men dressed in jeans and flannel and down vests and hunting caps perched on stools at the bar. Women sat at tables with their girlfriends drinking rum toddies. A laughing couple fed each other nachos. A fistful of older guys hunkered over the pool tables. The air smelled of cheese and beer and French fries. The décor was standard Colorado neighborhood pub fare with rawhide lampshades, a roaring fireplace in the center of the room, and trophy deer heads on the wall.

Tuck knew without having to ask that the Rusty Nail was a long way from Jillian's Chardonnay-drinking, Mozart-listening, hundred-dollar-haircut world. Sooner or later, she was going to realize that as well and head back to the big city. Even if the deed Blake had signed over to him never turned up. All Tuck had to do was wait her out. The house meant nothing to her and yet it meant so much to him. It was his last connection to Aimee.

"Ooh," she said, and nudged Tuck with her elbow. "Who's that pretty blond woman with Bill?"

"That's his fiancée, Lily Massey. She teaches high school math."

"And the guy in the suit talking to Will?"

Tuck's eyes followed her gaze. Trust Jillian to find the only man in the room dressed in a three-piece suit and carrying a briefcase. His flank felt odd where her elbow had dug into him, and he caught a whiff of her hair, which smelled like cucumbers. "That's Jefferson Baines. Celebrity real estate agent."

Jillian shot a look at Tuck. "I take that to mean he's a real estate agent to celebrities looking for a mountain getaway and not a celebrity himself."

"He kisses a lot of asses. You figure it out."

Jillian glanced back at Jefferson, tilted her head, and studied his ass. "He looks like he's good at it. That's an Armani he's wearing."

"Jefferson is a legend in his own mind." Tuck snorted. "He conned Sylvester Stallone into a ninety-nine-year lease on a lodge in Crystal Ridge. And rumor has it he sold Carmen Electra a ski condo in Estes Park and slept with her. But I'm betting he started that rumor himself. At least the last part."

"Hmm, I don't know about that," she said. "The Rolex at his wrist looks real."

"The guy's a total poser. He lives in a one-bedroom apartment on Donner Avenue. The floors are made out of laminate. What kind of real estate agent worth his salt lives in a place with laminate flooring?" Tuck noticed Jillian was giving him the strangest look. "Laminate is an insult. Here he is a real estate agent and he's got a place with faux wood that ain't gonna last."

"I've heard the opposite. I heard laminate was more durable than hardwood," she said.

"Vicious lies spread by the makers of laminate flooring," Tuck replied sagely.

"Let me get this straight. Jefferson Baines has weak wood." Jillian nodded. "I see. That's very enlightening. Good to know in case I'm ever in the market for strong wood."

A Machiavellian smile lit up her face. This was how she looked in the courtroom, he realized. Manipulating language to suit her needs. He felt led on.

Jillian nodded at the twin CPAs. "So, what kind of wood do Bill and Will have?"

"They inherited their mother's place on State Street. Soft wood in that area of town. Their floors are pine." He eyed her, wondering what she was up to. "But Bill's upgrading when he and Lily get married. They're going for oak in the home they're having built."

"How do you know?"

"I've been commissioned to build their cabinets."

"What about that guy?" She pointed to an effeminate-looking young man at the bar. "What kind of floor does he have?"

"Bamboo. Exotic but green. Why the sudden interest in flooring?"

"I've never given it much thought," she said. "But you make it sound so fascinating."

"You can tell a lot about someone by their flooring choices," Tuck said.

"Ah, I see." Jillian laughed and lowered her eyelashes. "So if you were building your own place, what kind of floors would you have, Tuck?"

He dropped his voice and met her eyes. "Mahogany all the way, Queenie. It's thick and hard and lasts forever."

"What about Sutter Godfrey?" She nodded toward the dapper old man as one of his cronies wheeled him through the door of the Rusty Nail. "He's got mahogany in the Peabody Mansion."

"Ah," Tuck said. "But it's very old wood. Termite riddled. Diseased wood can be very dangerous."

"Just for the record," Ridley said. "We've got tile throughout our entire house."

"Poor us, we've got no wood at all," Evie said in a mock mournful voice, and then grinned.

"Because you wore it out." Ridley tickled her lightly in the ribs.

Evie giggled.

"I suspect we're not talking about flooring anymore," Jillian said.

"I'm up for a good flooring discussion. What's on the table? Hardwood, laminate, tile, natural stone, granite, carpet?" Lexi Kilgore sidled up to their booth. "I'm sorry I'm late, Jillian. Customer came in at the last minute."

"Granite's good," Tuck mused. "I'd forgotten about granite."

Jillian sent him a chiding glance, making him feel like a laggard. "We've moved on, Tuck. Keep up."

"Can I sit with you?" Lexi asked, wedging herself in next to Jillian, leaving her with no choice but to scoot closer to Tuck.

Her thigh settled against his, and he could feel her body heat radiating through the layer of their clothes, seeping into his skin. He liked the contact, and his body responded, stirring in a way it hadn't stirred in a long time. It bothered the hell out of him that he liked it.

"How's the ankle, Tuck?" Lexi asked. "You took a nasty spill. Your face was so white that when Bill and Will helped Jillian get you to the truck, I thought you were going to pass out."

Tuck lifted his mug. "I'm cruising. Thanks for asking."

Jillian frowned. "You shouldn't mix painkillers and alcohol."

"Nope, I stopped taking the Vicodin this morning."

"It could still be in your system."

"It's only one beer, and look, it's not even a third gone. I'm good to go."

"Uh-huh." She didn't looked convinced.

"I am," he said defensively. Damn, but the woman could set his back up quicker than anyone he'd ever met.

"When are you going to start renovating the lake house?" Lexi asked. "You know I have to special-order that particular carpet she wanted—"

"I'll have to get back to you on that," Tuck interrupted, wishing she hadn't opened that can of worms.

"Carpet?" Jillian said. "You were planning on putting carpet in your own house?"

"That was before you showed up to contest my ownership."

"No granite? No wood at all?"

He glared. "Aimee's choice in flooring is off limits to you."

Silence engulfed the table. In the next room, pool balls clacked. On the jukebox, Shania Twain sang about feeling like a woman. Tuck felt like an asswipe.

Jillian downed her wine.

Lexi and Evie and Ridley all rushed to speak at once.

"Let's order," Ridley said. "I'm starving."

"You want another Chardonnay?" Evie asked Jillian. "I'm flagging down our waitress."

"Are you guys ready for the autumn festival?" Lexi chirped, and plastered a bubbly smile on her round face. "I can't believe it's next Saturday already. Where did the time go?"

Brandi trotted over and took the drink and food orders. Tuck tried to rouse some interest in her, but compared to the sharp, sleek woman beside him, the barmaid looked like a schoolgirl.

He thought about apologizing to Jillian for being so touchy. She'd simply been teasing him, and he'd bit her head off. Yes, he was still grieving his wife, but that didn't give him an excuse to be a rude jerk. He didn't know how to begin, so he busied himself with polishing off his beer and staring down the cleavage of her awesome fluffy white sweater.

"I probably should be getting home," Jillian said without looking at Tuck. "I'm still trying to plow my way through Sutter's open cases. It is a mess. I don't know how the man gets any business done."

"But we've got nachos coming," Ridley said. He could tell that his brother-in-law was trying to make up for Tuck's assholishness. "The Rusty Nail makes the best nachos in town."

Evie shot him a look and cleared her throat loudly.

"Besides the Bluebird, of course." He tightened his arm around her, clearly not interested in joining Tuck in the doghouse. "No one's a better cook than Evie."

Suck up, Tuck mouthed silently.

"I saw that, Tucker Manning." Evie shook a finger at him.

"Brandi." Ridley motioned when the waitress brought them the drinks and nachos. "Bring Tuck another beer. He needs some loosening up."

"No, no," Tuck said, but Brandi was already zooming off.

"Consider it, man," Ridley said. "She would wait on you hand and foot."

"Who would?" Jillian asked.

"Brandi the barmaid," Evie supplied. "Ridley's determined to play matchmaker for Tuck."

"Tuck's back on the market?" Lexi's eyes lit up. "I had no idea."

"It's been two years," Evie said. "He's only thirty. He needs to move on."

"Oh agreed, agreed." Lexi bounced in her seat.

Tuck groaned inwardly. He didn't want it getting out all over town that he might start dipping his toe in the dating pool again. Lexi was a sweet woman, but he wasn't the least bit interested in someone that damned bouncy. Was he really thinking about dipping his toe in the dating pool? He slid another glance at Jillian's exceptional cleavage.

Jillian cocked her head and studied Brandi as she took drink orders from a neighboring table. "She'd be perfect for you if you don't mind changing diapers."

"Hmm." Tuck sniffed the air. "Smells like jealousy in here to me."

"Please." Jillian laughed as if the idea was completely preposterous. "I have no romantic interest in you whatsoever."

"Really?" Lexi sounded hopeful and clasped her hands in her lap.

"Really," Jillian said emphatically.

God, how had he gotten himself into this conversation? Brandi came back and slid the beer across the table. She winked slyly at him. Tuck gulped and just dove right into the beer. Anything to keep from dealing with this.

Jillian crossed her leg underneath the table, and the tip of her shoe grazed his shin. He caught another whiff of her cucumber-scented hair and had the strangest urge for a garden salad. She smelled like lush, summer produce, and the thought of nibbling on her was making him hard.

"I think this is an exciting time," Evie said, leaning across the table. "Ridley and I are working on a baby. Jillian's just moved to town. Lexi's expanding her business to include window treatments, and my little brother Tuck has decided to come out of the shadows and return to the land of the living."

All eyes were on him. Tuck blew out his breath. It unnerved him. The thought of starting over, trying again. He wasn't sure he was ready. Hell, he wasn't sure he'd ever be ready.

"A toast." Evie lifted her glass and looked at Tuck pointedly. "To new beginnings."

Everyone raised their glasses and echoed, "To new beginnings."

"Hey," Lexi said to Evie after they clinked glasses. "Have you thought about window treatments for the nursery?"

And they were off, Evie and Lexi talking about babies and curtains with circus animals on them that matched the receiving blankets Evie had already bought.

Clearly an outsider in the conversation, Jillian leaned back against the seat, and strands of her hair trailed along Tuck's shoulder. To keep from yanking her into his arms and stealing a kiss, he made himself think about work. How was he going to finish the job Sutter had hired him to do with a broken ankle?

But no matter how hard he tired, Tuck couldn't keep his mind, or his eyes, off Jillian. He was in serious trouble here. It wasn't just her cleavage or the tickling strands of her hair against his skin or the cucumber scent of her invading his nostrils. It wasn't the pucker of her rich raspberry lips when she took a sip of wine or the way her slender neck curved into her shoulders or the heat of her long, firm body radiating through his that clouded his brain.

Okay, so maybe it was all those things, but it was something more as well, and he had no idea what it was or what to do about it.

He squirmed in his seat.

She looked over at him. "Are you okay?"

"Um . . . I gotta move my legs. Kinda cramped up here."

"Oh," Jillian murmured, and leaned over to touch Lexi's arm. "Could you let us out, please? Tuck wants to stretch his legs."

Lexi let them out and Jillian got up, stumbling a little in the process. Tuck put out a hand to steady her. She'd had only two glasses of Chardonnay. He didn't know if she was a lightweight in the booze department or if it was those high-heeled boots giving her the trouble. You had to admire a woman who stood five-foot-ten and still wore heels.

"Thanks," she said breathlessly, and moved away from

his hand. She reached for his crutches and passed them to him. "You know, I think I'm just going to call it a night."

"So soon?" Lexi said.

"Are you sure you should be driving?" Tuck asked.

She sized him up. "Like you could drive me home with a broken ankle?"

"We could walk. It's only a quarter of a mile."

"You're on crutches."

"I have tough underarms."

"It's downhill."

"I'm willing to risk it if you are."

"Hang out a little longer," Evie said. "We'll drop you off in a bit."

"You stay," she told Tuck. "Let Rid and Evie bring you home. I'll see you back at the house."

"You're not walking alone."

"What? Someone in Salvation is gonna mug me? You people don't even lock your doors."

"It's October. There still might be bears wandering about looking for some last-minute snacks before hibernating. I'd hate for you to be an appetizer."

Her eyes widened. "Oh. I hadn't thought of that. Okay, you can come." She retrieved her jacket from the coat rack, shrugged into it, then turned and headed for the door, her ass swaying seductively as she walked away.

Tuck hitched his crutches underneath his arms. *If she really is a jinx*, he thought, *I'm about to find out for sure.*

Chapter Twelve

All Jillian could figure out was that the house Chardonnay at the Rusty Nail had more kick to it than her usual label. She had no other excuse why her head was spinning sweetly and she was dumbly ambling down the road toward the lake house in the dark of night guided only by a sky filled with stars and Tucker Manning limping along beside her on crutches.

She'd had only two glasses. Why did she feel so unsteady?

Maybe it had nothing to do with the wine and everything to do with the delicious hunk of man beside you.

The air was crisp and clean, and she felt a little breathless. High altitude, she told herself, but whenever she sneaked a glance over at Tuck's profile, her pulse rate spiked. A shiver shot down her spine at the same time a moist heat rolled between her inner thighs.

Quick! Think about something else.

But her dumb, numb brain refused to cooperate. His scent hung in the air. Some kind of spicy cologne tinged with the yeasty aroma of beer and the musky fragrance of outdoor man. He was a far cry from the men she normally dated—smooth, polished, overly groomed men like

Alex or the muscle-bound, pretty-boy himbos who looked good in a Speedo but didn't think too much.

Tuck was a guy's guy. Good-looking for sure, but in a rugged, tousled way. He didn't shave half the time, his hair was just a tad past the point of needing a trim, and she'd never seen him in anything other than flannel and denim.

Oh wait, there was that time when she'd walked in and found him on the couch in only his underwear.

Anyway, she'd never been with a guy like this. Unabashedly blue collar to the bone. Sure, he'd had his Magic Man phase. She'd seen the article on him in *Architectural Digest,* gussied up in a tuxedo. He could give Alex Fredericks a run for his money. But that had just been a lark for him. This Tuck, this guy here with the broken ankle and wind-blown hair and whiskey-colored eyes, he was the real deal. He could hunt and fish and start a fire with his bare hands. No wonder he'd settled in Salvation. No matter where he'd been born and raised, he was Colorado to the bone.

And without even trying, he turned her on like no man ever had.

"Here we are." Tuck stopped walking at the top of Enchantment Lane. The streetlamps ended at this point. They both stood looking to where the road dipped before it disappeared in the darkness.

"I think we should have taken that ride from Evie and Ridley," she said.

"They're still at the Rusty Nail. They play in the trivia tournament at eight on Thursday nights."

"Ah," she said.

"So, you and Lexi. Friends?"

"I'm new in town. I was looking for someone to hang out with."

"You've got me," he said. "I'll hang with you."

"Yeah, here's the deal. I'm thinking you wouldn't be so good at the girl talk."

"You never know; I might surprise you. I grew up with sisters."

"But what if you're the one I want to talk about?" She slapped a hand over her mouth. Why had she said that? Damnable Chardonnay.

"You want to talk about me to Lexi Kilgore?"

She made a derisive noise. "Noo . . . it was just an example of a topic we couldn't talk about. Should we do this thing now before we slowly start dying of exposure?" Jillian asked, vigorously rubbing her upper arms to stay warm.

"Ready as I'll ever be." To descend the hill, he bravely thrust his crutches out in front of him, anchored them on the asphalt, and swung his body through. He used his good foot to hold a new spot while Jillian followed behind him.

"This is a piece of German chocolate," he said.

She held her breath, just waiting for him to fall on his ass. What had they been thinking coming out here alone in the dark?

Tuck tried the maneuver again, succeeding a second time. "Look, ma, no leg."

"Don't get cocky, buster."

"We'll be just fine unless we run into a bear."

"Tell me you're making this whole bear thing up just to make me nervous."

"Nope," he said cheerfully. "Bears are very real, and they can get really cranky if you come between them and a hearty meal."

"I'll make a mental note to avoid that."

"Sound's like a plan."

Up ahead she could see the lake house, and relief pushed through her. "We're almost there."

"With the steepest part of the landscape to traverse," Tuck observed.

"Here, I'll lead the way." Jillian marched off in front of him.

"Jillian," he called.

"Yeah?" She swiveled her head as she stepped over a cross-tie timber that lined the lake property from the curvaceous Enchantment Lane.

"Watch out for—"

But she didn't hear the rest of the warning. The heel of her boot caught on something in the dark, and she found herself stumbling headlong toward the ground.

She put out her palms to catch herself. Her knees kissed the cool damp earth at the same moment she heard the clatter of Tuck's crutches as they tumbled to the dirt; then she felt his strong arm slide around her waist. "What are you doing? You're gonna fall if—"

Too late.

He was already slipping and taking her all the way down with him.

Somehow, Tuck ended up flat on his back in the pine needles with Jillian stretched out across the length of him, his arm still locked securely around her waist. His chest was so broad and firm. His eyes so dark. His breath so warm against her skin.

"Brilliant move, Einstein," she muttered.

"How do you know this move wasn't highly planned and calculated?" he asked.

"Too graceless. Then again, you're a guy . . ." She hitched in her breath. "*Was* it planned?"

He laughed. "Are you kidding? I couldn't do that on purpose if I tried. Besides, pratfalls just aren't my style. Face it, you weren't the only one imbibing tonight."

They stared into each other's eyes, and Jillian suspected he knew as well as she did that the situation they were in had nothing to do with alcohol. She scrambled off of him before she did something wholly inappropriate and exceedingly stupid. She turned toward the house, blood pounding in her ears.

"Hey," Tuck called out. "You just going to leave me here?"

"Huh?" Jillian blinked. She'd been so focused on getting away from the hard heat of his body that she'd forgotten he was lying there like a turtle, unable to hop up or flip over on his own. "Oh yeah. Sorry."

She hurried back to him, knelt beside him, and helped lever him off the ground. She reached for his crutches. Thrust them at him.

Wind rustled through the pine trees and sent a shiver over her skin. She didn't want him thinking she was shivering because she was so close to him, even though she was. "It's cold out here," she said. "Let's get inside."

"Let's," he echoed.

In the darkness, she could barely see the porch.

"Next time we go out drinking," she said, "we should remember to put the porch light on."

"Good idea. Next time."

They rounded the side of the house, their boots making hollow noises as soon as their feet hit the redwood deck. The moon, which had been playing peep-eye with the clouds, burst forth from its hiding place in that moment, bathing the dock in a silvery glow.

It was a beautiful shot of an autumn lake in moonlight. She heard the sounds of the wind-blown water gently lapping the shore, a hoot of an owl from a nearby tree, a dog barking in the distance. She caught the scent of wood smoke in the air, along with the cool, crisp, languid odor of mountain water.

She stopped to suck in an awed breath. "This view is stunning."

"Yeah," he whispered. "It is."

Jillian didn't have to turn her head to know Tuck was looking at her and not the water. "It's romantic."

"That too."

"Did you and Aimee make love out here often?"

"A time or two," he surprised her by admitting. "But only in the summer. Aimee didn't like the cold much." His tone took on a wistful note.

"And yet she loved Colorado."

"In the summer mostly."

"You're lucky," she said.

"Lucky?" His voice sounded gravelly.

She swept her arm at his vista. "To have all this."

"What are you talking about? I have nothing. Not legally. Not until that deed turns up and I lost the most precious—" He broke off and maneuvered himself away from her.

She knew he was talking about his wife. She didn't mean to make him think about her, but she supposed when you love someone that much and lose them so young and tragically, you never really stop thinking about them. Jillian wondered what it would feel like to be so loved.

Jealousy bit into her, and she hated herself for being jealous of a dead woman. How pathetic was that?

"You've got a lot more than you think you do. You've got a great sister and brother-in-law who love you. You'll soon have a little niece or nephew on the way. You're doing a job you love. You're young and strong and gorgeous, and you have your whole life ahead of you if you could just let go of the past."

"Hey!" Tuck snapped. "You've got no right telling me what to do with my life."

Jillian held up her palms. Her heart was breaking for him and everything he'd lost, but the man was desperately in need of some tough love. "You did everything that was humanly possible to save her."

"Yes, I did." His tone was vicious.

"So let yourself off the hook. You're not the one who's dead, Tuck."

"It's so damned easy for you to say. You have no idea what it's like. You've never even been in love."

His accusation hurt, but it was true. "You're right. I'm the interloper, the stranger, the misfit. Story of my life. No one wants to hear what I have to say. I don't belong."

He drew an audible breath. "That's not what I meant."

She turned away from him, hugged herself in the cold, and walked out onto the dock. He was the damned Magic Man, and he didn't even realize it. Yeah, so life had taken his wife, kicked him hard in the balls, but he'd had something Jillian had never had.

Love.

A lump formed in her throat. No one had ever told Jillian that she was loved. At least not that she could remember. Not her mother, not her father, certainly not her stepmother, and there'd been no grandparents. No man had ever said the words to her. She told herself she didn't care, that it didn't matter, that she didn't need that kind of messy emotion in her life, but it was a lie. She wanted love more than anything. Wanted it so much that she kept putting herself in situations where she'd never get it, stacking the deck against herself in a self-fulfilling prophecy.

Stop feeling sorry for yourself. Suck it up. Get over it.

"Hey," he said.

Jillian did not turn around, but she heard him clopping across the wooden deck with his three-legged crutch walk. "Yeah?"

"Let's go inside. I'm freezing my ass off."

The petulant part of her wanted to tell him to go inside, that she didn't need him. She didn't need anybody. But she hadn't become a great prosecutor by holding on to resentment. The sensible part of her that knew how to make a plea bargain, the part of her that was shivering *her* ass off replied, "Okay."

They went inside together.

But once they were in the cottage with the door locked and the moonlight safely hidden behind the curtains, Jillian didn't know what to say or do next.

Tuck propped his crutches in the corner of the foyer and shrugged out of his coat. It was still early, Jillian realized as the Bavarian cuckoo clock mounted near the fireplace struck nine.

They looked at each other. The smell of wind and lake and pine trees flared in the short distance between them. She was looking at his lips and he was looking at hers and . . .

"You are not going to kiss me," she said.

"No." He leaned closer.

"It would be stupid."

"Agreed." Tuck was so close now that their lips were almost touching.

"We're strangers."

"But roommates."

"Strange roommates," she murmured.

"Very strange." He ran the back of his hand over her cheek.

"We're both in bad places in our lives."

"Terrible."

"We're embroiled in a property dispute." Jillian leaned toward him, closing the miniscule gap. "Kissing would be disastrous."

"Catastrophic." Tuck curled a lock of her hair around his index finger.

"I mean, where would we go from there?"

"Right."

"We're certainly not going to sleep together."

"Absolutely not."

"Never mind the sexual chemistry."

"Yeah, forget all about that." His palm was at the nape of her neck now, his fingers splayed through her hair.

Jillian kept telling herself, *No, no, no*, but all she could think about was that damned sex dream where Tuck had a starring role and how they'd been so ripe and hungry for each other.

God, it was hot in here. Like the frickin' Sahara Desert.

They were nose to nose. Her body was on fire, her blood boiling. Tuck's cheeks were flushed. Jillian suspected her own were as well.

"I'm going to step away from you right now," she said.

"Me too."

She didn't move.

Neither did he.

Their chests were pressed together. She felt her nipples harden beneath the lace of her bra. Damn her anyway. "I thought you were stepping off."

"I am."

"I'm waiting."

"I'm going." He didn't move.

Her breath was chugging through her lungs as if she was a ten-pack-a-day smoker. "Good-bye."

"See ya."

Then he snatched her into his arms and kissed her so hard her head spun. He speared his tongue past her lips, and she just let him. Not only let him, but parted her teeth and *encouraged* him to continue.

Dumb, dumb, dumb.

His flavor filled her mouth, enveloped her, flooded her.

Unbelievably, impossibly, he tasted exactly the way he had in her dream. Through his taste alone, she could have identified him blindfolded in a room filled with a hundred men. His fingers fisted in her hair, and he held her to him so tightly she couldn't move—didn't want to move.

Tuck plastered his other hand to her fanny, pulling her up flush against him and grinding his hips against hers, giving her full appreciation of his rock-hard erection.

Desire shot through her, stronger than before.

Break it off. Pull away. Stop this before it's too late.

Ah, but his kiss was drowning out that prudent voice, dissolving any last shred of resolve she might have. She nipped his bottom lip between her teeth.

He moaned low in his throat and maneuvered her

against the wall, probably to keep himself from being thrown off balance. She wished she had something more than a wall to stabilize her.

Tuck pressed his body into hers. Excitement shot blood through her veins at an alarming rate, and she hissed in her breath as he branded her neck with his dangerously hot tongue.

The kiss was hard. Savage. Every muscle in her body twitched in response. Jillian was so sure it would be gentle, tender. She didn't mind that the kiss wasn't what she expected. In fact, she liked the surprise.

His frantic tongue increased her desire for him. She cupped his face with both hands and kissed him back just as fiercely as he kissed her.

Tuck grunted, running his hand up underneath her shirt, his palm skimming her belly.

If Mutt hadn't picked that moment to come bounding in through the kitchen, a fast-food wrapper in his mouth, Jillian couldn't say what would have happened next.

But Mutt did come in and with his oversized tail wagging, wedged himself between Jillian and Tuck, breaking them apart.

"Someone's jealous," Tuck panted.

"Looks like that same someone's been rummaging in the trash," Jillian said breathlessly, her lips still tingling.

They stared at each other, and suddenly it all felt so wrong when seconds ago it had felt so right. She thought of all the reasons they couldn't be together, the least of which the fact that he was still hung up on his dead wife.

Tuck shoved a hand through his hair, looking sheepish. "About what just happened . . ."

"Big mistake." She rushed in to say it before he did.

"Huge."

"Gigantic."

"Monumental."

"Enormous."

"Epic."

Jillian stepped away from him, tugged down the hem of her sweater. "This can't happen again."

"Gotcha."

"I mean it."

He raised his palms. "Completely hands off."

She knelt to scratch Mutt's ears and willed her heart to stop pounding. She felt rather than saw Tuck hobble away.

She raised her head. "Tuck?"

He turned, looked at her. "Yeah?"

"It's nothing personal, you know. You're a great guy. I'm sure of it."

"You're not so bad yourself, Queenie."

"Why do you call me that?"

A smiled curled his lips. "Because you look so damned regal. So untouchable."

"The Ice Queen," she said, thinking about what her fellow lawyers said about her.

"Oh no, Queenie," he said. "You're regal as hell, but try as hard as you might to convince people otherwise, there ain't nothing cold about you."

"So Jillian is Tuck's temptress, huh?" Evie said to Ridley when they got home from the Rusty Nail just after ten o'clock.

"Yes, but don't tell him that I told you about his vision

quest. He'd be upset. He didn't like telling me that he'd had a sexual fantasy about someone other than Aimee."

Evie unbuttoned her blouse. "I like her, but she's nothing like Aimee."

"Is that good or bad?" Ridley asked, trailing her from the kitchen into their bedroom.

"I'm just saying she's not Tuck's normal type." Evie stripped off her blue jeans and paraded over to the toilet.

It still threw Ridley for a loop when she went to the bathroom in front of him. It wasn't that he minded. He liked seeing her naked anytime he could. He'd just grown up in a family that was very private about their bodies. When they'd first hooked up, the uninhibited way Evie shed her clothes both thrilled and shocked him. He wondered if they were going to have issues over nudity when they had kids or if becoming a mom would change her. Did he like the idea of her changing, or not? Honestly, the whole baby thing unnerved him. He wanted one, yeah, but the reality of it had him quaking in his boots.

Ridley stepped to the sink and wet his toothbrush. "Tuck believes she's a jinx."

"That's because you told him she was." Evie peeled off several squares of toilet paper.

"Hey, go easy on that stuff," he said. "With what the fertility treatments are costing us, we gotta cut every corner."

"Ridley, are you seriously suggesting that a couple of extra squares of toilet paper are going to put us in the poor house?" She flushed, then came over to elbow him away from the sink so she could wash her hands.

Sometimes it bugged him the way she encroached on his space, and he had to remind himself she grew up in the second position in a family with four kids, while it had been just him and his older brother. She was accustomed to having to jockey for everything she got in life, while Ridley, as the youngest of two, had pretty much had everything handed to him.

"You know, I was really prepared not to like her." Evie lathered her hands with peach-scented liquid soap. Little orange bubbles floated in the air between them. Ridley noticed how small and yet incredibly strong her fingers were—all that kneading and chopping and slicing. "And not because of all that jinx stuff. But you know what? I actually think she might be good for him."

"You're not worried he'll fall for her and she'll hurt your brother?" Ridley mouthed around his toothbrush, and kept brushing long past the point he was ready to rinse, waiting for Evie to move away from the sink.

His wife dried her hands on a peach-colored towel. "Honestly, I don't think he could get any worse than falling into Salvation Lake on the anniversary of Aimee's death. And she is so not Tuck's type—he likes them petite and sweet. I don't think there's much danger he'll fall in love with Jillian."

Ridley spit and rinsed. "So you did see the sizzle. There's megawatt sexual tension between those two."

"Oh yeah, they've got chemistry, but that's good. Hot sex is all he needs right now. The man's been celibate for two years. He could do a lot worse than Jillian as his transitional woman, but I'd hate to see her get hurt."

"I don't know," Ridley mumbled, feeling decidedly uneasy. "From everything I know about vision quests, she's either a temptress whose going to be his ruination or she's his destiny."

"You're reading too much into that vision stuff."

"Don't discount what you can't understand."

Evie sank her hands on her hips. "Did you do a vision quest when you met me?"

Ridley shrugged. His wife had that pick-a-fight look on her face and a pugilistic set to her shoulders. "Did you lock the back door?" he hedged.

"You did!"

He shook his head.

She advanced on him.

Grinning, Ridley backed up until his butt hit the bathroom wall. She looked so beautiful all naked and fiery eyed. "Come on, tell me. What did you see?"

"I saw a woman with the most amazing red hair." He reached out to twist a lock of her hair around his thumb. "And she was passionately whipping up a batch of the most delicious biscuits. I could taste them in the vision. Buttery, light, and flaky. I knew a woman who could make biscuits like that had to be an angel. I fell instantly in love."

"With me," she whispered.

"With the biscuits. You were just a side bonus."

"Ridley James Red Deer." She playfully swatted his shoulder. "What an awful thing to say to the woman who's going to be the mother of your children."

"Well, if that's the case, shouldn't we be working on making babies instead of standing here talking?" He snaked a hand around her waist and lifted her up into his arms.

"My big strong Indian brave." She sighed into his chest.

He took her mouth, kissing her firmly yet tenderly, letting her know just how much she meant to him. Things had been a little tense between them lately, and he wanted to sweep all that pressure away and just enjoy sex the way they used to before all the fertility treatments and ovulation charts.

Evie let loose a needy moan, and he carried her into their bedroom. His tongue swept her sweet, sweet mouth as he laid her down on the soft mattress. Blood rushed pell-mell to his cock, turning him to stone. God, he was hard for her.

She tasted so good. Better than the awesome biscuits she baked. He loved how petite she felt beside his bigness, how smooth she was to his roughness.

Two people couldn't be more opposite. He was a Native American man from the mountains. She was from an educated urban family. He'd gone to school on a reservation. She'd trained in Paris. While he was learning to hunt and fish and live off the land, she was speaking French and turning the simplest ingredients into elaborate meals. She was bossy; he was born to help. She was direct; he was oblique. She was fire. He was water.

And yet, in spite of their differences, they made it work. Who knew? Maybe it worked because of their differences. They had their ups and downs, sure, but they never got bored.

She wound her arms around his neck, and a shiver shot down his spine. His fiery woman made him burn. She peered into his eyes with a look that was pure Evie. "Take me, big man."

And so he did.

Thirty minutes later, they lay together, letting their ragged breathing return to normal. Evie rested her head on his chest. "Have you done a vision quest about our baby?"

Ridley hesitated, not wanting to get into this, but Evie was having none of his silence. She raised up on one elbow and looked down at him. "Rid?"

He sighed and put a hand over his eyes. "No."

"Why not?"

He cleared his throat and reached over to idly stroke her bare breast with the back of his finger, hoping to distract her, but she had the focus of a border collie herding sheep.

"Well?"

"I'm afraid of what I might see."

"Or not see." Her voice was serious.

"Yeah," he admitted.

"I want to go on a vision quest," she said.

Oh crap, what had he gotten himself into? "It's not that simple, Evie. You've got to believe in it for a vision quest to give you the guidance you're looking for. And it's not like magic. It doesn't make you psychic or foretell the future. You just see images, have dreams that guide you to make decisions."

"You sent Tuck on a vision quest without any hesitation."

"That was different. Tuck was desperate. And he had an open mind."

Evie sat up. "I'm desperate to know if we're going to have any children."

"Evie, we're gonna have kids, one way or another."

"What does that mean?"

"If we have to adopt, we will."

"I want my own kids," she whispered. "Our kids. I want to know what it feels like to be pregnant."

"Come on, you know you'd love an adopted child just as much as you'd love a biological one. You've got so much love to give, Evie."

"You're right, but still, I want to try. I want the full experience."

Ridley blew out his breath. "That's another reason I don't want you to go on a vision quest. I don't know if you could handle it if you didn't get the message you're searching for, and I can't bear seeing you hurt."

"I'm hurting now."

"I know."

"You're being stubborn about this."

"Maybe, but this is my spiritual practice, and you have to respect that. It's not a parlor trick." Glaring, he sat up. "You have to respect it."

"I can, I will, I promise, if you'll just go on a vision quest with me," she pleaded.

He hated to deny her, but it wasn't that simple. If she didn't see anything, she'd be disappointed. If she saw something that told her they couldn't have their own kids, she'd be crushed. He had to be the bad guy here, for her peace of mind. "I'm sorry, Evie. The answer is no."

"No?" Her voice quavered, full of tears. Damn those hormones that could change her mood so quickly.

"That's right," he said as calmly as he could. His inclination was to give in, but he had to stand his ground. "No."

"I'm not sure I can be around you right now."

"I accept your anger. It's healthy."

"Good, you can accept it on the couch." She shoved a

pillow at him. He knew she was just reacting to her fears, but still a man had only so much patience. "Go sleep on the couch. And you can sleep there until you agree to guide me on a vision quest."

Ridley jerked back the covers, stormed to his feet, and jammed the pillow under his arm. "Fine, but I've got to tell you that banishing me to the couch is certainly not the way to get the babies you want."

He slammed the bedroom door behind him and heard her burst into tears.

It was in his nature to go back inside, wrap his arms around her, tell her that he was sorry and that he'd do what she wanted. But on this matter, he knew he couldn't give in.

Not just for his sake, but for Evie's as well.

Chapter Thirteen

All right, all right, she was going to stop thinking about Tuck. Right here, right now. No more fantasies about him or that kiss.

Determinedly, Jillian sucked in her breath, dropped her purse into the bottom drawer of Sutter's antique desk, and plunked down into the rolling leather chair. She reached up to run her fingertips over her lips, trying to recapture the feel of Tuck's mouth on hers from the night before.

Great, you can't go two minutes without thinking about him.

Hell, she'd lain awake all night thinking about him.

Stop thinking about him. Now!

Right, right. Head in the game. Purposefully, she straightened the stack of papers in the in-box that didn't need straightening, looked up, and spied the ladder she'd moved to the corner yesterday while cleaning up the mess from Tuck's fall through the ceiling.

Immediately, she thought of Tuck and how he'd looked standing on that ladder.

Stop it.

She turned on her laptop and slid another glance at the ladder. She could smell Tuck's scent in the room.

Outdoorsy and masculine, mingling with the musty smell of old house and water-damaged Sheetrock.

It's just your imagination. You can't smell him.

All at once, the taste of him filled her mouth, and Jillian just *yearned* for him. His kiss had been such a heady combination of need and restraint, of tenderness and demand.

Knock it off. Get to work.

All right, all right. She cracked her knuckles, took a deep breath, and focused her attention on the computer screen.

But she knew the ladder was still there. Standing like a forgotten solider. A constant reminder of the man she was struggling to forget.

"Dammit," she muttered, pushing back her chair.

Jillian headed for the ladder with the intention of stuffing it into the adjoining supply room, but before she reached it, the office door opened and a beautiful young blonde stepped over the threshold.

"Hi," she said. "You must be Jillian Samuels, the new lawyer everyone in town is buzzing about."

"I haven't taken the Colorado bar yet, but, yes, I suppose I am."

The woman stepped across the room, her hand extended. "Lily Massey."

"Ah," Jillian said, shaking her hand. "Bill's fiancée."

She beamed. "I am."

"What can I do for you, Lily?" Jillian asked. "Or did you just stop by to say hi?" She hadn't been in town long, but she'd quickly learned people liked to pop in to get a good look at her and satisfy their curiosity. Or size her up before making their bets in the guess-when-she's-gonna-leave-town pool.

"I need to speak to you about my prenuptial agreement."

A real client. Good, good.

"Have a seat," she invited with a wave at the chair positioned in front of Sutter's desk.

Lily glanced up and eyed the hole in the ceiling. "What happened?"

"Long story."

Lily kept staring upward. "Are we safe?"

That was a loaded question. As a lawyer, she knew safety was an illusion. At any moment, you could step off the curb in front of a Tom Thumb delivery truck and get run down. You could fall through the attic and break your neck. You could drop dead of a brain tumor in the middle of Starbucks. And yet, she was certain that was not the answer Lily Massey was looking for.

"As long as we don't go into the attic." Jillian sat in the rolling leather desk chair, and Lily tentatively eased down across from her. "So you want to draw up a prenup?"

"No," she said. "I want you to tear it up."

"Excuse me?"

Sighing, Lily leaned back against the chair. "My father made me get one. I'm from L.A. Everyone gets a prenup. Dad insisted when he came up for our engagement party. He thinks he's protecting me but . . ." She trailed off.

"But?"

"He doesn't understand."

"As a lawyer, I'm afraid I have to side with your father. Do you have significant assets?"

"I've got a small trust fund, yes. But Bill has money of

his own. He's been saving for the right woman to come along."

"That's all very romantic but not terribly practical. This country's divorce rate is fifty percent."

"You're from a big city, too, aren't you?" Lily asked.

"Houston."

"You've never lived in a place like Salvation."

"That's true."

"You don't understand either. About small towns and people with integrity. When they give you their word, it's law."

"People in small towns don't have a lock on integrity. Proportionally, there's just as much greed and corruption in Salvation as there is in L.A."

Lily shook her head. "No, there's not. You'll see if you stay long enough. This is a special place. The people in it are special too."

Okay, so Lily was a bit delusional. She didn't seem to know the first thing about human nature.

"I'm guessing Bill is hassling you about the prenup?" Jillian ventured.

"No," she said. "Exactly the opposite. He cheerfully signed it."

"So what's the problem?"

"Bill didn't ask me to sign one."

"Why not?"

"He says what's his is mine. Don't you see?" Lily asked. "My prenup ruins everything."

Jillian leaned forward. "How so?"

"A prenuptial agreement says I expect the marriage to fail. I don't."

"It's just a legal document to protect you, worst-case scenario."

"I don't live my life that way." Lily shifted, crossing her legs at the knees. "Preparing for the worst and hoping for the best. I believe that if you prepare for the worst, then that's what you're going to get."

Jillian didn't expect Lily's comment to affect her like it did, but suddenly she experienced a yawning hollowness in the pit of her stomach. That's what she'd done her entire life. Prepare for the worst and hope for the best—that is, until she moved to Salvation. She hadn't prepared for anything. She'd broken her pattern and look where it had gotten her. Living in a house that in all likelihood she was going to lose, living with a man who made her feel things she didn't want to feel.

"Instead of destroying your prenup, why not just get Bill to draw one up of his own so you'll be on equal footing?"

Lily twirled the large marquis-cut diamond on the ring finger of her left hand. "He says he has faith in us, that he knows we're destined to be together. He's not afraid. He loves and trusts me."

"That's all well and good, but what's going to protect you if this marriage doesn't work out?"

"My faith will protect me. Faith in our love."

"You're basing this on emotions. Be practical. Think of your future," Jillian lobbied.

"Haven't you heard a word I've said?" Lily tilted her head. "I'm in this marriage for better or worse, for richer for poorer, in sickness and in health. Bill is the love of my life. Now, if you don't mind, would you please get the prenup? I'd like you to witness its destruction."

"If that's what you want." Jillian got up and headed for the file cabinet she'd spent the past week organizing.

"I'd also like you to attend our wedding so you can see for yourself that what Bill and I have is the real deal. It's on Christmas Eve at Thunder Mountain Lodge. The whole town's invited."

She's so naïve. "That's very kind of you, Lily."

"So you'll come? You will still be in Salvation by Christmas?"

Was this a challenge? Or was she just taking it that way? Why not go to the wedding? It wasn't like she had plans for Christmas Eve.

"We're doing it up big," Lily enticed. "A grand celebration for a big love."

"Sure, why not," Jillian accepted, her fingers walking through the files under the M, not really sure why she did.

"That's great. And, Jillian?"

"Yes?" She looked up, Lily's prenuptial agreement in her hand.

The young woman's smile was brilliant. "I hope someday you find *your* true love."

"I'M IN A PICKLE, Aim, and I don't know how to get out of it," Tuck spoke out loud to his dead wife. "I need your advice on what to do about Jillian."

Dead silence.

Normally when he talked to Aimee, he experienced a comforting peace wrap around him. He knew it was probably all in his mind, but nevertheless, when he talked, he imagined she was listening, and that made him feel better.

Not today.

Today he felt emptier than he had since he'd fallen into the lake on the anniversary of her death. It was a rotten sensation, and he wanted to run away from it, but there was nowhere to go, and it had nothing to do with the fact that he was held captive by the cast on his right leg. He couldn't run from his hobbled mind.

"Aimee?" he tested.

Nothing.

His chest ached. Restlessly, he shifted on the couch. "Are you gone?" he whispered.

From his pallet in the corner beside the fireplace, Mutt lifted his head and gave him an expectant look.

"It's okay, Muttster, go back to sleep."

The dog lowered his head, and Tuck tasted something salty on the back of his tongue. He swallowed, blinked, picked up the remote control, and flipped through the television channels in search of a diversion but found none. He couldn't concentrate on mindless daytime TV prattle.

"I'm sorry, Aim. I didn't mean to kiss her. But you've been gone for so long, and I'm so lonely and I miss what we had so much. I want that again. You were right when you told me that I'd want it again, but I didn't believe you. I don't want to want another woman. But I do."

Dammit. The salty taste was back in his mouth again. He clenched his jaw and swiped at his eyes with his sleeve.

"Aimee?" he murmured, reaching desperately for something he knew was long gone.

Mutt whined.

"When you're right, dog, you're right. There's no one here but me and you. I gotta let go. I know, I know . . . but seriously, how the hell does a guy do that? And what woman's gonna want me with all my emotional baggage?"

Mutt barked.

A knock sounded on the door.

Tuck blinked, scrubbed at his eyes, and took a deep breath, struggling to tamp down his emotions and hoping whoever was at the front door would just go away. After the fifth knock, he heard the door handle jiggle open.

"Tuck, you in here?" Ridley called from the doorway.

"Come in," Tuck hollered, shifting on the couch to a sitting position. "What's up?"

Ridley came through the door, bringing with him the smell of Bluebird cheeseburgers. "Lunch's up."

"Dude, how'd you know I was starving?"

"Your sister is omnipotent."

"Gimme." Tuck reached for the brown paper bag in Ridley's right hand, then spied the stack of wood his brother-in-law had tucked under his left arm. "What's that?"

Ridley tossed him the sack and sat down beside him on the couch. "A special project for you while you're laid up."

Tuck's ears pricked up with interest as he opened the paper bag, and the smell of grilled onions wafted into the room. He loved the idea of something to do while he was recuperating. "Special project?"

Mutt whined loudly and licked his lips.

Ridley laid the maple wood on the coffee table, fished a dog biscuit from the front pocket of his shirt, and tossed it to the dog. "Evie's Christmas gift from me. I want you to make it."

"Yeah?" Tuck eyed the expensive maple as he bit into his cheeseburger.

"Music box."

Tuck nodded, swallowed. "I'm with you."

"Cradle on top of the box. Cradle that swings. Intricate detail. Not gonna be easy."

Excitement pushed out the loneliness he'd been feeling before Ridley had walked in. He's been an architect and a carpenter, but he'd never tackled a woodworking project like this. All his skills had been plied on houses, not delicate crafts. Eagerness had him putting down the cheeseburger and picking up the maple. He wanted this. Needed it. "Plays Brahm's Lullaby?"

"George Michael's 'Faith'."

Tuck grinned at Ridley. "Dude, I'm so there."

TWO WEEKS PASSED with Jillian and Tuck tiptoeing around each other. Or rather Jillian tiptoed. Tuck sort of clumped about in his cast. Jillian made arrangements to take the Colorado bar exam and spent her spare time studying at Sutter's office or playing chess with Lexi. Tuck immersed himself in crafting Evie's music box. Neither one of them spoke again about the kiss they'd shared. In fact, they both did their best to avoid talking about anything personal.

They fell into the rhythm of roommates trying hard to give each other space. She got up at five-thirty each morning, went running with the dog, showered, and left the house before Tuck ever woke up. In the evenings, Tuck hung out at the Bluebird or at Evie and Ridley's.

The weekend before Halloween, Tuck finished the music box. He could see a hundred different ways he could have done it better, but he had to admit it wasn't half bad for his first attempt at crafting a music box. But once it was done, time weighed heavily on his hands. He wanted—needed—something else to occupy his mind while his ankle healed. That Saturday morning, when Jillian returned from her jog with Mutt, he announced, "I'm going stir-crazy. I need something to do. I'm going to strip the wallpaper off the kitchen, then texture and paint the walls."

"You can't do that," she said, toweling the perspiration from her neck. "Our property dispute hasn't been settled. Blake's will hasn't been probated."

"Look, the place needs renovating. Whether you end up living here or I end up with the place, it's got to be done. What's the harm in giving me something to do?"

"You'll want to decorate it your way, and if I end up with the place, I'll have to redo it."

"I tell you what, you can pick out the décor."

She narrowed her eyes. "Why would you do that? Is it because you know there really is no deed?"

"There's a deed."

"Then why?"

"You are the most distrustful woman I've ever met," he said. He tossed his head and his hair fell over his forehead. He needed a haircut, but she liked the rakish look longer hair gave him. "I'm bored and I'm desperate enough to let you paint the kitchen pink if that's what it takes."

"I won't paint the kitchen pink."

"I had no doubts. You're not a girly-girl."

"Fuchsia, maybe," she teased.

"So you wanna make a supply run to the hardware store in Boulder?" He smiled.

"Who pays for the material?"

"We split the cost."

"Again, why would you do that?"

"Occupational therapy. It's not any more expensive than material for some useless craft project."

He had a point. The charming grin—combined with the sexy hair—did her in. She ignored her prudent side, tossing caution out the window. It would be pretty damn nice to get rid of those ducks. "Yeah, okay. Let me get my purse."

BY NOON they'd only managed to steam off about a quarter of the mallard duck wallpaper. It was a painstaking process. Intrigued by the whole wallpaper peeling endeavor, Mutt kept getting underfoot, and they spent half their time shooing him away. Finally, Jillian got up and put the dog outside. "Go chase a squirrel or something."

She came back, and hands on hips, watched as Tuck meticulously steamed a section of aged yellow wallpaper. "Mallards in the kitchen. Imagine."

Tuck grunted. "It is a lake house."

"Who picked out that wallpaper?"

"Aimee's grandmother I imagine. This lake house was in the Townsend family for three generations."

Jillian pushed her bangs back off her forehead. "Then Blake goes and breaks the chain by leaving it to me."

"And then deeding it to me," he reminded her.

"Why would he do that?"

"There weren't any Townsends left to leave it to."

"No, I mean, seriously, why would he leave the place to me and then deed it to you? The brain tumor is the likely explanation, but I was with Blake the day before he died, and while he had been getting progressively forgetful, he didn't really seem impaired."

"I can't answer that."

"I mean, why didn't he just leave the place to you to begin with? Why drag me into it at all?"

"I don't know that either. Maybe because you were more like a daughter to him than his own daughter, and Aimee didn't have any kids to leave it to."

She stared at him. "How come you never had kids?"

"There wasn't time," he said sharply. "We wanted to, but Aimee . . ." He shook his head, didn't finish.

What in the hell was wrong with her? Why had she asked that? "I'm sorry. That was completely rude and none of my business. Would you like to break for a quick lunch?"

"Yeah." He straightened, turned off the steamer, and went to the sink to wash his hands, his cast thumping heavily against floor.

"You're limping less."

"It doesn't hurt as much as it did." Tuck wiped his hands on a cup towel. "I can sleep on my stomach again."

"That's good," Jillian murmured. Immediately, her mind went to the thought of him lying on the couch the way she'd found him that first morning almost a month earlier. She pushed the image from her mind and went to peer into the refrigerator. "We're out of groceries. You wanna just hit the Bluebird?"

"That'd take too much time. We have bread," Tuck

said. "And sliced cheese. We could have grilled cheese sandwiches."

"Clearly, you haven't tasted my cooking."

"Don't worry, Queenie, I'll handle it."

Jillian tucked her fingers into the back pockets of her jeans. "I wish you wouldn't call me that."

"Why not?" He twisted the tie off a loaf of wheat bread. "It suits you."

"That's a depressing thought."

"How come?"

"Queenie makes me feel as if you think I think I'm better than everyone else. I'm reserved with people. I know that, but it doesn't mean I think I'm better."

"I don't think that at all." He turned the gas burner on low.

"What do you think?"

"A queen is a woman who's foremost among others. Plus, you said you played chess with Blake, right?"

"Yes, it's my favorite game."

He gave her a look that said, *There you go*. "And what's the most powerful piece on the chess board?"

"The queen."

"Exactly."

"So when you call me Queenie, you're saying I'm powerful?"

"Yup."

Jillian couldn't help smiling. "Powerful, huh?"

"Far more than you know."

"I think I like that."

"That's what I've been trying to tell you. Wear your crown with no misgivings, Queenie." He winked at her and melted butter in a nonstick skillet.

He finished cooking the sandwiches and served them up. They sat at the bistro table in the breakfast nook. They hadn't sat here together like this since the morning after the first night Jillian spent at the lake house. From this vantage point, they could look out the window and see a section of the lake stretching out frosty green beyond the snow-covered pine trees.

Soft rock music poured from the radio in the kitchen window. They'd found a station they could both agree on. Delbert McClinton was singing "Givin' It Up for Your Love." The song had came out the year Jillian was born. She knew because the audio tape *The Jealous Kind* had been among her father's music collection when he'd died. As a teenager, she'd listened to his tapes over and over, trying to make a connection to the man she barely remembered. She shook her head, shook off the past.

"This is the best grilled cheese sandwich I've ever eaten," she told Tuck, surprised at how tasty it was. "What'd you do to give it that extra zing?"

"Mustard."

"Hmm."

"And not just any mustard," he said. "Grey Poupon."

"Should we be eating this in a Rolls-Royce?"

"I'm in the mood to slum it, how 'bout you, Queenie?"

"I've been slumming it for a very long time, Magic Man. Rolls-Royces are a bit beyond my budget. I was a county employee."

Tuck leaned back in his chair, stretching his long legs out in front of him, his eyes lingering on her face. Jillian glanced away, looking out the window to see a few black-headed sparrows perched on the bird feeder on the deck, pecking at sunflower seeds.

On the radio, The Lovin' Spoonful was playing "Do You Believe in Magic?" No, Jillian didn't. But she wished she could.

"You really planning on staying in Salvation?" Tuck dusted bread crumbs from the table onto his empty plate. "Even when the deed turns up?"

She was already getting attached. She was quickly growing to love the house, the mountains, the lake, the town. The fact that everyone treated her as though she were transient was bothersome. It made her feel a little unwelcome, even though the community was friendly. They had not embraced her fully.

Or could it be you haven't fully embraced them, and they're picking up on your emotional reserve?

She lifted her chin. "Yes, I am."

"Wait until after you've weathered a Colorado winter and see if you still feel the same way."

"What's the deal?" she asked. "You in the local pool to see how soon I'll leave town?"

"You know about that?"

"You better change your bet. I'm not leaving."

"That stubborn, huh?"

"Partly," she admitted. She met his gaze, and he was studying her with half-lidded eyes. "But mostly because I need this chance at Salvation."

"Pun intended I'm guessing."

"All my life I was so focused on being a prosecutor. It's all I ever thought about, all I ever worked toward," she said.

The Lovin' Spoonful posed their question again. Do you believe in magic? Such a stupid song.

"So when all the other little girls were talking about

being rock singers and movie stars and models, you said, hey, I wanna put the bad guys in jail?"

"Yes, yes, I did. I was quite enamored of *Law and Order,* but it went beyond that."

"In what way?"

"I was attracted to law because the roles are clear. I liked the responsibility and the authority. I'm a cards-on-the-table kind of gal. I like a career where preparation, caution, and constant questioning are valued. I like the fact that it's clear who the bad guys are and who the good guys are. I get off on the dangerous undercurrent inherent in criminal law. The courtroom is the only place where I felt like I truly belonged."

He smashed the bread crumbs on his plate with the pad of his thumb. "You're always thinking, aren't you? Trying to figure out everyone's angle."

"Always," she admitted.

"What's mine?"

"Huh?"

"If I was accused of a crime, how would you assess me?"

"I'm not sure this little analysis game is such a good idea," she said.

"Why?" He leaned closer, his eyes suddenly sharp, the languid expression completely disappearing. "Afraid you'll hurt my feelings?"

"Honestly? Yes."

"You think I'm that sensitive?"

"I value the friendship we've started to forge. I don't want to blow it."

"Like I almost blew it the night we walked home from the Rusty Nail."

"Yeah," she said. "Like that."

"I promise I won't get offended. I'd really like to know how I look through Queenie's eyes."

"Shouldn't we be getting back to the wallpaper?"

"We can steam and strip and talk all at the same time."

"Are you sure you really want to know?"

He raised his chin. "I do."

"No holds barred?"

His eyes glistened a challenge. "No holds barred."

"Even if it might sting?"

"That's what no holds barred means."

Jillian sucked in a breath. "Okay, here goes, but remember you asked for it."

Tuck stacked their plates in the kitchen sink, grabbed up the steamer, and went back to the wallpaper. "Go ahead, I'm listening."

Jillian took up a putty knife and came to stand beside him, prying off the paper he'd loosened with the steam. "In spite of having been the Magic Man," she said, "you're an underachiever."

"You've been talking to Evie."

"Yes, but I didn't have to talk to your sister to figure this out about you."

"No?"

"If you'd worked hard to become an architect, if designing those classrooms was so important, you wouldn't be here in Salvation, hiding out."

"Interesting theory, except maybe I don't view it as hiding out," he said.

"You don't. I get that, but it's part of what I'm basing my opinion on."

"So we're in agreement."

"You settle."

"What does that mean?"

"You settle for what's in front of you, because you don't want to tolerate the discomfort of desire."

"Now you sound exactly like Evie."

"Your sister has said something similar?" Jillian arched her eyebrows.

He moved to run the steamer over a different section of wallpaper. "Maybe."

"You remind me of an F. Scott Fitzgerald quote I read once."

"And what's that?" Warm steam rose up between them.

" 'The test of a first-rate intelligence is the ability to hold two opposed ideas in the mind at the same time and still retain the ability to function.' "

He turned and grinned at her as that irresistible lock of hair fell over his forehead again, making him look completely adorable. "Ah, Queenie, you're saying I'm smart?"

"I'm saying you straddle the fence."

"Not so."

"Please." She snorted. "Democrat or Republican?"

"What's that got to do with anything?"

"Just answer the question."

He shrugged. "I'm not married to either party. Depends on the candidate."

"My point exactly. You sway whichever way the wind blows." She peeled off a long strip of mallards.

"That's unfair."

"Paper or plastic?"

"No preference."

"Baseball or football?"

"I like them equally."

"Stem cell research—for or against?"

"I don't have all the facts. I can't make an informed decision without studying both sides of the issue."

"Aha!" Jillian crowed. "Beautifully proving F. Scott Fitzgerald's point."

"You're pretty competitive, aren't you?"

"You're the one who said you could take it."

"I might have been a bit hasty with that."

"You know why I think you quit being the Magic Man?"

"Um . . . because my wife got diagnosed with advanced ovarian cancer?"

"Aimee was just an excuse. I think you stopped being the Magic Man because you didn't know how to deal with being special," Jillian said, sliding the putty knife underneath a section of wallpaper and then peeling off the chunk. She dumped it in the big cardboard box they had sitting in the middle of the floor. "It was too much pressure. Being a star happened to you accidentally, right? You designed these classrooms and because of your designs, people learned better in your buildings. So there was this mystique about you and you weren't secure in your . . ."

Jillian stopped talking when she realized Tuck was frozen in place beside her and that he hadn't spoke or moved since she'd mentioned Aimee's name. And she knew then that somewhere, she'd crossed the line.

Nervously, her eyes flicked to his face.

His expression was pure stone.

"Tuck?"

"How dare you," he accused. "How dare you insinuate that I used my wife's illness to run out on my career. You don't know me. You have no idea how much I loved her or what I would have done for her. She was my life, my soul, my heart. I didn't give a damn about my fucking career. All I cared about was Aimee. And you dare to stand here and blather about—" Tuck broke off abruptly, clenching his fists at his sides.

Jillian felt as if she'd been kicked in the gut by a horse. She'd been too glib, too insensitive. What in the hell was wrong with her? She'd known better than to bring up Aimee's name and yet she'd done it anyway.

"Tuck . . . I . . ." She reached out to him.

He raised his palms, took a step back. "You know what? I can't do this. I can't have this conversation with you."

She backed up, hurt by his pain, disturbed that she'd caused it. Saddened that no one had ever loved her the way he had loved his wife and convinced that no one ever would. Why would they when she had it in her to say such inconsiderate things?

Tuck threw down the steamer, picked up his car keys from the hook by the back door, hunched his shoulders, and limped out.

Leaving Jillian feeling utterly abandoned.

Chapter Fourteen

Tuck tracked Ridley down at the Rusty Nail.

"I flipped out on Jillian," he said morosely, and peered into the beer he hadn't touched. "I flipped out and now I don't know how to go back and undo it."

"Do what I do—act like it never happened."

Tuck leaned back and gave his brother-in-law a long appraising glance. "And that works?"

"No, but it's my defense mechanism and I'm sticking to it."

"Even though it doesn't work."

Ridley took a slug off his longneck beer. "Yep."

"How long have you been sleeping on the couch?" Tuck asked.

"How did you know?"

"You've got that I-ain't-getting-any look about you."

"You should know."

"Point taken."

"Evie told you, huh?"

"Yep." Tuck took a sip of beer. "Why don't you just let her do this vision quest thing?"

"Yeah, because it turned out so well when you did it."

"Hey, you were right about Jillian. She is a jinx."

"No, I was wrong about that. She's not a jinx. I didn't

know your psyche well enough to interpret your vision. Honestly," Ridley said. "I think Jillian is the best thing that could have ever happened to you. Since she's been in Salvation, you've come alive again."

Tuck made a dismissive noise.

"You have."

"This arrangement isn't working. I gotta find a new place to live," Tuck said. "I feel like I've been backed into a corner with no way out. I'm choking."

"You're going to give up the house? Aimee's house?"

Tuck briefly closed his eyes, fighting off the barrage of emotions like a bullfighter dancing around the bull. He'd never experienced such a mix of feelings—anger, sadness, hope, regret, shame, denial, expectancy, loss, fear. He pressed his lips together, then said, "That deed's never going to turn up. For all I know, Sutter's previous assistant ran it through the shredder."

"Or Jillian did."

He shook his head. "She wouldn't do that. She wants the house, but she's a straight shooter."

"I'd invite you to stay with us, but I have no idea how long I'll be needing the couch."

"It's all right. I can find somewhere else. I shouldn't abuse your hospitality," Tuck said.

"You oughta call Jefferson Baines. He might know who's got a place to rent on this side of the mountain."

Tuck snorted and took another swallow of beer. "That pinhead?"

"He's a pinhead, yes, but he does know the real estate market around here."

"All the high-priced places."

"You can afford it."

"Hello? I'm no longer pulling down high six figures. Self-employed, remember? Lousy health insurance. Aimee's illness put a huge dent in my savings."

"Still, I know you've got *some* tucked back."

Tuck tightened his jaw. "That's earmarked for renovating the house."

"You know . . . ," Ridley started.

Tuck held up a hand to halt him. "Stop right there. I know what you're going to say, and I don't want to hear it."

"Okay."

They sat there not talking, just drinking. Tuck found himself thinking about what Jillian had said. She'd been right about everything, and that was why he'd overreacted. A guy didn't really like having a mirror held up to his face so he could see his flaws. Plus, he'd asked for it and then hadn't been able to take it. He *had* pulled in his head like a turtle; he *had* turned his back on life.

Still, something had been made abundantly clear to him. He had to get out of there, and the sooner the better. Because if he stayed at the lake house, he feared he might not be able to keep his hands off her.

And that would be such a bad thing?

Yes, yes it would, because he was coming to treasure the friendship they were forging, and he didn't want to do anything to screw it up. Staying in that house with her, when they were so clearly attracted to each other, well, it was just plain stupid.

Come Monday, he'd go see Baines and ask him to be on the lookout for a place for him to rent.

In the meantime, Tuck had to make sure to keep his mouth shut and his hands to himself.

* * *

JILLIAN WENT TO THE BLUEBIRD for dinner after spending the remainder of the day peeling off the kitchen wallpaper with only Mutt for company. Partially because there wasn't anything else to eat in the house besides lamb-flavored Eukanuba and partially because she was hoping to run into Tuck.

Disappointment washed over her when she discovered he wasn't there. She seated herself at the counter and was busy studying the menu when she felt someone come up behind her.

Tuck? His name immediately leapt into her mind.

Jillian turned, but it wasn't Tuck.

"Hello, we haven't met yet. My name's Jefferson Baines and you are..." The real estate agent extended his hand.

Jillian shook it. "Nice to meet you Jefferson. I'm Jillian Samuels."

"Jillian." He said her name like a used-car salesman and held it in his mouth for too long.

"Does anyone ever call you Jeff?"

"Only if they don't like breathing." He laughed heartily.

"Jefferson it is, then."

He leaned one elbow against the counter, slouching insouciantly, trying to look casual in spite of his Armani suit and Gucci loafers. "I've been seeing you around town."

"I just moved here a few weeks ago."

"I live halfway between Salvation and Thunder Mountain," he said. "Thunder Mountain is where all the action is, but Salvation does have its charms."

"It does."

"Word around town is that you're a lawyer."

"I am."

"You and I have something in common."

"We do?" He was the kind of guy the old Jillian might have been interested in once upon a time. Tall, handsome, career-focused, ambitious, well dressed.

"We're fellow Texans," he said. "I'm from Dallas. I hear you're from Houston."

She tilted her head so that her hair swung over her face. Not to be coy but to study him from behind her cloak of hair. He had cover-model good looks. You had to be careful of guys that gorgeous. Alex had taught her the truth of that lesson. "You heard correctly."

"It's quite a change," Jefferson went on. "From the big city to Salvation."

The guy couldn't claim scintillating conversationalist on his résumé. "Yes."

He leaned closer. "How are you adjusting to small-town life?"

"Just fine, thanks for asking."

"I also heard that you inherited the Townsend lake house."

"That's still in question."

"I heard Tucker Manning's laying claim to the place as well."

"You hear a lot."

"I keep my ear to the ground and my nose in the wind."

"You're quite the contortionist."

He laughed.

Jillian canted her head, trying to figure out his angle.

"You know," he said, "if it turns out the lake house

really does belong to Tuck, I've got a gorgeous place I could show you up on Thunder Mountain."

Ah, so this was really why he'd come over to her. Somehow she immediately liked him better, because he was trying to sell her some property instead of getting into her pants.

"That's good to know. I'll keep that in mind, Jefferson. Thanks for the information." She sent him her friendliest, "you're dismissed" expression.

He gave her another thousand-watt smile. "There's something else I was wondering about . . ."

"Oh yeah?"

"I've heard . . . I mean, it's none of my business . . . but there's a rumor going around . . ."

Jillian straightened and met his eyes. "What do you want to ask me, Jefferson?"

"Tucker's living in the house with you?"

"Uh-huh."

"With you, with you?"

"Excuse me?"

"I mean . . . . umm . . . uh . . . do you two have a thing going on?"

"We're roommates."

"That's it?"

"We're friends."

"And . . . er . . . nothing else?"

Jillian thought about the kiss Tuck had given her, and she plastered a smile on her face. It had been fourteen days since she and Tuck had walked home from the Rusty Nail together. Fourteen days since he'd kissed her in the foyer of the lake house. Fourteen days since he'd set her blood to boiling and her head to reeling. And nothing else had happened since then. Until today. Until their fight.

She knew how many days it had been, because she'd counted every last one of them by the hour. "Nope, nothing else."

"Then the speculation around town that you two are an item is just speculation?"

The last thing Jillian wanted was to add to the Salvation rumor mill. "Total fabrication."

"I thought so," Jefferson said. "I mean, Tuck is so hung up on his late wife. Some say he'll never get over her."

"Do tell."

"Yeah, he brought her to Salvation and became a carpenter even though he was making big bucks as an architect, just because she used to enjoy spending summers here as a kid. He gave up everything for her and then she died anyway. Stupid move, if you ask me, derailing your career like that."

"I think it sounds incredibly sweet and loving."

"That's why they say he'll never get over her. No one can take Aimee's place."

"I see."

"So you're unattached?" Jefferson leaned against the counter, and his eyes brightened.

A twinge of emotion that she couldn't identify knotted up tight against her rib cage. Jillian wasn't much interested in going out with Jefferson Baines, but that emotion—whatever the hell it was—had her holding up her bare ring finger. "Free as a bird."

He let out an audible breath, and that was the first time Jillian realized Jefferson was nervous about chatting her up. She softened a bit toward him. She knew some men found her intimidating. Her height and what Tuck called her regal appearance were the culprits. She had donned her queenly armor when Jefferson approached. Giving him the silver-cool tone she used when offering plea-bargain deals to defense lawyers, and he'd managed to hold his ground.

She felt a little sorry for him then and understood he wasn't as slick and glossy as he wanted to appear. She asked him to sit down and join her for a cup of coffee. He readily agreed. Jillian tried to take the real estate agent seriously, but whenever she looked at him, all she could think was *faux wood.*

And then she immediately thought of Tuck and envisioned smooth, hard, rich mahogany.

"So, what do you say?" Jefferson asked.

It was only then that she realized he'd asked her a question, and she had been so busy thinking about Tuck's favorite hardwood she hadn't heard. His head was cocked to one side, and he was looking at her earnestly, waiting for an answer to his question.

"Sure," Jillian said, pretending she knew what he was talking about.

Jefferson beamed. "Great. That's really great."

Crap, apparently she'd just agreed to something. But what?

Jillian smiled so as not to hurt his feelings if he realized she hadn't heard a word he said. "So, to recap . . ."

"I'll pick you up at seven Friday night."

She nodded, keeping the smile going. Apparently she'd just accepted a date with him. Well, fine. It was a good thing. Clearly nothing was going to happen with Tuck, and that was fine. She didn't want anything to happen with Tuck. She didn't want anything to happen with Jefferson, either, for that matter, but it didn't hurt to get out of the house. Especially since she and Tuck were around each other constantly.

"Jillian?" Jefferson asked.

"Right. Seven o'clock, Friday night. It's a date."

NEITHER ONE OF THEM mentioned what had happened on Saturday. They kept things light. Jillian spent what little time she hung around the house upstairs, while Tuck stayed downstairs. They barely saw each other. Which was perfect. Or so she told herself.

On Friday morning, Jillian got up earlier than usual, because Sutter actually had a new client coming into the office at seven-thirty to draft a will. She found Tuck at the bistro table eating scrambled eggs. He didn't offer to make her any.

She reached for a box of corn flakes from the cabinet, along with a spoon and a bowl, and came back to sit down across from him.

"Good morning," she said.

"Good morning." He didn't look up from the copy of *Sports Illustrated* he was reading.

She got up again to pour herself some coffee. "You want another cup?"

"I'm good."

"How's the ankle?" She sat back down, dismayed to see her corn flakes had already gone soggy.

"Couldn't be better."

"Did you let Mutt out?"

"Fed him too." He flipped the page of his magazine without ever looking up.

He looked so damned complacent that she had an irresistible urge to rattle his cage. "I'm meeting Jefferson Baines for dinner, so I won't be home until late."

Tuck's fork stopped halfway to his mouth, but he acted only mildly interested. "Oh yeah?"

"Yes." She couldn't quite meet his gaze. "He asked me out. We're going on a date."

"Have fun." He picked up his fork and went back to his eggs.

Disappointment curled inside her. "That's all you're going to say?"

"What? You want me to tell you not to go?"

"No, I just figured that you'd have something smart-ass to say about faux wood."

"I've already told you my opinion on Jefferson Baines. No need to repeat myself."

"So you don't care if I date him?" She left the bistro table to toss her soggy cornflakes into the sink.

"Why should I care? You're a grown woman. Date away."

"Fine. I will."

"Are you mad at me?"

"No, no." God, what was she saying? She was practically begging him to ask her not to go out with Jefferson. "Why would I be mad?"

"Great. Glad to hear it."

"Perfect, I'll just go, then."

"Have a good time."

"You can bet I will."

"Watch out for the Viagra."

"What?"

"Faux wood and all that." Tuck winked.

"You can be quite infuriating, you know that?"

"Right back at you," he said.

Jillian snatched up her purse and marched for the back door. Something, she didn't know what, told her to glance back over her shoulder.

She caught him, his eyes off the magazine and totally focused on her. What knocked her off guard was the way he was looking at her—as if a house he'd invested months in designing and building had just gone on the market.

TUCK COULDN'T BELIEVE JILLIAN was going out with Baines. If that's the kind of artificial show-off she went for, no wonder she'd never been in love.

"What do you care?" he growled under his breath as he pulled into the parking space at the Peabody Mansion. After he'd broken his ankle, he delayed the jobs that required going up on ladders. Sutter had told him to take his time getting back to repairing the old Victorian. His ankle wasn't a hundred percent, but Doc Couts had taken the cast off the day before, and he was healing well enough to get back to work. Especially since Ridley had promised to drop by and help him when he finished an electrical job he had on the other side of town. He was ready for this.

Or so he told himself. What he didn't admit was that he couldn't wait to be around Jillian again.

He went inside.

"Hey, Tuck, how's the ankle?" Lexi greeted him from the doorway of her flooring store.

"Much better, Lex, thanks." He looked at her, and she smiled at him kindly. Too kindly.

"I heard Jillian's going out with Jefferson," she said.

Ah, that explained the look on her face. She was feeling sorry for him. "Yeah," he said. "I heard the same thing."

"You're not jealous?" Lexi asked.

He shrugged. "Why would I be jealous?"

"Aren't you two sort of seeing each other?"

"No." He waved a hand. "Why? Did Jillian tell you that we were seeing each other?"

Lexi shook her head. "I just sort of assumed it. Since you were living together—"

"That's strictly by necessity," he rushed to interrupt her before she got any further. He didn't want any rumors starting. "Until this property dispute is settled. We're just roommates. It's strictly platonic."

"Are you sure? Because the way she looks at you sometimes . . ."

That pulled him up short. "Huh? How does Jillian look at me?"

"Kind of wistful. And lusty. Like she wants to jump your bones but she's afraid to get too close."

"Naw. You've misinterpreted the look. She's not interested in me that way," he insisted. "We're just friends."

Friends, huh? More like adversaries who drive each other crazy with sexual chemistry.

"Are you sure?" Lexi prodded.

"Positive."

"So then you're free tomorrow night?"

That gave him pause. "Why, Lexi Kilgore, are you asking me out?"

"Well, maybe, kind of. You see, I have this gift card

to Thunder Mountain Lodge, and it expires tomorrow if I don't use it, and there goes the fifty bucks for my last birthday from Gramma Louise. I really don't want to go alone. I was going to ask Jillian, but now she's going out with Jefferson."

"Is this a pity date?"

"Hey, you'll get a free meal."

Tuck looked at her. Lexi had always been nice to him. For three or four months after Aimee died, she had brought him casseroles once a week. She was a sweet woman with a bubbly personality, and if he hadn't been so broken up over losing his wife, they might have already gone out. Why not accept her invitation? Jillian was going out with Jefferson; he could have a date too.

"Lexi, I'd enjoy having dinner with you tomorrow night."

BY THE TIME Tuck got home from work, it was just after five o'clock. He and Ridley had spent the day replacing the Sheetrock in the ceiling of Sutter's office, but to his surprise, Jillian had left the building right after they'd started work, and she hadn't come back. So he was relieved to see her Sebring in the driveway when he arrived.

He walked in the door and heard the shower running. The sound of it—and the image that popped into his head of Jillian standing naked under the running water—caused his heart to thump loudly in his ears. The cottage had only one bathroom. He'd been planning on adding a second, but now he was glad he hadn't.

Sauntering into the hallway, he stripped off his shirt and tossed it into the built-in hamper. Okay, so it was an obvious move, but he wanted her to get an eyeful of his bare chest when she came out of the bathroom.

The water shut off.

A couple minutes later—while Tuck stood around trying to act like he'd just taken his shirt off—the bathroom door opened. Jillian emerged in a white bathrobe with her hair twisted up in a blue towel. In her hands, she held a pair of red silk thong panties.

She looked up, let out a little shriek, and fisted the panties in her hand. His groin tightened. "What the hell are you doing lurking in the hallway?"

"Had a dirty job today. I need a shower."

"That gives you the right to skulk?"

"It's my house. I can skulk if I want to."

"That's up for debate. It's been five weeks and still no deed. It's past time to get Blake's will probated."

"I wasn't skulking." He noticed her gaze skipped over his bare chest.

"Now you're a liar as well as a skulker." She seemed to just now remember she was holding the skimpy red panties. Quickly, she stuffed them in the pocket of her bathrobe.

"You wearing those for Jefferson Baines?" God, why had he said that? Now she was going to think that he was jealous. Which he was, but he didn't want her knowing it.

"What if I am?"

He stepped closer, blood racing, heart pounding so hard he was afraid she could hear it. He smelled the cucumbery scent of her shampoo. A droplet of water trailed down her neck. He watched it slide over her skin and disappear between her breasts. So far, he'd consciously avoided showering when she did. Usually, she showered in the mornings, and he took the evening. But tonight, she had a date, so she'd changed her routine. All to his advantage. She couldn't fault him. She was the one who'd gone off their schedule.

Jillian stood her ground. She wasn't easily intimidated. Her eyes met his, and she watched him warily as he walked toward the door.

And grazed her breast with his elbow.

She sucked in her breath. "Hey!"

"Sorry for the accidental boob graze."

"Accidental my ass—you did that on purpose."

"If you don't like getting your boob grazed, maybe you shouldn't stand in the hallway wearing nothing but a bathrobe."

"I don't get it," she said. "This morning you couldn't seem to care less that I was going out with Jefferson."

"I don't." He took in the haughty slope of her shoulders. The regal way she held her head. How the hallway light reflected a soft glow off the creamy complexion of her skin. Damn, but she was beautiful and sexy as hell. He kept thinking about what she'd look like in that red thong and how he'd like to be the one to take her out of them.

"Then why are you here? You know I'm getting ready for a date. Why not go to the Bluebird or the Rusty Nail until I'm out of the house?"

"Because," he said. "I have a date as well."

Chapter Fifteen

Jefferson told Jillian he'd made dinner reservations at Thunder Lodge on Thunder Mountain. It took almost an hour to drive the fifteen miles of winding mountain roads to the ski resort.

On the drive in his late-model black Lexus, Jefferson tried to engage Jillian in idle chitchat, which she didn't hear a word of because she kept thinking about Tuck and how he'd looked standing bare-chested in the hallway. It was the first time she'd seen him undressed since the morning she'd walked in and found him sleeping on the couch.

There was no doubt about it—the man had world-class pecs and biceps. He could be a swimsuit model if he so desired. She licked her lips, remembering how he'd looked standing there with the shadow of the bathroom door falling over him, the play of light delineating the striation of his muscles.

What in the hell had gotten into him? Was he jealous? She scarcely dared hope. Did he really have a date? Or had he made it all up?

When she thought about Tuck out on a date, *she* felt jealous. The first time he dates since his wife's death and it wasn't with her. Why did she want it so badly to be her?

"Do you like the music?" Jefferson asked.

For the first time, Jillian realized Vivaldi was spilling one of his seasons out of the stereo system. Why did she have a sudden craving to hear the Lovin' Spoonful sing "Do You Believe in Magic?"

"Lexi told me you like classical," Jefferson confessed. "She suggested Vivaldi."

"How kind of you to play it for me and to think to ask Lexi what kind of music I like." She smiled. "That's very considerate."

"I do my research when I take a lady out."

God, he sounded so cheesy. What was taking them so damned long to get to Thunder Mountain? "Uh-huh."

"See that house up there?" Jefferson pointed to a sprawling split-level log cabin hidden in the mountains.

"Mmm-hmm."

"I sold it as a summer place to Wolfgang Puck's nephew," he said proudly.

"That must have been interesting."

"He gave me a gift certificate to Wolfgang's restaurant for the next time I'm in Vegas. Would you like to go to Vegas with me sometime? You know, what happens in Vegas . . ."

"Stays in Vegas," she finished for him. "Yes, I've heard the slogan."

Jefferson swiveled his head and winked at her. "So, what do you say about a trip to Sin City? We could stay at the MGM Grand. Catch Blue Man Group onstage?"

"Let's see how one date goes."

"Gotcha."

It was all Jillian could do to keep from rolling her eyes. She shifted in the seat, angling her body away from his, and stared out the window to while away the time while Jefferson gave her a running commentary on who owned the houses they passed, how much the houses were worth, and who was likely or unlikely to have property on the market soon. The guy knew his business. She had to give him brownie points for that.

They rounded a curve, and in the rearview mirror, Jillian caught a glimpse of a pickup behind them that looked exactly like Tuck's. Her pulse accelerated. Was he following them?

But that was stupid. Tuck drove the number-one selling pickup truck in America. In silver, the most common color for vehicles. The chances of Tuck being behind them were very slim. So why did she feel a sudden burst of excitement?

Because you're starting to get hung up on the guy.

She wasn't. Was she?

She waited for the next curve to even out to see if she could catch another glimpse behind them, but the road just kept spiraling upward.

Be real. Why would Tuck be behind you?

Well, there was only one road up the mountain, and he'd said he had a date. It wasn't as if Salvation was flush with great first-date places. Most likely, anyone headed out for a date would go to either Boulder or up to Thunder Mountain, and the mountain had the better view.

"Almost there," Jefferson said, and reached across the car to touch her arm.

She drew back.

"Sorry," he apologized. "Did I overstep my boundaries?"

Jillian forced a smile. Honestly, he wasn't a bad guy, just overeager and not at all her type. "I've just been a little tense lately."

"Well, tonight is your night to relax. Thunder Lodge is known for their excellent wine list and romantic ambiance."

"Good to know." The thought of getting snockered was appealing, but the last thing she wanted was to lose her edge around Jefferson. He hadn't tried anything funny yet, but he had said that stupid crap about Vegas.

"Lily Massey and Bill Chambers are getting married up here."

"So I've heard. I've been invited."

"Really? You wanna go together?"

"One date at a time, Jefferson."

"Gotcha."

They arrived at the restaurant at last. Jefferson tossed his keys to the valet and offered her his arm, trying his best to be a good date. But Jillian just wasn't in the mood to appreciate his efforts. As he escorted her into the building, she couldn't help glancing over her shoulder to see if Tuck's pickup had arrived.

"This way," Jefferson said, and ushered her inside before she had time to see who was coming up the mountain.

The restaurant was quite elegant. White linen tablecloths. The waitstaff attired in traditional black uniforms with white aprons. A maître d' who seated them right away at a spectacular table by the window overlooking the ski run. An impressive wine list just as Jefferson had promised.

There was night skiing at the resort, and from where

they were seated, they could watch skiers sluice down the mountain. Fun classic rock from the fifties and sixties was being played on the slopes, and they could hear it inside the restaurant. It was a great place with the proper romantic atmosphere. The only trouble was, Jillian kept wishing she was there with someone else.

Tuck.

Just as the waiter arrived to take their drink orders, Jillian looked up from her menu to see Tuck and Lexi walk in. Her stomach lurched.

In his suit and tie, Tuck stole her breath away, and she had to admit Lexi looked quite lovely in a lavender skirt and blouse set. A waiter steered them toward the opposite side of the room, but Lexi headed their way. Tuck looked surprised and followed her over.

"Hello," Lexi greeted, sauntering up to their table. "Imagine running into you guys here."

Tuck clamped a hand on Jefferson's shoulder. "How you doing, buddy?"

"Tuck," Jefferson said. "I didn't know you and Lexi were dating."

Lexi beamed. "It's the first time we've gone out."

"Hey, why don't we all eat together?" Tuck suggested.

Jillian rummaged in her mind for an excuse why they should not share a table, but Lexi clapped her hands in that endearing way of hers and said, "Oh yes, that would be so fun."

Tuck was already pulling out Lexi's chair for her. Jillian shot him a withering glance. He grinned at her. She glared.

The waiter hovered.

"Instead of two glasses of cabernet," Jefferson instructed, "go ahead and bring us a bottle." Then he turned to Tuck. "This is our first date as well."

"Really?" Tuck popped open his linen napkin and spread it across his lap, all the while keeping his eyes trained on Jillian.

Lexi leaned over and whispered behind her palm to Jillian, "This is so much fun. Me being out with Tuck, you with Jefferson."

The excitement in her new friend's voice made Jillian glower at Tuck. What was he pulling? "Don't expect too much," Jillian whispered back, desperate to protect Lexi. "This is his first date since Aimee."

"Don't worry," Lexi whispered. "I know what I'm doing."

Jealousy, sharp and unexpected, sliced into her. From the ski slopes came the sound of "Do You Believe in Magic?"

"Hey," Tuck said. "They're playing our song."

Jillian stared at him. "Our song?"

"Your song?" Lexi raised an eyebrow.

"You have a song?" Jefferson asked.

"Yeah." Tuck held Jillian's gaze. "It was playing on the radio when we had our first fight. Remember?"

Oh, she remembered, all right. "That doesn't make it our song."

"It makes me think of our first fight. Doesn't that qualify as our song?"

"You can only have a song if you're a couple," Jillian said. "We're not a couple."

Several long minutes passed. Then the waiter returned with wine and took their food orders. Tuck and Jillian ordered filet mignon cooked medium. Jefferson and Lexi ordered the pheasant.

Jillian was sitting directly across from Tuck, and in spite of herself, she couldn't help noticing how sexy he looked freshly shaven and smelling of manly cologne. Jefferson's cologne had a floral undercurrent, but Tuck's was woodsy, earthy. She'd never seen him dressed in anything but flannel and jeans except for on the cover of *Architectural Digest*.

His eyes met hers across the table as if he could read her mind. He gave her a short, sly smile, and she felt as if she'd been lit on fire. White-hot embers of desire that had been burning inside her from the moment they had met sparked, flared.

When the bread basket came, Tuck and Jillian reached for it at the same time, and their hands touched. The heat of his hand short-circuited her hormones and she burned.

Yes. *Burned.*

For Tuck.

Blindly, she left the roll in the basket, drew her hand back, and reached for her wineglass instead. She took a big gulp, trying senselessly to put out the brushfire rolling through her.

"So tell us, Jefferson, what big real estate deals are you working on?" Tuck asked, smoothly buttering his bread, but the whole time he was talking and buttering, his gaze was on her. His whiskey-colored eyes were luminous, the pupils dilated in the candlelight. He parted his lush lips and very sensuously took a bite of bread.

"Well, Tuck . . ." Jefferson launched off on his latest project while Lexi asked eager questions.

But Jillian wasn't listening to Jefferson babble. All she could do was look at Tuck and think, *I want this man.*

Lexi fueled the conversation when talking houses turned into specifics and she got down to flooring and window treatments.

"What do you think of laminate flooring, Lexi?" Tuck asked, but he was still looking at Jillian.

She shot him a knock-it-off look.

Simultaneously, he slightly lifted his eyes and his shoulders.

"Laminate definitely has its place," Lexi said.

"Thank you." Jefferson raised his fork. "A lot of people look down their noses at laminate, but when you have three cats like I do, you appreciate something that, while looking like hardwood, is actually much more practical."

"Really?" Lexi's eyes widened. "I have three cats as well—Mandi, Andi, and Moe."

"Faux wood," Tuck mouthed to Jillian.

Jillian swung her foot and kicked Tuck under the table.

"Ow!"

"Oops, sorry, clumsy me."

"Watch the pointy-toed shoes, Queenie. My ankle still isn't one hundred percent."

"Queenie?" Lexi asked.

"Her nickname," Tuck explained.

"It's not my nickname," Jillian said hotly. "It's the insult Tuck likes to irritate me with."

"It's not an insult. If I was insulting you, I'd call you a bathroom hog."

"I don't hog the bathroom."

"I disagree. When I went to shower for my date with Lexi, guess what—no hot water."

"So you had to take a cold shower. Poor baby."

"Bathroom hog."

"Cry baby."

"Um . . . my pheasant is delicious," Lexi said to Jefferson. "How's yours?"

"Wonderful. So with three cats, what kind of flooring do you have?" Jefferson asked.

Tuck was glaring at her. Was he mad? He's the one who'd started this whole mess. Now here he was ruining dinner.

"Could you guys excuse me a minute? I need to make a phone call," Jillian said.

"Hurry back." Jefferson smiled.

Jillian darted to the alcove near the restroom; from here, she could see Tuck sitting at the table. She got out her cell phone and called his number.

He answered at the table.

"What in the hell are you doing?" she demanded.

"Hang on a minute." While she watched, he lowered the phone, said something to Lexi and Jefferson, then pushed back his chair, got up, and started sauntering toward her, all grin and swagger.

"Okay," he said into the phone, his eyes on her face across the length of the restaurant. "I'm back."

"What in the hell are you doing here?"

"Last time I checked, it's still a free country. You don't own Thunder Mountain." The closer he came to where she huddled in the alcove, the wider his grin grew.

"You asked Lexi out to make me jealous," Jillian accused.

"I did not," Tuck huffed. "Lexi asked me out."

"You are such a liar."

"She did. Go ask her. She had a birthday gift card to Thunder Lodge that was about to expire."

"You expect me to believe that coincidentally on the same day I was going out with Jefferson, Lexi had a gift card to the same restaurant where he was taking me?"

"It's the truth."

Was it? Tuck didn't seem the kind of guy who'd be unkind enough to ask Lexi out simply to use her as an excuse to spoil Jillian's date.

"Besides," he said, "you went out with Jefferson to make me jealous."

"I did not. I accidentally got roped into this."

"That might be true, but you sure went to a lot of trouble to make sure I knew all about it." Closer and closer he sauntered, those whiskey eyes drilling into her like lasers.

Jillian backed up. "Lexi's going to think you're interested in her."

"I'll make sure she knows we're just friends."

"Like we're just friends."

"Yeah." His voice was husky.

Tuck kept coming, looking at her as if he were stripping her clothes off with his eyes. What had happened to the man in mourning she'd been living with for the past several weeks?

Gone was the emotional barrier he'd erected. Hell, gone was any respect for her physical space as he walked right up to her, taking the cell phone from his ear and snapping it closed just as her butt bumped the wall behind her.

"You're being rude," she said. "Leaving your date alone."

"You left the table first. Your date is just as alone as mine." He was standing toe-to-toe with her, his mouth merely inches away. "And you kicked me. Now, that was rude."

She had an overwhelming urge to reach up, grab him by that expensive tie that looked like a holdover from his Magic Man days, tug him into the bathroom, and make out with him.

If it hadn't been for the waiter who came up behind Tuck, she might very well have done just that.

The waiter coughed.

Tuck swiveled his head but kept his body angled in Jillian's direction. "Yes?"

"Um, sir, the rest of your party left."

"Yeah?"

The waiter extended the check and cleared his throat. "They said you'd be paying the tab."

"SO WHAT HAPPENED LAST NIGHT?" Jillian asked Lexi the next morning. She stopped by the flooring store with Styrofoam cups filled with hot coffee and cream puffs from the Bluebird as a peace offering.

"Evie's cream puffs!" Lexi squealed and bit into one. "Oh, yummy. Thank you."

Jillian rested her hip against the edge of Lexi's counter and crossed her arms over her chest. "So, about last night . . . ?"

Lexi giggled and wiped powdered sugar from the end of her nose with the back of her hand. "That was rude of

Jefferson and me running out and leaving you with the check. I do apologize."

"No, no, it was rude of Tuck and me to go off and leave you guys at the table. Honestly, Lex, we didn't mean to hurt your feelings."

Lexi blinked at her. "What do you mean? My feelings weren't hurt."

"I thought you and Tuck . . . that you were interested in him."

Lexi laughed.

Puzzled, Jillian canted her head. "What's so funny?"

"I asked Tuck to take me to Thunder Mountain, because I was jealous of you dating Jefferson."

"You like Jefferson?"

"For ages. And in the two years he's lived on the mountain, he's never really noticed me. Sure, he comes in here and talks shop, but he's never seen me as anything more than a flooring supplier. Until last night." Her eyes sparkled.

"You don't have a crush on Tuck?"

"No."

"Really? I sort of thought you did."

"He's good-looking, sure, and very sexy but . . ." Lexi shook her head.

"But?"

"Tuck's a one-woman man."

"You mean he'll never get over Aimee?" An emotion she couldn't name burned Jillian's stomach.

"I mean he's a one-woman man," Lexi repeated. "I'm sorry you guys had a lousy time at dinner."

"We didn't have a lousy time."

"You two were fighting like cats and dogs."

"Fighting?" Jillian suppressed a laugh. Fighting was the last thing they'd been doing. Flirting like mad and having sex with their eyes across the table was more like it.

"Then when Jeff asked me—"

"Wait, wait, I thought he didn't let anyone call him Jeff."

"I told him that Jefferson was too stuffy. He looks like a big cuddly Jeff to me."

"Ookay." The man looked neither cuddly nor like a Jeff to Jillian, but there was no accounting for taste.

"Anyway, when Jeff asked me if I wanted to go back to his place and just let you guys fight it out, I couldn't resist. I hope you're not too upset about the tab thing. It was Jefferson's idea. And I have to admit, it felt kind of naughty." Lexi giggled again.

"No, no, no problem. We didn't mind paying. Tuck and I just . . . we were . . ."

"I know." Lexi nodded. "Embarrassed by your behavior."

That wasn't what she was going to say, but it would do.

"Guess what?" Lexi touched Jillian's forearm and lowered her voice. "Jeff and I had sex until dawn. I'm worn out, but I've never been happier."

AFTER THAT NIGHT at Thunder Lodge, things between Tuck and Jillian shifted. Rather than avoiding each other as they had been doing, they started spending more time together as renovations on the lake house progressed.

While they worked, they talked about all kind of things—politics, religion, celebrities, architecture, pet care, carpentry, and law. The only topics off limits were

Tuck's marriage and Jillian's childhood. She'd never been comfortable discussing it. In fact, Blake was the only one who'd known the entire sordid story.

Through their discussions, Jillian and Tuck got to know each other better and found out they had a lot more in common than they'd ever suspected. They both loved water parks and Rocky Road ice cream. They agreed George W. Bush was the worst president ever to hold the title commander in chief and that Craig Ferguson was much funnier than Conan O'Brien. They admitted recycling was a great thing to do, but they were both a bit lazy about it.

They discovered they shared an obsession with Court TV, and they enjoyed amateur stargazing. They had each seen *Les Miserables* on Broadway six times and realized to their surprise, that on one occasion, they'd actually been at the same theater showing. Tuck told her stories about what it was like growing up with three older sisters, while Jillian regaled him with tales of law school. He took her shopping for some "decent"—as he put it—winter clothing, declaring none of the things she'd brought from Texas would hold up to a Colorado snowstorm.

Every passing evening as they painted and hammered and plastered and tiled and talked, the house slowly began to take shape. Then on the Sunday before Thanksgiving, Tuck issued an invitation.

"Evie's having our annual family Thanksgiving feast at her house and you're invited," he said as they were putting new baseboards up in the living room.

In truth, she hadn't thought much about the upcoming holiday or how she would spend it. Usually, she hung out with Delaney, Tish, and Rachael, but this year, they all had their own celebrations, and she was so far away that when they'd called to invite her, she'd turned them down.

"You can meet my entire family."

That both pleased and intimidated her. "I don't know . . . ," she hedged.

"Come on," he said. "It'll be fun."

"You really want me there?"

"Not just me," he said. "Evie and Ridley too."

"Okay," she said, "I'll come."

Then Tuck rewarded her with a smile that lit up her heart, and she realized what a very dangerous thing that was.

Chapter Sixteen

Tuck had to admit he was nervous about bringing Jillian to Thanksgiving dinner. He didn't want anyone reading anything into the gesture, other than the fact that he and Jillian were simply roommates and good friends who enjoyed spending time together.

He'd told her about Evie's invitation because he couldn't stand the thought of her being alone. At least that's what he told himself. The truth was, he wanted her there. Wanted her with him, but he wasn't ready to face the implications of that desire, so he blocked it out.

But when his big family got together, he knew they could be a bit overwhelming. He and Jillian stood on Evie's front porch. He had Evie's music box to give to Ridley wrapped up in newspaper. He'd held on to the box until he'd received the musical apparatus programmed to play "Faith" that he'd ordered online. He'd installed it the day before.

Jillian had two bottles of wine tucked under her arm. Her contribution to the festivities because, as she'd told him in the truck on the way over, she didn't cook and who could compete with Evie on that score anyway?

Tuck leaned over to ring the doorbell.

"Wait, wait." She placed a restraining hand on his wrist. "How do I look?"

His gaze trailed over her, and he couldn't help but think how breathtaking she was. "Fabulous."

"No, really." She smoothed out the front of her burgundy dress with her palm. "The neckline isn't too low, is it?"

"It's perfect. They're going to love you."

Nervously, Jillian flicked out her tongue to moisten her lips. "How can you be so sure?"

Tuck reached out to give her forearm a comforting squeeze. "You've put away some of the toughest felons in Texas, Queenie. I assure you that you can handle my family."

"Yes, but I wasn't worried about impressing the felons of Texas."

"You don't have to impress them. Just be yourself."

"Okay." She took a deep breath and tucked a strand of hair behind her ear. "Go ahead. Ring the bell. I'm ready to run the gauntlet."

He couldn't help but be touched that she cared so much about what his family thought of her that it affected her emotional equilibrium. He'd never seen her looking so vulnerable. It made him want to put his arm around her waist and protect her from any and everyone. The impulse surprised him.

"Jillian," he whispered as he heard the door open. "Don't worry, sweetheart. Whatever happens, I've got your back."

HAD TUCK JUST CALLED HER SWEETHEART?

Jillian shook her head and blinked, unable to believe

her ears. Why had he called her sweetheart? Had he just slipped up? Or was there some hidden meaning to it?

But there was no time to ponder the questions. Ridley was greeting them at the door and ushering them over the threshold. Jillian stepped inside, and immediately her senses were assaulted with the sights, smells, and sounds of a large extended family gathered for a holiday celebration. Ridley took their coats and Jillian handed him the two bottles of Chardonnay she'd brought.

The dining room table was laden with food. Two gigantic turkeys. An industrial-size pan filled with cornbread stuffing, along with a serving tureen of giblet gravy. Side dishes galore—candied yams, fruit salads, vegetable casseroles, deviled eggs, mashed potatoes, macaroni and cheese, yeast rolls and cranberry sauce. And on the sideboard a bounty of desserts. Chocolate cake, peach cobbler, oatmeal cookies, and pies—apple, pumpkin, pecan, French silk, cherry, and rhubarb. There were soft drinks and lemonade for the kids. Wine, tea, and coffee for the adults.

The air was thick with the dizzying smells of sage and roasted turkey and cinnamon and nutmeg and onions and butter and garlic.

A half-dozen kids cavorted underfoot, giggling and running and playing tag. In the living room, the television was tuned to a college football game, and there were several men gathered around it.

Tuck took her by the elbow and introduced her. She met his father, James, who looked so much like Tuck it took her breath away. It was like having a snapshot into his future. Apparently at sixty, Tuck was still going to be a stunningly handsome man. She also said hello to Tuck's other brothers-in-law, Steve and Magnus. Steve, a native New Yorker, was of stocky build and average height, and he was as dark as Swedish-born Magnus was blond.

Next, Tuck took her to the kitchen. She shook hands with his other two sisters, Desiree and Sabrina. They looked a lot like Evie, both slender with classic features. Tuck's mom, Meredith, insisted on giving her a hug.

"And this is Grandmother Fairfield," Tuck said, taking her over to meet the matriarch of the clan. "We just call her Gran."

The minute Jillian laid eyes on the older woman, she knew this was who she had to prove herself to. She had to be in her mid-eighties, but her eyes were still sharp even though her shoulders were stooped.

"Tuck," Ridley said from the doorway of the kitchen. "Can I borrow you a minute to help me set up the extra table for the kids?"

"Sure thing," Tuck said, and then abandoned Jillian to his womenfolk. So much for having her back.

RIDLEY FURTIVELY PULLED TUCK into the garage and eyed the box nestled in the crook of his arm. "Is that it?"

"It is."

"Hang on." He locked the garage door so they wouldn't be interrupted by inquisitive nieces and nephews. He couldn't believe how nervous he was. The fact that Tuck had taken so long over the music box heightened his anxiety. He wanted this gift to be special. Tuck was a talented carpenter, but Ridley knew he'd never crafted anything like this before.

Tuck unwrapped the music box from the newspaper. Ridley held his breath.

"Your hands are shaking," Tuck said.

"Hell, I know." Ridley's voice was gruff.

"Don't drop it." Tuck settled the gleaming wooden box in his hands.

Ridley just stared. It far exceeded his expectations. The craftsmanship was exquisite, but more than that, it was as if Tuck has read his mind. Gently, he pushed his big thumb against the delicate cradle atop the music box. It swayed softly. A lump humped up in his throat. "Dude . . ."

"You like it?"

"Evie's gonna cry when she sees it."

"Is it what you wanted?"

"Dude . . . ," he said again. There was nothing else he could say. Evie was going to love the music box, and hopefully she would understand what he was trying to tell her with it. He carefully opened the box, and the cradle rocked as it played "Faith."

Just then, someone rapped on the garage door. "Rid? You need some help out there?"

It was Steve. Ridley unlocked the door, let him into the garage, and locked it behind him.

"What are you guys doing out here so clandestinely? Sneaking a smoke?" He looked hopeful.

"Gave it up," Ridley said. "Supposedly it lowers your sperm count."

"Hey, what's that?" Steve honed in on the music box cradle.

"Evie's Christmas present. That's what we were doing out here."

"That's beautiful." Steve reached for it. "Do you mind?"

Ridley handed it to him.

Steve traced a finger over the intricate scroll carvings. "Where'd you get it? This is first-class woodwork."

Ridley jerked a thumb at Tuck.

Steve's eyes met Tuck's. "You did this?"

"I was laid up with a broken ankle."

"This is amazing. I mean, I knew you were a talented carpenter, but damn, Tuck, you could make a mint off these."

"It's not that big of a deal," Tuck said.

Ridley wanted to poke him and tell him not to be so modest.

"I'm serious," Steve said. "I know a guy. Owns a gallery in SoHo. This might not be his thing, but I'm sure he can refer you to someone who would know how to represent it."

"Hey," Ridley said to Tuck. "You could have a whole new career."

"Rid, you mind if I take this back to the city with me? Show it to my guy, see if he's interested?" Steve asked.

"You better ask Tuck if he's interested."

"Well?" Steve arched his eyebrows.

Tuck shrugged. "It's Ridley's box."

Steve looked at Ridley again.

Ridley didn't want to part with the box, but if Steve could help get Tuck back in the mainstream flow of life, he'd make the sacrifice. "Just make damn sure you get it back to me safe and sound so I can give it to Evie on Christmas."

"You guys are coming to New York for the holiday, right?"

"I don't know." He and Evie hadn't cemented their Christmas plans.

"That's what Meredith and Jim are planning."

"We'll play it by ear."

Steve slapped Tuck on the back. "Damn, man, I still can't believe how good you are. Mark my words, my friend is going to go ape over this. Looks like the old Manning magic is back."

"CAN I DO ANYTHING TO HELP?" Jillian offered, feeling like the odd woman out in the kitchen filled with family members.

"You can make the poppy-seed dressing for the spinach salad," Evie said. "The recipe and the ingredients are on top of the microwave."

Happy to have a chore, she moved purposefully to the microwave and started making the poppy-seed dressing, only to become aware that Grandmother Fairfield was staring at her.

"So you're Tuck's roommate, huh?" the old lady asked.

"Yes, ma'am."

Gran snorted. "Roommates," she muttered. "In my day, we called it shacking up."

"Mrs. Fairfield," Jillian rushed to assure her. "Tuck and I really are just roommates and friends."

"Hmph," Gran said. "Who you trying to kid? I see the way he's looking at you."

Her comments startled Jillian. How did Tuck look at

her? Had his grandmother already picked up on the sexual chemistry between them? To distract herself, she took the cap off the white-wine vinegar. "I can assure you our relationship is strictly platonic."

"Maybe for now . . ."

"Mom," Tuck's mother thankfully intervened, "would you like me to escort you to the table? Evie's just about ready to serve dinner."

"Sorry about Gran," Evie whispered as her mother took her grandmother into the other room. "She's got strong opinions."

"I understand," Jillian said, and busied herself with adding sugar and poppy seeds to the white-wine vinegar.

A few minutes later, everyone was seated at the table while Tuck's father said grace over their meal. Afterward, everyone dove in and started passing plates around the table. It was a warm and friendly atmosphere until Gran, who was eyeing Jillian from across the Thanksgiving spread, said, "You're nothing like Aimee, nothing at all."

"Mother!" Tuck's mom scolded, while several other people chided, "Gran!"

"Well, she's not."

Tuck reached for Jillian's hand under the table and gave it a squeeze. She was amazed at what that one gesture did to her heart.

"When are you and Ridley going to give us some grandbabies?" Meredith asked Evie, taking Jillian out of the hot seat and putting Tuck's sister squarely in it.

"We're working on it, Mom."

"You're thirty-five and the clock is ticking."

"We know, we know." Evie's smile was tight, strained.

Jillian immediately felt sorry for her and guessed that she hadn't told her family about her infertility issues.

"What's the problem?" Gran narrowed her eyes at Ridley. "You shootin' blanks?"

"Gran!" the entire room exclaimed.

"Everyone else tiptoes around the truth. I just call 'em like I see 'em. I'm eighty-five. I don't have the time or patience for hem-hawing."

"The turkey is delicious, Evie," Jillian said.

"Hem-hawer," Gran accused.

Jillian met the older woman's gaze. "You don't want me to hem-haw. Okay, I'm calling it like I see it. You're a rude old lady."

The entire collective gasped.

"Nope." Gran grinned mischievously. "She's not a thing like that goodie-two-shoes Aimee. So what's the deal between you two?" She wagged a wrinkled finger between Tuck and Jillian. "Is it true love or just sex?"

"Not that it's any of your business, Mrs. Fairfield, but I'm not having sex with your grandson."

"Must be true love, then."

"I don't believe in the concept of true love."

"You don't believe in true love?" Gran stared at Jillian as if she'd stepped off a spaceship from another planet.

Everyone else at the table was gaping at her as well.

"I think the concept of destined love is a myth perpetuated by fairy tales and greeting cards."

"Then stay far away from my grandson, missy. He's been kicked around by life enough in his short time on earth. He doesn't need to go falling for a woman who doesn't believe in true love."

"Well, if believing in true love makes a person as

cranky and bitter as you are, then I'm happy to do without it," Jillian said.

The entire roomful of people fell silent, including the kids. Everyone looked at one another. Suddenly Jillian realized how rude she'd sounded.

Dear God, what had she done? What had she said? Why had she said it? She had no idea how to maneuver in a family. She had no right to be here. Chagrined, Jillian pulled her hand from Tuck's, jumped up from the table, grabbed her coat off the rack by the door, and ran outside as fast as her legs could carry her.

HUMILIATION TIGHTENED JILLIAN'S FACE. She was a horrible, horrible person. Baiting an old lady.

She stood in Evie and Ridley's backyard, staring at the snow-covered mountains, breathing hard and trying to calm her racing heart. She could see the ski lodge from here. Thunder Mountain was a sprawling winter tourist destination, not far from Salvation as the crow flies, but a thousand miles difference in tone and flavor. Salvation did not possess the ubiquitous overpriced mountain gear shops or celebrity-owned boutiques or chain restaurants or sprawling condo expansions or new-age healing centers that had sprung up around the resort.

Jillian caught a glimpse of Tuck from her peripheral vision as he followed her out the back door. He stood behind her, two thermoses clasped in his gloved hands. She couldn't look at him.

She heard the snow crunch under his boots as he walked toward her, and she could feel the heat of his gaze stinging the back of her neck. She cringed at what he must be thinking of her right now.

The smell of Thanksgiving hung in the air, smoked turkeys and roasted chestnuts and cranberry sauce. Cornbread stuffing and green-bean casserole and glazed carrots. It smelled like home. It smelled like family. And it was more than clear that she didn't belong.

She thought about the way Tuck's family had looked at her, and she'd just known what they were thinking. *You can't replace Aimee.* What is this woman doing here? She's not one of us.

Jillian had never belonged.

Not with her mother. Not with her father and her stepfamily. Honestly, not even with her friends Delaney, Tish, and Rachael. Even with them, she'd held herself in reserve, never really fully letting down her guard. The only person she'd ever allowed herself to have a strong emotional connection with was Blake, and that was simply because he'd been as lonely as she was.

Jillian had thought she kept up her guard to protect herself from getting hurt. What she now realized was that she'd never let people in because she was afraid that if they knew who she really was deep down inside, they wouldn't want anything to do with her. She felt like such a fraud, dressed in festive clothes, pretending to be someone she was not. Pretending to be the kind of woman who could successfully navigate holiday family gatherings and be accepted.

What did Tuck see in her? Why did he want to be her friend?

"Jilly?" he murmured.

She turned. He extended a thermos toward her. A lump of emotion knotted her throat.

"Coffee. Black as pitch just the way you like it."

She took the warm thermos, clutched it in her hands, dipped her head, unable to meet his gaze. "I'm sorry for the way I behaved in there. I don't know what came over me. I can't imagine what your family must think of me . . . um . . . coming unhinged like that. I truly am sorry. I'm ashamed of myself."

"Jillian." Her name on his lips was a gentle reprimand. "Look at me."

She tilted her chin up and met his warm, unwavering gaze.

"You've got nothing to be ashamed of. For one thing, Gran had it coming. For another thing, you're as entitled to your opinion as anyone in that room. If anything, I'm ashamed of the way they behaved. I hope you'll forgive them. Normally they're really not like that. They're just all worried about me—"

"I know, I know. You lost the love of your life, but I feel sorry for whoever you end up marrying, Tuck, because she'll never be able to live up to the sainted Aimee."

Silence fell.

Jillian remembered the day of their first fight. It had been about Aimee. She gulped. "Tuck, I apologize. I shouldn't have said that."

"It's all right," he said, twisting open the top of his thermos and taking a sip. "Aimee wasn't perfect. She had her faults. It's easy to forget now that she's gone."

Jillian followed his lead and took a sip of her own. She hardly dared believe he was able to talk about Aimee without getting defensive. "Is it terrible of me to want to hear what her faults were?"

"Not terrible at all." He smiled, but it didn't reach his soulful whiskey eyes. "Simply human. Okay, here goes. Aimee stole the covers at night. I'd end up shivering on one side of the bed, and she'd have the blankets heaped on top of her and tumbling off over on the other side to the floor."

"A real blanket hog, huh?"

"And she had the most irritating habit of chomping the ice in her drink. Crunch, crunch, crunch. Drove me around the bend."

"Ice-chomping blanket hog. How did you stay out of divorce court?" Jillian dared to tease.

"And Aimee had this way of laughing that ended in a snorting sound. I thought it was cute when we were dating, but after a couple of years, it got a little annoying."

"You loved her terribly, didn't you?"

"Yeah," he admitted. "I did. But she's gone and I'm still here, and I gotta find a way to live with it. I don't want the next woman I marry to feel as if she has to compete with Aimee's memory."

"You're right. Whoever this woman is, she deserves all of you, Tuck, and I say this from my heart as your friend. You deserve to love again without fear of being hurt. Life hurts but you shouldn't avoid living to keep from feeling pain. For one thing, it doesn't work."

"No?" He never looked away, never even blinked.

"Hurt and pain will always find you. And secondly . . ."

"Yeah?"

"You gotta have the pain in order to appreciate the pleasure and the joy life has to offer. Life is filled with contrasts for a reason. Hate and love. Shadows and light. On and off. Up and down. It's the paradox of a dual universe."

"And you say you're not spiritual? You're sounding a lot like Deepak Chopra to me."

"Okay, so I've done some reading, some spiritual exploration."

"So what's your excuse, Jillian? Why aren't you out there doing the carpe diem thing when it comes to dating, romance, and love?"

"Because," she said, finally admitting it to herself as she admitted it to him. "I've been living so long in the shadows that I've lost the ability to see the light. I don't want you to get lost in the darkness, Tuck. I care about you too much to let that happen."

"You . . ." The expression in his eyes flared, but she couldn't really read the emotion there. "You care about me?"

"Of course I care about you. We're friends, right?"

"Yeah. That's right. Friends."

"Friends," she echoed.

"And you don't believe in true love."

She shook her head.

He nodded. "So if we're friends, how about going skiing with me on Saturday at Thunder Mountain?"

"Um . . ." Did she want to go?

"Friends have fun together. Correct?"

"I suppose they do."

"Then let's go have some fun. Just you and me."

"You sure your ankle is up to it?"

"It's been seven weeks since I broke it. No better time to find out what shape I'm really in."

The back door opened at that moment, and Evie came out on the steps, coatless, arms wrapped around her, turkey apron still tied at her waist. She was shivering against the wind. "Come inside, you guys. It's time for pie."

Chapter Seventeen

"I love the way Jillian lit into your grandmother." Ridley chuckled to Evie once all the guests were gone and they were cleaning up the kitchen together. Ridley was washing the dishes, Evie drying them. "The old gal has been allowed to run roughshod over your family for too long."

"I was mortified."

"For Jillian?"

"For you."

"For me?" He cast a glance at her. "What for?"

"That shooting-blanks comment."

"We both know that's not true."

"Yeah." Evie blew out her breath. "I'm the one with the problem."

"It's not a problem. We've only been trying for a year. We'll get there, honey. You're just putting too much pressure on yourself."

Evie didn't answer and instead industriously dried one of the turkey platters Ridley had just handed to her. She wished she shared his optimism. But she was going on thirty-six. Already, the days of her viable eggs were numbered.

"Jillian is one fiery pistol." Ridley chuckled. "I just

wonder how much longer she and Tuck can keep this platonic relationship going."

"Speaking of fiery pistols . . ." Evie tossed the cup towel aside and snaked her arms around Ridley's waist, babies burning on her brain. "What do you say we leave the dishes until tomorrow and call it a night?" She stood on tiptoes to take his earlobe between her teeth.

"Come on, honey." He loosened her arms. "I'm exhausted, and we've both got to get up early in the morning. We can go one night without sex."

"But I'm ovulating."

"We did it last night and twice the day before."

"Excuse me. I didn't realize having sex with me had become such a chore for you." She turned away.

"Evie . . ." He grabbed her arm and pulled her back toward him. "Don't get mad."

"Ridley, you just don't seem to grasp how important this is to me."

"And you don't seem to realize all the pressure you're putting on me to perform. I'm only human. It's taking all the fun out of our lovemaking."

"You want me to relax?"

"I do."

"Then guide me on a vision quest. Reassure me that I will get pregnant, that babies *are* in our future."

Ridley exhaled in exasperation. "I've told you before that a vision quest is not the answer for you."

"I think you're being mean not letting me do this."

"And I think you're being unrealistic."

"Tuck had a vision of Jillian and now here she is. That's pretty powerful mojo."

"Exactly. It's not something you mess around with if you're unprepared for it."

"I'm your wife. Don't you love me?"

"Of course I love you. That's precisely the reason I don't want you to do it."

Evie yanked away from him in frustration. Why was he so adamant she not go on a vision quest? Why was he denying her this peek into the future?

"Hey, hey." He chased after her. "Come here."

"What?"

His arms went around her, and he lowered his head to kiss her. Evie didn't kiss him back.

"You forget all about the vision quest and I'll make love to you every night until you get pregnant. How's that?"

Evie looked into the dark eyes of the man she loved more than life itself. "Okay, all right, but tonight, I get to be on top. I heard it increases your chances of having a boy."

THE SNOW AT THE TOP of Thunder Mountain on Saturday morning was the finest skiing powder Jillian had ever seen. The day was perfect. Sun shining, no wind to speak of. The slopes smooth and tightly packed.

Below them on the black-diamond trails, expert skiers maneuvered over moguls, jumping and swishing in their colorful ski attire. A small flotilla of novice skiers followed an instructor down one of the easier, green-circle trails. And at the very bottom of the mountain, they could see the raw beginners snowplowing madly on the bunny slope. To their left, the ski lift deposited a new round of skiers and then circled back down for more.

Jillian wriggled her fingers into her ski gloves. *We're just here to have fun*, she kept telling herself. *It's nothing more than that. Not a date. Two friends out enjoying the mountain.*

"I'm tired of being a gaper. I'm ready for the milk run. Race you to the base." Tuck grinned and pulled his ski goggles down over his eyes. "Last one down buys lunch."

He took off.

Never one to resist a challenge, Jillian's competitive streak kicked in, and she shot after him.

He hopped over moguls like his ankle had never been compromised. Jillian's heart momentarily vaulted into her throat, but when she realized he could handle himself, she deftly maneuvered the mogul. Aha! She still had it.

Tuck had insisted she rent parabolic skis, and they were amazing. The hourglass shape gave her more speed and control, and they responded immediately to the slightest pressure. Technology had made great strides since the last time she'd been skiing in college during spring break with Delaney, Tish, and Rachael.

They raced, flying around trees, zipping down the hill, zigzagging over the granular surface soaring toward Thunder Lodge, the Chalet condos, the bank of metal lockers where skiers stashed their possessions. It felt decadent, this hedonistic, holiday, cold-weather dash, as if they'd shoplifted something money couldn't replace—time, a precious memory, happiness. They were still young, they were free, and Jillian basked in their very aliveness.

The snow was sugar, tempting and white. On their

skis, Jillian and Tuck raced, breathless and hungry, muscles charged and blood pumped with adrenaline. It was a glorious game, and Jillian realized that she did not play nearly often enough.

On the skis, on the mountain, pulling in the cold, crisp morning air, Jillian felt like someone else. It was as if she'd stepped into the body of another Jillian, this one lighter, giddier, silly even. Gone was Queenie and in her place was . . .

Who?

She didn't know, but she liked this new woman, this new sensation wrapping around her, crowding out the cloak of loneliness she'd worn for twenty-nine years. Something happened to her on the top of that mountain as she played snow tag with Tuck. Something she could not explain. Something that filled her with hope and expectancy. Something that made her soul sing.

Jillian spurred her body onward, eager to win, determined to beat him. She dug her poles into the snow, pushing faster, aiming for a shortcut, even though it was steeper than the path Tuck had taken. Jillian had never been afraid to assume risk in order to claim her prize.

But even so, they arrived at the base at exactly the same moment. No winner, no loser.

Equals.

It was, Jillian decided, the perfect ending to the perfect ski run. Grinning, she took off her ski cap and shook her head.

Tuck sucked in his breath. Jillian's face was turned in profile to him as she looked back at where they'd come from, her gaze drinking in the pine trees, the snow, the mountain vista.

She ran her fingers through her hair, and the wind tossed the ebony strands over her shoulder. She looked mind-shatteringly beautiful in her powder-blue snow-bunny suit that snugged her athletic body like a leather glove, hugging her breasts and womanly hips, nipping in at her sculpted waist.

He pushed his goggles up on his forehead. Her cheeks were flushed, her eyes hidden behind the darkly tinted lenses of her sunshades. The bright morning light warmed their skin. She tilted her head back to catch the sun full on, briefly shut her eyes, inhaled deeply, and then looked at him.

"I love the smell of snow," she breathed.

Hypnotized by the sight of her, Tuck could only nod. White snow, black hair, ripe body in blue clothes.

She pointed at the ski lodge. "Break for lunch?"

"Guess it's Dutch treat," he said.

"I'll pay."

"It's not a date and I didn't win the bet. We're friends. It's Dutch treat."

"Unless," she said, "I pick up lunch and you can pick up the tab for the hot toddies after the last run of the day."

"I can go for that."

They skied to the lodge, shrugged out of their gear, locked up their skis, and went inside. They were a little early for lunch, and the place was fairly empty, so the waitress showed them to a table in the lounge area. The television at the bar was tuned to *The Price Is Right*, but the sound was muted.

The smell of hearty, winter food scented the air—chili, pot roast, hunter's stew, chicken pot pie. Tuck ordered the chili, and Jillian went for the chicken pot pie.

"How's the ankle?" she asked.

"Good as new."

"I'm having a good time." She smiled at him over the rim of her coffee cup while they waited for their food order. "Thanks for inviting me."

"No problem. I'm enjoying the view." Tuck looked at her instead of out the window at the majestic mountain, letting her know he wasn't speaking about the scenery. He was confused by his own statement. They were forging a friendship. Why was he mucking things up with the insinuation that there could be more?

She briefly met his eyes, then quickly turned her gaze out the big picture window. She looked unsure of herself. He couldn't blame her. He was feeling as unsteady as a toddler taking his first steps. "Yes, it is beautiful."

"Gorgeous." He never took his eyes off her face.

She fingered the bracelet at her wrist as if it were a talisman she used to comfort herself when she was feeling off balance. He'd watched her perform the gesture before. She rubbed her fingers over it like a rosary. Whether she knew it or not, the woman had faith in something. A power beyond her.

A crackling fire in the fireplace near their table suddenly made a loud snapping noise and spilled a shower of sparks into the grate. She jumped, slightly startled. Then her gaze met Tuck's.

"Dry wood," he explained.

"Ah, we're back to the subject of wood again." Her eyes twinkled, teasing him. "It's a favorite of yours. A regular theme."

"What can I say? I'm a carpenter at heart." He chuckled. "Wood is my medium."

"Medium is fine with me. I've found that large is often not all it's cracked up to be."

Desire churned Tuck's stomach as he caught her sexual innuendo. He felt at once both concern and excitement. He wanted her, yes, but he wanted her friendship even more. The morning they'd just spent together convinced him of that. He wasn't going to jeopardize the good thing they had going.

Sex was sure to mess things up.

But the look in her eyes—the look that told him she wanted him as much as he wanted her—cut like razor wire and made him think, *What if, what if, what if?*

He was sitting next to her so they could both view the mountain through the picture window. He could see the pulse at the hollow of her throat fluttering. His own heart was fluttering too. His gaze dropped to her wrist again, watching as she twirled the silver and turquoise filigree bracelet.

"Where'd you get the bracelet?" he asked.

"Blake. He gave it to me for my law school graduation."

Tuck snorted, shook his head.

Jillian's chocolate brown eyes narrowed. "What does that snort mean?"

"He was far more of a father to you than he ever was to Aimee," Tuck said.

"And you resent that."

"Yeah. I do."

"From what Blake told me, Aimee was the one who'd cut him out of her life," she said.

Anger sparked inside him. "Blake was a shitty father."

"Maybe. I wasn't there. But he was the closest thing to a father I ever had. I'm saying that whatever went on between him and Aimee, it was a two-way street. Aimee wasn't all sweetness and light."

"Excuse me, are you disrespecting my dead wife?"

"That's not what I meant, but you do idolize her memory. No living woman could live up to Saint Aimee."

Tuck couldn't believe she was going there. "Don't," he said through clenched teeth. "Don't you say a word against her."

Her jaw tightened and she turned her head to look out the window. Tuck was startled to see unshed tears glistening at the corner of her eyes. Immediately, he felt contrite. Reaching out, he put his hand on her forearm.

She stiffened.

"Jillian," he murmured. "I don't want to fight with you. We've had such a great day. I just wanted . . ."

He looked down at her wrist, at the bracelet that represented the wall between them. His love for Aimee, her loyalty to Blake. Ghosts sat in the two vacant chairs at the table. Ghosts of the past, mucking up the promise of a hopeful future.

"Don't try to figure me out, Tucker Manning," she said. "Save your efforts."

"I can't." Tuck lifted a hand and slowly traced the back of one finger down the side of her cheek and along her tensed jaw.

He was encouraged when she didn't pull away. In fact, she swiveled her head around to meet his gaze full on.

"You fascinate me, Jillian Samuels," he said.

The breath left her lungs in a small sigh.

He knew he shouldn't do it, but he couldn't seem to stop himself. She looked so hurt, and he felt so compelled to smooth things over between them. He brushed his lips against hers. A breezy, hardly there kiss.

The touch of their mouths sent a shudder clean through him.

She sighed a second time.

He lowered his head, slid his arm around her back, pulled her closer, and kissed her more firmly.

Jillian parted her lips, but she didn't lean into him, and she kept her arms stiffly in her lap. Tuck touched the tip of his tongue to hers, but she closed her mouth and drew back.

"No," she whispered.

Tuck pulled his head away. "I . . . I . . ." He didn't know what he wanted to say. Words seemed empty, useless tools with which to try and scale this . . . this . . . *thing* between them. "Are you okay?"

She nodded, but her eyes never left his. Her body radiated a bizarre combination of self-discipline, anger, desire, and fierce melancholia.

The waitress interrupted, depositing their food on the table. The earthy aroma of cumin-rich chili scented the air between them.

He looked at Jillian, at the regal set to her shoulders and the hooded expression in her dark eyes, and he felt so inadequate. His heart hammered and his gut twisted and his mind spun. *What in the hell am I going to do about this feeling?*

Just as he was pondering that question, he got a glimpse of the weather report on the television. At the same time he noticed the ominous weather pattern outline on screen, the bartender took it off mute. From the looks of the Doppler radar, the blizzard would be slamming into them within the next three to four hours. Luckily, Salvation was only an hour's drive away, but they needed to get a move on in order to get down the mountain safely.

"Hunker down, folks," the weather forecaster announced. "Because within the next three hours, the blizzard of the decade is headed for Thunder Mountain all the way down to Boulder."

ALL DAY LONG, the talk at the Bluebird had been of the coming blizzard. By the time Evie closed the café early, the snow swirled like heavy lace throughout the town. She got home to find Ridley had stocked them up on firewood and supplies in case they lost electricity.

"I got a bastard of a headache," he told her. "I'm going to bed early. You coming?"

Evie went with him, but her mind was so keyed up she couldn't sleep. She kept thinking about the blizzard, about Thanksgiving dinner, about the babies she wanted so desperately, about the vision quest Ridley refused her. The more she thought about that last part, the more irritated she got.

By midnight, she was still wide awake, and the blizzard hadn't yet hit. Evie made the decision she'd been on the verge of making for weeks. She tiptoed out of bed and slipped into the sweat lodge.

She'd only been inside it once, right after he built it. She had to admit the symbol of her husband's spirituality bothered her on a gut level. Intellectually, she didn't care. She told herself she liked that he practiced what he believed. But emotionally? It made her feel left out. She didn't have faith in things unseen the way he did, and his adherence to this custom she didn't know or understand was a wedge between them.

You have to get over this. You're hoping to have a baby with him. Ridley's going to want to share his beliefs with his child, and you can't deprive him of that. It's time you understood your husband's faith.

She started a fire in the fire pit with the piñon wood, turned on the gas-powered sauna and battery-powered MP3 player. The sound of low, steady drumbeats spilled from the speakers. In the dark of midnight, with only the flickering firelight for a guide, Evie took off her coat and her flannel pajamas in the sweat lodge. It exuded the musky, masculine smell of her husband. Stripped naked, she sat on the bearskin rug.

After peppering Tuck with questions about his vision quest, Evie tried to emulate the conditions. She crossed her legs in lotus position. She inhaled deeply of the piñon wood smoke. She hummed a mantra—*baby, baby, baby.*

The temperature in the lodge grew hotter. Sweat beaded Evie's brow, her upper lip, the flat space between her breasts.

Baby, baby, baby.

The bearskin rug felt luxuriously sensual against her bare butt. Smoke swirled upward, funneling through the flue and out the hole in the roof.

Baby, baby, baby.

She waited. Prayed. Minutes passed. Finally an hour.

Nothing happened.

Her butt was growing numb, her entire body was now bathed in sweat, and the incessant drumbeating was getting on her nerves. What was she doing wrong?

You don't believe.

The thought came to her from the air, but it sounded exactly as if Ridley had said it. Startled, Evie looked toward the door. But it remained closed.

She thought of the baby she wanted. Wrapped her empty arms around her chest. She thought of her husband asleep in their king-sized bed. Tears pricked at the back of her eyelids.

You gotta have faith.

Evie took a deep, shuddering breath and let it out slowly. The languid, heated smoke snaked throughout her body. Her muscles relaxed; her head went comfortably numb.

Buzzy. She felt all warm and buzzy.

Smoke grew thicker inside the room. The smell of piñon wood was overpowering. And the drums, they just kept beating. *Pound, pound, pound.*

Baby, baby, baby.

Her eyelids drooped heavily. She coughed, blinked.

Then, in the haze of smoke, she saw something.

A baby.

Evie smiled immediately and joy contracted her stomach, but as she watched, a woman came and picked up the baby and disappeared into the cloud of smoke.

Then suddenly she was surrounded by children. Babies, toddlers, little boys and girls in Easter attire. They were standing on the lawn of the White House. It was the annual Easter Egg hunt. All the children had mothers who were carrying baskets heaped high with eggs.

And there was Evie, standing alone, watching the event take place all by herself. No child at her side, no baby in a stroller, no round pregnant belly like many of the young mothers. She realized suddenly that at thirty-five, she was the oldest woman on the White House lawn.

Tears spilled down her face, and a wrenching sob squeezed her throat. She looked down at the basket that she realized was looped over her right arm. Inside, atop the bright green artificial grass, were three tiny white eggs.

Evie threw back her head and howled with grief. The vision was clear enough. She did not have a lush full basket of eggs. There were no babies in her future, no children of her own flesh and blood to love. She was a failure as a woman.

The pain was horrible.

Evie drew her knees to her chest and let the tears flow. Ridley was right. She shouldn't have come in here. Shouldn't have seen what she'd just seen. Shouldn't have learned the truth this way. Alone. Without him to comfort her.

"Evie!"

She jerked her head toward the door. Saw her big man standing there with a deep frown cutting into his brow, anger tightening his jaw. With his wild, dark hair falling loose to his shoulders, he looked all the world like a surly black bear. Her heart galloped.

"What in the hell do you think you're doing in here?" Ridley growled.

In that moment, Evie knew she'd crossed the line and there was no way she could step back across.

Chapter Eighteen

For three days, Jillian and Tuck were trapped inside the lake house together while the blizzard of the decade raged outside.

On the second day, the electricity went out. Tuck kept the fire in the fireplace roaring. They played chess by candlelight. Jillian beat him seventeen games in a row before he vowed never to play her again. They roasted marshmallows over the blaze and brewed up hot chocolate over the gas stove. They listened to the weather report on the radio. They made stew and cornbread. They drank pots of coffee and sat huddled under a blanket, watching *When Harry Met Sally* on Tuck's DVD player until the batteries gave out.

"Do you think men and women can simply be friends?" Jillian asked him when the movie was over. They were sitting side by side on the couch, Mutt sleeping at their feet.

Tuck shrugged. "Sure."

"You don't buy into Harry's philosophy, then?"

"Nope."

She turned to look at him in the firelight. "Are we friends?"

"I like to think we are."

"I don't know. I think Harry made a valid point."

"Women and men can't really be friends?"

"Exactly. The issue of sex is always there."

Tuck looked into her eyes.

Tension permeated the room. Sexual tension. Taut and hot. Jillian glanced away and stared into the fireplace, focused on the flames flicking the wood, the smell of mesquite.

But no matter how hard she tried to direct her attention elsewhere, every cell in her body was acutely aware of the man sitting next to her. The sexy man she was stranded with in a snowbound cabin.

She fisted her hands against the tops of her thighs. Her throat felt tight, the set of her shoulders even tighter. Restlessly, she wriggled her toes inside her thick woolen socks. Even way across the couch, Jillian could feel the heat emanating off Tuck's body. The room smelled of him—musky, manly, magnificent.

"Fear and stubborn pride kept Harry and Sally apart when they could have, should have, been together much sooner," she said.

"Yeah," he said. "Stupid Harry, stupid Sally."

"Or," she said, "I suppose you could look at it from the opposite angle. They let sex spoil a wonderful friendship."

"You can't have a great love relationship and a great friendship at the same time?" Tuck asked. Then before she could answer, he said, "No, wait, you're the woman who doesn't believe in true love at all."

"It's not that I don't believe in love," Jillian said. "It's just that I don't believe it's some magical, fairy-dust kind of thing. Seriously, do you?"

"I used to. Once upon a time."

"And now?"

"I'm not so naïve. I thought true love would save me from pain. What I found out is that it causes more pain than you can possibly believe."

"Yeah," she said. "I suppose there is that."

They looked into each other's eyes, there in front of the flickering firelight.

"Come here," he murmured.

"What?"

He reached out and ran his fingertips along her shoulder, and she moved closer to him, anxious to feel his breath on her neck, to feel the beating of his heart beneath her palm.

She was someone new. Different. No longer a legal eagle from Houston. No longer that stepchild on the outside looking in. No longer the dirty mistress, the judge's ugly little secret standing on the doorstep on Christmas Eve dressed like a Victoria's Secret cowgirl.

Tuck just held her in the circle of his arms. Held her and looked straight into her. "You've never been valued the way you deserve."

"I'm no Magic Woman."

"You are."

"I've told you, I don't believe in magic."

"David Copperfield would be so disappointed."

"He knows there's no such thing as magic. He makes a living faking people out."

"Why are you so afraid to believe?" Tuck asked.

Jillian wrinkled her nose. "I hate getting my hopes dashed."

"There is something out there, Queenie." He tightened

his arms around her. "Something that can't be explained. I saw it in those learning centers I designed." And apparently in the music box he'd designed for Evie. It felt good, knowing the magic was back.

"Yeah, so why did you stop designing them?"

He drew in a deep breath. "You've got me there."

They sat there for a long time, snuggled up on the couch together, listening to the wind howl and Mutt snore.

Tuck played with a lock of her hair. She had such beautiful hair. Silky and straight. He had so many questions to ask her. They'd known each other almost two months, and he hadn't asked her the truly important things about her past.

"Tell me," he said. "Tell me about your pain. Tell me what makes it so hard for you to believe."

"It's a long sordid story," she said. "I'm sure you don't want to hear it."

He waved a hand at the bank of snow pressing heavily against the window. "It's not as if we're going anywhere. What was your childhood like? I've gotten the impression it wasn't good."

Jillian sighed, moved from the circle of his arms, and curled her legs underneath her. "I don't even remember my mother, and I barely remember my father."

"They're dead?"

"My father is. My mother . . ." She shrugged. "Who knows where she is?"

"You never tried to find out?"

"No."

"Why not?"

"She never wanted me."

He waited, not pressing, letting her tell her life story at her own pace.

She stared into the fire, seemingly hypnotized. When she spoke again, it was almost to herself. "My parents hooked up when they were quite young. My mother was eighteen, my father nineteen. From what I gleaned from my stepmother, they had a very tumultuous relationship. Then again, her version of things tend to get pretty skewed."

Tuck gave her his full attention.

Jillian pulled her knees to her chest and clasped her arms around her legs. The pensive look on her face told him she was leafing through her memories. "My dad was married to my stepmother when he got my mom pregnant. My mother didn't tell him about me. But having a baby didn't stop her from hanging out in bars and pool halls. She had an alcohol problem. I realize that now. I remember falling asleep on shuffle-board tables to the sound of Hank Williams and Merle Haggard on the jukebox and the smell of beer and cigarettes in the air. In the meantime, my dad had this whole other family I knew nothing about. Two other daughters. Legitimate daughters."

Tuck thought about his own stable, loving family. His parents who were still happily married after forty years. He'd been so lucky and he knew it.

"Then on Christmas Eve, when I was three years old, my mother left me on my father's porch with a letter of explanation pinned to my chest, rang the doorbell, and just drove away."

"Damn. That was cold-blooded."

"I don't remember that day, but I suppose in her mind she was doing the best thing for me."

"You must have felt so scared and lonely that you blocked it out." The thought of that three-year-old kid abandoned on a doorstep on Christmas Eve fisted anger inside him. What kind of person would do such a thing?

She blew out her breath, and that's all Tuck thought he was going to get out of her. He said nothing further. If she didn't want to talk about it, she didn't want to talk about it.

But then a few minutes later, she surprised him by saying, "My stepmother was very unhappy to suddenly have a third daughter to raise. I don't think that marriage was a happy one. My stepmother wasn't the most stable person emotionally, and my dad threw himself into his work. He'd leave before I woke up in the mornings, and often he wouldn't return until long after I was in bed. Like I said, I was really little, and I don't remember that much about him. The one clear memory I have of him was this one time he took me fishing, and he bought me this little pink tackle box with yellow daisies on it. In a dumb way, that was one of the reasons I was so excited about inheriting a lake house. So I could go fishing."

The vision of a little black-haired girl clutching a pink tackle box with daisies and a kid-sized rod and reel caused something inside him to unravel. "Aw, hell, Queenie."

Jillian paused again and glanced over at him. The raw pain on her face was almost unbearable.

In that moment, he saw past her beauty, beyond the dark enigmatic eyes that were often hooded to hide her thoughts. Beyond the high, feminine cheekbones, the thick black eyelashes, the regal nose. He saw beyond the promise of her beautiful mouth and the chin she kept clenched so firmly, as if she feared it would give away too much of her heart if she relaxed her hold.

"My dad died in a car crash when I was five. His secretary was in the passenger seat. She died too. My stepmother claimed they were having an affair." She shrugged again. "Maybe they were."

"What happened to you?"

"My stepmother raised me, but she treated me differently than her daughters. I suppose it's understandable under the circumstances, but a kid only knows she's being singled out, punished more often. Not long after my father died, my half sister Kaitlin and I were playing hair salon, and I whacked off Kaitlin's hair. My stepmother had a fit. It was Christmastime, and that year she put coal in my stocking. She told me I was a very bad girl and Santa didn't love me. Later on, she mellowed, or the doctor got her on the right medication, and she stopped being so mean, but those early years . . ." Jillian shook her head.

Quick anger pulsed through him that anyone could treat a child so cruelly. No wonder Jillian was locked up so tight and afraid to trust. She'd been betrayed in so many ways; he couldn't blame her.

"You're kidding me."

"I wish I were. One time when I was nine or ten, she just took off with her kids for the weekend and left me at home alone. During the day I was fine. In fact, I liked having the house to myself, even though I was supposed to clean the entire place while they were gone. But that night, a storm rolled in. I was in my bed upstairs, all alone. Not even a pet. My stepmother hated animals. Refused to let us have any. So I finally fall asleep, and in the middle of the night, I wake up and I'm sure I've heard a sound downstairs."

"You must have been terrified."

She nodded. "I lay there, not really knowing if I'd heard a sound or if it was something I dreamed. I held my breath, listening, hyper-alert to every creak of the house. My blood was strumming through my ears. Did I hear a noise or was it my imagination? But my mind was being so loud I couldn't hear. I didn't move, terrified that if someone was in the house, they'd hear me and come after me."

"That's horrible."

"There are lots of people in this world who had it worse. I know that. I had a roof over my head and food to eat. But I wanted out of there. I studied hard in school, luckily it came easy to me. I excelled. Got scholarships to college. Got my wish. Got the hell out of there. Graduated magna cum laude from law school."

It aroused something inside Tuck that she'd trusted him enough to tell him all this. He wanted to touch her, to comfort her for that long-ago pain, but he had no business, no right. Still, he couldn't just leave her with her shoulders tensed, her chin clenched, her mind ensnared in the past. He skimmed her forearm with his fingertips—briefly, lightly, just enough to let her know he cared.

"I'm sorry."

Tuck couldn't handle the swell of emotions flooding through him. He couldn't keep looking at Jillian. Instead, he got up and threw another log on the fire. When he turned, he saw tears reflected in her eyes.

It shook him. She was so strong, so brave. He didn't

think of her as the sort who cried. Unlike Aimee, who had bawled at Hallmark commercials.

"Jillian." He went to the couch and put his arms around her.

She blinked. "I'm sorry. I don't usually do this. I don't even talk about it."

"Thank you for telling me."

"It was so long ago. I got over it. I survived."

Tuck squeezed her tighter. "You never get over something like that."

Jillian made a noise, half bravado, half sorrow. "Hey, we all have our crosses to bear. You lost someone very precious to you."

Every cell in his body ached. He knew what it was like to suffer a great loss. She looked over at him. This shared intimacy forged a deeper understanding, a tighter bonding between them.

"Losing Aimee changed me forever, you know." He swallowed, unable to believe he was talking about his wife with her. "I'll never be the same."

"Right." She moved from him, dabbed at her eyes.

His arms felt strangely empty. He liked holding her, but he wasn't sure that he liked that he liked it.

"I think this calls for a stiff drink. You want something to drink?"

"I don't think we have anything stronger than Coke."

"Let me see." Tuck got up, grabbed the flashlight off the table, and rummaged around the kitchen. He thought there might be a beer or two in the fridge, but it was empty. He checked the kitchen cabinet. Nothing. Then he checked the cabinet over the stove.

Score!

"Look what I found," he said, coming to the archway between the kitchen and the living room and holding up a bottle of Baileys Irish Cream for her to see. "Irish coffee anyone?"

"Oh me, me." Jillian waved at him from the couch. "With this cold weather outside, I could use some warming up inside."

Tuck had to bite his tongue to keep from saying something raunchy and totally inappropriate. He concentrated on pouring the coffee and stirring in the Baileys and trying not to think about how much he wanted to kiss Jillian. He couldn't very well go back in there with a boner.

Think about carpentry.

Finger joint, butt hinge, tongue and groove.

Oh crap, that was only making things worse. He'd never realized before what erotic terminology his profession employed.

"Hey," she said, sashaying into the kitchen. "Can I help? Need me to hold the flashlight?"

"Yeah," he said, and passed her the flashlight. "Thank God for battery-powered coffeemakers."

"Thank God," she echoed.

She was standing so close that he could smell her unique Jillian scent. He was in serious trouble here, and there was nowhere to run.

And at that moment, Tuck realized running was the last thing on his mind.

TWO HOURS AND THREE Irish coffees later, Jillian was giggling like a teenager. They'd been playing truth or dare, and Tuck had just dared her to stand on her head.

"Ten years of yoga," she said from her upside-down position, with her back against the wall beside the fireplace.

"You win, pretzel lady. Come down before you get a headache."

Jillian dropped her feet to the floor and sat upright, combing her fingers through her hair.

Tuck laughed. He was at his most alluring. Dark eyes filled with anticipation, his mouth quirked up at one corner, warm, inviting, sexy.

And Jillian was at her most suggestible. Tipsy and snowed in with a sexy man she'd been having erotic dreams about for quite some time. In a flash of sudden knowledge that almost knocked the breath from her body, she recognized she was falling for him.

It was more than friendship. She wanted sex from him and lots of it.

His masculinity aroused her, his cleverness intrigued, his intricacy provoked her. She admired his dedication to family, his loyalty to this town, his empathy to his friends.

She considered what he'd revealed by talking so intimately about Aimee. She sipped at the Irish coffee long past the point where she should have stopped drinking. Her head spun and her heart pounded and she felt warm all over.

Wings of panic fluttered against her rib cage. The new understanding that her feelings for him had strengthened, deepened, altered her reality. She wanted to make love to him.

Now and for a long time to come.

Jillian was scared, terrified that this glimmer of joy she was feeling would evaporate if she studied it too hard.

How could she trust in this tenuous emotion? She'd let down her guard with Alex and look what happened.

But Tuck's not Alex and he isn't married.

No, he was worse. He was a widower still in love with his dead wife, and there was no way she could compete with a ghost.

Confusion wrapped her in its grasp, and the most she could manage was a simple, "Thank you."

Tuck said nothing, just sat there watching her in the firelight.

She didn't expect him to feel the same way about her. That was too much to hope for. But the hungry expression in his whiskey-colored eyes told her that at least he wanted her sexually. Wanted her quite badly, in fact. That was easy enough to read. His eyes roved over her body and his jaw tightened.

Jillian had spent her adult life telling herself sex was enough, but with Tuck, she didn't know if she could keep convincing herself that was true. She gulped, suddenly swallowed up by unexpected melancholia. Jillian shook her head, mentally warding off the sadness. She wanted him. She would take whatever she could get. If sex and friendship were all he had to offer, so be it. She didn't really believe in anything more than that.

"I . . . I need to go freshen up," she said, and set her mug down on the coffee table. "I'll be right back."

She rushed into the bathroom that Tuck had just finished renovating the week before. He'd textured the walls in Venetian plaster. The beautiful sage green color she'd picked out made her think of the prairie in springtime. Since the lights were out, they had candles going in every room, and the dancing flames enhanced the old-world look of the new décor.

Jillian washed up in the new copper sink he'd installed in the stylish yet rustic bathroom cabinetry he'd built himself. She splashed cold water over her face, trying to dampen the effects of the Baileys Irish Cream and snap herself out of the magical spell the blizzard seemed to have cast.

She stared at her reflection in the mirror and saw how wide and shiny her eyes looked. "I don't believe in magic," she told her reflection. "I don't, I don't, I don't."

But she did believe in great sex, and there was a handsome man out there, and it had been months since she'd had sex. There were condoms in her purse, and he seemed as interested as she, so why not take a gamble?

She left the bathroom and went to change from her sweater and jeans into a pair of silk sapphire blue lounging pajamas and a diaphanous matching bathrobe. She hesitated a moment when she remembered Alex had given her the pajamas and robe set, but then she thought, *What the hell?* They looked good on her no matter where she'd gotten them. The material flowed like water over her body, soft and fluid, and the neckline showed off just the right amount of cleavage.

Sexy but not blatantly so.

And that's when Jillian knew she was going to seduce him. She went back to the bathroom and brushed her teeth and then her hair. She put on just enough makeup to give her a fresh, dewy look—charcoal mascara, pink cream blush, cinnamon-flavored lip gloss—applying it as best she could in the restricted lighting. She peeled off the slouch socks she liked to wear around the house and went back to the bedroom in search of the blue feathered mules that matched the silk pajamas and robe.

Taking a deep breath, she affected her sexiest walk and sauntered back out into the living room, stopping long enough to open her purse, find the condoms, and slip them into the pocket of her robe.

Tuck didn't hear her approach. He was busy poking the red-hot embers and adding fresh logs to the grate. She paused a moment to admire him in the firelight.

Even in studious repose, the man exuded a rugged sexuality that took hold of Jillian and wouldn't let go. Maybe that was the very reason she wanted him so much. He brought a raw, primal realness into her world.

She ran her hands along the pajamas, the silky material rubbing against her body, the feel of it escalating her excitement. How she wanted him!

And how nervous she was that he might reject her.

Tentatively, she licked her lips, lowered her eyelashes, and stepped closer. She heard something clang to the floor, glanced over, and saw Tuck had dropped the poker, along with his jaw.

"Jesus, Jillian."

Startled, her hand flew to her throat. What? What had she done wrong? "Yes? What is it?"

He gulped. "It's just that . . . you look . . ."

"What?"

"So damned *hot*."

The gleam in his eyes sent a flush of pride pumping through her bloodstream. She couldn't ever remember a man making her feel quite this sexy. The air crackled with sexual tension.

They stared at each other.

Tuck smiled and closed the gap he'd opened when she'd taken him by surprise. "You never cease to amaze me."

"Is that a good thing or a bad thing?"

"Oh, trust me. It's a very good thing."

She ran her tongue over her lips.

"Are you as tipsy as I am?" he asked.

"No doubt."

Tuck splayed a palm to the nape of his neck. "I gotta admit, I'm feeling a little nervous."

"Me too."

"But excited."

"Same here."

"We don't have to do this."

"I know."

They never broke eye contact, just kept looking and looking and looking at each other.

She had started this, but Tuck was the one who crossed the line. He closed the remaining space between them, reaching out and pulling her up flush against him.

Jillian felt all the air leave her body in one long pent-up whoosh, and it was like she'd been holding her breath all her life, waiting, just waiting for this moment. Waiting for him.

Tuck kissed her with the enchantment only a magic man could deliver. Strong, confident, decisive, he made his move, boldly exploring her mouth with his hot tongue.

She felt a primal, dazzling need sewing her to him, strengthening her desire to see this thing through.

Their radiant energy grew, fused, swelled. She wrapped her arm around his neck, pulling him down closer. Her lips vibrated with receptiveness.

"You can say stop at any time and I'll pull the plug," he said. "I just want you to know that."

"Right back at you, but I don't want to pull the plug."

"Neither do I," he said. "But you need to know I haven't been with anyone since . . ."

Neither one of them wanted to say her name. Jillian nodded. "Yes, I understand."

"It's been over two years. I might not last five minutes."

"We're snowed in. We're not going anywhere."

He kissed her again. "Where shall we do this?"

"Let's start right here on the rug in front of the fire."

"Aw, you're just a big romantic at heart."

She smiled encouragingly.

Gently, Tuck ran his hand up under the hem of her top, his rough palm skimming her bare belly. With his other hand, he tilted her chin up and brought his mouth down on hers for another soul-searching kiss.

She melted into him.

Enveloped in each other, pasted together by contact at the shoulder, hand, leg, hip, and chest, Tuck and Jillian sealed their destiny and closed their fate.

She wrapped her arms around his waist, and he enfolded her to him. It felt as if their very cells were entwined. They were oblivious to everything on earth beyond themselves and this moment.

They had fallen down the well of each other. Tuck's energy filled Jillian with rapture. His masculine power rolled off every inch of her in glorious waves. He evoked in her a desire immeasurable, a thirst so vast all the oceans of the world evaporated in a single drop.

How was this possible? How could she have become so deliriously intoxicated with him?

Her emotions terrified her.

The air vibrated between them. One wrong move and they could fall off the earth. Their entire time together had been like this. A daring adventure, and now they were embarking on a dangerous affair.

At last Jillian understood why she'd hidden behind casual sex all these years. By keeping her affairs casual, she could gamble without risks. Feel without feeling.

But now all that had been stripped away. She was metaphorically naked. Fully exposed.

It felt glorious.

And scary as hell.

Chapter Nineteen

"Queenie." He smiled and pulled her closer, pressing his lips against the hollow of her throat. "You're so righteous and regal."

She was afraid then, in the circle of his arms. Afraid of losing this precious moment, of never getting it back. She wanted so much to hope for happily-ever-after, but she didn't believe in it.

He took her by the hand and led her upstairs to the bedroom. She meekly acquiesced. He seated her at the vanity, turning the chair around so she could watch him in the candlelight. She was supposed to be seducing him, but he was taking over, turning the tables on her.

While she watched, he stripped off his clothes. His bare, taut buttocks flexed as he moved, the pale skin contrasting the tan above his waist. She went breathless staring at his abs. Compelled, Jillian could not look away.

He was glorious. All biceps and triceps and glutes and hamstrings. Take that, Adonis. She couldn't ever remember having such a well-built lover. She would remember this body for a long time to come.

And his face!

Straight out of a fantasy. His jaw was square, his cheekbones prominent. His wheat-brown hair shining in the candlelight; the scruffy cut suited his dreamy, artistic nature. Architect, carpenter, a man who knew how to use his brains.

And his hands.

She got to her feet and slowly began to take off her clothes. She had performed lots of stripteases before, and she'd never been self-conscious. Not even the first time she'd tried it.

But now, she found herself hesitating, fumbling at her buttons, feeling unsure. What was wrong? What was different?

She rushed through the process, anxious to get it over with. He didn't seem to notice that he'd received the abbreviated version of her burlesque moves. Even the look of frank appreciation in his eyes when he saw her naked did nothing to allay her uneasiness.

He smiled tenderly.

"Tuck," she whispered, and he came across the room toward her and cupped her breasts in his warm palms. Her nipples became even harder beneath his hands, and he thumbed them ever so slightly.

They exhaled at the same time, breathing out each other's air.

She thought he was quivering, then realized it was her, shaking so hard her knees wobbled.

"Now," he said, "let's get comfortable."

He arranged the pillows on the bed, piling them high and then easing her down onto her back atop them. He lay on his side next to her and walked his fingers down her arm.

"How do you want to be touched right now?"

"Kid gloves," she whispered, and his eyes lit with such

feverish delight she knew he understood. "Feather fine. Lots and lots and lots of foreplay."

"I can do that." He reached out and with an incredibly light caress, grazed the base of his palm over her collarbone.

Jillian shivered.

His hand was a silken glide, his lips delicious. He swirled his fingers over her navel. Softly and sweetly he kissed the leaping pulse at her neck. He dropped down the length of her throat and then took tiny succulent nibbles.

Then his tongue went traveling south to the peaks of her jutting breasts. His tongue flicked out to lick over one nipple while his thumb achingly rubbed the other straining bud, drawing it in to the extraordinary blaze of his mouth.

His thigh tightened against her leg, and his abdominal muscles hardened to pure, smooth steel.

"Tuck," she whispered his name on a sigh. She loved his name. It rhymed so nicely with a very naughty word. *Tuck, Tuck, Tuck.* "Tuck, that feels so good."

Her eyes flew open and she lifted her head up off the mattress. She had to see what he was doing to make her feel so good. Her gaze latched on his lips as she watched him drawing her nipple in and out of his mouth.

She let her head fall back against the pillows. "Go lower."

He dipped his head, trailing his tongue down the middle of her chest to the flat of her sternum before he veered off into other territory, her nipples responding to his touch.

While his lips were finding her breasts, his hand was dancing around the juncture of her thighs. She parted her legs slightly, just enough to let him slip a finger or two between them.

He suckled first one nipple and then the other while strumming her clit lightly with an index finger.

She tilted her pelvis, arched her back. “More,” she begged. “More.”

And then his mouth and his fingers were in the same place, and he had moved around so that his head pointed south. His lips closed around the tiny throbbing head of her cleft while his fingers tickled the entrance of her womanhood.

His tongue laved her sensitive skin as he suckled her deeply. She writhed against him, trying to push her body into his, needing more. Barbed ribbons of fevered sensation unfurled straight to her throbbing sex. Her inner muscles contracted, rollicking with desire for him.

“Tuck,” she whispered weakly. “Tuck.”

“Yes, sweetheart. What do you want? Tell me what you need.”

“I want it all. I want everything.”

“Like this?”

“Yes,” she hissed as he moved his mouth back and forth, his hair a silky glide beneath her fingers. “Yes, yes, yes.”

Tuck worked his magic with his fingers while his tongue led her into uncharted territory. She was on sensory overload as he gently guided her to a paradise she’d only dreamed of before now.

But this wasn’t a dream. The warm wetness of his mouth, the sweet taste of his kiss still lingering on her tongue, the earthy smell of his masculine scent, the sound of the wind roaring outside the window. This new awareness of him awoke something inside her, and all the old failures and disappointments fell away.

He was beyond good-looking to her. He was pure life, pure joy. His mouth moved over her without caution or fear. He pushed Jillian past her knowledge of herself. She had never before been so physically possessed. His movements shook her world. The walls of the room seemed to ripple. Could a blizzard cause an earthquake?

No. The ground did not tremor, only her body.

She rode the flow of emotions, navigating the swell of pleasure and desire and discovery with accomplished ease. His warmth enveloped her, and she experienced a sense of safety with him that she'd rarely felt before.

He was lifting her up to a place she'd never known existed. She loved the adventure of him and was fascinated by this aspect.

Then she was seized by a sudden bittersweet feeling. This moment could not last. She closed her eyes, determined to ignore the sadness. Besides, this was all she needed. This brief slice of delight. She wasn't a commitment kind of gal. No reason to be sad. She was having fun, and he was doing some very nice things to her with his tongue.

Tuck's feet were pressed against the headboard, his long masculine legs parallel to her face. His hard shaft poked into her ribs.

She had a wicked thought and turned toward him, curling her spine outward while at the same time shifting her pelvis closer to his mouth and dipping her chin so she could lick the head of his penis with her tongue.

He gave a yelp of pleased surprise. His mouth was on

most her feminine lips while at the same time she stretched her own mouth over the expansive width of his penis.

His tongue was hot and wet. So was hers.

She swirled. He licked.

Up and down, around and around, they were both moaning and writhing, consumed by pleasure.

On and on they went. He on her, she on him. Licking, sucking, tasting. Glorious sensations rippled through her body, turning her inside out. They increased the tempo as the pressure built, rising to an inevitable crescendo.

Jillian mewled softly whenever he did something right, grunted when he made a wrong move. It didn't take him long to pick up her rhythms, to learn what she liked and give her more of it.

She took him deeper until she felt him pressing against the back of her throat, juicy and slick. She rolled her lips back, stretching wider to accommodate his bigness. She wanted to swallow all of him. She breathed in the heady smell of his sex.

He broke contact. "Jilly, I gotta have you now, but I don't have any condoms."

She moved around in bed to face him and looked into his proud face, reaching up to trace her finger along his cheek and feeling something monumental move inside her. It was an emotion unlike anything she'd ever felt before. She couldn't name it. She stopped trying to figure it out, just let it sweep her away.

"I have a condom," she said, "in the pocket of my pajama pants."

"I'll get it."

He retrieved it and hurried back. Then he was kissing her again. Her mouth, her nose, her eyelids, her ears. He was over her and around her and then, at long last, he was inside her.

"Jillian," he whispered her name, soft as an ocean breeze, caressing her with sound as he rotated his hips from side to side, maintaining tight, intense contact.

Now, with him deep in her moist wetness, she felt every twitch of his muscle. He lit her up inside. She had no thoughts beyond wanting him deeper, thrust to the hilt inside of her.

She wrapped her legs around his waist and rocked him into her. Her fingers gripped his buttocks, pushing him farther. Her turn to own him. Her turn for control.

Frenzy.

Everything was urgent and desperate and frantic. She felt like her breath encompassed the entire world. Need. Such need. To find, to press, to hurt, to soothe, to fly free.

They came together, and it was like pouring gasoline onto a fire. Infused, she could not tell where he began and she ended. No separation. Their connection was one hundred percent, and it filled the world. There was no space for anything else. Their oneness banged through their whole bodies. No moment existed in which they were not part of it, of each other.

She bristled with joy. It felt strong and resilient. It rippled through her body, burning her to a crisp. She was warm and gooey and completely scorched, and she loved it.

When it was over and they were two once more and Jillian lay panting in his arms, the total obliteration of what had just happened scared her witless.

Lucid thought surrendered to utter emotion. The

wipeout had been pure. Complete. Unadulterated lust had knocked her into a trance from which she feared there was no awakening.

OH SHIT, WHAT HAD HE DONE?

Tuck stared at the ceiling, listening to Jillian's soft, measured breathing beside him. He wasn't ready for this. Okay, so his body had been ready, but certainly not his mind, not his emotions.

You're just scared.

Hell, yes, he was scared. You bet your sweet ass he was scared.

It was the Baileys Irish Cream, the snow, the romance of the fireplace. It was *When Harry Met Sally*. It was her distractingly wonderful smell. It was the stew and the cornbread and the coziness of married life he missed. Tuck searched for something, anything to blame, except for the truth.

Himself.

They could put this behind them, he tried to convince himself. They could go back to being friends. This didn't have to get complicated or sticky. They were sophisticated adults.

It was a one-time thing. An error in judgment. It didn't have to define their relationship from here on out.

Except that Tuck yearned to reach across that bed, pull her to him, and make love to her all over again.

Don't do it; don't compound the mistake.

He had to get up. Get out of here. But there was nowhere to go. A blizzard wailed outside. They were stuck.

His hand reached across the bed and felt the warm,

round shape of her underneath the quilts. He turned on his side, propped himself up on his elbow, and stared down at her.

The night-light cast a soft glow over her sleeping features. His breathing grew shallow, and his eyes drank her in. This slumbering mystery woman who enticed him enough to make him forget about Aimee.

Guilt clamped down on him then. Guilt and shame. He didn't want to feel remorse, but there it was, doing battle with his desire.

And still, he couldn't stop wanting Jillian. She was so captivating, so alluring. She drew him in like a magnet. Any man would want to sleep with her. She was a temptress, and she didn't even try to be one. It was just innate in her DNA. Exotic and erotic.

He traced his gaze over her, comparing her long, leggy body to Aimee's. But there was no comparison. They were opposites in every way. Jillian dark and tall, Aimee blond and small. Jillian cynical and courageous. Aimee sweet and accepting.

He ran his hand along her body, learning the slope of her shoulders, memorizing the arc of her breast, the scoop of her waist, her taut, flat stomach.

"Tuck," she whispered his name like a prayer in the cold, dark of midnight. She was a warm beacon, opening her arms, welcoming him to her.

He was damned. He could not stay away from her heat, her vitality. He sought her lips and branded her with his kiss. She made a soft noise of approval low in her long, slender throat.

His hand found her nipple, and she shivered beneath his fingertips. She felt so good, so right, and yet he was so scared. Terrified of what he was getting into. It felt like quicksand. He was drowning, but he couldn't—wouldn't—turn back no matter how hard he tried.

Tuck tugged her to him, pressing his erection against her leg and running his hand down her spine, feeling each vertebra as his mouth trailed over her skin.

Jillian sighed and threaded her fingers through his hair.

Tuck slipped his hand down her back to the round smoothness of her butt. God, what a magnificent ass she possessed. Urgent need welled up in him, just as strong as before. Need he both regretted and longed for.

Kissing her hard, he stroked one hand along her buttocks, the other across her stomach, sending it lower until he slipped a palm between her thighs.

Her eyes were trained on his face. He could feel the heat of her gaze. He looked deeply into her, felt something slip inside him. Something brave and worrisome.

And then he found her sweet spot. She was warm and dripping wet for him. He groaned his approval.

Jillian whispered Tuck's name again and swallowed him up with her eyes.

He felt light-headed. He told himself it was the alcohol, but he knew it was not. Jillian that made him dizzy. His mind was filled with a hundred scenarios of how he wanted to make love to her next. Carry her into the bathroom, maybe bend her over the counter, let her watch in the mirror while he took her from behind. Or maybe hoist her legs on his shoulders and hang her head off the bed. Or perhaps stand on the floor, drag her to the edge of the mattress, tuck a pillow under her butt, and impale her completely. Or . . .

But before he could even finish imagining the next position, she was leaning over him, pushing him onto his back while she swung her leg over his waist and straddled him.

She bent her head and kissed him, spearing her tongue past lips that were parched for her. Hungrily, she ran her hands up his arms and pinned his wrists over his head, anchoring him to the bed. She eased her body down over his erect, throbbing shaft, and he sucked in his breath as her tongue stoked his passion.

The temptress moved over him, her flesh soft and moist and hot. God, she was glorious, and he reveled in the feel of her.

He was lost, swept away in a vortex of lust. A part of him, the part he didn't want to recognize, admitted he'd never felt this kind of desire before. Not with any other woman. Not even with Aimee.

Immediately he felt disloyal, and he would have lost his erection if the temptress hadn't chosen that moment to squeeze him tightly with her inner muscles.

He laughed aloud and she laughed with him, and in that moment, the temptress disappeared and it was just Jillian. His friend. Who had tonight become his lover.

Her hair was a tumble about her shoulders. Her dark eyes glazed with lust as fierce as his own. Her mouth was swollen from his rough kisses. He'd worked her over as fully as she was working him.

Raw, primal sex consumed them, and they tumbled about the bed, slinging pillows, mussing sheets, grappling and groaning and doing wild, wonderful things to each other.

"You . . . are . . . amazing," he managed to say, and

then he was atop her, pressing her into the mattress, kissing her again and again and again while outside the storm raged on a banshee bacchanal.

I want her. Not just now, but forever. Keep her always.

The thought rumbled in the back of his brain, but he was afraid to think it, to hope for it. He'd had magic once and he'd lost it. He was terrified to find it again in case it slipped through his fingers once more. He couldn't bear the pain of losing such a love again.

Not love, he tried to convince himself. Not love, just great sex. He refused to confuse the two.

He stopped moving, not knowing what to do. Trying to banish his thoughts and just go with the feeling. He closed his eyes, not wanting her to see the war going on inside him. Not wanting her to suspect that he was falling. He didn't want to fall.

Not again.

She wasn't the one. She couldn't be the one. She wasn't bound to stay in Salvation. And she didn't believe in magic.

He had to stop this before it was too late. Before he was too far gone. Abruptly, he rolled out from under her.

"What . . . ," she gasped. "Where . . ."

"I'm thirsty," he said, not looking at her. "You want some water?"

She reached up, wrapped her arms around his waist, and pressed her lips to his back. "I want you."

He got up, pulled the covers over her so he wouldn't have to see how wonderful she looked naked in the bed he'd shared with Aimee. "I don't want you to get cold."

"Tuck?" She sounded small and lonely, and he felt like

an utter bastard, but he couldn't make himself go back to her.

"You hungry? I could heat up some leftover stew."

"I'm hungry for you."

Like a coward, he left her there. He ran to the kitchen. He stuck a glass under the faucet and ran the water until it was overflowing.

And he never went back.

JILLIAN WAITED, wondering what had happened. When he didn't come back to bed after several long minutes, she got up and padded into the living room and found him sleeping on the couch.

She told herself she wasn't going to cry, and then she burst into tears. Wretched bastard. What was going on? She went back to bed and reached for the phone. To her amazement, she got a dial tone in the middle of the storm. Choking back the sobs, she called Delaney.

"Hello?" Delaney asked in a drowsy voice.

"You were asleep."

"Jilly?"

For the first time, Jillian looked at the clock. It was eleven o'clock mountain time. That meant it was midnight in Houston. "I'm sorry. I didn't realize how late it was. Please go back to sleep."

"What's wrong?"

"Nothing's wrong . . . I . . ."

"Are you crying?" Delaney sounded incredulous.

"I'm not crying." Jillian sniffled.

"I've never seen you cry. What's wrong? How can I help?"

"Nothing, everything's fine. Go back to sleep. I'll call you tomorrow."

"If you hang up this phone, Jillian Samuels, I'm coming to Colorado to kick your butt."

"You were totally wrong, Delaney. Tuck is not my Mr. Right."

"Oh, Jilly, what happened?"

"I . . . we . . ."

"Yes?"

"There's a blizzard here. We got snowed in together."

"Ah, you slept together."

"Well . . . yes. Then he freaked. Completely. Left the bed in the middle."

"The middle of what?"

"Sex."

"He left in the middle of sex?"

"He said he was thirsty. He went into the kitchen and never came back. I went looking for him. He's asleep on the couch. This is bad. This is very, very bad. Has Nick ever got up in the middle . . . ?"

"No," Delaney said adamantly. "Never."

"See? I told you. Tuck is not Mr. Right. Mr. Right would not get up in the middle."

"Maybe he's just scared."

"Like I'm not? Now I'm scared and mad."

"So how was it? Before he left in the middle."

"It was great, fantastic, the best ever—that's what's so frustrating," Jillian said, wanting desperately for Delaney to tell her that Tuck absolutely was her destiny and that all she needed was to wait for him to realize they were meant to be.

Instead, Delaney said, "Well, maybe he isn't the one."

"I dreamed about him while wearing the veil."

"Could just be a coincidence."

"I dream about the guy and then I meet him in real life. That doesn't seem like a coincidence. I mean, if anything is fated, it would seem like that would be a clear sign."

"So he is the one?"

She sighed. "I don't know. If he is, he's not cooperating. How did you know for certain Nick was the one? Wedding-veil thing aside. What made you ditch Evan and everything you had planned for Nick?"

"He came after me to stop me from having myself kidnapped at the wedding. He wanted to be the one to kidnap me."

"That is romantic." Jillian sighed.

"You can't compare Nick to your guy. Apples and oranges, Jilly. Tuck's a widower. You have to cut him some extra slack."

"I can't compete with a dead woman, Laney, and I shouldn't have to."

"No, no, you're right."

"I'm going to tell him the sex was all a mistake," Jillian said.

"Was it?"

"Well, he left in the middle, so obviously he thinks so. I'll beat him to the punch. I'll just tell him it was all a huge mistake. I'll blame the blizzard. I'll blame the Baileys . . ."

In the background, Jillian could hear Nick's low throaty voice whisper something sexy.

"It's okay; it's all right," Jillian said, feeling dismally lonely.

"Jillian, no, this is important. Talk to me. I'm listening. I'm here for you," Delaney reassured her.

"I know that, but just go make love to your husband and give him a hug for me for being the kind of guy who doesn't run away in the middle."

Chapter Twenty

Dumbass.

Tuck berated himself. He'd screwed up. Big-time.

He'd been snowed in a lake house mountain cabin for three days with an incredible woman who was his polar opposite in every way. Thing was, he'd just had the best sex of his life, and he felt guilty as sin. He'd loved Aimee with every bit of his heart, but making love to her had never been so . . . so . . . *all-consuming.* The way it was with Jillian.

And then he'd gotten up right in the middle of sex last night and just left her lying there. The sex was just too damn good. Impossibly good. Unbelievably good. That's what turned him inside out.

Jillian threw herself into lovemaking like it was a religion. She was fiercely devout. Dishing out wild, no-holds-barred sex with a fervency that stole the breath right out of his lungs. And yet at the same time, she tasted as sweet as cotton candy and as crisp as freshly laundered linen. An erotic combination of sultry-eyed temptress and honey-voiced waif. And the smell of her was all over him. Understated but persistent. Uniquely Jillian.

His Jillian.

Tuck groaned. No, no, he had to stop thinking like this. She wasn't his Jillian. Could never be his Jillian.

Why not? whispered a subversive part of him that wasn't playing by the rules. *Why not?*

He craved her. Ached for her. His body tensed and his mouth watered and he hungered to take her again and again and again. Nothing had ever had hold of him like that.

The bedroom door creaked opened, and he heard her pad into the living room. He should pretend to be asleep again like he'd done last night. It's what a smart man would have done.

But when was the last time he'd done anything smart?

He just lay there, staring at the ceiling, and when her head popped over the top of the couch, their eyes met. Glued.

She said nothing and neither did Tuck, but he was acutely aware of her eyes on his.

A long, uncomfortable pause ensued. The only sound between them was Mutt's doggy breathing as he slumbered on the floor in front of the fireplace.

Finally, Jillian drew in a deep breath. God, even the way she swallowed looked sexy. "How'd you sleep?"

"Fine, fine. You?"

"Peachy." She nodded.

She was lying and they both knew it. He'd heard her thrashing around all night, just as he'd been.

He swung his legs off the couch, sat up.

She sat down where his legs had just been. Her hair was mussed, and the sheet creases on her face shouldn't have made her look cute, but dammit, they did. She stared into the ashes of the spent fire, where a few coals smoldered, and dropped her hands into her lap. She wore the blue silk pajamas she'd worn last night. Even with that rumpled-no-makeup-just-rolled-out-of-bed thing she had going on, Jillian was stunning.

Her cheeks pinked under his scrutiny, and her eyelids lowered heavily. "About last night . . . ," she started, then stopped.

"Yeah?"

"I understand completely why you did what you did."

"You do?" That was amazing because Tuck didn't know why he'd done what he'd done.

"It was a mistake."

"Mistake," he echoed.

"We both know that. We don't want it to ruin our friendship, so let's just pretend it never happened. Okay?"

"Okay."

"That is what you want, right?"

"Yes, yes. If that's what you want too."

She nodded rapidly. "Oh yes, exactly. Big mistake."

"Bad."

"Terrible."

"Worst ever."

They looked at each other and both managed to summon up a weak laugh.

"Promise me it won't ever happen again," she said, "please."

"I promise."

"We won't even speak of it." She folded her arms across her chest and looked resolute.

"Speak of what?"

"There, that's it. Perfect."

Neither one of them said another word. Mutt raised his

head and looked at them as if their quietness had awakened him.

Tuck didn't rush to fill the silence, because he had no idea what to say or how to make things right. He didn't even know if he wanted to make things right. One thing he did know—he couldn't stop visualizing her on his bed, in his arms, her body lithe and supple and naked. Passionate and hungry and alive. And she'd looked at him as if he was the center of her universe; that look had been his undoing. That's what had scared the hell out of him.

Tuck was so damned confused. On the one hand, it was as if she'd been made to order. Rush delivery sex mate. Long, shapely legs. Exotic eyes dark as Swiss chocolate. Raspberry-flavored mouth. Silky ebony hair. A devilish tongue that roused the caveman inside him.

And a sweet, moist, tight feminine box that drove him mad with desire.

He wished like hell he hadn't walked out on her in the middle of sex last night. He wished he could go back and fix it. Part of him wanted to gather her in his arms, haul her back to bed, and start all over again. But another part of him—the cowardly part that had run out on her in the first place—held him back.

"Jillian, I . . . ," he started, but had no idea what else he was going to say. *She regrets it. Let it go. You told her you'd let it go, so let it frickin' go.* He cleared his throat. "Jilly—"

"Shh!" She raised a hand.

"What is it?"

"Listen."

Tuck cocked his head, listening. "I don't hear anything."

"Exactly. No wind."

The blizzard was over.

IT TOOK ALL MORNING and part of the afternoon for Tuck and Jillian to dig out of the snow, but once they had a path cleared to the road, they donned cross-country skis and took off.

Jillian glided off to Fielder's Market with Mutt for groceries. Tuck headed for Evie's house to corner his brother-in-law. He desperately needed a guy's perspective on this whole situation.

After he'd promised Jillian they wouldn't talk about it again, Tuck thought of a hundred questions he wanted to ask. For instance, had *any* of it been good for her? Because things had been pretty darned fantastic for him until he'd made like Foghorn Leghorn and chickened out.

Maybe he shouldn't have bailed. If he'd stayed in the bed with her last night, maybe he would have gotten her out of his system. As it was, he was totally obsessed with her. Dammit. She was tougher than he was, putting all this behind them. Dusting her hands of their lovemaking as if it never happened.

Grumbling under his breath, Tuck pushed himself faster with the ski poles, not even noticing how appealing the town looked bunked under the snow. He hoped Ridley had beer in the house. He was in the mood to knock back a couple of brews. Never mind that it was only three o'clock in the afternoon. He'd been snowed in with Jillian for three days, and he needed a release.

Aimee, he should think of Aimee. Aimee would help him forget Jillian.

Okay, okay, what did he love most about Aimee?

Tuck wracked his brain, and in that panic-stricken moment, realized he couldn't call up his wife's face. Whenever he tried to imagine Aimee, he saw Jillian. Instead of Aimee's blond locks twining down her back in soft curls, he saw Jillian and her patrician Cleopatra haircut. Black and straight and angled to her shoulders. He tried to remember how Aimee had felt in his arms all soft and round and girly. But instead, his fingers were recalling the touch of Jillian's strong, lithe, athlete body.

Jillian was in his head. Not just in his head but on his skin. He could smell her. Taste her. She'd invaded his senses like a dictator taking over a country.

Thankfully, he'd finally reached Evie and Ridley's house. He kicked off his skis and whammed his fist against their door.

Ridley answered, his hair down around his shoulders, looking comfortable in sweatpants and a red flannel shirt. "Dude," he said. "You look like hell. What happened?"

"What happened?" Tuck said, shouldering past his brother-in-law. "I've been snowed in for three days with Jillian Samuels. That's what happened."

"The plot thickens."

Tuck raked his gaze over Evie. "How'd you guys weather the storm?"

Ridley shut the door behind him. "Your sister and I have been snowed in as well. It started out sketchy. Just before the storm hit, I caught Evie in my sweat lodge. She'd had a vision that really upset her, but then I convinced the her dream was a good omen, not a bad one, and we straightened everything out. If things went as good as

I think they did, you might be an uncle in nine months. We stayed in bed the entire three days."

"Aw, come on, man." Tuck clamped his hands over his ears. "I don't want to hear that stuff about my sister."

Ridley grinned. "You're jealous because I got some and you didn't?"

"Well . . . ," Tuck said, trailing off.

"Huh?" Ridley blinked.

Tuck paced the tile floor of their living room in his ski boots. *Clump, clump, clump.* "It was the snow. The fireplace. The Baileys Irish Cream . . ."

"You and Jillian did it?" Ridley asked.

"Yes."

"Damn."

"What is it? What's wrong? Is it the jinx thing?"

Ridley laughed. "No. I was pretty well off base about the jinx thing. I owe your sister twenty bucks."

"Huh?"

"Evie bet me twenty bucks if you guys got snowed in together you'd end up in bed."

It was Tuck's turn to curse, but he said something a lot stronger than *damn*. "It was a mistake. A huge mistake."

"It was just sex, right? How big a mistake could it be? Unless you forgot to wear a condom."

"I wore a condom." He clenched his jaw and dropped down on the leather love seat. "It's not that."

"You want a beer?"

"Please."

Ridley retrieved the beer, popped the top, and pressed it into Tuck's hand, but after one swallow, Tuck didn't want it. His brother-in-law perched on the hearth, where he sat and just waited.

Tuck started talking. He told him everything. The kissing, the dancing, the watching of *When Harry Met Sally*, the downing of Baileys Irish Cream. The great sex. The really great sex that came after the sex. And the terrible sex where he got up in the middle of things and ran away.

"Wow," Ridley said after he'd finished. "You really screwed up."

"Tell me about it. Thing is, this morning, she wanted to forget all about it. Didn't even want to discuss it."

"Can you blame her?"

Misery crawled through him. He pulled a palm down his face. "What should I do?"

If anyone could help him think of a way through this sticky mess, it was Ridley. His brother-in-law could handle temperamental Evie when no one else on the planet seemed to be able to manage that trick. Tuck valued his opinion and his advice.

"Nothing," Ridley said sagely.

"Nothing?"

"Nothing."

"But I can't stop thinking about her, and I have to live with her, and how can I wake up every morning and see her and go to bed every night in a separate room and not touch her and . . ."

"Take a deep breath," Ridley advised.

"You, you're the one who caused all this. You put me in your sweat box—"

"Sweat lodge," he interrupted to correct Tuck.

"And you made me have this vision quest I wasn't even interested in having."

"You needed it."

"I have this pervy sex dream about her and then I meet her in the flesh. It's spooky. It's weird. The hairs on my arms go up every time I think about it. Then you tell me she's a jinx and to stay away from her. Then you come back and tell me you were wrong and that she's good for me, and and so I started thinking, maybe, *maybe* . . ." Tuck was getting light-headed from not pausing to breathe.

"Hey." Ridley shrugged. "I'm as fallible as the next guy."

"You could have told me that *before* I took your advice. Now she's looking at me as if I'm a leper, and I've ruined our friendship to boot."

Ridley got up, came across the room, and clamped a hand on Tuck's shoulder. "You, my friend, have a lot to learn about the fairer sex. I can't believe you were married for three years and never figured this stuff out."

"What do you mean?"

"Jillian's probably feeling exactly the same way you are. Worse maybe. You did get up and leave her in the middle of sex. What's she supposed to think? She's gotta be thinking she repulsed you somehow. So to save face this morning, she comes up with this let's-forget-all-about-it plan."

"You really think so?"

"Sure I do and—hey, are those *hickeys*?"

Tuck slapped a hand over his neck. "None of your business," he mumbled, remembering exactly when Jillian had stamped him with her love bites.

Ridley cocked his head and pretended to pout, but his eyes were twinkling with laughter. "Evie's never given me hickeys."

"Stop feeling jealous. If you want hickeys, ask her for hickeys."

"She says they're trashy."

"Then tell her to give you a hickey where no one can see it."

"Good idea."

"Could we get back to the issue at hand? What am I supposed to do about living with Jillian?"

Ridley pursed his lips and placed his hands on his hips. "Move out, I guess."

His brother-in-law said the words Tuck needed to hear. He knew he needed to hear them, but he still wished Ridley hadn't said it.

"You know, I've never seen you this affected by a woman since Aimee."

"I never . . ." Tuck paused, unable to believe what he was about to say. "I was torn in two when I lost Aimee. It was like I had my heart ripped out of my chest, but, Rid, when we were dating, I never felt this kind of torment. What Aimee and I had was quiet and calm and tender. This thing with Jillian—"

All teasing humor was gone in his brother-in-law's eyes. "Is true passion. That's why you walked out on her in the middle of sex—she scared the crap out of you."

A chill went straight through his bones. He didn't want to admit it. Didn't want to say it. Didn't want to feel it. He refused to betray Aimee's memory and what they'd shared.

"You were pretty young when you and Aimee got married," Ridley said.

"I loved her."

"I'm not saying you didn't love Aimee. I'm just saying there's more than one kind of love."

"I'm not in love with Jillian," Tuck insisted, but even as he said, it he felt something treacherous tighten his chest.

Ridley started humming 10cc's "I'm Not in Love."

"Knock it off." Tuck scowled.

He was not in love. He couldn't be in love. Aimee had been his soul mate. They'd both known it. You only get one soul mate. Right?

Ridley kept humming.

"I'm not in love," Tuck growled.

He wondered if Jillian believed in soul mates. She'd told him she didn't believe in magic, but what they'd shared last night—until he'd screwed things up—had been pretty damn magical, indeed.

And if he admitted it (which he didn't), then he'd have to confess (which he couldn't) that the sexual magic between them was stronger than what he'd shared with Aimee.

Tuck shoved the thought away. Jillian was just older, more experienced than Aimee had been. She knew tricks his sweet little bride had never dreamed of; that didn't mean anything except sex with Jillian had been great. No, beyond great. It had been . . . well . . . *magical*.

Jillian probably didn't think so. She'd been quick to deny it this morning. But what if Ridley was right? What if Jillian had just said those things to save face?

"Tuck?"

"Huh?"

"You might want to set that beer bottle down before you bust it in your hand," Ridley advised.

Tuck blinked at his brother-in-law. He'd zoned out, his mind caught in the past, worrying the dilemma. He'd forgotten he was at Ridley and Evie's house. He looked down and saw his hand was wrapped around the longneck Michelob bottle so tightly his knuckles had blanched white. He forced himself to relax his grip and settle the bottle onto a coaster resting on the end table.

"You need to tell her."

"Who?"

"Jillian."

"Tell her what?"

"How you really feel."

"I don't know how I feel."

"You do. You just don't want to admit it."

"I'm glad you're so all wise and all-knowing, Rid. Wanna tell me what I'm thinking right now?"

"You're thinking I should go screw myself."

"See, you *are* all-knowing."

Ridley shook a finger at him. "She got to you."

"I like her, sure. I'm not denying that. We're friends. Or we were. Now I don't know what we are." Longing mixed with despair, then did the tango with an odd combo of hope and resignation.

"Friendship's a great way to start a relationship."

"We didn't start out as friends. We started out as two people forced to share a space."

"No one forced you. You could have left the lake house at any time. You could have moved in with me and Evie. You had options. But you didn't choose to exercise them. There's a reason you didn't leave. Why?"

"I don't know, but whatever the reason, I can't stay there now."

"Granted. Not with the way you left things."

"We can't go back to being friends," he mused. "No matter how much we both might want to pretend this never happened. Harry was right."

"Harry? Who's Harry."

"When Harry Met Sally."

"Oh right, I agree with Harry. You can't stay there and go back to the way things were. So make a move. Either take it a step further and embrace the sex, or forget the friendship and give up the lake house. The deed has never shown up anyway. Just let it all go."

"It means letting go of Aimee," Tuck whispered.

Ridley's eyes were kind. "I know."

Leave or stay? Did he want to embrace the sex? Yes. He wanted it a lot. Jillian had reconnected Tuck with the part of himself that had stopped living the day Aimee had died, but was he really ready for such a huge step? On the other hand, was he ready to walk away from Salvation? Say good-bye to his memories? Was he ready to let Aimee go?

"Whichever one you choose, just quit ruminating about it. You're driving me nutty. We're sitting here after a break in the blizzard gabbing like girls when we should be outside getting stuff done while the sun's shining. Pathetic."

Just then the phone rang.

"Good to see we still have communication with the outside world," Ridley said, and picked up the phone. "Hello?"

Tuck took a swallow of the beer he didn't want.

"It's for you." Ridley handed the phone to him.

"Jillian?" he asked stupidly, nonsensically. There was no reason for her to call him here.

"Steve."

"Steve?"

Ridley handed him the phone. Tuck put it to his ear.

"Yo, my man," Steve said. "I finally got through. We've been trying to call you guys for days. Rang your house first, got no answer, thought you might be here."

"Blizzard just broke, cabin fever," Tuck explained.

"Everyone good?"

"We made it through all right."

"Good. Listen, I've got some great news for you about that music box."

"Yeah?"

"I showed it to my friend, but it wasn't something he handled, so he passed it off to a dealer who specializes in handmade curios. She displayed it in her shop. Customers went nuts over the box. I knew they would. Anyway, she received offers upward of twelve hundred dollars."

Tuck was stunned. "For a music box?"

"There's no substitute for craftsmanship. The dealer said it was like everyone who picked it up fell under its spell. Get this, she took orders."

"On my behalf?" Tuck didn't know if he liked that or not.

"For customized boxes."

"Before asking my permission?"

"Don't get mad. She got thirty-five special orders at twelve hundred dollars a piece. She hasn't taken any money. She told them she didn't know if the artist could deliver that quickly, so you're not obligated. I'm telling you, that music box is bewitched. The Magic Man rides again."

"Huh?" Tuck couldn't believe it.

"Listen, here's the best part. Stella Bagby—that's the dealer's name—is going overseas for the winter. She's willing to let you stay in her place in Midtown while you make the boxes and she's scouting out wholesale deals for the wood to maximize your profits."

"You want me to come back to Manhattan?"

"Just for the winter. Just until you get this new business established."

"You've put in a lot of effort on my behalf."

"Hey, you gave me a job when I sorely needed one. Plus, Desiree and the kids would love to have you so close. We miss you. Ridley and Evie have had you long enough."

"I'll think about it."

"Just let me know soon. Stella wants to sublet if you're not interested, and she leaves for Europe next week."

"That's not much time."

"The stars are aligned; it's time to make a move."

"Yeah. Thanks, Steve."

"Don't mention it. Either way, you're coming up for Christmas with Evie and Ridley, right?"

"Right."

"You bringing Jillian?"

"No."

"Ah, that's a shame. Des and I really liked her."

Me too. "Listen," he said. "I gotta go. Lots of postblizzard things to do."

"Don't leave me hanging too long."

"I'll call you tomorrow."

"Bye." Steve hung up.

"Crossroads," Ridley said as Tuck handed the phone back to him.

"Yeah." He felt stunned, overwhelmed. One minute he was talking to Ridley about moving out and just giving Jillian the lake house, and then suddenly there was this opportunity to move back to Manhattan and start his old life all over again.

"Inevitable and necessary," Ridley said cryptically.

"Huh?"

"It's part of the vision quest."

"What is?"

"The crossroads. Which way are you going to go? Who are you going to be? The decision is now, my friend."

"I'm not ready."

"Doesn't matter. The universe is ready for you to commit. One path or the other. New York or Salvation. Hold on to the past or embrace the future. The choice is yours."

Tuck sank down in the kitchen chair, his head spinning.

Just as quickly as he'd turn cosmic, Ridley was back to his practical, laid-back self. He walked to the coat rack, took down his parka, and shrugged into it. "I'm going out to chop firewood. You coming or are you getting your period?"

"Asshole." Tuck grinned.

Ridley cheerfully flipped him the bird and headed out the back door.

Tuck realized that he had firewood of his own that needed chopping. He trooped out the back door behind Ridley and snapped his skis back on, his thoughts on Jillian. He had an option now. A place to go if he left Salvation. But what was he going to do about his feelings for Jillian?

She was so different from Aimee. The two women were night and day and not just in their appearance.

Aimee had loved cooking and sewing and housekeeping. A homebody. An earth mother. She didn't have strong opinions except in regard to her father and his infidelity that had wrecked their family, and she rarely offered her advice or input. Decision making put her in a dither.

It used to drive him crazy when he'd ask her where she wanted to go for dinner and she'd shrug and say, "Wherever you want to go." It was as if she was defined only by him and his work. When they were married, he'd thought it was great. Thinking back, it felt one-sided. He'd been in charge of their marriage, and Aimee had been along for the ride. Look up *agreeable* in the dictionary and the description fit Aimee to a T.

Jillian had no interest in domestic chores. She did what had to be done in the housekeeping realm, but that was it. She had a dazzling, brilliant mind, and she wasn't afraid to use it. She had so many opinions she could open an Opinions R' Us franchise. Jillian would never allow herself to be defined by any man, and he admired the hell out of her for having her own life, her own will. If he was told to pick one word to describe her, he couldn't do it, although *gumption* would be on the list, along with *strong, argumentative, bold,* and *sexy*.

Aimee had never ruffled his feathers. Jillian stimulated him in a hundred different ways. Some good, some irritating, none of them boring.

But was he ready for anything more than friendship

and sex? Could he really put his heart on the line again? He was terrified that he could not.

And that was the deal. Jillian deserved someone who could give her his full love. Without reservation or hesitation. The fact he was hesitating said it all.

It was time to let go and walk away.

Manhattan was calling.

Chapter Twenty-one

Two days after the town dug out from the storm, Jillian came in the back door from work, set her briefcase on the kitchen table, and doffed her knit cap and gloves. "Hey, Tuck," she called out. "You'll never guess what happened today . . ."

Her words trailed off as she caught sight of him standing in the doorway, two big leather suitcases gripped in his hands.

"Tuck?" she asked tentatively. At the same time, it felt as if someone had smacked her in the back of the head with a two-by-four. "What's up?"

But she didn't have to ask. The look on his face, the set to his shoulders, she just *knew.*

"I'm moving out, Jillian." He set down the suitcases.

"Oh," she whispered, and felt something inside of her slide sideways. Things had been odd between them the past few days, but she'd put that down to the awkwardness of what had happened during the snowstorm. They still hadn't talked about it. She thought at some point they'd discuss it, define the new direction of their relationship. She'd been stepping back, giving him time. But clearly, there would be no talking. Tuck was moving out.

Her first impulse was to plead with him not to go, to

ask what she'd done wrong, to promise to change. But, of course, she did not do any of those things. She was the Ice Queen, the bulldog, the tough competent lawyer who never showed her tender side. She didn't whimper. She didn't beg. She wouldn't change simply to please a man.

Jillian pressed her lips together and took the hit. "I see."

They stared at each other.

"Where are you going?" she finally asked, her chest tightening. She was having trouble catching her breath.

"I have a place to stay in Manhattan."

"Manhattan?" She tried to keep her voice controlled. Not only was he moving out, but he was also moving away. She wouldn't see him again.

"You were right all along."

She moistened her lips with her tongue. Her throat felt parched. "I was?"

"I've been hiding out. It's time to start living again. I have a job making music boxes like the one I made for Evie."

"Oh," she repeated, and then said inanely, "It is a beautiful music box."

He shifted, his gaze never leaving her face, but he said nothing.

"Um, what about the lake house?"

"The deed's never going to turn up. Obviously Sutter lost it. Besides, Blake wanted you to have the house. I was being stubborn insisting on staying here. I realize that now. The place is yours, Jillian." His eyes clouded. "I . . . I want you to have it."

"Tuck . . ." She stopped, swallowed, tasted salt. "I'm the one who's been stubborn. This is your home; you lived here with your wife. I'm the interloper. The outsider. I should be the one to leave."

He shook his head. "You need this place, Jillian. It's given you a new start. Soon you'll take the bar exam, and I know you'll pass it. Then you'll eventually take over Sutter's law practice. Me?" He shrugged. "This house, the past, has been holding me back, keeping me from moving on with my life, and I wasn't able to see that until you showed up."

Sorrow jolted her straight to her soul. He was telling her that she'd given him the strength to leave. It served her right for daring to hope.

She'd known better. People always betrayed you or left you. Her mother had dumped her on her father's doorstep and run away. Then her father had died, leaving her to a bitter woman who resented having to raise her husband's illegitimate daughter. And, of course, there was Alex Fredericks, who'd betrayed her as well. Even her best friends had moved on with their lives, leaving her behind.

"I'm catching an early morning flight to New York."

"What's the rush?" she asked, cringing inwardly, terrified he could hear the sadness in her voice. Purposefully she shrugged, acting as if she didn't care. "I mean, it's trivia night at the Rusty Nail. We're supposed to play against Lexi and Jefferson, remember?"

"If I don't make it to New York by tomorrow, the woman's going to sublet her place to someone else. She's leaving for Europe and has to have the place rented before she takes off."

She hitched in a breath. "So this is good-bye?"

He nodded. "I just took Mutt out for a walk. He loves the snow."

"That he does."

Silence stretched between them.

"Mutt's another reason for you to keep the lake house." His eyes were all over her face, and she realized she hadn't broken his gaze either.

"So you already said good-bye to Mutt?"

"Yeah." His Adam's apple bobbed. "Brought him a juicy soup bone from the Bluebird. He's in the living room in front of the fire gnawing it up." His smile was slight.

"Thanks," she said, because she didn't know what else to say.

Finally, Tuck tore his gaze from hers and bent to pick up his suitcases, then paused. "For what it's worth?"

"Yes?" Her heart quickened. What was he going to say?

"The town pool betting on when you'd leave?"

"Yes?"

"I had today's date in the pot. Ironic, huh?"

"There goes your ten bucks." She struggled hard to keep her face neutral. She wasn't about to let him know how much she was hurting.

A horn honked outside.

"That's Ridley. He's driving me to the airport in Denver."

She nodded.

"Take care of yourself, Jillian." He looked wistful, but she refused to let it get to her.

"You too, Tuck."

"We still friends, Sally?"

"Friends," she echoed, but she knew it was a lie. They could never go back to being just friends.

Tuck stepped toward her and gave her a quick kiss on her cheek. A nice kiss. A friendly kiss. She wanted to slug him for it.

"Take care of yourself." Then without another word, he turned and walked out the door.

Jillian let him go. What else could she do? She stumbled to the living room and plunked down on the couch. The room was cold, but she was too depressed to get up and poke the embers, to add wood to the fire. Mutt, sensing her mood, came over and stuck his head in her lap. She reached out to scratch his ears. He whined his sympathy and she just broke.

The woman who never cried sat on the couch, thick tears rolling down her cheeks. She'd never had a feeling like this. Her friends had told her it was a good feeling, a wonderful feeling, but to Jillian it was pure torture.

She'd been denying it, avoiding it, pretending they were just friends, but after last night, she knew she was lying to herself. She was stone cold in love with Tuck Manning, and he wasn't able to love her back.

TWO WEEKS AFTER TUCK MOVED to Manhattan, Jillian sat on a barstool at the Bluebird, elbows on the counter, her chin propped morosely in her palms, trying her best not to think about how empty her life was now that he'd gone or how much she missed him. But it was particularly difficult when she kept picturing him totally naked, stretched out on the bed, head propped in his hand and him winking provocatively at her.

Why couldn't she get that damned man out of her head?

She clenched her teeth and pushed the cold scrambled

eggs she'd ordered but didn't possess the enthusiasm to eat around on her plate. The Bluebird was decorated for Christmas, tree in the corner, lights strung around the room, pine boughs and holly and mistletoe above the door.

Hands down, Tuck was the best lover she'd ever had, bar none. She doubted there was a better lover on the planet. At least for her. It seemed he'd known without her having to tell him exactly what she needed and when she needed it. Until the unpleasant part where he'd abandoned her in the middle.

And even as they were digging out of the snow and purposefully not discussing how they were feeling, Jillian had quelled an overwhelming urge to throw herself into his arms and tell him she wanted so much more than either sex or friendship.

She wanted the kind of love he'd had with Aimee. And then he'd just packed up and moved to New York without any notice after they'd made love. Every time she thought about it, she got a painful catch in the dead center of her chest.

"You can't ever replace Aimee in his eyes," she muttered under her breath. "There's no point in trying."

So many people had abandoned her in one way or another. She'd learned that she could not depend on anyone. There was no guide, no teacher, no authority that could save her. There was only herself.

She'd spent her life holding her feelings in reserve, afraid to trust, terrified that she'd be abandoned again if she dared to give away her heart. She realized now that she'd displaced her emotions into her career. She'd used her loyalty to law as a way to avoid false starts and stops in her personal life.

But when she lost Blake and quit her job, she found something else. Salvation. That's what she had to remember. The lake house, the town, the people. She'd survive without Tuck.

Now if only she could stop thinking about him.

Snap out of it. Focus on something else. Think about studying for the bar.

But the test seemed so far away. The lonely winter loomed long.

Evie came over. "Mind if I sit down?"

"Not at all."

Evie came around from the other side of the counter and plunked down on the barstool next to her. "Eggs that bad?"

Jillian shook her head. "It's not the food. It's me."

"I'm sorry about Tuck moving to Manhattan. I miss him too. I thought you guys were working on something."

She shrugged. "Hey, it wasn't meant to be."

Evie patted her hand.

"How are you and Ridley doing?" Jillian asked, eager to get the subject off her and Tuck. "Any news on the baby front?"

To her alarm, Evie's eyes misted with tears.

"What is it? What's wrong?"

Evie clenched her jaw. "I've been putting on a brave face, but"—she swallowed—"during the storm, I went and did this vision quest thing, and I got a bad omen. Ridley says it's a good omen, but I don't believe him. I think he was just trying to placate me."

"Vision quest? What are you talking about?"

Evie explained what a vision quest was and detailed what she'd seen.

"You know, I really don't believe in that sort of thing, Evie."

"I didn't either, but when Tuck . . ." Evie bit down on her bottom lip.

"When Tuck what?"

"On the second anniversary of Aimee's death, Ridley stuck Tuck in the sweat lodge and he had a vision."

"Good vision or bad vision?"

"It was about you."

"Really? What did he see?"

"You'll have to ask Tuck; he didn't talk to me about it. I got all this secondhand from Ridley."

"So this vision you had," Jillian said, switching the focus back to Evie. "What was the omen?"

"I'll probably never have kids, and I want them so badly. The thing is, it's affecting our marriage. Ridley tries and he's Mr. Optimistic, but, Jillian, I'm scared we won't survive this." A tear slipped down her cheek.

"Come on, you guys really love each other. You can work this out. Can't you?"

"I don't know if love is enough. I've tried to keep the faith but . . ." Evie swallowed visibly as the tears streamed faster down her face. "I got my period. I was so hoping that this month—this time—after all the love we made during the blizzard . . . but it's just not going to happen. Faith isn't going to change reality. Babies just aren't in the cards for us."

Evie's distress stilled Jillian's heart. She wasn't a big believer in the power of love in the first place, but to think that a couple as strong as Evie and Ridley couldn't overcome their problems confirmed every negative thing she'd ever believed about love.

"I'm sorry. So there's no hope left?"

Evie wiped at her eyes, tried to smile but failed miserably. "We're going to New York to spend Christmas with my sister Desiree and her family. I have an appointment with a celebrity fertility specialist. He helps movie stars in their fifties have babies. It's gonna cost us a big chunk of our savings, but I'm desperate. If this doesn't work . . ." She let her words trail off again.

"I wish you the best of luck."

At that moment, the bell over the door jangled. Bill Chambers and his fiancée Lily Massey came in, bundled in snowsuits and gazing romantically into each other's eyes. Jillian felt a twinge—part jealousy, part longing, part concern for Lily, who'd torn up her prenup agreement for this man. She had no legal protection now; she was banking her future on love.

"Jillian, hi!" Lily called out, and scurried across the room toward her, Bill following in her wake. "I've been looking all over for you."

"What's up?"

"We just wanted to give you this." Lily placed a white linen card in her hand. "An official invitation to our wedding on Christmas Eve. You're still planning on coming, right?"

Why not? It wasn't like she had anywhere else to go. "Sure."

"Evie and Ridley are bailing on us." Lily gave a pretend pout.

"Family thing," Evie said.

"We understand," Bill interjected.

"But we're sooo going to miss you," Lily said with her native California inflection.

The door opened again. Lexi and Jefferson came in laughing over some shared joke. Jillian had to admit they were a good-looking couple. Over the past few weeks, Lexi had been giving her daily updates on their romance. Apparently, things were hot and heavy.

She was in the midst of a love-a-thon.

Lexi and Jefferson came over and started chatting with Lily and Bill about the wedding. Evie got up and went back to work. Jillian felt like a fifth wheel. She was about to leave when Lexi leaned over to whispered, "How you holding up?"

"Fine, fine, why wouldn't I be?"

"I know how much you're missing Tuck. I can imagine how I'd feel if Jefferson was in New York and I was stuck here."

Jillian waved a hand. "Please, I'm fine."

Lexi looked skeptical. "Are you sure? 'Cause if you want a girls night out, just you and me closing down the Rusty Nail, say the word. I'm there for you."

Jillian shook her head.

The bell over the door jangled a third time. Everyone looked over to see Sutter Godfrey cross the threshold, leaning heavily on his cane but out of his wheelchair. The entire café clapped. "Way to walk it, Sutter," Dutch called from the kitchen.

Sutter waved away the accolades. His eyes met Jillian's.

"Ah," he said. "Just the lady I wanted to see."

WHILE SUTTER was dragging Jillian into the back room for a private conversation, Tuck was walking up 42nd Street. He'd been in Manhattan for two weeks and he'd yet to pick up a carving tool. He hadn't been able to work. The city noises kept him up at night. In the day, he'd stare out the window at the building across from him, seeing in his mind's eye Salvation Lake surrounded by the Rocky Mountains.

He tried to work, but his creativity fled. The wood felt cold, dead in his hands. He'd stare at the wood, willing inspiration, but nothing happened.

Stella Bagby's apartment was spacious by New York standards and was only three blocks from the hustle and bustle of Time's Square. The city was alive, dusted with snow, Christmas lights winking, people carrying brightly colored shopping bags. He used to love it here. The energy, the urgency, the audacity of the best city in the world.

But the Big Apple was no longer in his blood. His pulse didn't skip, his breathing didn't quicken, his mind didn't rev as he took it all in. His heart was still in Colorado.

He knew he looked out of place in his flannel, jeans, and work boots, but he didn't care. He walked at a Colorado pace, people zipping around him. He turned up Broadway, entered the throng of Times Square. He looked up at a theater marquis and saw to his surprise there was a revival of *Les Miserables*. Immediately he thought of Jillian.

It was their favorite musical.

His chest tightened. He glanced at his watch. The matinee started in fifteen minutes.

He imagined Jillian with him. He pictured them snuggled together in the balcony seating, whispering the lines to each other; they both knew the story so well. He wished he could share this with her.

"For old time's sake," he murmured, then walked up to the booth and bought a ticket.

WHILE TUCK WAS WALKING into *Les Miserables*, Jillian was sitting down across from Sutter in the back room of the Bluebird.

"What did you want to see me about?" she asked.

"I found this in a desk drawer at my home office," he said, pulling a manila envelope from the inside of his jacket and sliding it across the table to Jillian.

"You have a home office?"

"Didn't I mention that?" His eyes twinkled.

"No, you didn't."

"You've been doing a good job, and I thought it was time to give you this," he said as she removed the rubber band he'd wrapped around the envelope.

A bonus? she wondered. Or maybe he'd drawn up papers to make her his partner. Her pulse accelerated.

"I've been getting community reports. Everyone likes you. Business has picked up, which I'm sure you know. Smart of me to hire you."

She didn't mention that it had been her idea. She slit open the envelope with her finger, slid out the paper inside. Her breath hung in her lungs when she saw what it was.

The deed to the lake house. Made out to Tuck.

She looked up to meet his gaze. "You found it."

"I never lost it." His eyes were sharp. The old man was not a fool.

"You had it all along. But why—"

"There's a letter inside that envelope too." He nodded. "I think you should read it now."

She found the letter and opened it with trembling fingers. Even before she saw the familiar handwriting, she knew who it was from, and hot tears caught in the back of her throat.

My dearest Jillian,

I write this letter to you after having just received news that I have an inoperable brain tumor. At most, I have six months to live. You won't be reading this until after my death, but I ask you, my dear friend, please don't grieve. I'm with my darling Aimee now. I couldn't do right by her in life, but I feel with all my heart that in death we will be reunited.

You and I never talked about faith, and until I lost my daughter, I'm not sure I had much. I made many mistakes, hurt many people. But you were the one shining star in my screwed up world. I turned you into my surrogate daughter, and I loved you like a father.

I worry about you, Jillian. You've got such an emotional wall up. It's necessary in our profession to detach, to distance ourselves from the ugly world we deal in, but you've carried it too far. Whenever you do get involved with men, it's those wretched types like Alex Fredericks. I know you're afraid to take a chance on an honest, kind man you could really love. I don't want you to make the same mistakes I made. I want you to be able to love freely, wholeheartedly, without reservation or hesitation.

To that end, I must confess to a bit of subterfuge, and my old friend Sutter has agreed to play along.

Right after Aimee died, I had Hamilton Green draw up a will giving you the lake house. It was always my intention for you to have the place, but I figured that day would be a long time off. Today, the oncologist told me differently.

Even though you didn't bring your problems to me, I knew you were having a crisis of conscience over your affair with Fredericks. I also knew Tuck was grieving too hard and too long for Aimee. Maybe I shouldn't have let him stay in the lake house. Maybe if I'd pushed him, he would have started healing faster.

It doesn't matter. What does matter is that I realized you two were perfect for each other if you could only see it. Tuck is a good and honest man. You are a smart, strong woman who deserves to be loved.

Therefore, I'm deeding the house to Tuck, but I'm having Sutter "forget" to file the deed and then "lose" it. My hope with this little beyond-the-grave matchmaking is that Tuck will fight to stay in the house because of his ties to Aimee and you'll fight to keep it because you have nowhere else to go.

Yes, I knew Newsom was going to appoint Fredericks to take my place, and I knew the egotistical bastard would accept. I also knew he'd try to force you to knuckle under and that you had too much integrity to take it. I hope you can forgive me if I've caused you any distress. That was never my intention. The lake house is your life preserver, and Tuck can be your anchor if you can learn to see your way clear to each other.

But even if it doesn't work out between you two, I do know that you have found your way to Salvation.

With all my endearing love,

Blake

DURING INTERMISSION, Tuck wandered out into the lobby, his mind still on Jillian. He'd barely even noticed the actors on the stage.

A group of young tween girls were chatting avidly about the musical, but Tuck didn't pay much attention to them—that is, until he heard a familiar voice urging the girls to hurry and down their refreshments before the curtain went up on the final act.

His head jerked up, and he glanced over to see Aimee's mother, Margery, ushering her charges toward their seats. Their eyes met.

"Tuck," she said, and broke into an instant smile. "I didn't know you were back in Manhattan. Why didn't you give me a call?"

Without even knowing he was going to say it, Tuck said, "I . . . I don't know what I'm doing here, Margery."

She looked around him. "You're alone?"

"Yes."

"Girls, go on back to your seats. I'll be with you in a minute."

Giggling, the girls took off.

"Sorry," Margery said, drawing closer to him. "Field trip."

"You're still teaching at Andover?"

"In a Manning building," she said, referring to the classrooms he'd built in Albany. "I'm so happy you're back. You've been grieving too long. It's time to share your gift with the world again."

They stood in awkward silence, theater patrons pushing past them, headed back to the auditorium. She took his elbow and pulled him out of the flow of traffic.

"I miss her, Margery."

"I know you do, Tuck. I miss her, too, but you've got to move on. Are you dating anyone?"

He thought of Jillian, shook his head.

"Why not?"

"There was someone," he said. "But I blew it. I . . ."

She squeezed his forearm. "Are you in love with this woman?"

Miserably, he nodded. "I tried not to fall in love with her. I felt like I was cheating on Aimee. I came to the city. I wanted to start over, but . . ." He swept his hand at the theater. "I came here because she loves *Les Miz* like I do. I didn't know they were having a revival."

"Aimee hated *Les Miz*," Margery said. "She hated musicals. Loved plays, though."

"I know."

Another awkward pause.

"Look, Tuck. You're only thirty. You can spend the rest of your life grieving. If you've found someone, embrace it. Aimee would understand. If the roles were reversed, you'd want her to find love again, wouldn't you?"

"Yes, yes, sure."

"Okay, then." Margery smiled softly. "I've got to get back to my girls, and you need to get back to . . . what's her name?"

"Jillian Samuels."

"Oh." She sounded surprised. "Blake's surrogate daughter?"

"You know about Jillian?"

Margery nodded. "I suppose there's a kind of poetic justice to it."

"You're not angry?"

"Honey," Margery said, "when you get to be my age, you realize how truly rare unconditional love is, and when you can find it, you grab it with both hands. You have my blessings, and I believe you have Aimee's as well."

Tuck went back into the theater for the last act, but he couldn't concentrate on the story. All he could do was think of Jillian and how damned much he missed her. Margery was right. He was wrong.

How had he been so blind as to throw away love? It was such a rare and precious thing. He'd been damned lucky to have a second chance at it, and he'd just walked away.

Proud, stubborn, scared.

Yeah. he was scared. That's why he'd run. Terrified that if he dared love Jillian, he'd lose her the way he lost Aimee.

So what are you going to do about it? Stay here cowering or do something to show Jillian how much you love her?

Once the thought popped into his head, Tuck knew exactly what he had to do before he could return to her. He jumped up and ran from the theater, his heart pounding with hope.

Tuck ran down the street, dodging foot traffic, bent on

finding a store that sold the highest grade mahogany in town.

THREE DAYS BEFORE CHRISTMAS, as they were waiting in the lobby of the expensive, hot-shot Fifth Avenue fertility specialist's office, Ridley opened the sack containing Evie's Christmas present. He felt compelled to give it to her here, and Ridley was not a man who ignored his instincts.

She was leafing through a baby magazine and paused to look over at him. "Are you finally going to tell me what you've got in the bag?"

"It's the reason Tuck's in New York."

"What?" She put down the magazine.

"I asked Tuck to make it for your Christmas present. Steve saw it when they came over for Thanksgiving and insisted on showing it to some art dealers in town. They went ape over it, and now Tuck's been commissioned to make a boatload of them. That's why he came back to Manhattan. The magic is back. What's in the box is bedazzling people the way his classrooms did."

"And you're just now telling me this?"

"I didn't want to ruin the surprise." Ridley took the music box wrapped in green foil from the sack and passed it to her. "Open it."

Evie eyed her husband, wondering what in the world was going on. Things had been up and down with them, mainly because her emotions had been on a roller coaster. Ridley rolled with the punches, but sometimes he'd escape to the sweat lodge, and then she'd feel guilty for running him off with her fears.

"Babe, I just want you to know that whatever happens in there"—he nodded toward the doctor's office door—"I love you and I'm behind you one hundred percent."

"Thank you. That means the world to me."

He squeezed her hand. "Open the package."

A sweet, unexpected giddiness enveloped her, and she realized it had been a long time since she'd felt truly happy. She felt it now, in the squeeze of her husband's hand.

Evie undid the bow, lifted up the tape, slid the foil wrapping off. She opened the lid, and when she spied the cradle, her heart flip-flopped. "Oh my. This is so beautiful."

She lifted out the music box, watched the cradle rock. The carvings were intricate, delicate, sublime. "Tuck did this?"

Ridley nodded. "Your brother is an artist. He shouldn't be wasting his time making cabinets for tract homes. Steve feels the same way. It's why he brought him back to New York."

She opened the music box, and it began to play "Faith." Several people in the waiting room looked over at them.

"You gotta have faith, babe," Ridley whispered. "Faith in us. Faith in me. Faith in the baby who's coming our way."

Her nose clogged with tears. "Oh, Ridley, you're the best husband any woman could ask for."

"Mrs. Red Deer?" called the office nurse, dressed in cool, sage green scrubs, from the doorway. "We're ready for you now."

She handed the music box back to Ridley, and he

stowed it in the sack. It was still playing "Faith," as the nurse led them to the examination room.

The nurse asked Ridley to wait in the hallway while Evie got undressed and the nurse put her legs in the stirrups, covered her with a sheet, and let Ridley come into the room. He perched his big body on the thin-legged chair beside the examination table. Evie saw on his face that he was as worried as she.

"It's gonna be okay. We've got each other."

She nodded.

The door opened. The specialist came in. He introduced himself. Shook Ridley's hand. Then all business, he donned gloves, sat on the rolling stool, and went down at the end of the table to perform a pelvic exam on Evie while he questioned them about their fertility status.

Evie told him everything they'd tried. "We're desperate, Doctor," she admitted. "You're our last hope."

The specialist finished the exam, put the sheet back in place, snapped off the rubber gloves, and stood up. "I'm sorry, Mrs. Red Deer. I can't help you."

Despair unlike anything she'd ever felt swallowed Evie up whole. It was over. The dream she'd dared to dream. The vision quest was right. She had no eggs left in her basket. From the sack on the floor, the music box dinged one lone note of "Faith" and then fell silent.

Where the hell did faith get you? Sorrow stomped on her soul.

Ridley got to his feet, hands clenched at his sides. "Why not? What's wrong? Why can't you help us have a baby?"

"Because." The doctor's eyes met Evie's and he smiled. "You're already pregnant."

Chapter Twenty-two

On Christmas Eve, it took every ounce of courage Jillian possessed to drive herself up to Thunder Mountain for Bill and Lily's wedding. But once she was there, she had to admit it was a beautiful location for the ceremony, and it was the perfect time of year to get married at a ski resort.

The lights were beautiful, the decorations festive. Lily was breathtaking in her white floor-length wedding dress, carrying a bouquet of white calla lilies as her father escorted her down the aisle of the intimate chapel.

Then Jillian looked up and saw him.

Tuck.

She rubbed her eyes, sure it was a mirage, but no. There was Tuck in what looked like the tux he wore on the cover of *Architectural Digest.* The Magic Man of Manhattan. He must have gotten her message that Sutter had found the lake house deed.

This is just like *When Harry Met Sally*, she thought absurdly. Except in *When Harry Met Sally*, they got together in the end. She was holding out no such hope for herself and Tuck.

Most of the town of Salvation was at the reception that followed. Evie and Ridley were there as well, Ridley strutting like the proud papa-to-be that he was. They'd celebrated Christmas early with Evie's family, then flown home to break the good news of Evie's pregnancy to Ridley's folks and the rest of Salvation.

Jillian ended up seated at a table with Sutter Godfrey and his wife. The meal was pleasant. She ate without tasting it. The tables were cleared, the band started playing, and the bride and groom had their first dance. She hadn't spotted Tuck in the crowded dining room, and she was wondering if he'd already left when her cell phone rang. She took it out of her purse.

Sutter frowned at her. "It's bad manners to take a cell phone call at the table."

"You're right," she said, and got up to walk toward the alcove.

That's when she saw him and lost her breath. "Hello," she whispered into the cell phone, her eyes on tuxedoed Tuck with his cell phone to his ear.

"Hello, Sally," he said.

Her heart fluttered. "Why, hi there, Harry."

"You're looking quite beautiful."

"Not so shabby yourself. You clean up quite nicely." She walked toward him.

His grin reeled her in.

She shut her phone.

He held out his hand. "Care to dance?"

She was going to tell him no; she meant to tell him no, but then the band started playing "Do You Believe in Magic" and she just said, "I'd love to."

Tuck swept her onto the dance floor, his hand wrapped securely around her waist.

"I had no idea you were such a good dancer, Magic Man."

"You're not so bad yourself, Queenie."

"Did you slip the band a twenty to play this song?"

"It was a hundred."

"Big spender."

He spun her around the floor, then pulled her up close against him. "Nothing's too good for my girl."

"Your girl? Since when am I your girl?"

"Can we go somewhere and talk?"

Oh, how she wanted to hope. But she was so scared, so afraid to take that leap of faith.

"Please," he said. "I have a special Christmas present just for you."

"I don't know." She hesitated. "You did a number on me before."

He looked contrite. "Come on, Sally. Harry admits he behaved like a complete putz."

"Putz is putting it nicely," she said.

"Okay, I acted like a jerk."

"Just a jerk?"

"An ass. I was an ass."

She nodded. "True enough. What happened to your big career in Manhattan?"

"Mistake."

"How do you know this isn't the mistake?"

His eyes darkened. "Being with you was never a mistake."

"Coulda fooled me," she said lightly, but her heart was strumming. "The way you ran out of the bedroom on me that night during the blizzard."

"Forget putz, forget jerk, forget ass. I was a total chicken-shit tool."

"Mmm-hmm."

"I was scared, Jillian."

"And I wasn't?"

"You're gonna make me work for this, aren't you?"

"No one appreciates that which comes easily," she teased.

"Then you, Queenie, are supremely appreciated."

"That's all I needed to hear." She wrapped her arms around his neck, and he bent to kiss her. The minute their lips touched, she burst into flames of sexual delight. No way could she drag this out, even if she was having fun sassing him. All she wanted was to make love to him again.

"You know," he said, "they're giving sleigh rides around the resort."

"Really?"

"That sound like something you'd be interested in?"

"I might be persuaded."

Tuck escorted her out of the reception hall and led her outside, where the horse-drawn sleighs were waiting along with wool blankets and complimentary wassail. A valet also handed Tuck a box wrapped with silver paper and a bright blue foil bow.

Once they were away from the hubbub of the wedding celebration, he handed it to Jillian. "Your Christmas present."

"I . . . I didn't get you anything."

"You danced with me. You're on the sleigh with me. You're hearing me out. Those are the only gifts I need."

Sleigh bells on the horse jingled. The air smelled of

snow and pinecones. The heat from Jillian's body warmed him from the outside in.

"Tuck . . ."

"Go ahead. Open it."

She unwrapped the package, took the lid off the box, and sucked in her breath.

"I made it myself," he said.

"Oh, Tuck." Tears shone in her eyes as she took the tackle box, made from mahogany wood but painted pink with yellow daisies stenciled on it. Just like the tackle box her daddy had given her.

"Undo the clasps."

She opened the metal clasps, and when she lifted the lid, it started to play "Do You Believe in Magic?" "A music box tackle box?"

"Do you like it?"

She wiped away her tears with the back of her hand.

"Jillian?" Sudden panic clutched him. She was trembling, and he was terrified she felt cornered. It was the last thing Tuck wanted to make her feel.

"It's the most wonderful present I've ever gotten," she sobbed. "Oh dammit, Tuck, you've made me bawl."

He pulled a clean tissue from his pocket and passed it to her. She dabbed at her eyes. "What's this all about? What happened? What changed?"

"After we made love and I ran out on you—because I couldn't deal with the depth of my feelings—I understood you were right that day when you accused me of being an underachiever. I had used Aimee's illness as an excuse to escape my sudden celebrity. I realized that I had to face my past and deal with it before I could come to you free and ready to love again."

"And?"

He took her hand in his, squeezed it tight. "I tried to forget you. I fought to deny we were fated. I told myself it wasn't logical. I'd already had my one great romance, and lightning doesn't strike twice, but, Jillian, it did. It has."

"What are you saying, Tuck?"

"I had a vision of you," he admitted. "In a dream. In Ridley's sweat lodge. Long before we ever met."

Jillian's eyes widened. He was confessing it to her.

"It sounds stupid now, hearing myself saying it, but it's true. It was the night of the second anniversary of Aimee's death, and I was torn up."

He told her then what happened. How he'd fallen into the lake. How Ridley had rescued him and shoved him freezing wet into the sweat lodge and made him get naked and breathe smoke and take a vision quest.

"I saw you first in the dream and then we met," he said.

Tuck was afraid she was going to tell him he was nuts. Terrified she was going to tell the driver to stop the sleigh and walk off without him. Especially when he saw her trembling. He'd made a big mistake. He shouldn't have told her any of this. It was crazy; he knew it sounded nuts, but it was the truth, and he needed her to know why he felt the way he did.

"Jillian." He reached out to touch her shoulder. "Am I freaking you out?"

She shook her head and smiled at him through the mist of tears. Her lips parted. "I saw you too."

The breath fled from his lungs. "What?"

She nodded and then told him a fantastic story about a magic wedding veil.

"I didn't think you believed in stuff like that . . . I thought . . ."

"I always wanted to believe," she whispered, "but I was so scared to believe in case it wasn't real."

"I'm real," he said, and pulled her into his arms. "And I'm here."

"Oh, Tuck."

"I never thought I'd feel the magic again. I thought one shot at love was all you got in life. I held on to Aimee too long. I know that. I also know she'd want me to be happy. To love again. To have a family."

"Are you sure?"

"I'm tired of being among the walking wounded. You made me come alive again, Queenie. You challenged me, you nurtured me, you stood up for me. Even though you never said it, you showed me exactly how much you loved me. You make me want to be the man you see in me. You saved me, Jillian. In more ways than you can ever know."

"Tell me," she whispered.

"I love you," he said, and squeezed her tight.

He was ready to risk his heart again. Jillian was worth the gamble. He loved her so much. He still loved Aimee but in the soft way of memories. And his heart was big enough to have two great loves in his life. He was a lucky, lucky man to have found Jillian, and he told her so. Kissing her and whispering his love for her over and over and over. "I love, I love you, I love you."

"I love you too," she whispered. "And I want you to know I've never said that to anyone before."

"I know how hard this is for you. I treasure your ability to say it to me now." Tuck reached out, took her hands, and laced his fingers through hers. He put his head to her forehead and looked deeply into her eyes. "You hear me on this, Queenie? I love you."

Jillian nodded. She heard him. This man loved her. He not only told her, but he'd also showed her repeatedly, and she'd just been too scared to recognize what it was or admit to herself what she was feeling in return. Too afraid there wasn't really such a thing as love this deep and wonderful. But now it was here, and she was feeling it, and she felt so stupid for not believing, not understanding. Her friends had tried to tell her, but their words of encouragement had fallen on deaf ears. She had to find out for herself.

As she looked into Tuck's eyes as deeply as he was looking into hers, she felt her consciousness shift to a whole new level of being.

For Tuck had convinced her to trust. Trust was all she needed to believe in the true miracle of love.

"My Magic Man," she murmured, and kissed him from the very depths of her faithful soul.

Epilogue

It was time to let go.

Tuck knew that as surely as he knew he loved Jillian. Loving her didn't mean he loved Aimee less. He had room in his heart for two great loves in his life, and he realized his love for Aimee had been the love of his youth, his feelings pure and simple and, honestly, in retrospect, too dependent.

The love he felt for Jillian was more mature. It was the love of his adulthood. Stronger, more complex, more autonomous. Jillian made him change and grow in ways Aimee never had. He was ready for this grown-up kind of love. Ready and unafraid.

They walked somberly down the dock together on that first day of summer, Jillian carrying the urn with Blake's ashes. They were dressed in black jeans and sweaters, black boots, and black leather jackets. They climbed into the skiff and rowed out into the middle of the lake. Tuck remembered the last time he'd been out on the lake. So much had changed since that autumn day.

The sun was warm on their faces, but the air was still chilly. From the center of the water, they could see the lake house.

Tuck's eyes met Jillian's and she nodded. Slowly, with

great reverence, they said a prayer and then they said good-bye to Blake.

They sat for a long moment, not talking, just watching the water wash away the past and the sun slip down the horizon.

"It's time to go," Jillian said at last.

Tuck nodded. He dipped the oars into the water, rowing back to the lake house and giving thanks for the woman sitting across from him. Jillian had brought him back to life. He'd been emotionally dead when he'd met her, and she'd saved his soul.

The little craft glided over the gentle current, carrying them to shore. He docked the boat. Jillian climbed out and tied it up, and then she reached for his hand. He took it. Partners, the two of them.

And in each other's arms, they'd both found what they'd been searching for.

Salvation.

Dear Readers,

Writing the Wedding Veil Wishes has been such fun I hate to see the series end. If *Rocky Mountain Heat* (previously published as *All of Me*) is your introduction to the series, I envy you getting to meet the characters for the first time. To me, one of the most endearing things about Wedding Veil Wishes is the camaraderie between these four friends. In today's hectic work we all need our women friends to help us through the ups and downs life (and romance) often throws our way.

The adventure all started in *Long, Tall Texan* (previously published as *There Goes the Bride*) with Delaney Cartwright who finds that all important wish-fulfilling wedding veil in that mysterious little consignment shop in Houston, Texas. Having the courage to wish on that legendary veil for a way out of her high-society wedding led to Delaney's heart's true desire—sexy cop Nick Vinetti.

Delaney passed the veil on to wedding videographer Tish Gallagher in *Second Chance Hero* (previously published as *Once Smitten, Twice Shy*). Some sad life circumstances have broken Tish's heart and her habit of using shopping as a solace has gotten her into deep financial trouble. But when she wishes on the veil to get out of debt and ends up with a chance to film the wedding of the President's daughter, she's stunned to learn the groom is none other than Secret Service Agent Shane Tremont, the ex-husband she never stopped loving.

In *Valentine, Texas* (previously published as *Addicted to Love*), starry-eyed Rachael Henderson (who was born in Valentine, Texas, on Valentine's Day) is wishing on the veil to help her get rid of her foolish romantic notions. After all, she's been jilted at the altar—*twice*. The last time on the same day her parents informed her they're getting divorced after twenty-seven years. Disillusioned with love, she starts Romanceaholics Anonymous, only to discover the feelings she has for her childhood crush, Sheriff Brody Carlton, are anything but foolish.

And last but not least, is Jillian Samuels from *Rocky Mountain Heat* (previously published as *All of Me*) who never believed in true love or fairytale endings. She isn't about to wish on that veil until a cruel betrayal leaves her raw and aching. Pushed to the limit, she puts on the veil, falls asleep, and dreams of her beloved. The only problem is, widower Tuck Manner is still mourning the loss of his beloved wife.

It's with a fond farewell I bid Delaney, Tish, Rachael, and Jillian their happily-ever-after. And I hope, as you read their stories, they will inspire you to do some wishing of your very own.

May your life be filled with love,

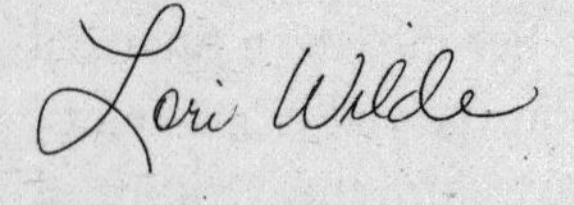

In Tish and Shane's story, can a lucky wedding veil—and a presidential wedding—bring these two ex-lovers back together?

Please turn the page for an excerpt from *Second Chance Hero* (previously published as *Once Smitten, Twice Shy*).

Chapter 1

From behind his high-end designer sunglasses, Secret Service agent Shane Tremont scanned the crowd gathered for the groundbreaking of the Nathan Benedict wing at the University of Texas campus.

His elbows were loose, his breathing regular, his stance commanding and self-confident. The perimeter had been secured. The crowd controlled. His Sig Sauer P229 357-caliber pistol nestled comfortably in his shoulder holster, freshly cleaned and loaded, along with a full capacity of ammunition clips stowed in the holster pockets and a bulletproof vest molded against his chest.

Although Nathan Benedict, the President of the United States, was being honored at his alma mater, he wasn't attending the ceremony. In Nathan's place was his twenty-two-year-old daughter, Elysee, who'd been entrusted with clipping the ceremonial ribbon in her father's absence.

Everyone loved sweet-natured Elysee, and it was Shane's job to guard her life with his own. His nerves might be relaxed, but his muscles were tense as coiled springs, cocked and ready for action.

The sky was clear and blue and balmy—the perfect mid-October afternoon in Texas. He was acutely aware of the political protesters. They carried signs scrawled with anti-Benedict sentiment. The Austin police held them at bay behind the picket line several hundred yards from the groundbreaking site.

Potential assassins, all of them. From the smiling young mother with a towheaded toddler in her lap to the elderly man leaning on a cane, to the trio of cocoa-skinned, dark-haired men gathered at the periphery of the crowd.

Shane narrowed his eyes and took a second look at the three men. They fit a profile that was politically correct to ignore, but he was Secret Service. Political correctness didn't figure into it. A whiff of Al-Qaeda and his adrenaline kicked into hyperdrive. He touched his earpiece and quietly mouthed a coded message that sent another Secret Service agent closer to the trio. Better safe than sorry.

"Everything okay?" Elysee laid a hand on his elbow.

"Yes, miss."

"Miss? Getting formal on me, Agent Tremont?" Her eyes twinkled.

"We're in public. I'm on high alert." He resisted the urge to smile.

"The crowd looks pretty tame to me."

"Protesters lined up on the sidewalk."

"Ubiquitous," she said. "I'm surprised. Usually there's more."

"It's because it's you here and not your father. Few are eager to protest a true lady."

"Why, Agent Tremont." A soft smile touched her lips. "What a gentlemanly thing to say."

He gave her a conspiratorial wink and her smile widened.

"Your tie's crooked," she said and reached up to give

his plain black necktie a gentle tug, then passed the flat of her hand over his shoulder. "There now. Spit-polish perfect."

"What does that mean?" he teased.

"I don't know. Just something my mother always said to my dad when she hustled him out the door each morning."

Shane and Elysee and her entourage were standing on a small platform suspended over the site of the groundbreaking. A fat yellow backhoe, along with several other heavy construction vehicles, sat with their engines powered up and running, ready to get to work as soon as Elysee sliced through the thick scarlet ribbon.

Some committee had decided a ballet of earthmoving equipment would be more cinematic than Elysee shoveling dirt. Although in the end, cinematography had turned out to be a nonissue. A devastating category four hurricane had just crashed ashore along the South Carolina coastline, pulling news crews eastward. Other than a few print journalists, the groundbreaking ceremony was devoid of the usual media brouhaha.

Shane swung his gaze back to the President's daughter. He had been assigned to her detail for the past thirteen months and in that time they'd become close friends. The relationship between a bodyguard and his protectee bore many similarities to that between a psychiatrist and his patient. Elysee told him things she couldn't tell anyone else. He listened, sympathized, and kept his mouth shut.

The intimacy had created a special connection. Shane liked her, even though she was seven years younger than he. This unexpected emotional bond wasn't something his training had fully prepared him for.

Elysee was petite and soft-spoken, with earnest opinions and tender sensibilities. She loved fully, completely, and without reservation, although men were always breaking her heart.

Shane couldn't understand why she hadn't become hardened or cynical about love. Her capacity to pick up her crumpled spirit and move on with the same degree of hope, trust, and optimism impressed him.

He thought of his ex-wife and his own heart—which was finally, finally starting to mend—swelled, testing the tentative seams of its emotional stitches. Two years divorced and thoughts of Tish still made him shaky. He'd loved her so damned much and she'd disappointed him so deeply. No pain had ever cut like Tish's secrecy and betrayal.

Many times over the past twenty-four months he'd tried to convince himself that he hated her. His anger was a red-hot flame he held close to his chest and stoked whenever his mind wandered to tender memories. But he couldn't hate her. Not really. Not when it counted.

Thing was, no matter how hard he tried to suppress his weakness, in the dark of midnight, he found himself longing for Tish and all that they'd lost.

He still ached for the feel of her curvy body nestled against his. Still longed to smell the spicy scent of her lush auburn hair. Still yearned to taste the rich flavor of her femininity lingering on his tongue. Even here, in the brightness of the noonday sun, surrounded by a crowd, he felt it.

Dry. Empty. Desperately alone.

The tip of his left thumb strayed to the back of his ring finger, feeling for the weight of the band that was no longer there. He swallowed past the unexpected lump in his throat.

Head in the game, Tremont.

Shane clenched his jaw to keep from thinking about Tish. Channeling all his attention onto safeguarding Elysee. This was his life now. Without a wife. Without a real home. The job was the only thing that defined him. He was a bodyguard, a protector, a sentinel. He was descended from war heroes. It was in his blood. In his very DNA.

The University of Texas chancellor stepped to the microphone and made a speech about Nathan Benedict and the dedication of the new Poli-Sci wing in his honor. Then he introduced Elysee.

A cheer went up. She *was* a crowd pleaser.

Elysee smiled and cameras clicked. An award-winning high school marching band that had been recruited for the event struck up "God Bless America." Shane's eyes never stopped assessing; his brain never ceased analyzing.

An assistant handed Elysee a pair of scissors so outrageously large that she had to grab onto them with both hands. Laughing, she raised the Gulliver-sized shears. Whenever she smiled, Elysee was transformed. Her bland blue eyes sparkled and her thin mouth widened and she tossed her hair in a carefree gesture. For one brief moment she looked as beautiful as any runway model.

Elysee snipped.

The thick red ribbon fell away.

The backhoe dipped for dirt at the same moment the bulldozer's blade went to ground and the road grader's engine revved.

The crowd, including the protesters behind the picket line, cheered again and applauded politely. Nearby, the backhoe operator was apparently having trouble with the equipment. It moved jerkily as its bucket rose. Elysee was perched precariously close to the platform's edge.

The backhoe arm swung wide.

In that instant Shane saw pure panic on the backhoe operator's face and realized the man had lost control of the machinery. The bucket zoomed straight for Elysee.

Shane reacted.

He felt no fear, only a solid determination to protect the President's daughter at all costs.

But it felt as if he were moving in slow motion, his legs locked in molasses, his arms slogging through ballistics gel. He lunged, flinging his body at Elysee.

He hit her with his shoulder. She cried out, fell to her knees.

Spinning, Shane turned to face the earthmoving equipment, hand simultaneously diving for his duty weapon at the same second the backhoe bucket sluiced through the air, slinging loamy soil.

His arm went up, gun raised.

The bucket caught his right hand, yanking him up off the platform. He heard the awful crunch, but the pain didn't immediately register. He was jerked from his feet. He tried to pull the trigger, not even knowing what he was shooting at, just reacting instinctively to danger. He'd kill for Elysee, if that's what it took.

But his fingers refused to comply. What the hell was wrong with his fingers? Shane frowned, puzzled.

The driver looked horrified as his gaze met Shane's. He was dangling from the bucket right before the operator's eyes as the man frantically grabbed levers and fumbled with controls.

Distantly, Shane heard Elysee screaming his name. Was she hurt? In pain? Had someone gotten to her? Was she being kidnapped? Was the runaway backhoe all a ruse to deflect attention from hostage takers? The questions pelted his mind, hard as stones.

People were running and screaming, rushing in all directions, ducking and dodging, tripping and falling. He feared a stampede.

Shane swiveled his head, trying to locate Elysee in the confusion. Why couldn't he feel the pistol in his hand? Dammit, why couldn't he feel his hand?

"Elysee!" Her name tore from his throat in a guttural growl.

The backhoe arm slung Shane up high, and then slammed him down hard onto the cab of the earthmoving vehicle.

Metal contacted with bone.

Pain exploded inside his skull, a starburst of bright searing light.

Then his vision went dark as he tumbled toward the hardpacked ground and slumped into the inky-black tunnel of unconsciousness.

Connect with us at Facebook.com/ReadForeverPub.

SECOND CHANCE HERO
by Lori Wilde

Tish Gallagher scores the job of a lifetime—too bad it brings her up close and personal with the man she's never stopped loving. Sure, their chemistry was hotter than a Texas summer, but their clashes were legendary, and no amount of longing will change that. (Previously published as *Once Smitten, Twice Shy*)

Follow @ReadForeverPub on Twitter and join the conversation using #ReadForever.

ROCKY MOUNTAIN HEAT
by Lori Wilde

Attorney Jillian Samuels doesn't believe in true love and has never wished for happily ever after. But when a searing betrayal leaves her jobless and heartbroken, a newly inherited cottage in Salvation, Colorado, seems to offer a fresh start. What she finds when she arrives shocks her: the most gorgeous and infuriating man she's ever met is living in her home! (Previously published as *All of Me*)

MY ONE AND ONLY COWBOY
by A.J. Pine

Sam Callahan, co-owner of the Meadow Valley guest ranch, is barely keeping his business in the black. But when a gorgeous blonde barges onto his property insisting he bought the place in a fraudulent sale—and that she's there to prove she still owns half the land—Sam realizes he's got much more to worry about. He could lose everything—including his heart. Includes a bonus novel by Carolyn Brown!

Find more great reads on Instagram with @ReadForeverPub.

CHRISTMAS WITH A COWBOY
by Carolyn Brown

A year ago, cowboy Maverick Callahan fell head-over-heels for an extraordinary woman he met while on vacation—a woman he was convinced he'd never see again. So when she appears on his doorstep like a Christmas miracle, Maverick is determined not to waste his lucky break. Includes a bonus novella by Sara Richardson!

A COWBOY FOR CHRISRMAS
by Sara Richardson

Darla Michaels has come up with the perfect way to save the town from a recent slump in tourism. But planning the first annual Cowboy Christmas Festival means she has to work with Ty Forrester, head of the town's rodeo association and an irresistible bull rider who keeps testing her keep-things-casual policy. Includes a bonus novella by R.C. Ryan!

Looking for more cowboys?
Forever brings the heat with these sexy studs.

BORN TO BE A COWBOY
by R.C. Ryan

When her aunt disappears not long after her shotgun wedding, Jessie Blair fears the worst. Unable to uncover answers on her own, she hopes lawyer/smooth-talking cowboy Finn Monroe can help solve the mystery—especially since danger seems to lurk around every corner. Finding protection in Finn's arms, Jessie experiences feelings she's never known before. But is love enough, when someone wants them both dead? Includes a bonus novella by A.J. Pine!

Discover bonus content and more on read-forever.com.

About the Author

Lori Wilde is the *New York Times* and *USA Today* bestselling author of over eighty romance novels. She is a three-time RITA award nominee, a four-time Romantic Times Reviewers' Choice nominee, and has won numerous other awards. She earned a bachelor's degree in nursing from Texas Christian University and holds a certificate in forensics. She is also a certified yoga instructor.

Her books have been translated into twenty-seven languages and featured in *Cosmopolitan*, *Redbook*, *Complete Woman*, *All You*, *Time*, and *Quick and Simple* magazines. She lives in Texas with her husband, Bill.

You can learn more at:
LoriWilde.com
Twitter @LoriWilde
Facebook.com/LoriWildeBooks
Instagram @LoriWilde02